ALEX SHAW has lived and worked in Ukraine, the former USSR, the Middle East, and Africa. He is the author of the number one international Kindle bestselling Aidan Snow SAS thrillers. His writing has also been published in several thriller anthologies alongside International Bestselling authors Stephen Leather and Matt Hilton. Alex, his wife and their two sons divide their time between Ukraine, England and Qatar.

🐦 @alexshawhetman
f /alex.shaw.982292
www.alexwshaw.co.uk

Also by Alex Shaw

Cold Blood
Cold Black
Cold East

Total Blackout

ALEX SHAW

ONE PLACE. MANY STORIES

HQ
An imprint of HarperCollins*Publishers* Ltd
1 London Bridge Street
London SE1 9GF

This paperback edition 2020

1

First published in Great Britain by
HQ, an imprint of HarperCollins*Publishers* Ltd 2020

ISBN: 9780008412265

Printed and bound in Great Britain by
CPI Group (UK) Ltd, Melksham, SN12 6TR

*For my wife Galia, my sons Alexander and Jonathan,
and our family in England and Ukraine.*

Prologue

Washington, DC

The co-conspirators stood on their balcony at The Hay-Adams. The White House was less than four hundred metres away. The balcony afforded them a grandstand view. Within minutes Maksim Oleniuk and Chen Yan, the founders of Blackline PMC, were going to launch the largest attack on the United States of America since the Japanese attack on Pearl Harbor, perhaps the biggest attack ever on the country. Maksim Oleniuk certainly hoped so. He looked down and smiled at the Chinese oligarch who had funded his dream of striking the US. It had been her finances – billions amassed from minerals and electronics, in partnership with his access and expertise as a former Russian Military Intelligence Officer, which had created this paradigm-shifting moment. Oleniuk found his partner highly attractive but understood she was the very last person in the world he should approach. He sipped his chilled champagne and wondered if she could read his mind.

'What are you thinking of?' Yan asked, surprising him, making his face colour in the gloom. Her American accent was flawless, perfected whilst she gained an MBA at the New York Institute of Technology. It put Oleniuk's Russo-British accent to shame.

'I am just thinking that never have parents given birth to such a powerful child.'

She inclined her head, a stoic expression on her face. 'Our child will live and die in the same instant, yet leave an eternal legacy.'

'Legacy,' Oleniuk repeated. It was something he had strived to create and the perfect word for the occasion.

They stood like expectant parents, the former GRU officer rocking from foot to foot and the Chinese billionaire stock-still, but both were nervous, excited and scared of what was to come.

The timing of the detonation had been mandated to utilise empty airspace, or airspace as empty as it ever could be over the continental United States. The location was hugely symbolic; the US seat of power deliberately selected, politically central rather than geographically so. Oleniuk's scientists had stated the risk of damage to the retina was small yet did exist if they were to stare directly at the epicentre of the detonation with the naked eye. For this reason, Oleniuk and Yan wore wrap-around sunglasses with specifically engineered lenses shielding their eyes. They gazed out over the balcony at the empty air a mile above the floodlit White House.

At exactly five a.m. there was a flash so quick that if the pair had not known exactly where to look it would have been missed, then a silent, purple detonation flowered. It bloomed like a monstrous, inverted Fourth of July firework. Its petals spread earthwards and then faded to be replaced by a mauve glow, creating a spectral false dawn.

Oleniuk felt the tingling sensation he had been warned to expect wash over him, as each individual hair on his body stood up on end. At that very moment, as if choreographed, every single light around the pair vanished. The White House lights disappeared, the floodlights on the lawn were no more and the stately residence of the President of the United States of America was plunged into darkness.

The glow started to fade; the night sky now taking on the

appearance of the bruised eye of a heavyweight boxer, before it gradually became black once more. The co-conspirators removed their protective eyewear. They had delivered a form of vengeance like no other the modern world had ever seen and, ignoring ancient, fanciful tales of vengeful gods, the single most powerful.

Oleniuk put his arm around Yan. 'We have done it.'

She did not reply; however, she did give him a sideways glance. Oleniuk quickly moved his arm. 'I am sorry. I was overcome with emotion in the moment. I do apologise.'

'It is understandable, given the circumstances.'

They continued to gaze at the capital city of the United States – dark, silent but not dead. The majority of the population were safely asleep and those who weren't would interpret the loss of power as a citywide outage, a total blackout.

Chapter 1

Two days earlier

Camden, Maine, United States

The assassin was Russian, one of their best. He had to be to make the shot. His hide was in an elevated position on a hill, half a click away from the target. It was the closest he was prepared to go, given the timescale and his schedule. Three targets to hit in three consecutive days. A reckless order in the Russian Army and certainly an unheard-of contract on the private circuit. But he was the best, and he had accepted. And he was now on target number two.

The ever-changing eddies and the elevation made the shot challenging. It was a job for a two-man team, a shooter and a spotter, but the assassin had always preferred to work alone. The assassin was not acquainted with failure; this was something that simply did not enter his thought process. Preparing to fail started with a failure to prepare, and Ruslan Akulov never failed to prepare.

His target was on time. He tracked him in his crosshairs. The man exited the rear of the house through a pair of double-height patio doors, sipping his Pinot Gris, blissfully unaware of the Russian's presence. Retired senator Clifford Piper lived in a sprawling mansion overlooking the town of Camden, Maine. The deck, where he stood now and would soon fall upon, commanded panoramic views of the harbour, West Penobscot Bay, and the evergreen islands.

Akulov had seen mansions before, castle-like homes constructed for the rich and corrupt, which dotted the outskirts of Moscow like mushrooms, while the rest of the population lived in shacks or high-rise concrete boxes. Never before, however, had he encountered one in a setting as spectacular as this. He agreed the panorama was impressive, but the man was not. He knew all about Piper. He hated him. As a senator Piper had preached his own brand of American imperialism, damning all those who dared speak out against Uncle Sam. He was a hawk, voraciously attacking Venezuela, North Korea, Russia, and China. He threw his words like missiles from the safety of Washington, a coward who would not dare repeat his slurs in the face of the enemy.

But, had he been punished for the innumerable deaths his rhetoric had caused or the hatred his words had incited? No. The senator had been allowed to retire to his mansion, and his three-million-dollar view. Not bad for a dacha, or as the Americans called them "vacation properties". The Russian let a sneer form on his face. The property would be vacated soon enough. He had watched his target, and knew his routine well. Piper took a glass of wine at eleven o'clock each morning on his deck in order to appreciate his view. Akulov had also enjoyed the vista. The ocean – like him – was a contradiction. By turns calm and violent. Not that he was naturally a violent soul, but he employed violence in the defence of his country.

The target was a widower, his wife having perished along with twenty-eight other Americans a year before, in a terrorist attack in Jakarta. But for the Jakarta team this had been a failure. Bitter fate had intervened in his employer's plans, made the senator succumb to food poisoning and unable to leave his hotel suite to join the bus tour. The bus his wife was on, the bus that had been boarded by gunmen who slaughtered every passenger. Grief-stricken, the senator had resigned and retired. The Jakarta team's failure ensured that Piper was added to the hit list given to Akulov, and Akulov did not fail.

The maid appeared. She stood by her master's side. She held his hand. Through open curtains, the Russian had observed the old man consoling himself by screwing her. It had not been at all arousing but Akulov had made himself watch, much like a wildlife photographer cataloguing the mating rituals of primates. Piper had grunted; the maid had not.

Mercifully at that precise moment the pair were only talking. At this distance, in the open, he could not hear the sounds escaping their lips, but he imagined they were the sickening words lovers pass to one and other. It wasn't his business. He didn't care what was or was not being said, what was or was not being promised. But what about the late wife? Would she have wanted her husband to become a monk or would she have approved of his new bedfellow? Piper looked contented, and had done so each day the assassin had observed him. Even now he continued to sip his wine, oblivious to the fact that a single .338 Lapua Magnum round from the Russian's suppressed rifle was seconds away from entering his chest and ripping out his heart.

Akulov adjusted the scope of his German sniper rifle. In ordinary times, Piper's death would be seen as a clear message to his country's leader, but these were about to become extraordinary times. The senator's death today would be ignored by tomorrow, and perhaps not be investigated until months after his death – if at all.

Akulov had not entertained the idea of killing the woman, even though strategically it made sense. She was the only other person in the house and leaving her alive would mean the alarm was raised that much faster, but he had no desire kill her. She was an innocent, a civilian and that went against his code. Besides, he mused, her relationship with Piper was sufferance enough. The maid stepped away and walked back into the house. Moments later her rotund shadow crossed a kitchen window.

Now Akulov steadied his breathing, watched the sway of the large trees dotting the property and the direction of the gulls as the grey-haired, potbellied Piper raised his wine glass to his mouth for the last time. Akulov made his final adjustments and calculations then gently squeezed the trigger. The .338 round rocketed towards the unwary enemy of Mother Russia, tore through his torso, punched out a fist-sized hole and kept going before it drilled itself into the timber-clad wall of the mansion.

Jack Tate didn't see the blue flashing lights in his rear-view mirror immediately; he was lost in the lyrics of Bruce Springsteen's "Born to Run". As the song drew to a close, he heard the sirens and then saw the police vehicle gaining ominously behind him. Tate swore; he couldn't believe that after all his years of training and active service, he'd made such a rookie mistake. He knew the drill; he pulled the Chevrolet Tahoe over on the shoulder, powered down the window, turned off the engine, and placed his hands in clear sight on the top of the steering wheel. As a police officer stepped out of the liveried Crown Victoria, the next song on Tate's radio started. He tried not to laugh – it was the Eagles' classic "Desperado".

The officer drew level with Tate's window but stayed several paces back, as procedure dictated. He asked him to switch off his music and then hand over his driver's licence and insurance documents. He spoke to Tate without checking them. 'Is this your vehicle, sir?'

'No.'

'Who does it belong to?'

'The rental company.'

'I see.'

'So what did I do wrong?'

The officer's brow furrowed and he took a moment to form his next question: 'You're British?'

'From London,' Tate replied, as the warm August air overcame the lingering cold of the Tahoe's climate control.

'You were ten miles an hour above the limit back there. We've had a lot of accidents on this stretch of road over the years. People see the view, get too excited and then . . . well, it's not a pretty sight.'

'I understand.'

The officer nodded. 'And what is your destination today?'

'Camden.'

'Business or pleasure?'

'Just a holiday.'

'Holiday?'

'Vacation.'

'On your own?'

Now it was Tate's turn to frown; these questions didn't seem to be usual for a traffic violation. 'Yes, on my own.'

The officer gestured with his left hand, the one holding Tate's documents, whilst his right slid towards his belt and rested on the butt of his firearm. 'This is a large vehicle for one person.'

'The rental company was out of stock. They gave me a free upgrade.'

'Stay in the vehicle, sir. I'll be back in a moment.'

Still holding Tate's documents, the officer backed away to his patrol car, where his colleague had been talking on the radio. Via his mirror Tate saw a brief exchange between the two before they approached the SUV, each angling for a different side of the Tahoe, weapons drawn. Tate frowned. Every instinct he had, every part of his training, told him to hightail it out of there, put the car into drive and pull away, wheels spinning, leaving the officers choking in the dust . . . but he was on holiday, not on deployment, and these were police officers not enemy combatants.

'Step out of the vehicle with your arms raised and place your hands on the vehicle!' the second officer barked.

Tate sighed. This wasn't what he needed, and unlike the cops back home, they were armed. He had no choice but to comply. This was where mistakes happened; this was where he was putting his life in the hands of men in uniform he didn't know, trusting them and trusting their training. It wasn't the first time he'd had more than one loaded weapon pointed at him. Tate slowly opened the door and shuffled around the side of the SUV as the roadside dust danced at his feet and the sun warmed his back. He kept his eyes firmly fixed front and centre, and watched the armed men approach via their reflection in his window.

'I'm going to search you now,' said the first officer. 'Are you carrying any drugs, needles, or concealed weapons?'

'No.'

Tate felt the officer pat him down before he said, 'Place your hands behind your back.'

Tate thought he knew what was coming next, but neither officer recited the Miranda to him or advised him of his rights. This he also found off. The nearest officer cuffed his wrists tightly, the left cuff pressing snugly against his metal watchstrap, forcing his Rolex further up his arm. Tate asked, 'Can you tell me what you think I've done?'

Neither officer spoke as they frogmarched him to the Crown Victoria. They opened the back, pushed him in, and shut the door. A moment later, the Crown Victoria's "Interceptor Pack" engine growled, and, with lights flashing, the driver navigated the flow of traffic heading towards Camden.

The officers were silent, tense. One kept his eyes on the road whilst the other repeatedly glanced back at Tate. The rear of the car was stuffy, and Tate tried to get himself comfortable, as the handcuffs dug into his wrists and ended up forcing him to lean sideways. He should have been worried, sitting cuffed in the back of a US police cruiser, but he wasn't. The emotion that he felt the most at that exact moment was annoyance. The cops had made a mistake. It was clear that this was about much more than speeding; that would have earnt him a ticket, a financial slap on the wrist – not steel cuffs. They'd picked on the wrong man. He'd enjoy telling them so, but there was no point in saying anything now. He'd not say a word until they'd arrived at the station, attempted to process him and realised their error. There would be an embarrassing "no hard feelings" conversation where the local law enforcement officers would try to persuade him that Maine was an exceptionally safe place to spend his vacation.

He allowed himself a bitter smile as he gazed out of the window at the sparkling sea below. This wasn't how he'd planned to arrive in Camden but at least the views did not disappoint.

After some scenic driving and negotiating the small roads, the police cruiser came to a halt outside a single-storey red-brick building. Cautiously, the two officers hustled him out of the car, through a column-adorned porch – which to Tate seemed like an architectural afterthought – and into the Camden PD station. An officer stood behind a processing desk at the front of the office. Posters were stuck on the walls: a mixture of tourist information, photographs depicting the local countryside and text-heavy notices. The desk officer glanced down at his desk then back up again and nodded at his colleagues. He looked worried and his voice sounded it too. 'Belongings?'

'In his vehicle,' one of the officers replied.

'I'll take his watch.'

The officer on Tate's left undid the strap and handed the watch to the desk officer. The man's eyebrows rose as he noted the brand before he placed it into a Ziploc-type plastic bag then put this under the counter. 'OK. Room one.'

Tate remained a compliant, silent witness to the unfolding events and let himself be pushed further into the station, past the desk and into the open-plan interior. The office door opened and a large figure stepped out, folded his arms and looked on as Tate was led through a door on the right. Inside was a narrow corridor with three steel doors on one side. The nearest was open.

The two officers locked him inside and left him alone.

The room was lit with a fluorescent bulb contained in a wire cage, which starkly illuminated a metal table in the centre space. The table was affixed to the concrete floor with steel pins, as were two chairs, one either side of the table – one facing the door and one facing away. 'Welcome to Camden,' Tate muttered to himself and shook his head. It was by no means the first time he'd been in a police interview room, but it was the first time he'd been in one as an innocent man.

Still cuffed, Tate sat at the table facing the door. In the British Army, he was used to planning operations and, for this, intelligence gathering was crucial, but here there was no intel to collect. He'd assessed the situation but could come up with no other explanation for his incarceration other than the fact that he'd been picked up in error. A case of mistaken identity. Someone who matched his description had done something, and something serious at that. So why hadn't he been read his rights? Why hadn't he been Mirandized? It still made no sense to Tate. He tried to get comfortable on the metal chair, managed to slouch a little and kick his legs out underneath. He closed his eyes and let his mind wander to the first time he'd been in a police cell. Even all these years later it still made him chuckle.

It had been on a family pilgrimage to North Wales to see his mother's cousin. He and his brother hated going. They'd stay for a week, several times a year. With parents who didn't approve of Game Boys, the brothers passed the long car journey playing "car cricket". His brother was always "in bat" first. The boys would stare out of the rear windows of the Volvo looking for pubs. Once they spotted one, they'd read the name or look at the gaudy sign hanging outside. For each "leg" that appeared in the pub name (physical or pictorial) the person in bat scored a "run" up to the maximum of six per pub. If the name did not contain any legs, the player in bat was "out", and the other player was now "in bat". Pubs such as "The Coach & Horses" and "The

Highwayman" always scored a "six" as there were either horses in the name or on the sign. Some pub names caused arguments, some made them laugh, and some did both – "The Cock" had been one of these. Their father said he preferred "legless pubs"; their mother tutted.

In Wales they played with a local friend – Richie Williams. He lived across the road and according to their mother was a bad influence. The boys would kick a ball about or go exploring with Richie. On several occasions they'd been chased away from the fairway of the Prestatyn Golf Club. But this last trip had been different. His brother had not wanted to go out – he was sixteen and studying for his GCSEs – but fourteen-year-old Jack did. He'd sneaked out to meet Richie and that was where, according to his parents, his problems started.

Richie boasted that he knew where the Golf Club kept the fireworks ready for their Summer Ball. He dared Jack to break in and take a rocket. And Jack did. But Jack, who never backed down from a dare, didn't stop at just one rocket. Jack took four rockets and two display-size Catherine wheels. That night he shimmied onto the roof of the local Tesco's superstore and set up his own display. The CCTV cameras had alerted the local police to their activity but not before Richie and Jack had set off the fireworks.

As Jack sprinted across the car park he was illuminated, not by blossoming fireworks but by the full beams of a North Wales Police Range Rover. That night was the first time he had been put in a police cell and it was the last time he had seen Richie Williams. It was also the last time they ever went to Prestatyn. That event had been the beginning of the end of his relationship with his parents. They weren't his real parents; he'd been in long-term foster care with them. He didn't miss them, as much as missed their son, his brother. And that was the reason he was on a road trip in the US.

Tate's eyes snapped open as the door creaked. The desk officer entered. 'I've got to take your prints – Chief Donoghue's orders. Will there be an issue?'

'No issue at all.'

'British?'

'English.'

'Like the Queen.' The officer had a legal pad-sized black plastic case in his hand. He retrieved a card. It had a printed table on it, columns to receive the inky print of each digit. 'Hold up your hands.' Tate did so and the officer inked the tips of each finger with a spongy implement from his case. 'Now on the card, roll each fingertip slowly once, from left to right.'

Tate complied. Once satisfied with the prints, the officer abruptly stood and left the room. Tate stared at his dirtied fingers, thought about rubbing the ink off onto his jeans but couldn't be bothered. Instead he stood up and wiped them on the clean, whitewashed wall directly next to the door. It was like finger-painting, a childish but satisfying act of defiance. Tate sat again. He didn't know how long he'd be stuck in the room for. How long would it take the local authorities to realise their mistake? One of the army's many mottos had been "eat when you can and sleep when you can" because you never know when you'll get another chance. There was no food, so Tate closed his eyes and tried to sleep. Fleetingly the stolen fireworks again bloomed in his memory and then he woke with a start, his neck stiff and his head groggy.

'Get up and follow me.' It was the desk officer again.

The officer led Tate out of the cell, back into the open-plan squad room, along the full length of the space and through a door into the big office at the back. The large man he'd seen earlier was sitting at a desk. He nodded Tate into the empty chair opposite him.

'I'm Chief Donoghue of the Camden Police Department. Care to tell me, Mr Tate, the reason for your presence in Maine?'

Tate examined his inky fingertips. 'Vacation.'

'That's what you told my men. But I'd like to know the real

reason.' Donoghue leaned back in his chair and laced his fingers in his lap. Tate noted that his bulk was muscle rather than fat. He had the look of an old soldier – a short, no-nonsense haircut and a stern brow. 'You see the thing is, Mr Tate, we think you may be just the person we have been looking for.'

Tate remained silent. In his experience, men in authority liked to hear the sound of their own voice, regardless of how much power they had. And this was Donoghue's desk, in Donoghue's town. He took in Donoghue's office. The same white walls as his holding cell but here the concrete floor was covered with grey carpeting. The wall directly behind displayed several framed certificates as though to confirm his legitimacy to all those sitting in Tate's seat. The desk itself was bare save for a laptop and a blue Maine PD coffee cup. There was a modern coffee station on a unit, and a coffee table with two comfy chairs.

'What job do you do back in the UK?' Donoghue asked.

'I'm a Human Resources consultant.'

'And the name of your employer is?'

'Fir Tree Consulting.'

'Branches everywhere? That's cute,' Donoghue said without humour. 'Can you verify that?'

'I've probably got a business card in my wallet somewhere. It's in my car, but I'm sure your men have already checked it.'

'You've got an attitude there, Mr Tate.'

'That's right, Chief Donoghue; we are both wasting our time here.'

'Do you have an issue with authority figures, Mr Tate?'

Tate shrugged. 'Not when I see one.'

The police chief's nostrils flared, but his tone remained neutral. 'You are doing what, exactly, during your vacation here?'

'Driving around, taking in the sights.'

'How long do you plan to be in the US for?'

'Like it says on my car rental agreement, a month.'

'That's a long vacation.'

'There's a lot to see.'

'Did you serve, Mr Tate?'

'You mean like a waiter?'

Donoghue pursed his lips. 'You know what I mean.'

Tate shrugged again. 'You've got my details and my prints. I imagine that you'll have a pretty good file on me soon enough.'

'Is that how you want to play this? Really?' Donoghue's eyes narrowed. 'Why are you being so unhelpful, Mr Tate?'

Tate sighed. 'Yes, I served.'

'Where?'

'Afghanistan.'

'Infantry?'

'Yes.'

'See much action?'

'More than I would have liked. What am I being charged with?'

'Nothing at the moment, apart from driving in excess of the speed limit.'

'So why haven't I been read my rights?'

'You may or you may not be aware that the *Amended PATRIOT Act* provides me with increased powers to hold and question "persons of interest" without charge. You, Mr Tate, are a person of interest.'

'I'm honoured you find me so interesting, but I still don't know what this is all about.'

'OK.' Donoghue pursed his lips again. 'At lunchtime today, a prominent local resident was murdered. It looks like a contract killing. A single shot was fired. I'm still awaiting confirmation on the type of round used, but it was pretty big – we believe some sort of sniper rifle.'

Tate's eyebrows rose. It *was* something serious. 'And you think I have something to do with this?'

'Something, or maybe nothing, or maybe everything. An SUV, like the one you were driving, was seen leaving the area. A surveillance camera captured a suspect fitting your description.'

'Who was the murder victim?'

'A retired senator by the name of Clifford Piper; you ever heard of him?'

Tate shook his head. The only Piper that flashed in his mind was the wrestler – "Rowdy" Roddy Piper.

'His wife was killed last year in a terrorist attack. He retired afterwards.'

Tate vaguely remembered the headlines. 'I've never heard of him, and I wasn't there. My SUV has a tracker, and you can check that against your intel.'

'Intel?'

'Your reports.'

'Yep, see, I know what "intel" means. I'm just surprised that you'd use that term. I don't think you are who you say you are, Mr Tate.'

'So you are going to hold me until what, you decide that I didn't shoot a senator with a Barrett?'

'Who said anything about a Barrett, Mr Tate?'

Tate remained silent for a moment; he was tired and snappy. 'It's the most reliable 0.50 rifle, in my opinion, and it's what I'd use if I wanted to make sure of hitting a target with one round. One large round. There's a pretty good suppressor available for it too, and in a semi-urban environment you want to make as little noise as possible.'

'Ha,' Donoghue said with a knowing nod.

Tate was getting bored; he wanted to be on his way. 'You don't have the murder weapon – just a large hole and a deformed round. And the fact that you didn't mention anyone as having heard the shot leads me to believe that the shooter used a suppressor. A 0.50 calibre makes a hell of a bang without one.'

'What did you do in Afghanistan, Mr Tate?'

'I soldiered.'

'What exactly did you do in Afghanistan?'

'I can't tell you.'

'Oh, yes you can. Weren't you listening to me? The *Amended PATRIOT Act* gives me—'

Tate stood. 'Yes, I heard.'

Donoghue got to his feet with surprising speed. 'Where the hell do you think you are going? Sit down!'

The two men sized each other up, Donoghue incensed, Tate impassive. A loud knock on the office door, followed quickly by an officer entering the room broke the standoff.

'Chief, this is urgent.'

'On my way. Officer Kent, please escort Mr Tate back to his holding cell. He won't be any trouble, will you, Tate?'

'None at all,' Tate said flatly.

Chapter 2

Camden, Maine

Oleg Sokol gazed out over the waves and breathed in the fresh sea breeze. Camden was so different to his native Sochi, but the sea air smelled the same. He saw birds soar on thermals and smiled at the sound of their excited calls. Oleg's surname "Sokol" meant falcon in Russian, and he too wished he could fly carefree and enjoy the beauty of the bay and the August sunshine, but alas, this was neither the time nor the place. Oleg's time in Maine would abruptly end with the coming attack. Many innocent people, of course, would perhaps perish in the aftermath and although he did feel for them, there was nothing he could do, so it was not his concern. His concern was whether the technology he had helped design in the laboratory would work in the field.

He watched a yacht out in the bay, its crew delightfully unaware that in thirty-eight hours the world as they knew it would vanish. Vanish for how long he did not know. Could the US rebuild, re-plug and reboot in six months, a year? He shook his head, as the vessel tacked to head south along the coast. Perhaps thirty-eight hours was all the crew had left.

'Good afternoon.' The voice that interrupted his thoughts was cheery.

'Good afternoon,' Oleg said.

'Is that a Russian accent I detect there?' the elderly woman asked.

'Yes, it is.' Oleg had once been a naturally friendly person. As a student learning English he had longed to meet native English speakers so he could practise, explore new words and improve his understanding. That Oleg would have been overjoyed to be overseas in the US. He would have been chatty and gregarious and engaging, but that was not the Oleg of today. He had a mission to conduct, and talking to anyone could put that at risk. He looked down at the old woman; her hair was ice white and immaculately styled. She wore a vivid pink blouse over equally bright, lime-green slacks, a sturdy pair of hiking boots, and a day sack on her back.

'And what brings you here?'

Camden was a town of only five thousand permanent residents, and each summer up to ten thousand more took up places in vacation homes and rentals. Yet even at the height of the tourist season it was all but impossible not to draw attention to himself. The locals were, like Oleg, naturally friendly people.

'I am here just to relax for a while. I work in Washington, so it is nice to get away from the city.'

The old woman smiled. 'I love it here – in the summer, that is. In winter I go down to Florida or go on cruises.'

Oleg smiled. He liked cruises and had once taken a train from Moscow to Kyiv, then cruised down the river Dnipro to the Black Sea resort town of Odessa where he'd proposed to his wife. He felt a sadness, and then didn't want to say anything more.

The old lady carried on talking, unaware of the distant grief behind his smile. 'Hill walking is what I love. Give me a good hill and I am happy. Tomorrow a group of us are walking down to Rockport and back. The weather forecast says that it'll be clear skies and sunshine. Well, goodbye.'

'Good luck and goodbye,' Oleg said as he watched the woman walk away. He noticed a cuddly panda keychain hung off the back of the day sack. He took a further five minutes to enjoy the scenery before trudging back up the path towards his Tahoe. It would be interesting to see how many yachts and other vessels arrived after the attack and how, if at all, they were affected. He pulled his encrypted sat phone out of his trouser pocket and read the message sent from his employer. The plan was unchanged. His team was to monitor the aftermath of the attack before falling back to the regional operating base six hours after the event.

Oleg checked his watch; he had time for one extra supply run. He'd drive past the inn, turn up Conway Road and go to Hannaford Supermarket. He may even buy a few bottles of Wild Turkey to take back home; they'd skyrocket in price once the stock in stores ran out and production ended.

Camden Police Station, Maine

'How's the coffee?' Donoghue asked.

'Good. Thanks,' Tate replied, four hours after the last time he'd faced the chief.

'I thought you Brits drank tea.'

'That's just the women; real men drink coffee.'

The police chief nodded. 'See this?' He pointed to a couple of sheets of letter-sized paper on his desk. 'This is all we got from running your prints through the system. Now the first sheet here is what I was meant to see . . . mundane details about your entry into the US and movements, et cetera. But the second is what I managed to see after I called an old buddy of mine who owes me a favour, and that's what took the time.'

'Am I still a person of interest, Chief?'

'You are an interesting person, Mr Tate. You were in the SAS.'

Tate frowned. 'Was I?'

Donoghue nodded. 'That's why I couldn't get much on you. It was classified, but the three lines I did eventually get from my buddy, who is connected, really opened my eyes.' Donoghue looked down at the paper for effect. 'You joined the Parachute Regiment straight from school and then three years later passed

SAS selection. After seventeen years you left the army and took a job with Hush Hearing. And that is as much as I got. So the question I still have is this, why is a former member of an elite Special Forces unit in my town at the same time as a gunman?'

'Happenchance.'

'You see, Tate, I still have an issue here. The tracker on your Tahoe says you were near the scene of the Piper shooting. Care to explain?'

'This morning I drove from Bangor to Camden.'

'And did you stop anywhere?'

'Yes. I needed a piss.'

'Did anyone see you?'

'I hope not; I was pissing in the bushes.'

'You think this is funny, Tate? Some type of joke?'

'No, I don't.' Tate fixed Donoghue with his steel-grey eyes. 'But I do think that your belief I had anything to do with this is hilarious. I insist that you call the British Embassy in Washington and notify them that I am being held, without charge.'

'Now you're giving me orders?' Donoghue folded his arms in an attempt to curb his irritation. 'OK, we'll do as you say and call them, like you were a US citizen with constitutional rights.'

'Thank you.'

'Who do you really work for?'

'Ask for Simon Hunter; he's the Commercial Attaché. I met him on a trade mission last year. He'll vouch for me.'

'I'm sure he will.' A thin smile appeared on Donoghue's lips. 'You see, I looked at your tracker data twice, in fact, after it was brought to my attention that you were near Piper's place and that you did stop. But then I realised that you couldn't be the shooter, as you were stationary for less than a minute.'

'I see.' Tate was annoyed; Donoghue had been fishing and now knew about Simon Hunter.

'And then, of course, your tracker had the SUV outside a pizza parlour thirty miles away at the time of the first shooting.'

'First shooting?' Tate said, surprised.

Donoghue ignored the interruption. 'We contacted the restaurant and sent them your mugshot. They confirmed you were there eating the entire time the tracker shows the Tahoe as stationary.'

'That's because I was.' Tate was terse. 'How many shootings have there been?'

'Two. One yesterday and one today with the same MO – a single .338-calibre round. You see, whilst you were cooling your jets in my holding cell we got the second round identified. It's a confirmed match to the first. Not a .50 cal, as you said, but a .338, and still big enough to all but split the victims in two.' Donoghue shook his head. 'No one ever gets shot in Maine, but now we've got a maniac on the loose with a Magnum calibre rifle.'

Tate nodded. He'd made a mistake. 'Of course.'

'Of course what?'

'Of course it was a .338. I wasn't thinking earlier.'

The police chief folded his arms across his large chest. 'OK, I'll bite. Go on.'

'Two shootings, in two days with the same rifle, so unless this was some type of "tag team" operation, it's reasonable to assume both were carried out by the same shooter. Correct?'

The police chief nodded.

'And the targets were in urban environments?'

'Well, as urban as small-town Maine gets. The men were at home, in their gardens, nice green places. What's your point?'

'The shooter may have been able to conceal himself, and subdue the sound of the kill shot, but how did he hide his rifle?'

'You mean as he moved to and from where he took the shot?'

'Yes.'

'He carried it in a bag?'

'But how big was the bag? Rifles aren't known as "longs" in the British Army for nothing. A guy carrying a bag as long as a pool cue would be noticed.'

'Simple. He disassembled it.'

22

Tate closed his eyes for a moment, thinking, visualising and then carried on, 'But, as far as I know, there are only two types of precision rifles that can be broken down in the field quickly and reassembled. One is used by the US Army and another by about a dozen different international police units.'

'So that narrows down the weapon used and where it came from? But, Tate, there has to be millions of the one used by the US Army floating around.'

'It wasn't that one.'

'Why not?'

'The Remington MSR has a barrel that can be removed to change the weapon's calibre, not for concealment. And the accuracy of the Remington isn't what I'd call that of a *precision* rifle because the barrel can be changed. Things get misaligned – the scope, the barrel and the action.'

'I get it. It's the other one and this helps me because it's what, rarer?'

'Especially in .338 calibre. Very rare. You're looking for a shooter using a German sniper rifle, a Blaser R93 LRS2. It's the LRS2 variant that uses the .338 Lapua Magnum rounds. The same as you analysed. Big holes, without the weight of a .50 cal, they were designed for the war in Afghanistan. And then getting a suppressor for this, which I imagine is not sold commercially in the US, is extremely hard.'

'And what if you're wrong again, Mr Tate?'

'I never make two mistakes on the same day.'

'OK.' Donoghue flipped open his laptop and pressed a few keys with his large fingers. 'Tell me the name of that rifle again?'

'A Blaser R93 LRS2.'

'I'm going to look it up as I've never seen one.'

A question formed in Tate's head as the police chief checked his Google results. 'Are there any links between the victims?'

Donoghue didn't look up. 'Not that we know of. The first was a banker by the name of Darren Sant; the second was Senator Piper.'

'And these shootings happened in the Camden area?'

'The first in Rockport – just down from us – and then today's was in Camden.' Donoghue's expression changed. 'Now that's interesting.'

'You've found something?'

Stabbing his screen with his index finger, Donoghue spoke. 'On *Wikiwand* I've found a list of "users" of this rifle. And the nearest to us here is the New Jersey State Police. I'm going to call them and pick their brains.' Donoghue finally looked up. He cleared his throat. 'Look, Mr Tate, I feel I owe you an apology.'

'I see.' Tate smiled thinly.

Donoghue continued, 'If a thing is too good to be true then it usually is, and hauling you in for this was just that. The FBI and the national news crews are going to be swarming all over me come lunchtime tomorrow. You are free to go, and your rental car has been brought around the front of the lot.'

'Good.' Tate stood.

The police chief extended his hand. 'No hard feelings? You were speeding, after all.'

'OK,' Tate said with more enthusiasm than he felt. The man had ruined his day, but he was a man in uniform and he had a job to do.

'Where are you planning on going now?'

'I've got a reservation at the Elm Street Inn.'

Donoghue smiled wryly. 'I live just across the road. Mind you, when I moved in, the place was called something else and they hadn't made the bar what it is now. The wife's not happy about it, but I am.'

'If I see you there, I'll buy you a beer.'

'Would you be attempting to bribe a police officer, Mr Tate?'

Tate smiled. 'I don't know. How good is the local beer?'

'Good. And thanks for your help identifying the rifle, if you're right.'

'I am.'

24

Chapter 3

Camden, Maine

Donoghue waived the speeding ticket, so all Tate had to do was sign for his watch. He left the air-conditioned cool of the police station. Outside, the late afternoon was still warm, and particles of dust danced in the sun as he opened the driver's door of the Tahoe. The built-up interior heat hit him. He sighed. It hadn't been parked in the shade. He climbed into the stuffy cabin, powered down both front windows and switched on the satellite navigation. He was finally on holiday again.

Fresh air blew on his face as he took Mechanic Street and then Elm before arriving at the inn minutes later. Elm Street Inn consisted of three white buildings, clad, as was the norm in New England, in white wooden planking. Two buildings were long two-storey accommodation blocks sitting at right angles to each other across a parking lot. The third, which had been the original house on the property, sat squat and heavily extended, facing the street. There was a grassy area to the right of both accommodation blocks with a screened-off section concealing a pool.

Tate brought the SUV to a halt at reception and stepped out. Having lost most of the day at the pleasure of the local police, he'd arrived much later than planned. He stretched and gave the inn a quick 360, noticing a large figure in jeans and a black polo shirt who seemed to be taking photographs of the parking lot. Tate squinted in the sunlight . . . no, the man was taking photos of the cars. Tate raised an eyebrow, entered reception and gave the old guy behind the counter his name.

'Ah, our guest from England?' the elderly guy asked in a chirpy voice and not waiting for Tate to answer said, 'Been over a few times myself; Pop was stationed there in the war. Very pretty place, England. Which part are you from?'

'Camden.'

'Camden?' the old guy said with a frown.

'Camden, London. And it's not as pretty as Camden, Maine.'

The door behind Tate swung open and the photographer entered. He nodded at the receptionist and said in Russian-accented English, 'Number seven.'

'Right you are, sir.' The receptionist handed him a key.

Tate eyed the large man. And large was an understatement – he was huge. He had several inches on him in both height and shoulder width. His hair was cut short, but not in any way that could be called stylish. It certainly wasn't the work of a trained barber. Tate noted his boots were well worn, whilst there were still shop-creases in his dark blue Levi's and black Ralph Lauren polo shirt. The man nodded curtly before exiting again. Tate watched him stride away. He recognised his upright, chest-first bearing as that of a soldier, or at least someone who had until recently been one. Questions formed in Tate's mind and as if to answer at least the first, the old man spoke.

'We got a pair of Russians staying with us; came up from Portland way the day before yesterday. He's the biggest. I'm Joe.'

'Jack, Jack Tate.'

'That's lucky, because we have a reservation in your name.' Joe smiled at his own joke as if it wasn't the first time he had told it. 'Well, Jack, if you'll just let me take a look at your passport and credit card, I'll see about giving you your room. Oh and if you can write the details of your vehicle on this form here?'

'Is there anywhere to eat around here?' Tate asked as his details were tapped into an ancient-looking computer.

'Sure is; didn't you see "Eric's" on Elm? It's the restaurant and bar attached to this place. Same owner, great food, great chef – I'm the chef. You like oysters?'

'I do, but the last lot I had were faulty.'

'Faulty?' Joe repeated.

'Yep, I had five but only three of them worked.'

Tate watched Joe's face go blank for a moment before he started to snigger. 'At my age, I imagine most of 'em would have been faulty.' He handed Tate a key. 'Here, room number six, next to our Russian friends in the building on the left. Now you go and drop off your things, and I'll see you a bit later at Eric's.'

'Thanks.'

Tate returned to the parking lot and drove the fifty feet to the accommodation block. Hefting out his bag from the trunk, he scanned the doors for number six. A few minutes later, he had located his room, thrown his bag on the floor, and was looking out of the window, across the car park to the view of the dense woodland. Tate shook his head and smiled; Camden, Maine, was definitely more to his liking than Camden, London, even if a rogue gunman was on the prowl.

Tate stayed motionless and took in the scene for a minute before undressing and stepping into the bathroom. He pulled the cord for the light. The bulb flickered for a moment before it went out with a small clink. Tate sighed, relocated the waste bin, and used it to prop the door open before turning on the shower.

Oleg sighed as the bartender plonked a plate piled high with food in front of his colleague.

'Double bacon cheeseburger with slaw and fries. Extra onion rings.'

'Thank you.' The large Russian rubbed his hands together in appreciation.

'Will that be all?'

'Yes, it is all.'

'Enjoy your meal.' The bartender retreated.

'You eat far too much. You'll be fat and unfit by the time you hit fifty,' Oleg stated.

Sergei sneered at his older colleague. 'In twenty more years, Oleg, when I am old like you, I will worry. But today I will eat good, hot American food because the day after tomorrow I will not be able to.'

Oleg glanced warily around the room. 'You are also as discreet as a T-62 battle tank!'

'I am sorry. Now can I finally eat?'

The pair lapsed into silence as the large Russian devoured his meal. Oleg slowly drank his beer. The quality was good, and he had to drink it to keep up the appearance of a man on vacation, but he also knew that it dulled his senses and he did not wish to miss anything that may be of note for his mission.

'And nothing has changed?' Sergei asked, wiping his mouth with a red paper napkin.

'I've received no call. Everything is going to plan. We stay to observe the attack and then we pull out six hours afterwards.'

'And then we shall return to Russia as national heroes whilst America falls to its knees.'

Oleg's eyes widened. 'You must say no more!'

Sergei chuckled. 'You think anyone here speaks Russian?'

'They may! For the next thirty-five hours we must not let our guard down.'

'In thirty-five hours, no one will be worrying about anything they overheard you or I say, even if they could understand Russian.'

For once there was logic in Sergei's words, but Oleg did not want to tempt fate. The man made him feel uncomfortable. Oleg drank his draught beer and continued to observe the bar and its patrons. What would happen to this place and the many thousands like it, he wondered, not just on a technical but also on a societal standpoint? A myriad of unanswered questions trooped through his mind, like soldiers at a Moscow military parade. Would the local grid or emergency generators turn on? Would the bar be used as a meeting point? Would the bar share its food and water supplies with stranded guests and needy locals? And what about criminal gangs? Would they take over and jockey for power with the powerless authorities?

These questions were his concern. These were his part of the mission.

Refreshed after a nap, Tate entered Eric's and took a stool at the end of the bar. It was early evening but a Saturday night nonetheless, yet fewer than half of the dozen or so tables were occupied. He spotted the big Russian sitting at a corner table with another man. They were facing out across the room. It was the exact spot he would have chosen, out of habit. It provided a clear line of sight to the exit; no one could approach without being seen. But the Russians had taken it first. It was puzzling, especially the way they were not facing each other but out across the room, almost as though they were waiting for a cabaret show.

If the large man was military, or military trained, was the second? He was older, grey haired yet from Tate's swift analysis seemed too soft to be an officer. He eyed Tate suspiciously. So what did that make him? Tate sighed and shook his head a little. He was on holiday, and by the look of the large Russian's brand-new clothes, so were they. Tate needed to relax and enjoy his downtime. He'd been ordered to take a month off to relax, unwind, and if he didn't, he knew his boss wouldn't be happy. He turned his head away slowly, not wanting to draw any more attention to himself.

'What can I get you?'

Tate was taken aback for a moment by the barmaid. He made

a conscious effort not to stare at her cleavage. 'Just a beer will do for now.'

'Draught or bottle?'

'What's best?'

The barmaid popped a bottle and placed it on a mat in front of him.

'Thanks.' Tate studied the bottle. The beer was labelled "King Titus" and brewed by the Maine Beer Company. Tate took a sip and nodded in appreciation. 'Will you have one?'

She shook her head. 'Too early for me. Are you staying here?'

'Yes.' He took a greedy slug of his beer.

The woman raised her eyebrows. 'You're the guy from London.'

'Close. Camden.' She frowned and Tate explained, 'Camden's a borough of London.'

'Funny, I never knew that.'

Tate took another swig. 'There's probably a word for people who travel to find their town's twin. I don't know it though.'

'There's another Camden in New Jersey, but that place is apparently the second most dangerous city in the US, and the poorest, according to an article I read.'

'A bit different from here then.'

'A lot different.'

'I'm Jack.'

'Sara.'

'Nice to meet you.'

'I'm glad you think so.' Sara turned away and served another customer.

'Have you seen the menu yet, Jack?' Joe asked, entering the bar from the kitchen door.

'Nope. Sara didn't give me one.'

'You said you just wanted a beer,' she snapped from the other end of the bar.

'To drink, but I'm also hungry.'

Sara smiled without sincerity and handed him a leatherette

folder. 'Here we are, sir. Please let me know what you would like to order.'

'Thank you.'

'Joe, can you take over for a minute?'

'Sure.'

Sara exited the bar and Joe shrugged. 'She's a bit . . . what's the word? Agitated at the moment.'

Tate nodded; it was no skin off his nose. 'So what would you recommend?'

Joe leaned forward and placed his index finger on an item. 'That. It's something I concocted myself. Seafood stew.'

Tate nodded. 'What's in it?'

'Scallops, haddock, and shrimp . . . with a dash of chilli. It goes surprisingly well with a bottle of white wine.'

'Sold.'

'On the stew?'

'On both.'

'Great, but I thought you were drinking beer?'

'I'm on holiday. I'll throw caution to the wind.' He finished the beer in two gulps.

Sara reappeared; Joe gave her a mock salute and returned to the kitchen.

'So what do people do around here for fun on a Saturday night?' Tate asked.

'Go into town, drink too much and fall over, or get on their boats, drink too much and fall overboard. You want another?'

'Nice, you should work for the Camden tourist board.'

'I've had a long day,' Sara said.

'Tell me about it.'

'OK, I will.' Tate rolled his eyes, but she continued to talk. 'My ex-boyfriend woke me up drunk at four a.m. like he has done nearly every morning for the past week. Hollering at my window and ringing my bell. Then, when he finally decided to leave, he slashed the tyres on my car, which meant I had to take a taxi to the grocery store. Then when I got back, I found out the meat supplier hadn't made his delivery, so I had to then spend an hour calling other suppliers to be able to serve my guests this evening.'

'I'm sorry.'

Sara folded her arms. 'So tell me about your day.'

'I drove down from Bangor, and then got arrested and thrown in a cell by your very efficient Camden PD.'

'So are you a dangerous criminal?'

He smiled. 'A case of mistaken identity.'

Sara exchanged his old bottle for a new one. 'I'm sorry, I'm just tired.'

'Hey, I'm a Londoner. Anything less than a slap in the face is viewed as politeness in my local boozer.'

'Boozer?'

'Pub.' Tate swigged his beer. 'Did you get your tyres fixed?'

'Yes. Why, were you offering to fix 'em?'

'I was.'

'Are you a car mechanic?'

'No, but I can have a look.'

Joe appeared with a plate. Sara pointed across the room. 'Take that spare table over there. I don't encourage eating at the bar. It makes the place look messy.'

'Fine,' Tate said with a shrug and shifted to the table. It was nearer to the Russians.

Joe deposited a large bowl. 'Enjoy.'

'Thanks.'

'Here.' Sara placed a bottle of Sauvignon Blanc and a glass on the table.

Tate watched her walk back to the bar. There was a noise from the corner and he saw the large Russian also assessing Sara. He nudged the second Russian and said something Tate couldn't quite make out. The older man remained silent.

Tate started to eat. He'd always liked fish and chips and, as a teenager, had a Saturday job at the local chippy. Back then some places still used newspaper to wrap the food in, well the outer layer at least. He remembered wrapping his brother's order in page 3 of *The Sun* on more than one occasion to try to embarrass him. Whether he noticed the bare breasts of the page 3 girl or not he never mentioned it. Tate hadn't been the best younger brother in the world and certainly far from the best son, but he and his brother had a strong bond. Tate took a sip of wine then continued to eat. What he was eating now shamed the simple fish and chips, and there wasn't a mushy pea in sight.

A group entered the bar. A family. The parents appeared to be in their late fifties. Their two daughters, tall, mid to late teens. All four were dressed in matching blue hiking shirts, khaki shorts and sturdy boots. Tate noticed the big Russian obviously ogling the girls as they took a table.

'Dad, can we order now? I'm hungry,' one of the two girls said, from behind her iPhone.

Tate ate his meal and thought again how the world had changed since he was a kid. They hadn't had iPads and iPhones; they'd had to make do with conning their parents out of change for the pinball machine or the pool table whenever they'd been treated to a pub lunch. He frowned; actually at the girls' age he'd already joined the army whilst his brother had studiously studied for his A levels. Tate looked at the family again. The two kids absorbed in their screens, seemingly oblivious to where they were or who they were with, whilst the parents checked a large tourist map. Meanwhile the eyes of the smaller, older Russian continuously roved the room.

Tate finished his meal and wiped his mouth on a napkin. Out of the corner of his eye he saw the older Russian jerk, as though poked with a cattle prod, and then thrust his hand into his jacket pocket. He pulled out a mobile phone, pressed it to his ear and turned away from the room. Moments later he rose to his feet and said something to the big Russian who stood and towered over him. They exchanged a few words. The older Russian's voice was low, almost inaudible, but Tate caught the other say in Russian, "That is why he is needed on this mission." He slapped the older Russian on the back and they left the bar.

There was something odd about the Russian's coded language and their behaviour, something that brought back bad memories. Tate drained his wine glass, left cash for his food and drink on the table, waited for a minute and then, on impulse, followed the men. As he stepped outside, he saw the duo reach the other side of the parking lot. They inspected a Winnebago belonging to another guest. After some finger pointing and gesticulation, they moved towards an SUV. In the dim sodium lights, Tate could just make out a second Chevrolet Tahoe, which was the same colour as his own, parked next to his.

His brain, although fuzzy from several beers and the best part of a bottle of wine, tried to remind him of something. It came to him suddenly. The police had stopped him because he was driving the same car as the suspected killer . . . No. Tate stopped himself. He was overthinking the situation again, chasing ghosts, allowing thoughts of his last operation in Ukraine to get the better of him. He was on holiday, and besides, neither of the Russians bore any resemblance to him.

The stench of cigarette smoke filled his nostrils and he heard a voice. 'What are you looking at?' Tate turned as Sara stepped out of the shadows by a rear door. 'Are you spying on them?'

'Just getting some fresh air.'

'I know, I know. I've been meaning to quit.' She dropped the cigarette on the tarmac and ground it into the path with her foot.

'It's bad for your lungs.'

'Mine look pretty healthy, don't ya think?'

'I can't give you a medical opinion.'

'Huh.'

The pair stood in silence staring at each other for a long moment before Tate spoke. 'I'm going to take a walk, then go to bed.'

'A walk, at night?'

'Yeah, I'm English; we like to walk.'

'There's nothing to see. At night I mean. Drop by the office in morning and I'll give you a tourist map.'

'OK, I will.'

'Goodnight.'

Tate watched her step back into the inn, stood for a moment then headed for the road. The inn was a way out of town, unlike the other places he could have booked, which were both more expensive and touristy. It was a fifteen-minute walk, he imagined, straight down Elm Street to the town centre. Directly across Elm he saw ornate sweeping gates standing either side of a road that curved one way then another. He could see houses set back from the road with drives and lawns. It looked respectable, and he remembered Chief Donoghue saying he lived opposite the inn.

Tate turned and started walking towards town. He breathed in the cooling evening air and tasted both the sea and the trees, or was he just being fanciful? He'd gone no more than a dozen steps when bright headlights appeared from the direction of town, accompanied by the whine of a turbocharged engine and the rhythmic throb of music. The lights were lost momentarily in a dip before the car crested the top. There was no pavement on his side of the road and Tate was forced to scamper backwards onto the grass as the Nissan flew past, well in excess of the speed limit.

Its exhaust banged and popped as the car slowed and came to a tyre-squealing halt and then reversed back the way it had come until it was level with him. It was a cobalt blue, highly customised Skyline straight out of a "Fast & Furious" movie. The windows were heavily tinted. The driver's powered down. From the gloom inside a head peered out. The driver had long hair, tied back with a bandana with a back-to-front, black baseball cap crammed on top. Tate met the driver's red-rimmed eyes. The driver glared at him, as though assessing him before he snickered, floored the gas to spin the tyres and roared towards the road directly opposite the inn, the quiet respectable road where Donoghue allegedly lived.

Even here in quiet, picturesque Maine it appeared there were idiots marking their territory, and marking the road with rubber, but he didn't care why. Tate carried on walking, away from the smell of gasoline and rubber. He wanted to make the most of the last light of the day, but his mind wanted to go back to the Russians at the inn. Who were they and why were they there? He remembered the last time he had seen Russian military officers; it had been in Ukraine several years before, and they hadn't been friendly.

Chapter 4

Five years ago

Mariupol, Ukraine

It had taken the seven-man team Tate was part of less than four hours to reach the Russian-occupied Ukrainian city of Novoazovsk from Mariupol. Led by a former Ukrainian Spetsnaz officer, Victor Boyko, they'd scurried across fields and taken paths through the woods but on nearing the town had been forced to use an insurgent checkpoint. Dressed in mismatched camouflage fatigues, each had a white band affixed to the left arm of their field jackets to distinguish them as fellow members of the DNR – the Russian-backed and funded Donetsk People's Republic. Carrying gifts, they'd passed with smiles; a team returning from a successful incursion into Ukrainian-controlled territory.

But the men with Tate were not DNR, they were members of "The Shadows". A pro-Ukrainian partisan group who had attacked Russian fuel depots, cut supply lines, eliminated key personnel, and most recently hijacked a shipment of anti-tank weapons. What the group lacked, however, was the kind of intel that only the intelligence arm of a nation state could provide, and that was where Tate entered the frame.

Tate had been seconded to a clandestine unit known only as "E Squadron". Operated by the Secret Intelligence Service, it utilised serving members of the UK Special Forces for ad hoc missions that were deemed too sensitive for overt British government action. Tate's ability to pass for Russian, and his tenure with the SAS, made him the first choice to lead the direct-action part of their current fully deniable mission in Ukraine. Whilst Tate's mission controller – his SIS officer brother Simon Hunter – sat safely in the British Embassy in Kyiv, Tate was sweating at the sharp end in the heat of a Ukrainian high summer.

Satellite intelligence had confirmed that an assault group numbering in excess of thirty members of Russia's Baltic Fleet Spetsnaz Unit were barracked in Novoazovsk. Further intel indicated that they were planning an imminent amphibious assault on Mariupol in preparation for the establishment of a "land bridge" to Russian-controlled Crimea.

Leaving the unsuspecting militants at the checkpoint behind, Boyko had led the group further into occupied territory to an abandoned dacha – a tumbledown summerhouse, where their heavy weapons had been cached in a tarpaulin-covered hole under rusting agricultural equipment. Boyko had done little to suppress his pride as he showed Tate four packing crates containing anti-tank weapons, a mixture of units of the RPG-30 Kryuk (Hook), and the RPG-28 Klyukva (Cranberry). The RPGs had been designed to defeat modern armour so, Boyko confirmed, a crumbling concrete building would prove no problem. The two-storey, blocky Soviet building had once been a local government administrative office and was the largest structure in the street.

Tate and Boyko had taken turns watching the Baltic base while the remainder of the team lay low in the woods behind the OP – the observation post. During the course of the day, there had been movement outside the target building – regular Russian troops bringing food supplies and irregular militants scrounging. Given short shrift by the professionals, the militants had wandered off complaining loudly. The weather, an oppressively hot Ukrainian summer, had made them sweat during the day but now thankfully as evening approached had dropped to a less antagonising level, and more importantly the mosquitos had drifted away. Tate scratched a bite on his arm; he'd remember to use more DEET next time. Checking his watch, he calculated that there was only one more hour of Ukrainian daylight left.

Lying prone in the ruined house, Tate studied the base through a pair of field glasses. As the heat made the dusty tarmac shimmer, he counted the number of Russian troops outside the building. Four stood around smoking and idly chatting in the shade of the entrance porch while a further two, shirtless, worked on the engine of an APC – armoured personnel carrier, which sat hood up on the grassy verge. The relaxed posture of the men belied their identity and purpose. These were members of the Baltic Fleet Spetsnaz unit, and they were preparing for combat. Like Tate, they were Special Ops operators who knew the risks associated with their jobs; unlike Tate they were about to be tasked with taking by force a friendly city. Tate had no qualms in taking them out if it meant safeguarding the residents of Mariupol.

The mission was black, deniable. If Tate became compromised, neither the SIS nor the Ukrainian government would be coming to his rescue. And any scent of British involvement would cause an international incident. Tate knew if captured, he would have to rely on his Russian language skills to talk his way out; but up against Russian Spetsnaz, there was little chance of this. Tate wasn't planning on messing up; neither were the men around him. The Shadows consisted of not only Ukrainians, but also Georgians with previous experience of Russia's aggression, Chechens no longer loyal to Kadyrov, Poles and Lithuanians, wanting to protect their cousins, and Russians who did not believe the Kremlin's lies. The Shadows were, in effect, a "Ukrainian Foreign Legion".

Tate took a momentary breather to wipe his face when a sound reached his ears – distant, amorphous, and becoming louder. Like approaching thunder but regular, repetitive, mechanical, manmade. A low rumble, heavy engines.

'Armoured vehicles!' Boyko confirmed, appearing at Tate's shoulder. Tate hoped it was APCs rather than anything heavier. Boyko read his mind. 'Our rockets should be able to penetrate their plates. Have no worries.'

'Train, fight easy,' Tate said.

'Is that a motto of yours?'

'I borrowed it from General Alexander Suvorov.'

'For a Russian he was a wise man.'

'He's not here – he must be.' Tate adjusted his field glasses to point at the far end of the street. He saw a dust cloud, and then the unmistakable shape of a Russian BMP-2 emerged. It was a light-armoured vehicle, faster than a tank and suited to urban warfare. Fitted with a 30mm auto cannon, a coaxial 7.62mm PKT machine gun, and an ATGM missile launcher; it was a deadly piece of hardware. 'And here comes the worst.'

A note of worry sounded in the Ukrainian's voice. 'Your intelligence stated it would be no more than two vehicles.'

'Yep, and here we have an armoured column.' Tate started to count. The first two vehicles were BMP-2s. The next four were T-80 battle tanks, a model Russia had officially mothballed in December 2013 and in amongst these were two soft-sided green Kamaz military trucks.

'This is not good,' Boyko murmured. 'Do you think this will be part of the assault?'

'Not the first wave; that'll use guile, not strength – hence the Spetsnaz. The armour will roll in later.'

The column became ominously larger as it grew nearer. The

two BMP-2s came to a halt over in front of the APC as the tanks and trucks carried on past the OP and deeper into the city.

'You were right, I think,' the Ukrainian said, slapping Tate on the back.

'True, but what was in those trucks?'

'I do not care – it did not stop here.'

Tate let out a sigh of relief; although they were armed with the correct weapons to defeat battle tanks, it would not be possible to knock one off at a time without receiving heavy and sustained incoming fire for their trouble. A figure climbed out of the lead vehicle. Tate adjusted his focus to bring the newcomer's face into sharp profile. A new intel package had arrived the night before, and this included an image of the intelligence officer from Moscow. The face Tate saw now matched a digital photograph from the pack. 'Target confirmed. That's Maksim Oleniuk.'

The troops, who had been smoking, dropped their cigarettes and snapped to attention, exchanging salutes with the man in charge. Oleniuk inspected the APC. He tapped the hood with his palm and spoke to the men working on it before he turned on his heels and entered the building.

As a former officer, Boyko was not used to taking orders and Tate could sense him becoming impatient at his side. The engine of the APC came to life. There was whooping as the soldiers congratulated their mechanics. More men now stepped out of the building to inspect the vehicle, joined by the crews of the BMP-2s.

'We are ready,' Boyko announced deliberately. 'Just give us the order.'

Tate nodded. Killing was never easy, but if neutralising these professional soldiers safeguarded the innocent residents of Mariupol, there was no real alternative. He checked his watch. There was now about forty minutes of sunlight left. The Russians would at least get fed and watered before they launched their attack, and that would be when they were at their most vulnerable.

Tate looked at the Ukrainian and tapped his watch. 'Tell your men, ten minutes. Then engage.'

'OK.' Boyko let a smile split his dirt-stained face. He squeezed Tate's shoulder and scurried backward out of the rear of the house and into the grassy field beyond. He would join the rest of his men who would now become three two-man fire teams.

Tate looked on like an angel of death; every man visible to him would be dead within the next quarter of an hour. He had the power; he could give the order to abort or he could warn the Russians. Tate did neither, as he counted down the ten minutes and waited. He heard a distant sound, an engine, low and laboured. It sounded like a heavy truck. He searched the road, with his field glasses, in both directions and saw nothing. And then it stopped. The evening became still again, and then it wasn't . . .

There was a distinctive whoosh from behind and to the south of him, and then an all but inaudible keening as the first grenade whistled on an arc through the darkening Ukrainian August evening and then finally a thunderous explosion. The APC was hurled upwards and then crashed against the wall of the base, like a plaything thrown by a giant, petulant child. There was a moment of silence before flames engulfed the heavy troop transporter and leached up the walls.

The next RPG landed next to the side wall, ripping a gaping hole in the concrete. Figures ran out of the building into the dying daylight in time to see more grenades turn the remaining two armoured vehicles into expensive pieces of scrap metal. Angry shouts and gunfire now added to the mix as the Spetsnaz tried to resist the surprise attack, returned fire into the field and tried to escape the kill zone, but it was futile as RPGs tore into the concrete walls around them.

Tate continued to observe, knowing the images of the dead and dying would join the show reel of ghouls who haunted him when he slept. He'd seen enough. Unable to bring in his own weapons, Tate had an AK-47 on the floor of the OP next to him. It was simple yet lethal and had been the mainstay of the Russian infantry for generations.

Grabbing the AK, Tate carefully crabbed from the broken window at the front of the house to the collapsed rear wall and the open field. He froze. Movement. In the field, but in the wrong direction. He dropped to the floor. Russians. A group who had not been hit by the attack, had not been in the target building, and had been unsighted by either Tate or Victor Boyko, were now flanking The Shadows' firing positions.

The realisation struck Tate that he was in danger of being cut off from his group. He was alone in the house, the OP, whilst the three two-man fire teams were in the field behind. And then he saw the Russians were being led by the intelligence officer from Moscow, Maksim Oleniuk. How had he escaped the attack on the base? Tate barely had time to count the twelve men, spaced out, weapons up, advancing on The Shadows. More than enough to launch their own assault and outnumbering The Shadows two to one.

Tate had to react; he had to try to even the odds. His group were low tech, no radios or comms. Mobile phones only and urgent messages sent via WhatsApp. Boyko had boasted to him that with end-to-end encryption, the free service was more secure than the Russians' own military network. But Tate didn't carry a phone, in case he was compromised. Tate glanced around the shattered farmhouse, the rubble wall, the caved-in roof and the staircase leading to the first floor. He'd ruled out the first floor as an OP because it was too exposed from the road but from the fields there was half a section of interior wall he could use as a shield.

Tate darted across the open space inside the house to the steps, all the while expecting to be cut down by a Russian round. None came. There were irregular gaps between the steps but soon he was at the top. He knew The Shadows would keep on firing until they had exhausted all of their grenades or came under sustained attack. They would discard all heavy weapons when they retreated in order to exfil faster. He could still hear the shells so he knew they had not bugged out yet and the Russians knew this too.

Tate flattened himself on the bare wooden boards of the first floor. The exterior front wall of the room here had broken away when the roof caved in, leaving a hole that could be seen from the Russian base. Tate looked up, out of the building at the base. He could see no one moving, no one alive. Rising to his haunches he moved to the back of the space, and using the intact part of the interior wall as a shield he peered out.

He had an elevated view of the field and the Russians moving within it. Unseen like tigers in a forest they stealthily traversed the chest-high crops, including old sunflowers that had grown never to be picked. And past the Russians he could see Victor Boyko and his men. Tate switched the fire selector on the Kalashnikov to single shot, made himself as small as he could and looked down the iron sights.

Broader and slower than his men, although still moving with skilled steps, Maksim Oleniuk was an easy target. Tate had had no time to test-fire the weapon, and AKs were generally used for short bursts or spray-and-pray attacks to supress an enemy with volume of fire, not accuracy. It was a weapon that could be thrown around, buried in mud and then immediately used; it was the Tonka Toy of assault rifles. But Tate was not playing. He breathed out slowly and squeezed the trigger. The single 7.62mm round tore towards the Russian officer and blew away the head of a sunflower to his right. Tate swore.

Oleniuk turned, unclear about the direction of the shot, eyes searching for an attacker but at his own eye level, and then he carried on forward. Tate sighted again, acquired Oleniuk's head and squeezed the trigger . . . at the very same moment, the Russian stopped dead and turned his face upwards. For the briefest of moments, it may have only been milliseconds, Oleniuk was staring directly at him. The 7.62mm round tore up the distance between the two men and struck just as Oleniuk jerked to one side. The round hit the man's neck, blood flowed and the intelligence officer dropped to the ground.

Tate wasted no time and acquired a second Russian. This one he hit first time in his upper back, punching the man forward into the crops. He didn't care if the man was dead or alive. Tate ducked as he started to take incoming fire. A volley of rounds sailed past him but one caught the top of the wall and kicked up a chip of concrete. Tate let out a breath and flicked the selector switch to "burst". This would allow three rounds to leave the rifle with each pull of the trigger. It was less accurate as the recoil would in effect be trebled but he needed a higher rate of suppressive fire. He moved as far to the right as he could and popped up again. This time he sent a burst at a soldier who was facing Tate's farmhouse and scanning for targets. The Russian jerked as all three rounds shredded his chest.

The RPGs had stopped and Tate saw The Shadows were exfiltrating from their positions and returning fire to the Russians in the field as they did so. He saw one go down from Russian fire and fall across an empty launch tube. Tate had bought some time, and just hoped it was enough for the rest to get away. But he still needed to escape himself. They had agreed on an ERV – an emergency rendezvous – two clicks past the woods at the next abandoned village, hopefully far enough away that the Russians would have given up any pursuit. Tate sought out one more target but didn't open fire as the man was moving away with the remaining Russians on a tangent that took them away from his exfil route.

Tate took the steps down, weapon up, to the ground floor. Taking a deep breath, he burst out of the cover of the farmhouse and into the field, looking for targets, looking for trouble and finding it. Rounds whipped past his head and he threw himself down onto the warm Ukrainian earth. He pushed himself backwards with his feet, his back flat to the ground. A Russian soldier burst through the crops immediately above him. Tate sent a burst into his face before the man had time to react. Tate rolled away, got to his feet and traversed the field as quickly as he could.

Once again the sound of mechanical thunder approached, but the T-80 battle tanks were too late. Tate and his comrades slipped away into the Ukrainian night, like shadows.

Chapter 5

Present day

Northport, Maine

The last light of the day made the walls of the house glow like an old sepia postcard. The house was a modest 1930s' two-bedroom cottage on Atlantic Highway between the towns of Northport and Belfast. What wasn't modest, however, was the twenty-acre oceanfront grounds. Mature trees, enough to be considered a private wood, lined the property on three sides affording total privacy for retired general Richard Leavesley and his wife. In high summer it was a verdant idyll and, according to photographs taken by the couple's daughter and helpfully posted on Facebook, became a myriad of reds and oranges in the autumn and a stark, sharp, Christmas card winter landscape when the snows came.

Akulov much preferred this place over the soulless timber monstrosity designed by the banker from Boston and Piper's mansion. But the Russian was not in the US to meet interesting people and discuss architecture with them; he was in the US to kill them. The old soldier was the last on his list of targets in Maine.

For this hit he would again use the Blaser. It had worked well thus far and he saw no reason to change his choice of weapon in an attempt to conceal the pattern of kills. The targets were on the list for various reasons but fundamentally, each man had wronged his employer and each was to be eliminated. But none of this mattered much to Akulov – soon the US would not have the capacity to investigate.

Even without the hasty change of schedule, this was the most challenging of his three hits. Not because, like him, the target was former military but for the simple fact that Akulov had a greater risk of exposure. During his initial reconnaissance trip he had parked in the only available place to him, the car park of the Hideaway Diner a five-minute walk directly along the Atlantic Highway. Among the tourists, he'd taken a while to eat and assess the possibilities of using the parking lot again but found the family running the establishment to be too attentive. His long and intensive training meant that he could sound and look American whenever he spoke English. What he could not do, however, was materialise and dematerialise at will.

Again the internet, and America's reliance on it, came to his aid. He'd run an untraceable "real estate" search on his encrypted phone. A property less than a mile away, on the same stretch of road, was advertised for sale. The listing, including full photography, confirmed that it was masked from the highway by a tree-lined meandering driveway, set back in the trees, and most importantly that it was available immediately. Real estate agency code for "empty". Akulov paid for his meal, left a tip not because he wanted to – he wasn't a fan of fatty American fare – but because if he didn't, he'd be remembered.

Coming to a halt in the turning circle he casually stepped out of his black Tahoe, advanced towards the front door of the vacant house and rang the bell. From within the whitewashed, timber-clad walls came a cheap, electronic chime that was at odds with the not insubstantial price being asked for the property. But apart from the bell, the rustling of the leaves in the breeze and the distant hum of the highway, no other sounds reached his tactically trained ears. Still playing the part of a potential buyer, Akulov walked the perimeter of the house, peering in windows and gently pressing the back door. Finally he placed his left ear against a glass pane and listened. Nothing. No hum of life. He straightened up and using the bottom of his dark blue polo shirt rubbed away any oils or imprint from his ear on the glass. Ears were almost as unique as fingerprints and he was certainly not going to leave any trace he had been here.

Five minutes later, after repositioning the Tahoe so that it faced back up the driveway and was hidden in the lea of the house, he used a set of lock picks on the back door. Once inside he'd scouted the house to confirm that it was empty.

Akulov never failed to prepare but the timescale in which he had to undertake this chain of assassinations was challenging. His preferred approach would have been to watch each target exclusively, establishing a hide – an observation post – and then once the best time had been assessed he'd take the shot. A single shot, any more would risk the origin of the round being identified. That is how he had worked in Grozny, that is how he had worked in eastern Ukraine and that is how most recently he had taken out a leading ISIL commander in Syria. But three targets in three consecutive days had now, on the whim of his employer, become three targets in two days. It was a totally unacceptable and rash request to any operator on the private circuit. But his employer knew he was the best, and so did he. As such he saw it as a challenge to his ability, and he had accepted.

He'd had to create three hides and use them simultaneously. The hides overlooking both targets number one and two had been less problematic. Rolling hills with thick vegetation had afforded the cover and well-used parking lots had camouflaged the SUV. He had come and gone in turn dressed as a hiker and then casually as a tourist – jeans and a dark polo shirt. He had also favoured a dark green, cotton balaclava in place of camo face paint. One moment it was on and the next it was off, as was his thick woodland camo smock. His Blaser remained safely stowed, broken down, in a customised case and compartment in the trunk of the Tahoe, until the final time he needed to use the hide.

Having found a route that took him painfully slowly through woodland and then grounds of the adjoining property, with its own extensive woods and an orchard, Akulov had observed and recorded his target's schedule. The general and his wife enjoyed having their evening meal at a steel garden set on the sloping lawn. They would then either go inside or remain sitting, drinking, chatting and reading until it was time to watch the summer sunset. It was very romantic, Akulov imagined. Sometime afterwards, the general's wife would retire inside, leaving her husband to sit in the warm night air. And that was when Akulov would end the old soldier's campaign.

A day earlier than planned and with the dappled light of the high-summer evening starting to fade, Akulov lay among the trees watching. Having switched his smock for a ghillie suit, a coverall adorned with loose strips of burlap chosen to match the hues of the foliage in the surrounding wood, and customised by interlacing long grasses, leaves and stems from the area into the garment's loose-weave fabric, he was invisible. As close to invisible, that was, as a human can be if they are immobile. Certainly he would stick out like the red star atop the Kremlin's Spasskaya Tower if looked at with an infrared scope, but he took the chance that a retired general, enjoying a pleasant evening in his own garden, would not happen to have one by his side. And even so Akulov would take his chances that he could get his shot in first before the target raised the alarm.

Akulov watched the general's wife, a handsome woman whose auburn hair seemed a shade too vivid to be natural, touch her husband on the shoulder before she sauntered back to the house. His target was alone. It was time to complete this part of his mission and move on. Again he would not kill the partner. The woman had willingly married a soldier and had known that at any time during his deployment her husband could be snatched away from her. He was a target and it was not up to him to decide when he ceased to be so. No. That decision had been made by the man's enemies. And one such enemy had ordered Akulov to end the man's life.

Akulov steadied his breathing and let his finger take first pressure on the Blaser's trigger. He started to squeeze but then a faint sound stopped him. His finger froze. A bark. A dog. Somewhere. Remaining immobile, senses on full alert, he listened. It barked again. He analysed the tone, the pitch. He cast his mind back. The house that lay between his target's property and the empty house, where he'd hid the Tahoe, was animal-free. No pet dogs, no children. As far as he could tell adults only. He heard the bark again, but now it was less audible, fainter, further away. Meanwhile Akulov's target, retired general Richard Leavesley, was still in his chair, still facing the ocean, still alive. And then he wasn't.

Akulov exhaled, squeezed the sturdy metal trigger, the .338 Lapua Magnum round entered Leavesley's left temple and exited through the right taking with it most of the retired general's brain, skull and face. The body was hurled sideways by the impact and the chair fell. The retort of the shot, lessened by the bulbous suppressor and deadened by the surrounding thick foliage, nevertheless flared as a firework in Akulov's ears. The Russian term for a firework display was a "salute" and this had been his salute to the target, the retired soldier had died a soldier's death.

Akulov did not move for several minutes. His eyes scanned the scene ahead, and his ears hunted for sounds of approaching feet. The dead general's wife had seemingly not heard the shot that had ended her husband's life. Akulov slowly crawled backwards far enough until he found the ejected shell case, which had landed just past his right elbow. Palming this he continued to crawl until he was behind a large tree and only then risked rolling over onto his back and sitting up. He pocketed the shell case, slowly got to his feet and holding the long rifle casually across his body stealthily retraced his route back to the safety of his SUV.

He reached the border of the first neighbouring property and paused before pulling away the loose boards in the all-but-hidden green-painted wooden fence marking the boundary. He listened. No sounds. The boards came away easily, affixed by nails that were now wobbling in holes purposely made too big. Akulov stepped over through the fence and replaced the boards. He crouched. His exfiltration route took him through more trees until he was forced to squeeze in the narrow gap between a garage and an exterior wall and then cross the second fence into the woodland that reached up to the property line of the empty house.

On his haunches he edged forward and then he froze, immobile, made of stone. The dog barked again. And it was nearer. Much nearer. He could hear movement up ahead in the garden, and muffled voices and then an excited bark. Akulov swung the ungainly rifle up as quickly as he could, both the length of the barrel and the suppressor slowing its travel. The foliage in front of him quivered as a dark, round object flew towards him. *Grenade!* a voice inside his head yelled . . . but that made no sense here. The object hit him in the chest and he realised it was a dark coloured rubber ball. And then the foliage exploded and the large, panting face of a golden retriever appeared.

The dog came to a sudden halt, cocked its head to one side and let out a quizzical bark. Akulov smiled, a gesture unseen under his balaclava. He dared not make a sound and he couldn't move his hands without moving the rifle. He willed the dog to get bored and retreat. It didn't. The dog edged forward, sniffing, and now its tail started to wag. Its nose nudged the webbing of his suit as it inspected the foliage attached to it and then it pushed its head down between Akulov's feet, opened its mouth and grabbed the ball with its teeth before it bounded away.

Akulov let out his breath slowly. He had three options: go back, stay where he was or move forward. He decided to stay put, for now. Noise attracted attention but more often than not it was movement that gave away position. Minutes passed and he heard the dog jumping around on the grass on the other side of the shrubs and the voices of a young boy and an older man calling the dog, and then a car door slammed and the noises stopped.

Akulov waited until he was sure that the garden was deserted before he moved once more. He exited the trees and squeezed along the three-foot-wide gap between the garage and the wall and then paused a beat, listened again before he made for the fence, removed yet more loose boards and escaped into the woods beyond. He checked his watch as he reached the far side of the woods. It was eight forty-five and the fading light filtering through the trees now made it difficult for him to see, but also harder for him to be seen. Pulling back the chain-link fence he had strategically cut to make entry, Akulov appeared in the garden of the empty property. But this time it wasn't empty. Akulov went prone in the grass.

Down the incline of the driveway and hidden from its entrance were two vehicles. One was his black Tahoe, and the other was a larger, dull red Ford pick-up truck. He didn't want to kill the occupants of the truck unless he had to. The truck had reversed in. It was facing him. Its lights were off. He could see that the back door of the house was open. A dim light at a first-floor window caught his attention. It was bouncing erratically, a torch An empty house, visited at night by someone entering via the back and using a torch? Akulov sighed. He had planned his mission down to the minutest detail but what he had not, could not have imagined was that the very same empty property that had appealed to him had also attracted intruders, thieves. And thieves were untrained and unpredictable.

The sight on the Blaser was stock. It was permanently affixed to the barrel so that when broken down and reassembled the rifle remained aligned, highly accurate, and that was the reason he had chosen that very model. But the scope was not set up for extreme low light levels. He had a dedicated NVG scope and barrel combination for that, but that was in a case, and the case was in the Tahoe and the vehicle was sixty feet in front of him.

Lights flared in a second room. Two distinct lights now were moving at the same time, a team of two? Unless he was running a solo operation, Akulov would have put at least one man as a sentry. He trained his scope on the Ford. It was the double-cab version with seating for five. The driver's window was open to the evening air and the seat was empty, but the passenger seat was not. Camouflaged almost as well as himself, a figure sat stock-still. His clothes were dark and blended into the interior gloom of the cab. So was this a three-man team? A useful number, perhaps harder to detect, but surely a four-man team could lift more from the house.

And then the fourth man appeared from behind the Tahoe. He walked around the whole length of the vehicle and then passed in front of the pick-up before he opened the driver's door. Akulov noted that they had disabled the interior light, which was a precaution he too would have taken; perhaps they had some training or, failing that, innate awareness.

Two men appeared from the back door of the house. They both carried a large sports bag in each hand and from the way they were walking, the bags looked to be heavy. The bagmen placed the haul on the truck bed before going back inside. Akulov cast his mind back to when he'd searched the house. He had a mental inventory of its contents. The house was sparsely furnished. It was decorated to sell, the old and expensive pieces of furniture – he imagined – having been taken by the current owners. As such it felt like a show home, a stage set. So what were the men removing from the house in bags? He'd wait for them to leave. He didn't care . . . but then he did.

The two bagmen reappeared with two more bags each, heaved them onto the truck bed, and paused for a moment before pulling a cover tight across the space. The truck started up, a rumble of throaty thunder in the quiet night air. Not a vehicle he would have chosen for its stealth capabilities but perhaps it was the load-carrying capacity it had been selected for? The two bagmen got in the back of the cab. The Ford pulled forward. Its lights were off and then it stopped. The driver clambered down. He took a step away from the truck. The passenger got out too and joined him. As did the bagmen. There was a conversation. It was quiet but appeared heated as the driver was gesticulating towards the Tahoe.

Eventually one of the bagmen shrugged, put his hand in his pocket, brandished something too small for Akulov to identify and approached the driver's door of the Tahoe. He inserted it into the lock. Anger and regret surged through Akulov. They could not take his ride, and they must not gain access to what was inside. He had made a mistake leaving his kit there. His anger increased, but now with himself. They had become a threat he had to liquidate.

The bagman made short work of the Tahoe's lock. The door swung open and the interior light came on. All four men were either looking at or moving to the large, black SUV. Akulov had no choice. The Blaser's clip held five rounds. He had four left, and four targets, but the rifle was a straight-pull bolt action, which was faster to reload than a standard bolt action rifle but agonisingly slow compared to even a semiautomatic. The question was, how many could he get before they moved? He had more rounds in the SUV and a compact Glock 19 on a leg holster, but this was an unsilenced backup weapon. The men were moving; he had no choice. Speed and aggression were needed.

He lined the driver up in his sights, aimed squarely between the man's shoulder blades and squeezed the trigger. Sounding like a heavy car door slamming, the supressed round took milliseconds to reach its target. The driver was propelled forward and landed face first on the grass. The passenger saw him go down, swung around, puzzled, shocked. Akulov had already ratcheted another round into the chamber and this hit the man in the chest. The passenger was lifted back and off his feet. He landed, sprawled against the Tahoe's front grille like roadkill.

The second bagman's right hand started to move towards his pocket, his eyes wide and whiter than his face in the failing light as he searched for the source of the gunfire. Akulov fired again. The man's head exploded and the round carried on to hit the wooden-clad house behind. Meanwhile, the first bagman had dropped behind the open door of the Tahoe. Akulov fired his last round. It hit the middle of the door . . . and didn't go through. He swore in his native Russian. A handgun appeared over the top of the door and two loud, unsuppressed shots were fired blindly in his general direction. The Kevlar panels insisted upon by Akulov's employer to be fitted to all of the vehicles used to safeguard the operation may now be exactly what compromised his part of it.

Akulov rolled away from the rifle, then crawled to his left and retrieved his Glock from its holster. He had a full fifteen-round clip, which was more than enough to defeat the target but every round fired either by him or the bagman was another scream of help in the night. But then the night became silent. The bagman was behind the car door and Akulov knew he'd be panicking, assessing his options.

The obvious play was to climb in the SUV, shut the door and drive away, but attempting to bypass the electronic ignition would take time. The second option would be to get back inside the house, and then that gave him more options: hide, find a vantage point to attack, find an exit route. The third option was the fastest way to end it all, and the most foolhardy, but would the bagman really charge Akulov's position? That left the fourth option: surrender. But surrender took more courage than fighting or running as the bagman would be putting his life in his attacker's hands.

Akulov gave the bagman no choice. He trained his Glock on the space under the open door and fired a volley of four quick shots. He then got to his feet and sprinted to the left again, to flank the target. He dropped to his haunches to minimise his profile and aimed the Glock. There was no movement from the bagman. The air was silent save for the ringing in Akulov's ears. The firefight had lasted less than two minutes.

He rose to his feet and approached the SUV. He kept his Glock trained on the crumpled body behind the door, but let his eyes dart to the other fallen men. None of them moved; none of them made a sound. He kicked the bagman with his foot. The bagman's head was resting on the doorjamb and his gun arm was inside. A Glock 17, standard police issue, had fallen into the footwell. He used his boot again and pushed the body out of the cabin. This time the bagman groaned as his head hit the ground and Akulov put a round through his forehead. Akulov went to each body in turn. There was no need for a close inspection; he could tell from the entry wounds and the lack of a head – in the second bagman's case – that all the men were dead. He didn't search any of the bodies for ID, or even look at their faces.

Akulov checked his watch and knew that he had only minutes before neighbours and law enforcement arrived on the scene. The unsuppressed gunfire, he imagined, had also brought the general's wife into the garden to make her own discovery. And that would create one hell of a show. There was no way he wanted to drive back past her place. He retrieved his rifle, didn't break it down, just stowed it in the trunk. He stepped over to the pick-up, unlatched the cover, pulled the corner back and inspected the truck bed. It revealed one of the bags. He tugged down the zip.

It was packed with bricks of one-hundred-dollar bills. Each brick was held tight by a Federal Reserve $10,000 strap. He felt his pulse rise, higher than it had during the firefight. He carried out a hurried mental calculation. It was a life-changing amount, for most people. American dollars were a global currency, but how much would they be worth after the attack? But the cash was free, the spoils of war.

Akulov quickly grabbed the nearest bag but as he hefted it up from the truck bed he heard a sound, and then voices. He smiled ruefully; he'd run out of time. He slung the single bag into the back of the Tahoe and closed the boot. Quickly and quietly, he clambered into the driver's seat. The Tahoe rumbled on start-up – nothing he could do about that – and drove slowly up the drive. He rounded the trees just as figures with flashlights appeared on the highway at the entrance to the property. He flicked his lights on to full beam to dazzle them and pushed the gas pedal flat.

The Tahoe's V8 growled, the tyres bit as they made the transition from gravel to tarmac and then the heavy SUV catapulted itself north, away from the carnage, away from the dead and towards his extraction point.

Chapter 6

Camden, Maine

Tate didn't know what it was that woke him. He lay still on the bed, eyes wide open, staring at a crack of pale sunlight that had slipped between the curtains of his hotel room. Even before he checked his watch he knew it was early; he was still on Camden time – Camden UK that was. He rolled out of bed and padded naked to the bathroom. He showered and felt more alive. Wrapped in a bath towel, he brushed his teeth and carried out a self-assessment. He looked tired, or perhaps he just looked old. He'd never thought he would reach thirty-five. He was glad he had all his hair. That had been one of his greatest fears as a kid – going bald. He and his brother used to chat about it. He smiled.

A year after officially leaving the SAS his fitness hadn't diminished; if anything, he had trained harder. He had to because his new, highly specialised role demanded it. But for now he was on holiday and allowed to relax, paid to in fact; however, the problem was that he couldn't. Something inside would not let go.

Shootings, both professional and amateur, intentional and unintentional happened all the time, true more so in the states than the UK, but even here a chain of professional hits was unusual. Especially in Maine. Especially when he was in Maine.

Little wonder the police chief had been sceptical. Tate mentally shrugged. Sometimes coincidences were just that. He dressed and headed for the door. His stomach was rumbling but he knew that save for an all-night diner he was too early for breakfast, and during his walk the night before he'd not seen a single one.

Outside the light was flat, pale, causing shapeless shadows around the vehicles and buildings as though a shimmering sheet had been thrown over the world. Directly in front of his door sat his hire car – the black Chevrolet Tahoe. Next to that sat another, and another. Three black Tahoes, his and the two driven by the Russian guests. A row of three, like a line of tanks waiting to advance on an unsuspecting enemy. His SUV had a small rental sticker in the rear window; the others did not. Tate's mind drifted back to the words of the police officer who had pulled him over, 'This is a large vehicle for one person.' And here were three Tahoes in a row, each being driven by a single person.

Tate cast a glance at the window of the Russians' room, the curtains closed and the lights out. They had two SUVs but one room. Military men thought nothing of sharing a room, a dormitory with twenty, thirty other soldiers all coughing, farting and flicking their bogies, and they travelled in vehicles packed like sardines in tins to full capacity. And that was the contradiction here. Two men, seemingly working together, seemingly military or ex-military, sharing a room but using two separate large vehicles?

Tate let out a long sigh. Anything could look dodgy, unusual, out of place if you looked too long at it, and two different cars probably just meant they'd come from two different places. But then again . . .

Tate's eyes fell on the three SUVs. With the exception of the rental sticker they looked exactly the same, clones even down to the rims. He consigned the plates of the Russian SUVs to memory and then crouched down and surveyed the underside of his rented Tahoe. He then compared it to the underside of the nearest one being used by the Russians. The ride height appeared to be the same but yes, there were differences. He then checked the next. In the gloomy light he could make out that both of the Russian vehicles had uprated suspension made to compensate for a heavier load or perhaps the rigours of "off roading". The Tahoe could handle bumps, sand and snow but nothing that would warrant upgraded suspension. But then if you'd gone to the trouble of upgrading the suspension, why not raise the ride height and add larger rims and tyres? Why keep the street rims and stock tyres? Unless the idea was for the vehicle to look stock, like a sleeper.

Had the engines been uprated too? Without popping the hood he had no way to check. Tate frowned. The two Russian vehicles were armoured; they had to be. Without checking the shut-lines very carefully or banging his palm against the panels he couldn't be sure, but he would wager good money on it. This was the only logical explanation. But who rode around in vehicles augmented with ballistic glass and panelling? The rich and famous, VIPs, mafia bosses? If this was Mexico City or Moscow, he wouldn't have found it odd, but in the car park of a three-star Maine inn?

Tate stood and walked away towards the road. Past the dark windows of the reception and bar. He reached the road and stopped. A little after five on a Sunday morning, Camden was asleep around him. He'd retrace his route from the night before into town and back. Perhaps he'd even head to the harbour to see if any of the fishing boats were coming back and then perhaps walk along the coastal path whilst it was tourist-free. But first he had a call to make and a question to ask. He retrieved his encrypted iPhone from his pocket, brought the screen up but then a shape shimmered in the distance. The ever-increasing morning sun now hit the polished roof like a mirror. A car, a Camden PD patrol car. Its roof lights silently rotated and flashed for a couple of seconds as it came to a halt in front of him.

The window powered down. Chief Donoghue looked up. He appeared tired. 'Get in.'

It sounded like a command, one soldier to another, not a

friendly request. Tate didn't bother to question it until he'd climbed in, negotiated the extra law enforcement panels jutting out from the dashboard, and shut the door. 'You arresting me for jaywalking?'

Donoghue checked the rear mirror and the car pulled away. 'Guilty conscience?'

'Always.'

Donoghue worked the wheel. The car made a tight turn and headed back in the direction it had come, back to Camden. Tate glanced at the police chief, and tried to read his face. 'What gives so early on a Sunday?'

'I'm going to talk to you frankly, Mr Tate. I'd appreciate the courtesy of you helping me. This is a small department in a small town and we just don't have access to the experts with the right skill sets.'

'And you think I have those skill sets?'

'Tate, I know you have them.'

'OK.' Tate tried to be noncommittal. 'So where are you taking me, Chief?'

'There's been another shooting, an assassination. Same MO, same weapon we believe – but the ballistics have not come back yet.'

Tate whistled. 'The third in three days?'

'The third in two days – this happened last night.'

'Two hits in the same day? That's highly—'

'Unusual?' Donoghue cut him off.

'Unheard of.'

'This one was different, maybe it was poor planning or bad luck but the shooter was interrupted.' Donoghue explained the crime scene at the two properties at Northport, bordering the Atlantic Highway; that a large black SUV had been seen speeding away from the second crime scene and lastly who the victims had been.

'A retired general and what, a bunch of crooks?'

'Crooks certainly but they may well be the same crew who held up an armoured car in Boston a month ago. Too coincidental for any other explanation. Look, even though we may be looking at the same perp as the previous two shootings, these crime scenes come under the jurisdiction of Northport. They're covered in tape and techs and they're waiting for the FBI and the whole works. Northport's given me copies of the crime scene photos. I want you to look at them, and they're back at my office.'

The PD cruiser retraced Tate's journey of the day before but in reverse. They pulled up in front of the columns. Donoghue opened up, let Tate in and then locked the main door again. Without waiting he strode to his office and took a seat behind his desk. He nodded at the coffee station. 'Help yourself.'

'Thanks.' Tate took a mug and poured a full cup of tepid coffee. Black was OK but he preferred his with a dollop of cream.

'Here.' Donoghue pushed a letter-sized manila folder across his desk.

Tate sat, took the folder and opened it. There were two sets of 10x8 prints, each set collated with a paperclip. The first were of the retired general. They showed the position of his body from several different angles. Tate didn't know what religious denomination the general had been but it was going to be a closed-casket affair. 'Single gunshot, to the head. A heavy round, the bullet exited and took his face with it. He never heard it or felt it.' Tate looked up. 'Have the local PD found the shooter's LUP – where the shot was taken?'

'Nope. But obviously it's somewhere in the woods on the property. I'm sure they'll find it.'

'All they'll find will be a few flattened twigs and broken leaves.'

'Because?'

'He's good, elite in fact; he took the shot undetected and then exfilled.'

'Which takes us to those.' Donoghue nodded at the second set of prints.

Tate put the shots of retired general Richard Leavesley to one side and spread out the rest. Four more victims, two with large holes in them, and two without heads. 'So these three were hit with a large-calibre round – from the same rifle I imagine – and this one by a smaller round, probably a 9mm but several times.'

'That much we know. But the why – is what I need to know.'

Tate nodded. 'The rifle we think he's using, the Blaser, has a five-round clip. That's one round for the general and four more. Now our shooter encounters four new, unexpected targets—'

'Whoa. How do you know they were unexpected? These guys had bags of money at the ready, could have been to pay the shooter. Again, too much of a coincidence otherwise.'

'Did he take the cash?'

'Not sure yet. Five sports bags stuffed with hundred-dollar bills in Federal Reserve $10,000 straps were recovered at the scene.'

'That's an awful lot of paper money for one guy to move, physically and financially. Cash is no longer king.' Tate shrugged. 'I don't know why these four victims were there, but it wasn't for him. So he surprises them and he's got four rounds for four targets. Now that's tight, even for our guy and especially with a straight-pull rifle. He missed one of them.'

'So he switched to a backup weapon?'

Tate nodded. 'If he'd known there were more targets, he'd have had at least a second clip. And we know the Blaser was supressed.'

'There was a phone call made to the Northport PD. Reporting gunshots.'

'The backup weapon.'

Donoghue retrieved a map from his drawer, laid it on the table and pointed with a thick index finger. 'That's Atlantic Highway running between Northport and Belfast. The general's house was here, and here – roughly a mile away – is where the shootout took place.' Tate leaned forward, studied the map, as the police chief continued, 'So our shooter sets up here, takes the shot, somehow exfils without alerting the general's wife then walks a mile along a highway back to his vehicle? That is nonsensical. No one walks the highway especially without being seen.'

Tate ran his finger along the map between the two locations. 'He went through the trees, a straight line. Bang – he takes the first kill shot here and then exfils to his vehicle here.'

'Directly through a neighbouring property?'

'That's what I would have done, if I had done it.'

Now Donoghue nodded. His desk phone rang. He held up his hand, made a quieting motion to Tate and then sat and answered it. Tate took the hint, picked up his mug, wandered away from the desk and drank his coffee. It was cold and bitter but he could taste the caffeine. Donoghue listened, didn't ask questions, thanked the caller and then ended the call. 'That was my counterpart at Northport. They've found what looks like three .338 rounds, one they dug out of a wall and five 9mm rounds.'

'That was quick.'

'The chief in Northport has more funding than me.' He laced his heavy hands across his stomach and sat back wearily. 'So it appears our shooter fired just three rifle rounds at the second location.'

Tate looked at the photographs again of the four men dressed in dark clothing, and the images showing their relative positions. The scene had been illuminated by arc lights so he could make out the detail well. He tried to visualise in which order the men fell. He closed his eyes. The house was on the left and to the right of that a red pick-up was parked but in between the pair was a vehicle-sized space. And that was odd. Why park further away from the house than they had to? No that was where the Tahoe had been.

'Tate, it's me who's been up all night and you're sleeping?'

His eyes snapped open, a connection made. 'I don't think he fired only four rounds in total. He emptied his clip – he wanted it to stay quiet but then he had no choice.'

'Because he missed? In that case we'll find the fifth round.'

'He took them out one at a time. The last one had time to move, to shield himself.'

'Where?'

'Behind the shooter's SUV. Think about it. This assassin, a guy who comes and goes like a ghost, discovers a larger force blocking his escape. What does he do?'

'He takes them out and gets the hell out of there, just like he did.'

'And risks things going noisy? No. He waits for them to leave, but then they force him to act.'

'How, they see him?'

'No, they're thieves. They try to take his ride.'

'So he risked, like you said, being compromised over an SUV?'

'Exactly. He could have got another vehicle, but there had to be something about that vehicle or something inside it that he couldn't afford to lose.'

'Yeah, OK. The fact is that our shooter murdered five citizens last night – four of them over a damn car? This is one cold-blooded perp. What matters to me is finding him, stopping him from killing again. He's attached to his Tahoe? Good, that's why we have a BOLO out for a black Tahoe.'

'Not just any Tahoe, an armour-plated one.'

'Wait, what?'

'A Tahoe fitted with ballistic plates.'

'I know what one is I just wanted to know why you would say that.'

'There are three black Tahoes at my hotel.'

'Those I am aware of. Two are driven by the Russians guests – the hotel's CCTV footage shows that they were parked, in plain sight, when each of the previous shootings took place. That's why we eliminated them from our inquiries and why we questioned you.'

'And those same two Tahoes at the hotel, driven by the Russians, are armour-plated.'

'You know this how?'

'I checked out their suspension – compared it to my own. It's beefed up, enhanced, reinforced.'

'You know about cars?'

'Enough to get by.' In the SAS Tate had been in mobility group, therefore trained in motor mechanics, but he didn't feel the need to mention this.

'Why do you think all this is linked, the Russians' Tahoes and the shooter's?'

'Because I don't think the shooter missed the last guy in black. I think the guy was hiding behind an armour-plated Tahoe and the .338 round couldn't get to him.'

'So now we're looking for a Tahoe with what a bullet hole in it?'

'Yes.'

Donoghue raised his hands to his face and rubbed it with both palms. 'Right.'

'Right?'

'Right, let's follow your hunch.' Donoghue stood. 'We're going back to the hotel and we're talking to those Russians.'

They drove in silence back to the inn. Donoghue seemed too tired to waste his energy on extraneous conversation and if humming along to music wasn't an option, Tate preferred to travel in silence. They pulled slowly into the car park, coming to a halt level with reception but blocking the exit for any vehicles to the road.

'They've gone,' Tate stated.

Donoghue nodded. He took a moment to collect his thoughts then said, 'I'll check the CCTV. At least then we'll see exactly when they left.' Donoghue pressed the gas pedal and steered the Crown Victoria over to a parking spot immediately outside reception. 'Thank you for your time this morning, Mr Tate.'

Tate took this as his cue that he was no longer needed and got out of the car. His stomach rumbled again, but now that it was after seven he knew that the inn would be open. He entered via the reception door to see the place deserted save for Sara who was behind the bar making notes on a piece of paper.

'Good morning.'

'Hi. One for breakfast?'

'Unless you want to join me?'

She shook her head. 'I'm doing intermittent fasting. I don't eat till eleven.'

Tate had been told by his first girlfriend never to mention a woman's weight, this included comments about any diet she may or may not be on. So he didn't. 'The chief is outside. He wants to see your CCTV footage.'

'Chief Donoghue?'

'I didn't mean a leader of the Panawahpskek Indians.'

'Someone's swallowed a guidebook. And they're called "Native Americans", not Indians.' She nodded to a pot of coffee. 'If I can trust you to be left alone for five minutes, help yourself to a coffee and a paper.'

Tate poured himself his second coffee of the day – this time there was cream – then took a seat at the bar. The coffee was much better than Donoghue's. As Tate drank he reflected on the events of the past two days. It certainly had not been the sleepy, relaxing holiday he'd expected. There was a stack of newspapers at the end of the bar. He pulled over one that claimed to be national and browsed the front page. Nothing of much interest: worries about a potential storm somewhere over the Gulf of Mexico, the US president's views on a new hybrid car plant in Detroit and at the bottom, almost as an afterthought, a report on the death of retired senator Clifford Piper.

He read the paragraph under the headline and turned to page four where the report carried on but now focused on the senator's record, the loss of his wife and what he had meant for the country. It was a "puff piece" and he learned nothing new. Although it listed his death as a murder, the word "assassination" had not been used. Tate wondered what the paper would say tomorrow after the third kill had hit the news.

He drank the rest of his coffee as he flicked through the

broadsheet until he came to the business section. There was a brief report on a contract signed with the US Department of Defense for next-generation body armour. Even when he'd been in the Regiment, soldiers were always complaining about their kit. Tate sighed. Trust the Americans to get the good stuff first. He closed the paper and put it back on the top of the pile and then remembered the phone call he was going to make. He pulled his encrypted iPhone from his jeans pocket but before he could dial, Sara returned.

'What's this all about?'

'What?' He played dumb.

She folded her arms. 'Why is Chief Donoghue so interested in my Russian guests?'

'He didn't tell you?' Tate didn't want to lie, especially if it put Sara or anyone else in danger.

'Would I be asking you if he had?'

'There was another shooting last night.'

Sara gasped. 'Where?'

'Northport. Eyewitnesses saw a black SUV hightailing it away.'

'And Donoghue wants to eliminate the two that were parked on my property?'

'Three – remember I have one too. But yes.'

'I see.' She shuddered. 'So what will you have to eat?'

'You haven't given me a menu.'

Chapter 7

College Park Airport, Washington, DC

College Park Airport was the world's oldest continuously operated airport, opened for Wilbur Wright by the United States Army Signal Corps in 1909 as a training ground to instruct military officers and others how to fly in the US government's first airplane. The significance of the airport was not lost on Maksim Oleniuk, but he didn't know if he could say the same for his men.

The former GRU intelligence officer stood in the centre of the hangar as his contracted assassin walked down the airstairs carrying two bulky black bags. Even from this distance Oleniuk could see the strength the man possessed although he was no more than six foot tall. The assassin did not seem at all fazed, Oleniuk noted, to see him. The assassin headed directly for his paymaster and laid down his bags. The one on the right made a metallic clunk whilst the other thudded. Oleniuk had no reason to care what the man had carried with him. The assassin was a professional, a former member of the classified, elite Russian GRU Spetsnaz group known only as "The Werewolves". A unit that officially had never existed. He had been their most proficient sniper and what he had in his bags would be exactly what he needed to remain so.

'Akulov, I trust you have no issues to report regarding your work in Maine?'

'No, sir,' Akulov replied. He was not standing at attention but nevertheless was respectful to the man who currently paid him.

'That is as I thought. Two tasks in one day is not an issue for a Werewolf. And you were the best. You still are.'

Akulov nodded.

Oleniuk thrust his right hand into his inside jacket pocket, a move that would cause many to flinch, but he saw that Akulov retained eye contact with him and seemed relaxed. Oleniuk himself felt a little unnerved by the man. His hand held out a sheet of paper, not a pistol. 'Here are your new orders.'

Akulov took the sheet, unfolded it and read. 'This has to be undertaken by when?'

'The first this afternoon. The others tomorrow. An OP has been set up for you for the first, there is nothing further you need plan for.'

'Yes, sir.'

'And if there is any collateral damage, do not let it concern you. They are expendable.'

'Expendable?'

Oleniuk noticed the assassin's eyes narrow and a hint of a frown appear on his brow. 'They are of no consequence. This is war.'

'I see.'

'But you must liquidate all targets.'

'I understand.'

'You may store your bags in the locker in the corner and retrieve more ordinance if required. Contact me when my orders are complete. That is all.' Oleniuk turned and walked back to his office in the corner of the hangar. Unseen by the assassin a wide grin split his face. His plan and his revenge were one step closer to completion.

* * *

Camden, Maine

Tate walked the twenty minutes down Elm Street towards central Camden, which on the tourist maps was referred to as the "High Street Historic District". Verdant trees lined Elm peppered every few feet by large, wooden-clad houses in varying shades of blues and whites. It was almost as though he were in an impressionistic painting. As he neared the town centre the trees became larger and the buildings became red brick. The first of these was a squat structure that housed the municipal offices and the Camden Opera House. Tate paused. He enjoyed music but had never understood opera. Perhaps he was a philistine but the thought of sitting for three hours whilst a fat Italian man tried to serenade a fat Italian woman wasn't his cup of tea.

He smirked remembering the time he'd gone to the Kyiv Opera House with his brother to meet an asset, a Russian agent who'd refused to rendezvous in any other place they'd suggested as it was too dangerous for him. Dressed in tuxedos the three stood at the bar during the intermission, sipping Ukrainian Koblevo cognac. Tate had found it hard to keep a straight face as he remembered innumerable clichéd spy films, but the meeting had been successful; the asset had informed them of plans for a Russian military column to enter the occupied Luhansk oblast.

Tate wandered away from the opera house and crossed the street into Camden Village Green. He sat on a spare bench, retrieved his iPhone and this time he did place his call. The day desk at GCHQ – the British Government Communications Headquarters – answered on the second ring. He was asked for his agent identity code before being put through to the duty officer. Tate recited from memory the registration numbers of the Russian SUVs and asked for the details to be sent to him. He ended the call and kept his iPhone in his hand, his finger hovering over the keypad as he contemplated whether to ring his brother or not.

Despite the warmth of the sun and the smiling faces of those he had encountered on his walk, a sense of melancholy had started to engulf him. And although he had not addressed it, he knew why. It was late August. Almost three years before in late August his foster parents had been murdered. It had hit him hard but by no means as hard as it had struck Simon Hunter, their son by birth. Tate had been overseas, himself on a clandestine mission, at the time of the terrorist attack that had claimed their lives. Out of contact, he'd returned to the news that an IED, hidden in a panel van, had exploded in Camden Market. Two men had been seen leaving the van moments before, one of these a nineteen-year-old Chechen, was wearing a suicide vest. He ran into the centre of the market's crowded street before detonating it.

Tate's parents, who had taken to routinely visiting the market twice a month, had been instantly killed by the blast from the van, as had eleven other pedestrians. Eighteen more died and an equal number were injured, by the suicide bomber. Amongst the dead was an off-duty fireman manning a collection table for a local charity. A radical Islamic Chechen group had claimed responsibility for the attack, although why specifically Camden Market had been targeted was not explained.

Tate knew of the group. The fact that they had managed to get a *Shahid* – the Arabic term for martyr – to the UK and launch an attack meant that they had become a significant and ongoing threat to the UK, and had to be eradicated. Battling those above him who, rightfully so, claimed that he was too personally invested in their demise, Tate's brother had obtained permission to task E Squadron. Tate joined the deniable unit for the personal mission. They entered Chechnya and terminated the group's senior leadership with extreme prejudice and without further incident. But revenge had not brought their parents back and the world would never know that it had been the United Kingdom who had ended the careers of the terrorists.

A week later, over his breakfast of Alpen, Tate had snorted with derision at the Russian president on TV who at a press conference praised the FSB for liquidating a terrorist cell in Grozny.

The electronic ping of an incoming email brought Tate back to the present. He opened it. Efficient as ever, GCHQ had obtained the registration details of the two Tahoes. They were leased by a company registered in the Cayman Islands called "LTZ Invest". It sounded like a nonsense name for a shell company. Tate carried out a quick internet search and found nothing on the company, apart from their Cayman Island registered address. A dead end but telling nonetheless. He put his phone away. He decided not to call his brother. He'd surprise him when he turned up in Washington. He'd hurry things up and get there by mid-week, after a stop in New York.

Tate got up and continued his walk. He'd heard of a little bar with views of the harbour, which looked interesting. It was a tourist spot and it was high time he became a detached tourist. And he also wanted to sink a few drinks.

Georgetown, Washington, DC

Simon Hunter gazed out of the window of his rented Georgetown townhouse at his neighbour walking a poodle. Hunter sighed. The weekend was slowly drawing to a close. Sunday was his favourite day, a time to relax before a busy working week, and as the Head of Station, Washington, for the British Secret Intelligence Service, his working week was busy. As a boy, Sundays had always been special. His parents would let him and his brother sleep in and then they'd be treated to a full English breakfast washed down with milky tea, all prepared by Dad, who only ever seemed to cook once a week.

If it wasn't raining, they'd go to the park; otherwise he and Jack would persuade Dad to let them watch the WWE highlight show. Hunter missed his parents, and he missed his brother Jack. But unlike his childhood and his parents, he'd be seeing his brother again. SIS had informed Hunter immediately that his brother had entered the country. Jack Tate was an SIS field agent, while Hunter was an intelligence officer – his position declared to the US authorities. The ambassador knew he was "Six", but in both his social and private life, Hunter remained First Secretary, Regional Affairs – a position that just involved him smiling at foreign dignitaries.

Even his girlfriend, Terri, who was upstairs snoozing, didn't know his true role. Hunter had told Terri little about his family, and he certainly had never mentioned his brother to her, for the simple reason that, like himself, what Jack Tate did was covered by the Official Secrets Act.

Hunter hated hiding his real life from her, and that included his brother's existence. Hunter had always thought of Jack as his real brother. When his father had brought Jack home, Hunter had been ten and a lonely only child. The bond had formed instantly but unlike adopting a small child, Hunter's parents had decided to foster Jack and let him decide later if he wanted to be officially adopted, to become a Hunter. It hadn't mattered to Simon Hunter that his brother had a different surname and Jack never mentioned it either. When Jack left school to join the army, he'd traded one non-biological family for another and had still remained Jack Tate. And Hunter was fine with that.

Outside, a fat man in a tracksuit wobbled on the sidewalk, attempting to reduce his bulk. Hunter approved. He rose before dawn most days to go for a run, but never on a Sunday. Since being assigned to the British Embassy in Washington and meeting Terri, his Sundays were different. Today they'd gone for a walk, without any real destination in mind, before having a liquid lunch and staggering home. He'd run off the booze tomorrow, he told himself.

He strode back into the lounge, switched on the TV, and selected a TiVoed WWE highlight show. A guilty pleasure.

He lost himself in the world of sports entertainment for the next half-hour until he heard footsteps on the stairs. Terri appeared, her tousled blonde hair hanging across her face. She was dressed in the yellow Hulkamania T-shirt she'd bought him.

Hunter grinned. Terri padded toward him as brilliant rays of evening sunlight fell across her, silhouetting her and confirming she was naked beneath the T-shirt. She dropped into his lap and put her arms around his neck. He kissed the top of her head, enjoying the closeness of the woman he loved. 'What do you fancy doing tonight?'

'You.'

'I thought, perhaps, we could go a grab a bite at that place you like?'

She looked up at him. 'Which place?'

'You know, the one that does the huge calzones.'

'Yeah, that narrows it down, not.'

'The one with the Russian waiter.'

'Boris the Pervert?'

Hunter chuckled; the man had roving eyes. 'That's the one.'

'I don't want to go out again. Let's order takeout and stay in.' Terri pushed herself up and walked away. In the doorway she took off the T-shirt and threw it at him. 'Help me work up an appetite?'

Akulov was not at all surprised that he had been tasked to undertake another immediate assassination. The weekend, and Sundays especially, were his favoured time to operate. This was because at these times, more so than any other – with the exception of public holidays – targets were usually to be found off-guard, relaxed, or simply drunk. Sunday afternoons were preferable. His target, the Englishman, was completely unaware as he screwed the blonde that he was less than a minute away from a violent death.

Akulov wasn't a spiteful man; he would let his target go out with a bang before another bang ended his life. The issue, however, was that he refused to take the life of the naked woman beneath the target. She would not become what Oleniuk and the Americans called "collateral damage". He did not like the phrase. Wasn't it the title of an old Schwarzenegger movie? He liked American action movies – guns, explosions, and semi-naked women.

He readjusted his position. The woman was stunning, and he imagined expensive – obviously a fantastic lay. Once this was all over he'd spend some money on women and vodka, blonde women and Russian vodka. He'd have his pick, as always, but one woman in particular came to mind. Her name was Tatiana, and like him she worked for Oleniuk and was in Washington. His mind flicked briefly back to a weekend they had spent together, over a year before, and then Monday morning had come and she was sent off on assignment.

He blinked, reprimanded himself for giving in to his emotions, and brought his focus back to the present. He continued to watch his target's copulating, this time getting aroused, and silently congratulated the Englishman on his technique and stamina. After another two minutes of athletic rutting, the target's back straightened up and his head rose. The Russian waited a beat then applied pressure to his trigger . . . a single suppressed round from the Blaser hurtled through the open space between the two buildings, tore apart the glazing of the window opposite, and exploded the target's head before it bored into the heavy wooden headboard.

Akulov was impressed; the German-made Blaser had certainly proved to be a wonderful weapon.

Chapter 8

Georgetown, Washington, DC

'Oh my God . . . oh my God!' Terri screamed as Hunter fell on her. She lay still for several moments, unable to think, unable to move as his weight and warmth gently suffocated her. A moment frozen in time that seemed to linger forever but in reality lasted no more than a handful of seconds. The room was silent, save for her ragged breaths as a gentle breeze blew in through the window.

'Does that mean I hit the spot?' Hunter asked lazily as he rolled off.

'Y . . . Yes . . . you did.' Her voice was still strained, as she panted for breath.

'Glad to be of service.'

'Not bad for an old man.'

'Old? I'm thirty-seven!'

'Sorry, very old!'

'Cheeky cow.'

'Simon, you know I love it when you talk dirty.' She rolled to her left and grabbed their half-drunk bottle of Californian white and took a large swig. She nimbly straddled him, looked down and then blew her mouthful of wine over his head and chest. 'Cow indeed!'

Hunter burst out laughing. 'And your udders are first rate!'

'Udders?' She ground her hips into him, then bent forward and gently bit his lower lip. 'I'll show you udders!'

As he lay next to the woman he now knew he loved, Simon Hunter was happier than he'd been since he was a child. Twice his life had been ripped apart, when he'd lost those he'd cared for, and he had doubted if he would ever achieve true happiness. He didn't know what it was; perhaps the two bottles of wine they had managed to put away since lunch had made him philosophical but Hunter found himself reliving his past like an old man. Shit. His thoughts were all over the place. Old man. He loved Terri, he really did, but that was what she called him. In jest. He was thirty-seven now and although Terri joked that he was an old man he did not consider himself to be one, no old men were "Boomers" like his dad . . .

His feelings for Terri had troubled him at first as the scars caused by his past somehow seemed to be more livid. He'd not told Terri about either event, not wanting to saddle her with his sadness. He'd lost an ex, his first love – Sofia Antonova. She'd died at the wheel in a fatal car crash. But lying there he felt guilty about remembering her. He had loved her, and he hadn't been a kid – they'd been in their twenties. Occasionally over the years he'd dreamed that she was alive, and with him. He sighed. He had to forget her, if he was going to move on.

But he couldn't forget his parents. It was late August and the anniversary of their deaths was approaching. Yet all this was the past; Terri was with him in the present and he hoped she would be a large part of his future.

Perhaps soon, if Terri felt the same way about him as he did about her, he would have to have "the conversation" – after she had been fully vetted of course, where he would come clean and tell her what he really did at the British Embassy in Washington. He was a fool for not openly declaring his relationship to the SIS, and knew that if found out he would receive a reprimand but he hadn't wanted to go through what he saw as the humiliation of potentially vetting Terri only to lose her. Beside him Terri started to gently snore. Hunter cracked a wide smile; perhaps he should record it so that finally she'd believe him? The gentle sounds of a Washington summer evening wafted in on the air as he closed his eyes, drifting off into what he hoped would for once be happy dreams . . .

He didn't know how long he'd been asleep for but far away Hunter heard a duck quacking. He was a boy, walking with his parents in the park. He tossed a chunk of bread to a mallard and another bird jostled for a piece of its own, but the quacking persisted and grew louder. It was rhythmic, it was mechanical . . .

'That friggin' phone!' an irritated, but sleepy voice mumbled.

Hunter opened his eyes; he'd been asleep, dreaming. The quacking was the ring tone, which he found funny, of his secure iPhone on the bedside cabinet.

'Ignore it,' Terri ordered tersely.

'I can't.' Hunter stretched for the phone, grabbing it as it rang off. He looked at the display, a colleague from the embassy. He was about to return the call when a text message arrived, a single word, a code word he had never received before and had hoped he never would. It was a security protocol introduced two years before to battle the ever-growing sophistication of foreign intelligence agencies and enemies of the Crown. Awake, alert, with all thought of sleep vanquished, his chest was tight. 'I need to get to the embassy.'

'Now?'

'Now.' Hunter sat up. 'Something has come up.'

'Again?' Terri reached for him.

Hunter got out of bed. 'I'm serious. I'm needed there.'

'What is it? What's happening?'

'Terri, I've got to go.'

'Ugh.' She pushed her head back into the pillow. 'You are a diplomat not friggin' 007.'

'I know. I love you.' Hunter dressed in fresh boxers and socks then grabbed a pair of chinos. He searched the room for a top. Terri threw the Hulkamania T-shirt at him. He shook his head and retrieved a blue oxford shirt from the wardrobe.

'How long will you be?'

He shrugged. 'Sorry, I really don't know. I'll call you.'

'You've abandoned me!' Terri declared dramatically. She closed her eyes and pulled the covers back up.

Still in a state of shock, Hunter got into his eight-year-old Land Rover Defender. The code word meant that a member of the diplomatic mission had been killed. He knew nothing more than that, and there was no way he was going to risk making a telephone call. Secure or not, he had no doubt that somewhere, someone could listen in to his every word. He swung the boxy 4×4 away from the kerb and powered up the deserted street, the diesel engine roaring like an angry lion. At this time of day, he'd make the office in seven minutes, less if he put his foot down.

The British Embassy, on the corner of Massachusetts Avenue and Observatory Circle, was an unremarkable red-brick building that reminded Hunter of a comprehensive school. Usually lined with parked cars, Observatory Circle was all but empty. Hunter noticed a solitary taxi stood at the corner facing Massachusetts, the driver apparently killing time or waiting for a fare or whatever else taxi drivers did. Hunter brought his Land Rover to a halt at the barrier, and a security guard checked his ID before waving him through. After pulling into the parking lot, he quickly made his way into the embassy building itself. The front desk was manned by Karen King, one of the locally hired support staff. She had a worried expression on her face.

'Hi, Karen.' Hunter forced a smile as the American did the same.

'Everyone is in the conference room.'

'Thanks.' He marched along the hallway then peered through the door. He saw that "everyone" amounted to half a dozen junior staff. He continued on to his own office but was intercepted by

Eric Filler, the Cultural Attaché. Hunter liked the man, despite that fact that he was known for his notoriously bad short-term memory, which resulted in him constantly misplacing memos, his reading glasses and his phone. Filler was dressed in khaki cargo shorts and a baggy yellow polo shirt, all but unrecognisable without his bespoke Savile Row suit. Hunter asked him, 'What's happened?'

Filler took Hunter by the shoulder and led him into his office, two doors down. He sat heavily before his desk. A sprinkling of Post-it Notes with scribbled reminders cluttered the workspace. 'Dudley Smith is dead.'

Hunter sat, shocked. 'How?'

'He was shot.'

'What?'

'The police are still trying to determine exactly what happened.'

Hunter blinked; this was horrible. 'And Dawn?'

Filler smiled ruefully. 'He wasn't with his wife; he was off humping that blonde girl from the coffee shop.'

The impact of the news started to sink in . . . Dudley Smith was the Military Attaché, the highest representative of the British armed forces in the United States of America. Hunter had known about the man's wandering eye but this was different. All single diplomats in sensitive positions had been specifically warned that anyone they became "involved with" needed to be vetted, something that Hunter himself had guiltily failed to do with Terri, to safeguard against extortion from criminals and foreign agents. For Smith this also safeguarded against sullying the reputation of HM Armed Forces. And on top of all this he was a married man. 'He told me they just met for coffee.'

'He lied.'

'How? I mean why? Who?' Hunter was still in a state of disbelief.

'Those are the questions the police will be asking us all, but I was hoping you had some idea.'

'Without any details from the police, it's all speculation. Get shot back home it's a big thing, but here everyone and his granny has a gun. For all we know, it could have been an accident, or a robbery.'

'Or "coffee girl's" jealous boyfriend?' Filler pronounced.

'Shit.'

'Shit indeed.'

Both diplomats were shaken. The death of a colleague was not something they ever got used to dealing with. Hunter asked, 'Where's the boss?'

'Karen couldn't raise him. That's why she called me and why I sent out the alert.'

'Any idea where he might be?'

'On his bike?' Anthony Tudor, the United Kingdom's Ambassador to the United States of America, was known to disappear – official functions permitting – at the weekends. He loved bicycles and hated cities. Filler checked his watch. 'I'll start the briefing in twenty minutes. In the meantime, I'm going to speak to the police to see if there is anything extra they can tell us.'

Hunter nodded. In the absence of the ambassador, as the most senior diplomat, Filler was in charge. He knew he had to contact the Foreign Office but would wait until he was fully briefed.

Washington, DC

Li Tam had been a registered taxi driver for twenty years, ever since immigrating to the US. He had worked hard, providing a good home for his wife and putting his daughter through college. Friends and family saw him as the poster boy for the American Dream, the epitome of honest, hard work. But they were all wrong.

Li Tam was not a taxi driver. Before being transferred to his new master, Li Tam had been an agent of the Chinese Ministry of State Security, a spy. With a sub sandwich in his hands and his light turned off, Li Tam seemed like a man taking a few minutes of "me time" before searching for his next fare. This also was wrong. Li Tam was observing the British Embassy and mentally ticking off who had or had not arrived for the crisis meeting. It had been almost ninety minutes now since the alarm had been raised, and all but three of the diplomatic staff had turned up.

Worryingly for Li Tam, this hadn't included the ambassador. Li Tam counted the staff in and he counted them out again. Yes, he was sure. The British Ambassador had not been in the building. It was time to let the Russians know that the mission had a kink.

'*Da?*' Maksim Oleniuk said, through a mouthful of filet mignon.

'We do not have the ambassador.'

'What?' Oleniuk spluttered and reached for his wine.

'He did not come to the embassy, and he is not at his residence.'

'*Suka!*' Oleniuk cursed in Russian. 'He must be found; we have a matter of hours left before the event!'

'I am aware of that.'

'I have new orders for you. Collect my man and take him to this location.'

Li Tam listened as Oleniuk dictated a Georgetown address. 'Understood.'

Oleniuk ended the call. He clicked his fingers for the cheque. A Hispanic server quickly handed him a piece of paper inside a leather wallet. Without examining the amount, Oleniuk thrust three hundred-dollar bills inside and left. Years of planning had been put into this project and now it all seemed to be unravelling. Someone would pay, and it would not be him. He stepped onto the sidewalk and the rear passenger door of the limousine was opened by one of his men. Oleniuk paused to take in the view of the boulevard, lit up and humming with nightlife, before he clambered inside and they pulled away.

Through the tinted, ballistic glass he watched late-night Washington go about its business. Let them live tonight, he mused, as tomorrow they will have nothing to enjoy. He checked his wristwatch and corrected himself; tomorrow was already here in Moscow.

It was Oleniuk's belief that for too long Russia had been the butt of jokes, the once powerful nation made pauper by the collective actions of the international community. They had meddled with her affairs, unfairly attacking her trade and business links all because she had liberated lands that had rightfully been hers. Crimea was Russian land! It never was and never should have been part of Ukraine, yet the international community could not see this. They had sided with Ukraine, which in his opinion was a made-up place, not a sovereign country, and because of this would forever be his enemy and an enemy of Mother Russia.

But he, like Russia, had bided his time. Pretending to fawn over canapés at innumerable society events, laughing at jokes told by buffoons with wives like baboons. One aspect of the operation irked him; the world and his homeland would never know that it was he – a true Russian patriot – who had eliminated Russia's enemies and masterminded the attack that had brought the United States to its knees.

Oleniuk had been a GRU officer, a soldier, a planner but believed most of all that he would be remembered as a leader. After leaving the Russian military he had continued to follow the development of military technology, and with extensive funding from his Chinese billionaire partner, had privately taken over certain research programs, which the long-standing Russian president had insisted be scrapped. Whilst the Russian state concentrated on bankrupting itself by producing quicker tanks, larger submarines and stealthier fast jets, Oleniuk had restarted the electromagnetic pulse (EMP) program. Unburdened from the shackles of the moribund post-Soviet state, five years of continuing research and Chinese cooperation had resulted in an operational weapon. A unit that could be delivered by an airframe and detonated unseen a mile above its target.

But Oleniuk had not shared his breakthrough with Russia. He knew the Russian military and intelligence apparatus inside out. The officers and men on the ground were hardworking, trustworthy, but the higher up the ranks you went the higher the frequency of imbecility was to be found. In short those in power would squander his weapon, his technology and his chance to make a difference. It was his weapon now, not theirs, and he alone would decide how it was used. And as a patriot, he had made the decision that it would be used to get his motherland out from under the yoke of the United States of America.

Oleniuk knew the technology was limited. An EMP weapon was a single-use force multiplier. He had been assured that the technology could not be copied, or reverse engineered but within months its effects could be counteracted. Nation states would rush to create their own shielding, rendering all but the poorest adversaries susceptible to an EMP attack. Perhaps he should order another unit be detonated over Afghanistan as payback for all the Soviet lives lost in the 1980s?

But no. Such thoughts were corrosive. The EMP strike was a one-off event, with a fall guy and a concrete strategy to ensure no blowback. Meticulously detailed fake intelligence was in place to paint North Korea as the aggressor.

His billionaire Chinese partner, a woman well respected by "the party" would persuade China that it must come to the aid of its strategic trading partner – the US – and rebuild their now defunct industries and infrastructure. Trillions were to be made. In the meantime, China, with the tacit agreement of the international community, and before the US was in a position to do so, would invade North Korea and once and for all bring to heel the embarrassing Third World dictatorship on their door-step. Overnight the regional paradigm would shift, as would the balance of global power.

The vast sum of money to be made and the will to bloody the nose of the US was enough for his Chinese partner, but Oleniuk had a far loftier goal. Oleniuk knew that the ailing health and popularity of the Russian president may be enough to see him win one more term in office but after that the strongman would be a spent force. Oleniuk had been out of the military for five years, in public life for that five and in five more would have enough wealth and political capital to take the Kremlin. He would be leader of a new, resurgent Russia.

The EMP technology, and the resulting power plays derived from it would kick-start his new Russia but it would be his mind and eventually the work of his men that would bolster this. In any endeavour what was bigger than the game were the rules, and he who controlled the rules decided who played the game and how.

Revenge was Oleniuk's salient motive. The hit list encapsulated this. Curated by Oleniuk, it contained a list of enemies of the Russian state. Several had been taken care of in Maine, one already eliminated in Washington and two more to go. But there was another name on the list. A third man to kill. A personal enemy. A man whose actions had wounded him, twice. His name was etched into his very being. His direct actions had come very close to destroying Oleniuk, turning him to drink, to despair, to the edge of suicide. Two of the men still to kill were serving diplomats at the British Embassy in Washington, DC; one of them was his nemesis.

Oleniuk rubbed his neck and felt for the scar he'd received in Mariupol. It was the result of the second time the man had wronged him.

Chapter 9

British Embassy, Washington, DC
The mood was subdued as the embassy staff ambled out of the meeting room. Filler had pushed the briefing back twice – once as he awaited more details from the police and then again as he awaited the arrival of Detective Jon Chang from the DC Metro Police. Chang had insisted on talking to the embassy staff in person, in his capacity of liaison officer. He gave the basic facts as he saw them – Smith had been shot by a gunman while visiting a friend's apartment. Chang stated that a two-man DC team would return to the embassy in the morning to interview all staff.

'We need to talk,' Chang announced.

'We can go to my office,' Filler replied and led the way.

Once all three men were seated, Chang addressed Filler and Hunter. 'I didn't want to say this in front of the rest of your staff. We now believe this was a professional hit.'

'What makes you think that, Detective?' Filler asked, barely suppressing his surprise.

'The shooter used a high-calibre round from a silenced weapon,' Chang stated bluntly. 'He wasn't a gangbanger, and this wasn't a home invasion or a crime of passion. This was a serious weapon, used in a professional manner. This was an assassination.'

Hunter's mind raced. Diplomats had died in accidents or been murdered in robberies, but this was the first time for decades a British diplomat had been assassinated. It was unthinkable. 'If this was a "hit", the killer knew where to find Smith.'

'Exactly,' Chang said.

Hunter understood the implications. 'Smith must have been under surveillance. Which means a team, not a lone gunman. Which hints at who? A terrorist group or a foreign intelligence service?'

'I hope it was terrorists.' Filler blew out his cheeks. 'The last thing we need is a shooting war with anyone!'

'But we have to look into all possibilities,' Chang confirmed. 'Now, can you tell me where your ambassador is?'

Filler shook his head. 'I can't.'

Chang quizzically raised a heavy eyebrow. 'You can't or you won't?'

Filler shot Hunter a glance before he replied. 'We can't. We have not been able to contact Ambassador Tudor since yesterday.'

'What?' Chang was incredulous.

'We don't keep him on a lead.'

'But you have protocols?'

'Yes, we do.' Filler folded his arms. 'The ambassador always has both a mobile and a satellite phone with him. He informs us when and where he is going. On this occasion he said he was going away for the weekend. The issue is that we can't raise him on either of his phones.'

'He's a high-value target if there ever was one,' Chang stated, flatly.

'Which is why,' Hunter declared, 'I wish to officially request that your department help us find him.'

'You want to file a missing person report, now?'

'Yes.' It was something he and Filler had discussed; it was not like Anthony Tudor to be incognito for so long. Not only were his phones unanswered but the name of the guesthouse he was apparently staying at did not exist.

'Of course.' The detective tried to hide his irritation with a thin smile. 'Let me go back to my car. I think I have the relevant form in my briefcase. If not, I'll run along and get one.'

College Park Airport, Washington, DC

Li Tam had never met the huge Russian before, but the man had presented himself at the correct address. He had hefted a heavy-looking, man-sized package into the trunk of Tam's taxi. It was obvious to Li Tam what the bag contained, but he made no comment as it meant nothing to him.

The pair had not spoken at all during the journey across the city. The Russian had used Tam like a taxi driver, which he ironically did not like. Tam reversed the taxi into a space directly outside a hangar. The Russian clambered out of his seat, popped the trunk, collected his heavy cargo, and left without saying a word. Tam watched in the rear-view mirror as the Russian was let inside and the door quickly shut behind him.

Tam knew that the hangar, and the adjoining one, were leased by a Chinese-owned company. It was one of many such places that dotted the United States to be used, when required, by his real employer. He knew neither why he had gotten in bed with the Russians nor why he had been loaned to them. He only understood that his orders were to follow all instructions from his Russian contact, or risk being recalled to Beijing. The life he had adopted in the US was far more comfortable than any he could expect in his native China, so he complied. In the US, he was treated by many as just another immigrant in a cosmopolitan nation of immigrants, and although he knew he was being watched by his own people, he felt a sense of freedom in his actions and activities. At least he had until his current orders had arrived.

Tam yawned; he was old and exhausted. Checking his watch he realised he'd been working now for twenty hours straight. If he did not rest soon, he'd be a danger behind the wheel; he had to protect his cover as a taxi driver. Tam chuckled to himself and rubbed his face with his hands. No, he actually no longer had to protect his charade. Come daybreak, no one would care if he was a real taxi driver or not. No one would pay any attention to how he drove, just that he had a vehicle that could be driven.

He lifted his iPhone and called his Russian contact again. It rang out without affording him the opportunity to leave a voicemail. It was a quarter to ten in the evening. Tam wet his lips as he pondered his situation. So be it; if he had no further instructions, he would sleep in the car until he was needed. It would not be the first time and the back seat was surprisingly voluminous. Tam started the engine. He'd find somewhere nearby to park, out of the glare of potential passers-by or surveillance cameras. He didn't want to draw any further attention to the hangar.

Chapter 10

Camden, Maine

Tate had decided to take the day to explore Camden. He'd hit a restaurant on the waterfront, called The Waterfront, before finding Laite Memorial Beach and then finally hiking up and down the Mount Battie Trail. Pushing his empty plate away, he reflected that the food at the inn was better than it had any right to be. He took a long pull on his beer. The place was emptier than the night before and the Russians had not yet returned. He'd eaten at the bar. Sara wasn't around and Joe hadn't told him to take a table.

'Another?' Joe nodded at the almost empty pint glass, his second so far.

Tate flashed Joe a thumbs up. 'Why not.'

The door opened and a large figure entered. Donoghue. He was out of uniform and joined Tate at the bar. 'I'll have the same.'

Neither man spoke until both draught beers were pulled, placed in front of them and they'd both had a swig. Joe drifted to the other end of the bar and busied himself polishing a glass. Tate asked, 'What's the latest?'

Donoghue nodded and took a second larger pull before he spoke. 'We caught up with the Russians. Checked the cars – like you said ballistic plates. We checked their documents, checked their ID's. All genuine, all in order. No laws broken, not even a speeding ticket.'

'I see,' Tate said, and drank some more.

'But I dug a little deeper. No law against having armour plating or "pimping your ride", but I'll admit it's a little strange that the lease company has ten – all the same colour.'

'And when you questioned the pair, what were they like?'

Donoghue cast Tate a look. 'Hell, why not. I can tell you. The big one had a smile on his face, like he found the situation amusing, and the older guy was talkative but a little timid. Both were polite and non-confrontational.'

'And did you search the Tahoes?'

'We did; they invited us to. Apart from an empty custom storage box in the trunk of each, nothing unusual, nothing amiss.' Donoghue drank again. 'So nothing whatsoever to link the pair of them, or their vehicles, to the shooter. And before you ask, we don't have the plate number of his SUV, and we have no evidence that it either was or wasn't armour-plated.'

'It was.'

'We'll see.'

'Any news on the shooter?'

'None at all. It's like both he and his vehicle were beamed up by Scotty.' The police chief finished his pint with one long pull. 'Tate, thanks for your input this morning. Now I'm finally going to go home and get some sleep. Oh and thanks for the beer – it's on you.'

'Glad to be of service,' Tate said to Donoghue's back as he headed to the door.

Without asking, Joe placed a new pint in front of Tate. 'And that one's from me.'

'Thanks, but what for?'

'Entertainment purposes. I couldn't help but overhear what you two were talking about.'

'A-ha.' Tate drank.

'I'm not going to say anything, but I don't trust those Russian fellas.'

Tate didn't reply. He finished his pint and decided four was enough. He checked his Rolex, almost ten. Time to turn in. He wanted to hit the road by mid-morning. After that, the events of Camden, Maine, however odd, would be behind him.

The cloying odour of cigarette smoke carried on the breeze and he heard a voice. 'What are you doing?'

'Going to bed.' Tate turned as Sara appeared from the shadow of the rear door. 'Your night off?'

'I needed some head space – know what I mean?'

Tate smirked. He supposed he did. 'I'm leaving tomorrow.'

'And?'

'I just wanted to say goodbye, oh and report a blown bulb in my bathroom.'

Sara sighed. 'Sorry. The wiring here can be an issue.'

'Look, I need a favour.'

Sara took a step closer and the light hit her face. 'What?'

Tate became serious. 'Those Russians, what do you know about them?'

'Nothing.'

'Nothing at all?'

'Well, we have their credit card details and photocopies of their passports.'

'When did they arrive?'

'Two days ago; I checked them in.'

'You don't just work in the bar then?'

'I'm the owner, didn't you know?'

'No. But I do now. Can I see the stuff you have on them?'

'Why? Are you a policeman, or a private dick?'

Tate smirked. 'I'm a dick but just a concerned citizen.'

'First Donoghue, and now you asking has got me curious. Tell me who you really are and I'll think about opening up the reception computer and having a look. You don't look like any HR consultant I've ever met.'

'How many have you met?'

'I'm waiting.'

'Look. I'm with the British Foreign Office, and they may be of interest to us. And that's really all I can say. Either you trust me or you don't.'

Sara sighed again. 'Well that makes as much sense as anything. And I do know you're British.'

'And only you and I would know,' Tate added, with a smile.

'C'mon, before I change my mind.'

Tate followed her into reception. 'Is there anything special about any of the cars in the lot?'

'What do you mean by "special"?' she asked as she logged in to the workstation.

'I don't know. The big guy—'

'Sergei.'

'You remembered his name?'

'He hit on me.'

'Congratulations.'

'Thanks?'

'Anyway, he was taking pictures of the parked cars the day I arrived.'

Sara shrugged. 'Perhaps our models are different to his back home? I bet he certainly hasn't seen many like mine, in the flesh.'

'What do you have?'

'It's like you, old and British. A 1966 Mini Cooper S. Import. It belonged to my father; he gave it to me.'

'I'm surprised he didn't keep it for himself.'

'He didn't need it anymore; he died of lung cancer.'

'Sorry.'

'Don't be, most people have lost someone. Have you?'

Tate lied, 'I've got no one to lose.'

'Parents?'

'Foster parents, whom I haven't seen for ten years.' Technically true.

'Brothers, sisters?'

'Only child.' Which again was technically true.

'Wife?'

'No.'

The workstation made a whirring sound. 'This thing is as ancient as Joe, but he likes it so who am I to complain? You know, he's so old-fashioned that he refuses to use a cell phone.'

'So what does he use, carrier pigeons?'

Sara was confused. 'No, he has a ham radio set. He chats to people all over the world on that. OK, here are their passports. I can't show you their credit card details.'

'Very wise.' Tate scooted around the desk, and looked over the top of her head. He could smell cigarette smoke but now also the stronger scent of her shampoo. 'Can I print these out, the passport details?'

'Why?'

'Because I think that there is something off about your Russian guests. I don't know what it is, but I've got some sort of sixth sense about people.'

'This "sixth sense", do you use it for your work at the British Foreign Office?'

'I do.'

She clicked the print button, turned and then cocked her head to one side. With a half-smile, she asked, 'What is that sense telling you about me?'

'It's telling me to thank you for the printout and say goodnight.'

Sara opened her mouth to speak but then headlights abruptly burst in through the open door and rap music blared from the parking lot. 'Shit.'

'I agree; I never know what they are talking about.'

'It's Clint, my ex; I told him to stop coming around.'

'He listens to rap?'

'Yep.'

'What is he, twelve?'

'No, he's a real Maine gangsta.'

The music abruptly stopped and Clint called out, 'Sara! You there, Sara? I just want to talk!'

Sara looked up into Tate's eyes. 'Help me?'

Tate shrugged. 'Always happy to help a damsel in distress.'

She gave him a peck on the cheek. 'Thanks.'

'You're very welcome.'

Sara took his hand and led them out to the parking lot, where they were greeted by a long-haired figure leaning against a customised Nissan. It was the same car as the night before and the same driver. Tate bit his tongue. Clint's hair was again held back with a bandana and baseball cap configuration but now Tate could see his jeans, which were as loose as a tent around his legs.

'Who is that?' Clint pointed an accusatory finger.

'Jack; he's from England.'

Clint pushed himself off the car and took two languid paces forward and gesticulated expressively with his arms. 'So what? Are you, like, "doing" him now?'

'I plan to.' She let go of Tate's hand, cupped his face, and kissed him on the lips. Her lips were moist and soft. Tate felt her tongue slip inside his mouth. He didn't resist and placed his hands on her bum, which he'd been wanting to do for the past two days. She pulled away, slowly – then spun abruptly to face her ex. 'There, Clint. Is that what you wanted to see? It's over; don't you get it? Now leave me alone.'

Clint bristled. 'Get outta my way! I'm going to show him what happens if you mess with Clint Donoghue!'

'Donoghue?' Tate repeated. 'Like, Chief of Police Donoghue?'

He strutted as he spoke. 'Yeah, that's right. So you ain't gonna get the better of me.'

'He's also a black belt in karate,' Sara said, slight concern now evident in her voice.

'So you're the "Maine Man"? I'm sure your father is very proud of you, Clint.'

'He is,' Clint replied not understanding the irony. 'So come on, Jack . . . Jack England – let's see what you've got!'

Tate let his body relax as he tried to ignore the adrenalin rush. Clint was no serious threat, but he hadn't been in a fistfight for a while, well for a week at least. The fact that he knew the kid was trained in karate made it easier for him to predict what was coming at him. A couple of quick punches and some showboating kicks he imagined, moves that looked good in a dojo but meant very little in a real fight against a highly trained soldier. He decided to give Clint another chance but still take the kid down a peg or two. 'Clint, go home and go to bed. No one loves an idiot.'

'What did you call me?' Clint launched himself at Tate but telegraphed his attack. His left fist jabbed out as a dummy before his right fist, a straight punch, hurtled towards Tate's face. Tate took a step sideways, and with both arms working at once, his right palm forced Clint's arm down while the back of his left fist slammed into Clint's nose. It was an effective counter and used Clint's own momentum against him. Clint obviously hadn't expected to be punched and stumbled back a step, but before he could understand what was happening, Tate grabbed him by the shoulders and threw him into the Nissan. Clint landed on the hood, leaving a dent before rolling off onto the tarmac.

'Go home, Clint; sleep it off.'

Clint stumbled to his feet, shook his head and felt his nose with his right hand. Pulling his hand away, his eyes widened as he saw his hand was now bloody. 'You busted my nose, man!' He took a step and checked the Nissan. 'You damaged my car! That's criminal damage!'

'No, Clint. You fell and your head hit the car. You are a very clumsy person. Now as we say back home, piss off!'

'Screw you!' Clint charged forward. Incensed. Arms and legs jerking as he changed from stance to stance. 'I'm gonna kill you!'

Tate adopted his own stance, more upright than Clint's. It was based on a mixture of techniques taught by the SAS. Clint again feinted with his left fist but then immediately threw another left then a quick right. Tate blocked both strikes. Clint dropped and twisted his hips and wound up to deliver a giant kick with his right leg. Tate let the leg get halfway then kicked out with his own leg. His heel collided with Clint's approaching shin. Clint howled and fell forward. Hitting the ground, he grabbed his leg. A trained fighter would have stopped at that point, claimed a victory, maybe even claimed the girl and walked away . . . but Tate wasn't a trained fighter, he was a trained killer. Tate followed Clint to the ground, knees landing on his chest, pinning him. Tate's hands grabbed the kid's neck.

'Stop!' Sara yelled.

Tate took a deep breath. Released his grip but then delivered a swift jab to Clint's jaw with the palm of his hand. 'Go to sleep, Clint.'

There was a clapping from across the parking lot. Tate looked up. The Russians were there, and they had been watching. Tate rolled Clint into the recovery position and got to his feet.

Tate could see Sara was shocked. She knelt down next to her ex-boyfriend. 'Will he be all right?'

'He'll wake up in a while. He'll have a stiff jaw for a few days, I don't think I've broken his leg, or his nose, but I'm not a doctor.'

'What are you?'

'Just a bureaucrat on holiday.'

'Where did you learn to fight like that?'

'The WWE – I was a huge fan of Rob Van Dam,' Tate said flatly. 'How did you know I could beat him?'

'I didn't.'

'Well, thank you and goodnight.' Tate shook his head and walked towards his room taking long controlled breaths. The two Russians were looking on.

'Rap is crap,' Sergei, the big Russian said, with a smile as Tate passed him.

Tate nodded and searched for his key. As he did so, the two men switched to Russian. Tate opened his door, stepped into the room, and pretended to close the door behind him, but left a small gap so he could listen in on the conversation.

'He has training,' Sergei stated. 'Do you think he knows anything?'

'I do not think so,' the older Russian replied. 'That would be a preposterous coincidence; however, the question is will he cause us any problems tomorrow?'

'If he attempts to take one of our cars, I'll shoot him. No man, no problem,' Sergei said.

There was a pause then the older Russian asked, 'What type of Nissan is that?'

'It's a Skyline, an old one.'

'How old?'

'A 1990 model perhaps. It's an R32 GT-R – but it has lots of wiring. And the owner, I imagine, has added more. It definitely will not start tomorrow, Oleg.'

'I agree. Not many will start. The Winnebago is diesel, which may have a better chance.'

Tate heard the Russians moving away and a moment later their door opened, closed and the key turned in the lock. Nothing made sense. Why were they interested in cars? Why were they now interested in him? And was shooting him an idle threat? Tate didn't want to find out, but what he did want to find out about was what was happening tomorrow.

He locked his door and hefted a chair in front of it for extra security. It wasn't much but it would slow anyone down a pace who tried to break the door down and would allow him time to respond. He yawned; it had been a long day. He'd rested sure, and exercised, but he'd also drunk too much and then danced with the gangsta. He shouldn't have hit the kid as hard as he had.

Tate traipsed to the bathroom, haphazardly undressing, and as he did so forgot about the folded printouts in his jeans pocket. He flicked the light switch and nothing happened. He rolled his eyes and remembered that the bulb had blown. Tate moved the waste bin, again using it to prop the door open, and then brushed his teeth. Two minutes later he emerged minty-mouthed, but still tired. He ignored his pile of clothes and lay on the bed. He rolled onto his left side, facing the window and the door. He was asleep within two minutes.

Tate sat up with a start and, for a moment, couldn't understand where he was. He heard voices outside and looked at his watch, a mechanical Rolex he'd bought ten years before. He could just make out the time; it was five past four. He lay back down and closed his eyes. He needed his sleep. The only thing that would make him get up now, he thought dreamily, was the woman who worked at the bar – correction, he reminded himself – the woman who owned the bar.

He started to drift off and then he heard Russian voices. Instantly alert, Tate ripped off his sheets, leapt out of bed, and positioned himself by the side of the door, expecting it to be broken down at any moment. There was more noise outside, but his door remained firmly shut. He waited a while longer before chancing a glance out of the curtained window. He saw the two Russians loading suitcases into their identical vehicles, a hard-shell Samsonite each by the look of it and then a second case. It was the second case that made him stare harder: it looked custom, not a piece of regular luggage.

The large Russian lifted his with ease but the second Russian's case slipped from his grasp and hit the ground. It burst open on impact and Tate saw the unmistakable shape of an assault rifle inside, several spare magazines and a pair of grenades encased in a foam cut-out base. In a comic mime, the two Russians berated each other until the larger one closed the case and hefted it into the SUV. Tate retrieved his encrypted smartphone and started to record the scene unfolding in front of him in HD video.

In a country where the right to keep and bear arms was sacrosanct, the rifle and magazines by themselves were not unusual but the grenades were, and then of course the two men were Russian nationals not US citizens. This made both the weapons and their ownership illegal. What were they up to? The Russians finished loading, got into their Tahoes, and drove off.

Tate backed away from the window. Had he discovered something? He pressed a button on his iPhone and speed-dialled the day desk at GCHQ. He was asked for his agent identity code before being put through to the duty officer.

'Has there been any chatter at all about an imminent terrorist attack on US soil?' He leaned against the wall and peered through the small gap between the curtain and window frame at the car park.

'Please wait; checking for any flash traffic,' the clipped female voice replied. The line became quiet as the duty officer speed-read the incoming traffic for her shift thus far, signals intelligence taken mostly from the US-controlled Echelon network. She knew better than to ask why the information was needed or where the agent was calling from. 'Nothing. Nothing at all. The US is quiet.'

Whether it was lack of sleep, alcohol or both making him paranoid, Tate didn't know, but something was happening that no one seemed to know about. He spoke to the officer again. 'I need you to connect me to a number.'

'Go ahead.'

Tate relayed a telephone number from memory. It was the number of his controller at SIS, the British Secret Intelligence Service, more commonly referred to as MI6. Tate waited as the call was routed via GCHQ, providing an added layer of electronic protection to Pamela Newman. She answered on the third ring, 'Newman.'

'It's Jack.'

'Can't sleep?'

'Ha ha.'

'You'd better tell me what's so important. You are meant to be on holiday, remember?'

Tate started to explain but soon realised he sounded a little manic. 'I've got their passport details and video footage of them.'

'Jack, you know how I feel about hunches, especially yours?'

'Yes I do.' Newman had told him they were not just the stuff of badly written detective dramas. An operative had to observe and interpret, and sometimes this could not be put into words.

'Send me all you have; I'll mark it as "most urgent" for our techies to look at. I'll get back to you if I get anything interesting.'

The line went dead. Tate sighed. Could he ever switch off? Yes, he reminded himself he could, but then things went wrong, like getting stopped for speeding. This month off, his first time off in a year, was meant to get him away from the job, to recharge after yet another extended operation, but now it looked like he was in the middle of something else. He checked his watch; it was twenty to five and still an hour before daybreak. Tate sighed heavily; that was all the sleep he was getting tonight then.

He retrieved the printouts from his jeans, placed them on the vanity table next to his bed and switched the light on. Making sure that the papers were square and flat, he photographed them before sending the jpegs in a secure email to London.

Tate walked into the bathroom and started the shower, cursing the missing light bulb. He ran through what he had seen, but none of it made sense. He didn't know much about the US car market. How many black Tahoes could there be in Camden? What was the link between the murder victims? What were the Russians doing?

He stood under the water, thinking until he heard his phone ring. He struggled out across the slick tiles and grabbed the iPhone. 'Tate.'

'Jack, we got a hit on the faces in the passports. Are you sitting down?'

'Shoot.'

'Both of them are former GRU.'

'Russian Military Intelligence?' Tate sat on the bed. 'Not the Russian Foreign Intelligence Service?'

'Definitely GRU, not SVR. That, however . . .' At the other end of the line he heard an urgent male voice call her name. 'Sorry, Jack, one moment.' The sound became muffled for a moment and he couldn't hear what was being discussed. 'I'm going to have to call you back.'

'Fine, I'm here all night.' The call ended and Tate was left looking at his blank iPhone. He got up from the bed, stepped back into the shower and rinsed off the accumulated fluff that had stuck to his dripping feet and legs.

Chapter 11

Washington, DC

A silent, purple detonation flowered. It bloomed like a monstrous, inverted Fourth of July firework. Its petals spread earthwards and then faded to be replaced by a mauve glow, creating a spectral false dawn.

Oleniuk felt the tingling sensation he had been warned to expect wash over him, as each individual hair on his body stood up on end.

At that very moment, as if choreographed, every single light around the pair vanished. The White House lights disappeared, the floodlights on the lawn were no more and the stately residence of the President of the United States of America was plunged into darkness.

The glow started to fade; the night sky now taking on the appearance of the bruised eye of a heavyweight boxer, before it gradually became black once more. The co-conspirators removed their protective eyewear. They had delivered a form of vengeance like no other the modern world had ever seen and, ignoring ancient, fanciful tales of vengeful gods, the single most powerful.

Oleniuk put his arm around Yan. 'We have done it.'

She did not reply; however, she did give him a sideways glance.

Oleniuk quickly moved his arm. 'I was overcome with emotion in the moment. I do apologise.'

'It is understandable, given the circumstances.'

They continued to gaze at the capital city of the United States – dark, silent but not dead. The majority of the population were safely asleep and those who weren't would interpret the loss of power as a citywide outage, a total blackout.

They would, however, struggle to explain why everything with wires, everything electronic, had instantaneously and catastrophically failed.

No sirens broke the unnatural silence, but a dull thud and a shrieking of metal did. Oleniuk looked earthwards. There was cursing from the street below; a limousine had come to a halt, striking the back of a taxi. Both drivers were out of their vehicles and berating each other. Just past the collision a pair of identical, black SUVs were parked within the hotel's turning circle.

'Time to leave,' Yan stated.

'Where will you go?'

'It is better for you that I do not tell you.' She thrust out her right hand; it held her champagne glass. 'Goodbye, Max, we shall see each other again when the operation is fully completed and everything has settled.'

Oleniuk took her glass. 'Goodbye. Safe travels.'

Yan left the balcony, navigated her way deftly through the darkened room and then took the stairs down to the lobby. Oleniuk watched as she climbed into the first Tahoe. Its light switched on and it drove away, the only moving light in a sea of darkness.

Alone now, a euphoric giddiness overtook Oleniuk as he slowly set down both glasses. With a trembling hand, he lifted the cold, sweaty bottle of champagne from the ice bucket. He drank greedily, raggedly, directly from its neck. He had never felt so powerful, so alive. He was a vengeful god.

The home of his enemy, the White House, now reduced to a spectre in the pre-dawn gloom, scowled at Oleniuk as he turned on his heels and made his way carefully downstairs to his own EMP-proofed Tahoe. He now had a few hours before the fun and games really began.

Camden, Maine

When the phone rang this time, Tate was dry and sitting on his bed wearing a green cotton outdoor shirt, black jeans and a pair of boots. 'Tate.'

'Sorry I cut you off. Now as I was saying we got a hit on the faces in the passports. Both are GRU. Sergei Yesikov, until recently, was a member of 561st OMRP – Baltic Fleet Spetsnaz.'

Tate felt his pulse increase. His last mission in Ukraine with E Squadron had targeted the Baltic Fleet Spetsnaz. 'And the other one?'

'Oleg Sokol, curiously used to work at—' The call dropped out, and at the same time the lights cut out.

Tate dived to the floor; immediately his training screaming at him that he was under imminent attack. Hell, why was he unarmed? They'd jammed his phone signal and pulled the switch on the electrics.

But nothing happened. No flashbang was hurled through the window to subdue him, no shaped charge was blown to obliterate the door, and no armed Russians rushed into his room. Around him Camden was still asleep.

Tate leopard-crawled across the room into the bathroom and only then did he stand. He checked his iPhone but the screen was blank. He pressed the power button, but nothing happened. Tate frowned. When he'd received the call from Newman he'd had sixty-two per cent of his battery remaining. So what had happened to it? He checked it for damage – none. His OtterBox Defender was one of the strongest phone cases on the market; he'd never even cracked the screen, but now the handset would not power up.

His mouth moved silently as his brain tried to process what

he was seeing. A jammer would deny his service, a conventional attack would damage the transmitter but none of this would turn his phone off. He went to the door, risked opening it.

On the other side of the car park a silver Ford Explorer was moving soundlessly. It jerked to a sudden halt. The driver stepped out, kicked the front tyre and popped the bonnet open. A passenger emerged and started to walk around the car with her mobile phone held up at arm's length. Tate frowned. In the grey, pre-dawn light he could make out that both passenger and driver were dressed for hiking wearing boots, khaki shorts and shirts. So what had happened? Had they been setting off for the day when the Ford had cut out?

He stepped back into the darkness of his doorway. He wanted to observe without being seen. So their car wouldn't start and the woman's phone couldn't get a signal. Could the phone even switch on?

A figure dressed in a suit appeared from another room, and ignoring the stricken Ford made his way to a BMW. He pressed his fob and then tried to open the door. He tried again and pulled the handle before he fiddled with the fob and opened the car with the manual key. And then nothing happened. A minute passed before he got out again and, clearly unable to make the BMW start, wandered over to the couple by the Explorer. For one car to refuse to start was unfortunate; for two to fail to start was unusual, but was it a coincidence or was something happening here that Tate just did not understand? He remembered the words of the older Russian: "Not many will start. The Winnebago is diesel, which may have a better chance."

Where was the Winnebago? He couldn't see it. Strange. He went back into his room and collected his wallet and passport from the bedside cabinet. He buttoned his passport into his left chest shirt pocket and pushed his wallet in the side pocket of his jeans. He left his dead phone where it was but picked up the remote key fob for his Tahoe and once outside attempted to blip the doors open. Nothing happened. He tried again. Again nothing. He looked at the fob, depressed the button again. There was no red light to say the unit was working. He slid the inbuilt metal key out of the fob and opened the driver's door. A mechanical thud released the door and he got inside.

He looked at the door light – it hadn't switched on. He checked the roof light – it was switched to "door". He flicked it to "on". It didn't switch on. He found the alarm light, watched it and waited for it to blink. It didn't. Finally Tate tried the ignition. No trace of a spark, no low groan. Tate got out of the Tahoe and manually locked it.

A second couple now appeared, also hikers or walkers or perhaps just one of those middle-aged couples who enjoy wearing matching "active wear". Their vehicle too was dead. Tate liked a puzzle as much as the next man, liked finding the clues before Columbo, but here he had no frame of reference.

All these items had circuitry, all these items used some type of wire . . . A cold, black fear gripped Tate.

He looked skyward for a sign, for a mushroom cloud, for any sign of a nuclear detonation. There was a slight breeze, but he could see no strange glow, no strange cloud and felt no unexplained heat. All the circuitry had failed and the only thing he knew that could do that would be the electromagnetic pulse from a nuclear detonation.

Tate saw that the curtains in the window of the Russians' room were open. He moved to their door and swiftly darted his head forward and then back. The room looked empty. He looked again now but for longer, feeling more confident that he wasn't about to be blasted through the glass by a 9mm. By what he could see in the pre-dawn gloom, the room looked to be clinically clean – the twin beds had been stripped down to their mattresses yet he couldn't see any trace of the bedding on the floor.

Tate turned and for the first time noticed a third black Chevy Tahoe was parked, in the deep shadows past the far end of the other accommodation block. It was an unpaved access space, he presumed for the maintenance staff. He walked directly towards it, trying to provoke a response. It would either move or it wouldn't. He drew nearer and noted that the number plate did not belong to either of the two Russian SUVs. Was it just a popular model or was that too much of a coincidence? He carried on towards the SUV and now saw a sticker in the windscreen for a rental company. He sighed and then he heard someone curse.

Outside the reception Joe was shaking his head and looking skywards, as though for divine intervention. Tate jogged over to him and said, with more calm than he felt, 'What d'ya know, Joe?'

'All I know is that the power's out and I can't get the damn backup generator to work.'

Tate took a deep breath; this would be interesting. 'Joe, I think this is more serious than the power. I think it's some type of attack.'

Joe's eyebrows came alive and tried to leave his face. 'On the hotel?'

Tate quickly explained about the effects of an EMP and what could cause it.

'Son of a bitch,' Joe said, shaking his head.

Tate had an idea. 'Sara said you had a ham radio set?'

'Sure do. I talk to people all over the world on that.'

'Do you have any friends in the UK?'

'You bet I do.'

'Can you try to contact one of them for me?'

'You betcha!' Joe sprang out of the chair. 'Follow me.'

Joe led them through the back of the reception area, along a corridor, and up a flight of stairs. He opened a door to a room, which overlooked the road. It was not much bigger than one of the standard hotel rooms, but there was a metal box sitting on the stand next to the television. 'It isn't much, but it's home.'

'You live here?'

'Yep. OK then, let's see what we can do.' Joe pulled a chair over and sat in front of the box. He undid the clasps to reveal his pride and joy. 'It runs on battery or mains power. I take it out with me sometimes. There's nothing better than sitting on top of Mount Battie and broadcasting to the world.'

Tate dragged over a second chair. 'Let's just hope we can broadcast to the UK.'

'Yup.' Joe turned on the set and beamed when a red light appeared. 'Now we're cooking.' He twiddled a dial and started to speak. There was nothing for a while and then a croaky elderly voice spoke.

'Hello, General Custer! Thank heavens you are safe!'

'General Custer?' Tate mouthed.

'It's my handle. Reading you loud and clear, Bombardier.'

'Well, I must say, I'm very glad to hear you. I've just had my fix of BBC Hard Talk interrupted by a news flash. It all sounded very ominous to me.'

'Can I?' asked Tate.

Joe nodded. 'Bombardier, I have a friend with me from the UK. He's going to talk to you now.'

'Bombardier, my name is Jack Tate. Can you hear me?'

'Yes, Mr Tate.'

'Good, now I need you to listen to me. I work for the SIS.'

'SIS?'

'MI6, I'm an agent for MI6.' Even most Brits didn't know it was actually called SIS; Tate blamed Ian Fleming.

'Ooh, how exciting.'

'Can you tell me what you've seen on the news?'

'Well, it's on all the channels now – breaking news. Something has caused the power to go out over the US. I've got the television on here watching it. Of course, they don't have any video footage yet.'

Tate tried to process the information. 'Has there been any mention of a nuclear weapon?'

'A nuclear weapon?' The voice from England rose a key.

'Yes.'

'No. One expert said that something exploded in the atmosphere above the continental United States, but he thought it may have been a meteorite.' The line became static for a moment.

'Oh, heavens above!'

'Bombardier,' Tate said, 'are you still there?'

'Yes. And you?'

'I hope so. Can you tell me any more about the attack?'

'Let me look.' There was silence and then Bombardier spoke again: 'OK, the satellites say that the power is off all across the continental United States of America. We're sending the RAF over to take a look. Nothing is coming out of the US at all – no transmission except yours.'

'OK, Bombardier, I need you to call my office for me. You need to speak to my boss; her name is Pamela Newman. Have you got that?'

Tate heard a scratching at the other end. 'Just writing that down.'

'Tell her that Jack Tate is active and is going after the Russians. OK?'

'Going after the Ru—' The set cut out.

Tate looked at the handset in disbelief.

Joe threw his hands up in the air. 'The damn battery!'

Tate went back to the window. The street outside looked the same, but he now saw a large figure crossing the road and purposefully walking towards the hotel. 'Joe, where's Sara?'

'She took a sleeping tablet and said she didn't want to be disturbed unless there was an emergency.'

Tate gave Joe a look. 'I think this qualifies.'

'Yes, of course.' Joe remained still for a moment and looked at Tate. 'So you're a real-life spy?'

'Yes, but it's not all sex and fast cars.'

'No?'

'Sometimes the cars are slow. Now go and wake Sara.'

* * *

Donoghue met Tate by the reception desk. 'My son's got two black eyes, a swollen nose, a dislocated jaw, a badly bruised shin, a dented Nissan, and a huge ego.'

Tate said nothing.

'No one in Camden would have dared give the little bastard a beating, except you. So I'm going to thank you.'

'Does your patrol car work?'

Donoghue frowned at Tate's question. 'No, it does not, and nor does my personal vehicle or my wife's. I don't know about Clint's Skyline. Do you know what's happening?'

'The US has been attacked.'

'What?'

As Tate explained, the chief of police stayed silent. 'When I took this job, I vowed I'd protect this place. I said that whatever happened in the future, Camden would be safe.'

'It is, for now.'

Donoghue frowned. 'How do you know all this?'

'Joe got his ham radio working; we spoke to someone in the UK. He was watching it on a BBC News channel.'

'Who was covering it here?'

'No one. There are no electronic signals coming out of the US. Chief, what's your emergency plan?'

'Disaster plan?'

'Yes.'

'We have the citizens assemble in the car park next to police headquarters.'

'And how do you let them know?'

'Telephone calls to first responders and announcements from the PA address system on top of our police cruisers' – he shook his head – 'which now will not work.'

'They may; I don't know. Joe's radio set worked, but that was kept in a metal box.'

'But cars are metal boxes.'

Tate shrugged. 'I'm not a scientist.'

'Who are you, Jack Tate?'

'Secret Intelligence Service.'

'MI6?' When Tate nodded, Donoghue continued, 'I knew it. So you were on an assignment?'

'No, I really was on holiday – I was ordered to take some time off. Look, there's something else I haven't told you: I overheard the Russians last night saying how cars wouldn't work today. They knew it was coming.'

'You speak Russian?'

'*Da.*'

Donoghue ran his hand through his mane of salt-and-pepper hair. 'How are the Russians related to this attack, unless it's the Russians who are attacking us? And how in the hell did they arrange it?'

'I have no idea, but if we grab the Russians we can find out.'

'Agreed. Are they still here?'

'No.'

'Great plan, Tate.'

'Yep. Where are the rest of your men?'

'According to the roster yesterday, one was on an early morning patrol and the others don't clock in until seven a.m.' He looked at his watch. 'Damn, even this is busted.'

Tate checked his Rolex. 'It's six. Look, somehow you need to get the town together to brief them. Nothing stops panic spreading better than facts and a friendly face.'

'You think I have a friendly face, Tate?'

'No I don't, so I suggest you get someone else to brief them, maybe the mayor or someone.'

'The mayor is on vacation.'

'You make the address then, but try to smile a bit.'

Donoghue heard a voice call, 'Chief!' He turned his head and saw an officer riding a pink bicycle. With a screeching of brakes, the bike stopped and the officer stumbled as he dismounted.

'Tate, this is Officer Edger.'

'Nice wheels,' Tate said.

'It's my daughter's,' the diminutive officer replied.

'Steve, do you know what's going on?' Donoghue asked.

'Some sort of power outage?'

'Yes and no.'

Tate looked out across the car park. First at his Tahoe and then at the other. 'I think we need to check Joe's paperwork.'

Chapter 12

Washington, DC

Li Tam had slept for longer than he had intended to but had still been on the road in time to see the detonation. His radio, set to his favourite station, had been playing jazz and the soothing, husky sounds of a saxophone filled the taxi as he had headed back to central Washington. The sky had still been dark but some streaks of light appeared over the horizon. As the music continued to float around his ears, he had imagined himself playing in a band before an adoring crowd. Lights started appearing in buildings and more cars joined the road. He'd stared up at the sky and smiled; understanding what was about to happen.

The clock on his dash informed him there were just a couple of minutes to go – he'd hummed to the tune on the radio and tapped his fingers on the wheel. A semi-truck ambled directly in front of him, its red taillights glowering at him like eyes of an angry dragon . . . and then it had happened . . . a greenish flash in the sky. The taxi had shuddered and the radio had died. Li Tam had coasted to the side of the road and switched off the engine.

Now not a single light shone, not a single car moved. Up ahead the semi had also stopped. The bemused driver was still looking in the open hood. Li Tam stretched and climbed out of the taxi. He felt the mild pre-dawn chill as he opened his zipper and urinated on the side of the road. The Russians had not called him. He decided that now he had done enough for them. If they wanted him, they could call him like normal people. He would go home and await further instructions there. His family needed him but to get back to them he had to take a chance and drive through central Washington.

Tam took a deep breath, stared up at the heavens and flashed a thumbs up as he imagined one of his nation's own spy satellites smiling down at him. He got back into the taxi and turned the ignition. The car started the first time, his lamps the only manmade light he could see. He was thankful that the scientists had been proved right. Their technology – both the EMP device and the EMP shielding fitted to his taxi – worked.

His journey was not quite what Li Tam had expected. A few morning commuters were up and about; some waited in vain for buses, while others walked or cycled. The important Washington worker bees had not noticed that they'd been the victims of a targeted EMP. To them, the power was out and that was all. A man in a suit stepped into the road, directly in front of the taxi, and attempted to hail him. Tam drove on. In his rear-view mirror he saw the man waving his arms, his yells muted by the car's thick, bulletproof glass. Tam chuckled; these Americans were overfed, overindulged, and overinflated fools. The man's actions were a warning, however, that he had to get out of the city soon.

He turned the taxi into Corcoran Street NW and slammed on his brakes. The narrow, townhouse-lined thoroughfare was blocked by an ambulance and a pair of police patrol cars standing at irregular angles. The officers had been leaning over the hood of the nearest one, studying a map, but on hearing the taxi, their heads had snapped left. Tam put the car into reverse and pressed the gas. The taxi shot backward, barely missing parked cars on either side of the one-way street.

The officers held up their hands and started to shout. An object banged against the trunk of the taxi, and Tam felt the tyres roll over something soft. He jerked the wheel right, bouncing up over the kerb as he saw what he had hit. It was a body, a body dressed in a dark blue police uniform. Tam heard a shout and saw another officer on the sidewalk, his service pistol raised and trained at him. He was yelling, but Tam filtered out the words as he searched for an escape route. He tugged at his wheel, put the car into drive, and slammed the gas pedal just as something flashed in his vision. The taxi leapt forward, darted through a gap between the parked cars, and collided with a large, leafy tree.

Tam was thrown forward. No airbag inflated to arrest his progress and his forehead hit the wheel with a thud. The edges of Li Tam's vision dimmed, became grey, and then his world went black.

'What do we have here?' Detective Jon Chang asked the patrolman as he regarded the unconscious suspect lying on the stretcher.

'That jerk ran over my colleague with a darn taxi, Detective.'

'How is he?'

'His leg is busted up pretty bad; it'll need to be set. Or at least that's what the paramedic said.'

Chang pursed his lips. The ambulance had come to a halt in the middle of Corcoran Street NW, as had the two patrol cars following it, as though they had suddenly run out of gas; they certainly hadn't been parked. The violent suspect they had been escorting at the time was still subdued and drooling, but now he and his stretcher had been placed on the sidewalk, corralled next to the taxi driver. Chang was tired. Unable to sleep after returning from the British Embassy, he had tried to catch up with paperwork at his home office when the lights all over the city had gone out. And then he had heard the commotion on the street below, as vehicles stopped dead in their tracks. Something was up. He glanced at the patrolman's name badge. 'Milligan, have you been able to raise anyone over the radio?'

'No,' Milligan replied. 'And my cell doesn't work either.'

Nothing made sense to Chang. 'How many cars have you seen moving this morning, I mean since the power went out?'

Milligan pointed at the taxi. 'This was the first.'

'So everything that relies somehow on electronics has failed?'

'Has it?'

'Nothing in my house works, not even the toaster.' Chang looked skyward. 'The only thing I know that would wipe out all the electrics is the EMP blast from a nuclear detonation.'

'As in a nuclear bomb?' Milligan's face lost its colour. 'You think we've been nuked?'

'No I don't.' Chang had recently been to an FBI lecture on developments in terror tactics; stolen nukes had been right at the top. 'Look where we are, Milligan, in the middle of Washington within spitting distance of the White House. If we'd been hit with a nuke, this would be ground zero. We'd already have been vaporised.'

'Then what?'

Chang raised his arms. 'The chances are it's an EMP. Someone has hit us with a non-nuclear EMP device.'

'Isn't that what they used in that old movie, *The Matrix*?' the young patrolman asked.

'I never liked Keanu Reeves, too oily, but the ex-wife did.'

'Yeah, I remember now,' Milligan continued. 'They fired an electrical charge and it knocked everything out, except their own ships.'

Now it was Chang's turn to frown. He stared first at the taxi driver and then at the taxi and somewhere inside his detective's head a light flicked on. Chang took two brisk steps toward the taxi, reached inside, and pulled the hood release toggle. The hood, dented from the impact with the tree, moved but did not open fully. 'Help me with this.' Milligan took hold of the edge and heaved. There was a creaking and a scraping but it opened. Chang peered inside. 'Do you know anything about cars?'

'I know how to drive them. I prefer horses to horsepower.' Chang gave him a quizzical glance. 'I'm from Idaho – my parents were cowboys.'

'Yeehaw,' Chang said flatly and studied the engine bay. He pointed with his finger. 'This part's been reinforced. It's meant to be a crumple zone and should have deformed on impact with that tree. It didn't. The engine's much larger than regular, that's for sure. You see these wires?'

'Yes.'

'They are extremely well insulated; in fact, they look more like miniature undersea cables than wires.'

'So what are you saying? This taxi was EMP proof?'

'EMP *proofed*.' Chang straightened and stretched. 'The only vehicle you've seen that can move today has uprated features and non-standard wiring. My bet is that the driver knew what was coming, and he knew how to prevent it from frying his electronics.'

'Are you sure? I mean an EMP attack. It's a huge jump.'

'Hypothesis, not assumption.'

'What?'

'It's what we detectives do; it's a hypothesis based on evidence.'

'How would a taxi driver know about an EMP attack?'

'A genuine taxi driver wouldn't.'

'Maybe he's not really a taxi driver?'

'You're learning, Milligan.' Chang climbed into the taxi and turned the key in the ignition. The car started on the first attempt, the engine producing a satisfying growl. He put the stick into reverse and backed away from the tree. Everything seemed to be working. Chang checked the wheel; yep, there was no airbag – more non-standard wiring took its place. He killed the ignition and got out. 'This is not a real taxi; it's not a civilian vehicle.'

'What is it then?'

'That is what I need to figure out.' Chang stroked the roof. 'But until then, it's mine.'

Camden, Maine

It had been Sergei's idea to change the plates on the SUV and add the sticker to the window. Oleg had held his breath when the Englishman had approached, but hiding in plain sight had seemed to work. "The best camouflage is often the simplest," Sergei had assured him. And for once Oleg realised that the younger, brutish Russian had skills and knowledge that he himself did not. Oleg had been on the roof for the detonation of the EMP and annoyed that he was not in Washington. He had seen a purple shimmer on the horizon but then relocated into an empty ground-floor room.

By now, all of the guests had made an appearance, and Sara was talking to them. The chief of police left the reception building with the Englishman and the officer who'd arrived earlier on a child's pedal bike. They had their heads down as they walked across the parking lot, but then the new arrival quickly looked up at the Tahoe. Time to go. He had a Glock 19 secured to his side in a pancake holster, which he would use if pushed. He watched the three men enter the other accommodation block. The two policemen took the ground floor while the Englishman went up the stairs to the top. They were being methodical and would eventually reach him or flush him out.

Oleg knew what he had to do. He waited until all three men were inside rooms before he opened the door and bolted for the Tahoe.

Tate heard a car door slam and ran out of the room he'd been searching. He then heard an engine and saw the SUV start to move. Tate shouted, 'He's in the Tahoe!'

Guests drifted towards it, curious at first and then waving and shouting. The SUV continued to travel slowly across the lot as Tate all but fell down the stairs in his haste to reach it. Donoghue burst out of the ground floor, shortly followed by Edger, both brandishing their service Glocks. The guests scattered as Donoghue got in the path of the SUV and aimed at the driver behind the windscreen. The Tahoe stopped.

'Step out of the vehicle. Step out of the vehicle, now!'

The Tahoe crabbed sideways and tried to go around Donoghue. Edger then got in front of the SUV. 'Stop or I will shoot!'

The Tahoe continued to move; Edger pulled the trigger.

'No!' Tate shouted, but it was too late. The 9mm round ricocheted off the hood panel and hit Edger. The policeman fell and the Tahoe left the parking lot.

The sun exploded above the horizon as Oleg hit Elm Street; meteorologically, a new and beautiful day had started, but he doubted many Americans would view it as such. He sighed. He had no choice in his actions; his employer was a partner in the attack on the hated US, and as a former serving member of the GRU's weapons research directorate, he had been paid very handsomely to continue his work. Serving Oleniuk rather than the Russian state had its benefits, and now all he had to do was merely observe and record the aftermath.

He took no delight in the liquidation of other humans. His work had been geared to killing the machines of war, not the men inside them, but after years of research working alongside those who did, his compassion had been blunted. Wars and disease, which had ravaged the globe, taught those who survived that it was a dog-eat-dog world and those who did not fight would be left eating nothing but dog.

Tate knelt down beside Edger. 'Stay still; I've had combat medical training.'

'I wasn't planning on running after him,' the officer croaked.

'You were lucky; the angle it hit your left thigh – a through and through. It may have clipped the edge of a bone, but I doubt it.'

'And how is that lucky?'

'If it had hit an artery, you would have bled out,' Donoghue added.

Edger grimaced before he spoke again. 'Why did my bullet bounce off?'

'Armour plating,' Tate said.

'Is he OK?' Sara asked, joining them.

'He'll be fine.' What he didn't add was *on any normal day.* 'Chief, help me get him to his feet.'

Donoghue bent down and the pair hauled Edger to a standing position. The officer yelled as he put weight on his injured leg.

'Don't use your left leg.'

'Thanks for the reminder.'

Tate looked at the crowd of guests. 'Has anyone got any medical training?'

Like schoolchildren, a hand went up, then another. Tate pointed at the two volunteers. 'Take him into a room and dress the wound.' He turned to Sara; their eyes locked. 'I presume you have a first-aid kit?'

'Yes.'

'Give it to them.'

'Hey, don't I get a say in this?' Edger grumbled.

'No. Once it's been patched up, you'll be mobile but until then we've got to prevent any infection.'

'My gun?'

Tate saw the Glock 17 lying a few feet away; it had been hurled from Edger's hand by the fall. Tate took a step and picked it up. 'I'll be borrowing this.'

'You what?' The chief of police advanced on Tate.

'Listen, you know who I am; you know my training. Look at what's happening here. Who do you think is safer using this: me or him?'

'I'm the chief of police!' Donoghue bristled. 'It's my town, and I get to decide who carries a police-issue firearm!'

Tate didn't need a pissing contest, not now. 'So deputise me. Surely your *Amended PATRIOT Act* that you are so fond of gives you the power to do so?'

Donoghue shook his head. 'Smug British . . . OK you are a deputy.' Donoghue seemed to become aware that the guests were waiting for him to address them. 'I need you all to listen to me. Some type of attack has happened on the United States, which has taken down the national power grid. An electronic blast of . . . er . . . electrons.' He cleared his throat. 'Secondly, we think that the Russian guests who were here are somehow involved. Any questions?'

'How do you know this?' a man in boxer shorts and a dress shirt asked.

Donoghue explained and then added, 'The entire US has been unplugged. You must check your cars. If they start, I'd advise you to try to get home now. You've got the rest of today until people start to panic.'

'And what if our cars don't work?' a woman with unruly red hair asked, aghast.

'Then you have to stay here. As the chief of police for Camden, I can assure you that my citizens are on your side and will help you in whatever way they can.'

Tate looked around at the faces of the hotel guests, innocents attacked, and to what end? Donoghue's words were true; when things went south, they went south fast. When the last spate of terror attacks had hit the UK, he'd been at the SAS barracks, sealed off from the real world. The British government used all available resources, including its small regiment of elite soldiers, to keep order among the civilian population and prevent any opportunistic attacks on the UK's major cities. But as with Northern Ireland before, people resented troops on the streets. Tate took Sara's arm and guided her away from the crowd of guests as a thought struck him. It was the first time he'd spoken to her alone, since the night before. 'Have you checked your car?'

'For what?'

'Does it start?'

'I don't know.'

'It's vintage, fewer electronic parts that could have been damaged.'

She looked at him with a strange expression on her face. 'You scared me last night. The way you attacked Clint was—'

'Necessary,' Tate said, cutting her off. 'He wouldn't back down.'

Sara nodded. 'No one ever says no to him.'

'So he learned something. Now can I see your car?'

'This way.'

They walked around the side of the reception building, and Sara pointed at a garage door. 'It's electric, too heavy for me to open.'

Tate turned the handle and pushed near the top of the "up-and-over" door. It shifted a bit; he pushed more and then crouched and pulled the bottom up. The door gained momentum, slid up and back on its runners and there was the early-model Mini. 'Keys?'

'In the car. This is Camden, Maine.'

'Right.' Tate opened the driver's door, which was on the UK side. He racked the seat back as far as it would go and looked at the controls, ignition switch, and manual choke. He loved cars and that was one of the reasons he'd joined the mobility troop within the SAS. 'Get in.'

'Hold on a moment there – no one drives this but me! And I can't leave my guests; and what about my property?'

'Sara will be staying here,' Donoghue said in his no-nonsense voice as he appeared in the open garage door. 'Tate, you drive. I'll ride shotgun.'

'Hello?' Sara raised her voice. 'It's my car!'

'Sara, I'm sorry; this is police business and we need to commandeer your vehicle.'

'Fine,' Sara said, 'but if it comes back with as much as a scratch on it!'

'You've got my card details, Sara – charge me for hiring it!' Tate said, with a wink.

'You know the card reader doesn't work.'

Donoghue eased himself into the dark red leather seat and shut the door. 'We're going to find the Russians?'

'We're going to stop the Russians.' Tate let out the choke and then slowly placed his hand on the key. 'Here goes; come on, old girl, do this for England.'

'You do know that BMW now owns Mini?'

'More's the shame.' Tate grinned and turned the key. The car coughed, then coughed again and then caught. He depressed the accelerator and the sweet sound of the Cooper S filled the garage. Taking off the handbrake, he manoeuvred the classic pocket rocket out of the garage and onto the road, unseen by the guests in the parking lot on the other side. 'Which way would he go?'

'Turn left. It'll take you straight through town and out the other side, the way you came yesterday. No more large towns until you hit Belfast; keep going after that and you'll eventually arrive in Canada.'

'And right?'

'A few small towns, some big ones, and then Boston.'

'And a lot of worried people without power.'

'And that's going to be a huge problem.'

Tate shrugged. 'I can't think about that now, and neither should you. We have to cut away and focus on the mission.' Tate accelerated north on Elm Street.

Chapter 13

Georgetown, Washington, DC

Simon Hunter stood in the bedroom, washed and dressed. He had to focus on finding the ambassador, but first of all, he needed to find his cell. 'Have you seen my iPhone?'

'No.'

Hunter was puzzled; if it wasn't in his pocket, it was usually by the side of the bed. 'Are you sure?'

'Are you accusing me of hiding it?'

'Yes.' Hunter continued to search and found it under a pillow. The screen was blank. He pressed the "on" button – nothing. Great, no power and no charge. No matter, he had to get to the embassy. Eric Filler had agreed to check the ambassador's residence and was going to text him if their boss was still AWOL. Hunter cursed himself. Something wasn't right. He should never have left the embassy or gone to bed; he should have been out looking, but Terri was waiting for him and damn it all, he had a life outside of work. 'I'm leaving now. I have to get to the office – they need me.'

'I need you,' Terri said theatrically.

Hunter smirked. 'You need to get to work too.'

'I don't start until nine. I'm not crazy like you.'

'That's very true.' He kissed her on the forehead and went downstairs. His laptop was in the lounge where he always left it. On a whim, he sat and tried to power it on. Nothing happened. He'd charged it the day before; it should have worked. Mystified, Hunter popped the laptop into its leather carrycase and left the house. Outside, a black SUV cruised past. He recognised the model as some bulky Chevy. Cars in the US were huge. They were like driving armchairs; he doubted they'd fit on UK roads or in UK parking spaces. He walked down the path to his cherished, diplomatic Land Rover Defender and opened the door. Outwardly, the overall design of the boxy British legend had barely altered in seventy years. Under the skin, however, electronics now replaced a wire and a prayer.

A sudden screech of tyres made him look up. The SUV had reappeared, pulled up, and blocked in the Defender. Before Hunter had time to react, a pair of large men bore down on him. The first was holding a silenced 9mm pistol.

'Get back in the house, Simon.' The words were English, the accent Russian.

Hunter's eyes flicked toward the Land Rover, betraying his thoughts of escape.

The second man skirted the vehicle and slammed the door shut, trapping the laptop bag within. 'He said go inside.'

'OK . . . OK.' Hunter's heart pounded in his chest. 'I'm putting my hand in my pocket for my key.'

'If it is not a key, I will shoot you here in the street, like a dog,' the first Russian said.

Shaking, Hunter retrieved his key and fumbled with the lock. As he pushed the door open, he knew what he had to do. There was no way he could escape but she could. 'Terri! Run to the back door now!'

'Stupid.' The Russian grabbed Hunter's head with one meaty hand and with a second, plunged a syringe into the diplomat's neck. Hunter dropped onto his parquet floor like a stone.

With supreme effort, Li Tam opened his eyes. The August sunlight dazzled him, making them snap shut once more. He could hear voices, although they were distant and the words were indistinct. His neck was numb and his head throbbed. Where was he? He tried to remember and, slowly this time, opened his eyes. Grey shapes, colours bleached away by the seemingly blistering sunlight, gradually gained colour and clarity as his senses adjusted, but the throbbing in his head increased. Tam stayed stock-still, confused, not aware of his surroundings or the reason he had been injured. A shadow fell, followed by the face that had caused it – a Chinese face.

'Keep quiet and I'll get you out of here.' The language was Mandarin, the accent Hong Kong.

The man moved away, his place now taken by a paramedic. Tam tried to speak, but his mouth was dry. The medic leaned down and poured droplets of water from a bottle into his mouth.

'Thank you,' Tam croaked. 'What happened?'

'You can't remember?'

Tam frowned; it caused him pain. 'Not fully.'

'My name's Frank. I'm a paramedic. What's your name?'

'Li Tam.'

Frank shone a light into Tam's eyes. 'Look left, right, up and now down. Do you feel pain anywhere apart from your head and neck?'

'My right leg . . . my ankle.'

'OK, that was probably the pedals. Can you move your feet for me?'

'Yes.'

'The fact you can feel pain in your legs and move them is good; it indicates there is no underlying spinal injury. But you do have whiplash and a concussion. The fact you lost consciousness and cannot remember the event indicates to me that it may well be serious. We need to get you to a hospital, but our vehicles won't start.'

Tam remembered . . . everything. His mission, the EMP, being cornered by the police and then attempting to escape.

'I'll take him in the taxi,' the Mandarin speaker said, now reappearing in Tam's vision but speaking English.

'What about your man, Detective Chang?'

The Mandarin speaker glanced over to the ambulance. Inside, the injured officer lay on a gurney while Milligan chatted to him. 'I presume he needs to keep that leg extended? There'll be no room with my suspect in the back and he won't squeeze into the front. I'll make a second trip.'

'Looks like we have no other option. I need to stay here but I'll put a neck brace on our patient before we move him.'

'Knock yourself out, Frank.'

Frank gently secured Tam's neck in a foam collar, and with the help of a colleague, eased Tam carefully to his feet.

'Hold out your arms,' the Mandarin speaker, whom the paramedic had called Detective Chang, said.

Tam complied, confused, and a pair of police-issue handcuffs were snapped onto his wrists. Chang and Frank led him to the taxi and eased him into the back seat. The ignition started and the taxi started to move off.

'How are you feeling?' Chang continued speaking in Mandarin.

With a dry mouth and a throat that felt as though it had been cut, Tam replied, also in Mandarin, 'Like I have been run over by a train. Who are you?'

'A friend. I need to get you to safety.'

Was he an actual police detective? Tam felt dizzy. He was finding it hard to think. 'Why am I cuffed?'

'Appearances. I had to get you out of there without the local cops suspecting anything. Understand? Now where do you want me to take you?'

Tam didn't want to go home; he didn't want to draw attention to his family. He needed help and the Russians were best placed to provide that. 'The airport.'

'Which one?' Chang asked.

'College Park.'

Chang threaded the taxi through a tight gap between a delivery van and USPS truck. 'It's a great day – look at all this. The attack worked.'

'Yes.' The fog in Tam's head was starting to lift, an increase of pain delivering an increase in clarity. He made eye contact with Chang via the rear-view mirror. Was the detective really another paid agent? Tam had lost a lot of time; he'd been compromised. He had to get back to where he'd started the day, College Park Airport. Tam switched to English. 'Where is my cell phone?'

Chang said, 'I have your sat phone.'

The taxi slowed as Chang started to make a turn towards a bay outside Washington Hospital. The parking lot was half-full with cars. Several of them had their hoods up as owners struggled to get them started. A sole ambulance stood by the entrance doors.

There was a shooting pain in Tam's right ankle as it took his weight. 'I need to get to the airport. I do not need medical attention.'

'OK.' Chang turned back onto the road.

Chang's eyes flicked between the road and Tam in the rear-view mirror as he drove away from the hospital. The roads were still empty but now there were more pedestrians on the streets, and few attempted to flag him down. He was trying to think what his next move should be. Take the taxi driver in to his station or go to the airport and see what else he could uncover, but either way he had to grill him whilst they were alone.

'I need my phone. I have to report in.'

Chang held it up but did not give it to Tam. 'I've been ordered to take over from you.'

'What?'

'I'm to replace you. Will that be an issue?'

'Under whose authority?'

'Your boss.'

'No. No, no. The Russians are running this; we are not meant to be in any contact with—'

'The Russians?' Chang blurted before he could control his surprise. He realised he'd made a mistake; he'd pushed it too far. But his suspicions had been proved right, in his mind at least. A foreign nation had attacked, and it was Russia. Tam looked angry; he'd been duped. Chang pulled the taxi into a side street, turned in his seat and withdrew his police-issue Glock. The last thing he wanted now was for the guy to attack him. There was an uneasy silence as, masks off, they eyed each other. 'Tell me about yourself, Li Tam. Have you been spying on us for a long time?'

Tam tried to change tactics. 'Please, I need my phone to call my wife and daughter to say I'm not dead.'

'And then call up for new orders?'

'I need to get home; they will be worried.'

'That's nice. I had a wife and a daughter once.'

Tam's face softened momentarily. 'Did you lose them in an accident?'

'No, I lost them to drink. Tell me about your mission, Tam. Tell me and perhaps we can cut a deal.'

Tam didn't reply.

'C'mon, Tam, I know you are connected to the power outage, and I know it's much more than just a power outage. We both know it's an EMP.'

'I do not understand.'

'You understand perfectly well; you can't backtrack now. You've slipped up. I know who you are.' Chang pointed the Glock. 'Thank you for the EMP-proofed taxi. It's exactly what I needed.'

Li Tam's eyes flickered before he spoke. 'I do not know anything about cars; it belongs to my boss.'

'I'll check that out.'

'You are making a mistake. I am just a taxi driver.'

Chang now held up Tam's sat phone, with his other hand. 'This works. How is it that you have both a working car and a working sat phone? I mean, how many everyday people even have a sat phone? The last time I used one was on a training course with the feds on disaster management.'

Tam's eyes flickered again. 'You are with the FBI?'

'Not yet,' Chang conceded, 'but that is who I am going to give you to. It would be better for you to come clean with me, here and now.'

'Otherwise what will you do?'

Chang could feel his anger rise; the little turd knew that he had the upper hand. He tried to keep his voice level. 'As I said, tell me what you know then maybe we can cut a deal; after all, you are just a small fish in this giant pond and we need to get the whales.'

'I'm allergic to seafood.'

Chang counted to ten as Tam looked on impassively before he spoke again. 'What were you doing in Washington?'

'Picking up fares, driving them around.'

'Working as a taxi driver?'

'Working as a taxi driver,' Tam repeated.

'Tell me about Russia.'

'It is a big country.'

'Now you listen to me!' Chang raised his voice. 'You are going to tell me what you know.'

Chang had a short fuse. It was his weakness and something that had stalled his promotion. He had been trained in advance questioning techniques, but he guessed if Li Tam was a foreign agent he had been trained to resist interrogation far more brutal than anything he, as a police detective, could hurl at him.

'I am a taxi driver. I am a US citizen. I know my rights.'

Chang's patience failed. He leant back, grabbed the smaller man by his shirt collar and pulled him forward. Tam fell into the footwell, his knees landing heavily on the hard rubber matting and jarring his neck. Tam grunted.

Again, Chang stared at Tam. Tam returned his gaze. The car, and indeed the side street outside, were eerily devoid of any manmade noise.

'Now, listen to me . . .' Tam's sat phone vibrated. Chang studied the screen. Curiously, a number was displayed. He put his left hand partway over the mic and spoke a single word of a single syllable. 'Yes?'

'Go back to the embassy. Keep watching for Tudor.'

'Yes.' The call ended and Chang stared first at the phone and then at Tam as realisation passed through the fog of fatigue inside his head. How could he have been so slow?

Chapter 14

Washington Street, Camden, Maine

On any normal August morning, it would be too early for people to be worrying about their cars in Camden, but not today. Unaware of what was going on or why, residents and visitors alike descended upon the two open-air municipal car parks placed on either side of Washington Street. Many of the cars were less than ten years old and relied heavily on microprocessors, complicated circuitry, and miles of wires.

Sergei sat behind darkened windows in the corner of the car park and monitored the situation. The two car parks had one hundred and seventy-four spaces in all, and most of these were full. He hadn't bothered to count the exact number. He would, if pushed, make up a number. He had a smile on his square face; the Camden Police Headquarters was next to the car park and showed no signs of life. No patrol vehicles parked outside and no noises within. From time to time people banged on the door, but to no avail. It was as if the police had deserted them, but Sergei knew the truth. The police, like everyone else, would be getting to work on foot.

A car grumbled to life and Sergei moved his eyes, nothing else. It was a yellow Honda Civic that had been hidden underneath some sort of protective cover. Was it to protect the paintwork stone chips or because the owner liked the look and didn't want to splash out for carbon fibre? Sergei didn't have a clue, but what he did know was that the vehicle started! A small cheer went up from the other vehicle owners. Slowly, Sergei raised his digital SLR and focused the long lens on the vehicle as it drove away. The car park became silent again. His technology had worked, but then he had never doubted it.

He started to feel warm as the morning sun hit his passenger window; his car would soon be a hothouse without an open window or air conditioning. He looked at his digital watch; 07:00, four hours until they pulled out. Sergei rolled his eyes. This was going to be boring. He had never enjoyed the surveillance aspect of the job; he was much happier with a weapon or fighting with his fists, but his experience and command of English had put him on this mission.

Another car moved. This time it was German – a BMW X5. Sergei photographed it and frowned. Why had that car started when it was full of modern electronics? Was the EMP not as powerful as they had been led to believe? This was why they'd been placed in Camden, to assess the effectiveness of the EMP's outer splash, at this distance from its detonation. Sergei stifled a yawn. Getting up at the arse-crack of dawn, so that he could be in position unnoticed by those checking their cars had been necessary, if unpleasant.

Several other motorists now started to speak to the driver, and then one banged on the door. Sergei nodded; this is how it would start. Fights would break out over working cars and only the strong or the armed would survive. An angry shout, and the driver pulled away with a screech of tyres. Yes, it was about to get interesting. Sergei opened his glove compartment; the light went on and illuminated a Glock, two spare magazines, and two grenades. No one was going to take his car.

He checked his watch. It was time to move to his next location to observe. Sergei started up the Tahoe, gaining many excited looks, and then squealed out of the parking lot. Five minutes later he slowly pulled into the supermarket, turned left, driving to the furthest space away from the entrance. In his experience all those making a beeline for the store would turn in the opposite direction and stop directly outside the store's wide, double doors. He turned off the engine and waited.

Within fifteen minutes he had been rewarded by the arrival of six vehicles. One was an ancient Chevy pick-up, two were motorbikes driven by men with beards and leather, and the last three were Nineties-era sedans. None of them were as reliant on technology as more modern vehicles. As he had predicted each vehicle had driven close to the front door whereupon the driver peered inside the store.

As he observed, the elderly driver of the ancient Chevy started to chat with the two bikers. He was too far away to either hear or read their lips, but he had a fair idea of what was about to happen. The Chevy backed up to the metal security doors, the two bikers then hooked up a pair of chains from the back, and the pick-up tried to move away. Without electricity, no alarm bells rang, no lights flashed, and no calls to either a security company or the police were made. The doors started to give; they bent at the bottom until a gap formed wide enough for a man to enter. And then all six drivers proceeded to loot the store.

Camden Hills State Park, Maine

The emergency rendezvous was just off the coast road in Camden Hills State Park. Oleg had driven quickly through Camden, stopping for nothing and almost running over a second police officer. This one had been standing on the highway next to his useless Crown Victoria and attempting to wave him down. Oleg made a mental note of the model as he accelerated past.

Five minutes later, he pulled into the park, becoming invisible from the road. He got out and stretched his legs before opening the trunk and checking his equipment. He had two satellite phones; one was Russian military and the other an Iridium. Layers of protective material inserted into every panel of the SUV shielded the phones from the EMP. The material was similar to that used in space suits to protect astronauts from solar radiation. This was technology Oleg knew and understood; a layer of metal was sandwiched inside strong layers of boPET polyester film, which protected the metal from damage. In theory, any energy released by an EMP would hit it and not the electronics underneath.

So far, everything he had tested had worked. It would make for an interesting report when he presented this to his employer; he had submitted his primary findings via his military sat phone.

Oleg heard footfall. He quickly shut the trunk of the car as a pair of hikers stepped out.

'Good morning,' the first said with a smile on his face.

'Good morning,' Oleg replied warily.

'It's a beautiful day for a hike,' the second said.

'Yes it is,' he agreed. From the matching hiking boots and shirts, Oleg concluded that the middle-aged couple were husband and wife.

'Well, we mustn't keep you,' the husband said. 'Enjoy your hike.'

The wife smiled at him and the pair strode towards the main road. Oleg watched them go with a quizzical frown; did they not know what had happened? There was nothing he could say to help them. He shrugged. He was reminded of the Amish. They would not be affected one iota by the EMP, unless, of course, they sold their crops to buyers outside the community. Perhaps they would even agree with the EMP's deployment as it would herald a return to a simpler more God-fearing existence.

The Mini Cooper S tore along the coast road, its speed and handling not consistent with its age. Tate knew that part of the sensation of speed was an illusion because they were almost sitting on the road, but he enjoyed it nevertheless.

'Your son—'

Donoghue interrupted him: '—is a product of my wife's first marriage.'

'I see.'

'He's a waste of space, just like his father was.'

'You knew him?'

'Sure, he was the high school jock. I was always second best, and that's part of the reason why I enlisted – to be the best.'

From Donoghue's bearing, it had been immediately obvious to Tate that he was ex-military. 'What were you?'

'MP. Except when I mustered out I walked right into the job here. Camden was so quiet it was almost like an active retirement.'

'And then this happened.'

'Yep.'

Tate saw a figure ahead and slowed. It was a man in uniform waving at them.

'That's Brian Kent!' Donoghue said with relief. 'He should have been back at the station by now.'

As they drew nearer, Tate recognised the officer who had stopped him for speeding. Tate brought the Mini to a halt next to him. Kent put his hand on the roof of the small car and bent down to the window. 'Chief, Mr Tate, what are you doing in Sara's car?'

Donoghue ignored his officer's question. 'Brian, have you seen any other vehicles this morning?'

'Just one, a black Tahoe.'

Donoghue and Tate exchanged glances. Tate spoke. 'How long ago was that?'

'Ten minutes, maybe fifteen. I dunno, my watch is busted, but he was in a hell of a hurry. Damn near ran me over! He was heading north. Chief, can you tell me what's going on? My Vic just stopped, the cut-out is dead, and my radio is down.'

'Brian, we've been attacked by some sort of bomb that stops electronics from working. It's called an EMP.'

'An EMP? Yeah, that's a good one, Chief; I've watched *The Matrix* too.'

'No, Kent, it's true,' Tate stated.

'What?' Kent was confused.

'Brian, stay with your car – that's an order.'

Without waiting for Kent to reply, Tate floored the accelerator pedal. The Mini squealed north, leaving a bemused police officer and two lines of rubber in its wake.

College Park Airport, Washington, DC

Maksim Oleniuk blew a smoke ring and watched it lazily drift apart before he spoke. 'You have done well, Tatiana.'

'Thank you,' Terri replied.

Oleniuk smiled. 'I have to hand it to you: your American English is flawless. It is only your cheekbones that betray your Russian roots.'

'Thank you again.'

'To be able to open one's mouth and converse in a foreign language, as though it were one's own, without a trace of an accent, is a rare gift. Would you believe that after four years at my English boarding school and a further three at Oxford, I was still called "the Russian"? I could never escape my lineage. You have. Bravo. But practice can make perfect, which is why, whenever I can I like to speak in the language of Shakespeare.' Oleniuk shifted his bulk behind the utilitarian metal desk and his left hand subconsciously fingered his neck. 'And Hunter does not suspect a thing. This is correct?'

'Correct.'

'Excellent.' Oleniuk could see the woman was uneasy. Simon Hunter was unconscious, on a military cot in a partitioned area of the hangar. Her part of the mission was over, or so she had believed.

'What happens now?' she asked.

Oleniuk remained silent as he inhaled deeply on his cigarette.

'They call this a civilised country, yet I am not allowed to enjoy a smoke after a delicious meal? That is the height of incivility, don't you agree?'

'I have never smoked.'

'Not even after sex?' He raised an eyebrow, suggestively. Terri didn't reply. Oleniuk stabbed his cigarette out into an overflowing ashtray. 'What happens now is that America crumbles.'

'I meant what happens to me?'

'I know.' Oleniuk leaned back in his seat and let his eyes undress her. 'You, of course, will be reassigned. There is no benefit to Blackline in having you in Washington at this time. It is the perfect opportunity for you to disappear. Terri Bowser will be consigned to history, one of the many who vanished when the United States went to pot.'

'And what will happen to Simon?'

'Hunter.' Oleniuk noted she was referring to the prisoner by his first name. It had to be nipped in the bud. He had not and would not tell anyone the true reason why Terri had been assigned to Simon Hunter. 'Hunter will be taken to a specialist facility where he will be interrogated. He is a valuable operational British asset who unfortunately vanished, with his American girlfriend, on the day of the attack. We have not captured a real British spy for a decade. I am sure he has many secrets to spill about the operations and inner workings of British Intelligence.'

There was a sharp knock on the thin steel door. One of the large Russians who had taken Terri from Simon's townhouse now stood behind her. 'He is awake.'

'Then we had better say good morning to him.' Oleniuk pointed at Terri. 'Bind her hands. Terri, I feel our best course of action is if you keep up your pretence a little longer.'

With neither word nor warning, the commando took Terri by the shoulders and lifted her up from the chair. He took a new pair of plastic ties from his pocket and bound her wrists together. Oleniuk stood, took a step forward, and slapped her hard across the face. Terri cried out, the sound amplified within the steel shell of the hangar. Her eyes tightened with resentment. Oleniuk's mouth turned up to form a narrow smile.

He led them out of the small office and into the main hangar room. At the back of the hangar and on either side sat prefabricated cabins used as detention cells by Oleniuk. In between these and facing the rear doors stood a white Bell 407. Nearer the middle of the hangar and to one side was a rest area. It contained several military cots and was watched over by the other man who had snatched the pair. Oleniuk clenched his fists as he battled the inner fury he felt at finally being in the same room as the man he despised: Simon Hunter. Oleniuk had to hold himself back, like a great reef holding the power of the ocean at bay. Those before him must see only calm, still waters and not the tumultuous, raging white horses.

He violently and suddenly shoved Terri forward so that she fell on top of Hunter. 'Good morning, Simon. Did you sleep well?'

Head thick with sedatives, Hunter's stomach lurched at the sight of Terri. They had taken her too! He held her, his face becoming a mask of anger as he took in the red welt on her cheek. Looking up, his expression changed as he battled to keep the signs of recognition from his face. Even though they had never met, he knew Oleniuk and knew he'd officially died five years ago in Mariupol. 'If you've done anything to her, there will be hell to pay!'

'I have done nothing yet, and that is how it will stay as long as you cooperate.'

'Under whose authority are you holding me here? I am a member of Her Majesty's diplomatic mission to the United States of America. I demand that you release us this instant!'

'It is very un-British to make demands, old boy. Don't you think?'

Hunter caressed Terri's face; the fear in her eyes made his stomach knot. 'What do you want?'

'Everything.'

'What do you think I know?'

'We shall start with something easy. What is the location of your ambassador?' Hunter shook his head slowly and a wry smile split the man's lips. 'Well?'

'You've asked me the one question I cannot answer.'

'Oh? Cannot or will not, Simon?'

'Cannot, Mister . . .'

'You may call me Max.'

That confirmed it. The Russian was Oleniuk, but how and why was he here? 'I cannot answer that question, Max. I do not know where the British Ambassador is. No one does. We filed a missing person report with the Metro Police early this morning.'

Oleniuk's eyes narrowed. 'You did?'

'We have not been able to contact him since Saturday morning, and of course now the power is out.'

'*Suka!*' Oleniuk's frustration had him subconsciously switch back to Russian. He addressed the guard in the same language as he stalked away across the hangar: 'Put them in the cell!'

His hit list was almost complete; Akulov had taken out targets across Maine and now Washington, but two more remained, and Anthony Tudor, the British Ambassador to the United States of America, was one of them.

Oleniuk had lobbied for Tudor's assassination during his tenure as the British Ambassador to Moscow, but at the time he had been overruled by his own chief within the GRU. Now he had the power to correct, as he saw it, a past error. It wasn't the fact that Tudor was missing that had made his anger flare; it was the fact that it was Hunter who had told him. Hunter the man he hated more than any other man alive.

He needed to control his rage; that would come later and with it as much psychological and physical pain as Hunter could bear. Oleniuk stepped out into the heat of the parking bay. The airport was still. He closed his eyes and listened intensely – absolute silence. It was calming. He inhaled deeply and his rage dissipated.

He walked around the corner of the hangar and faced the airfield. There were again no signs of life. None of the small private planes and helicopters had moved. None of them could, except for his own Bell, which sat safely out of sight, and a pair of Gulfstream G650ERs in the much larger hangar next door. All three airframes had been protected by the EMP shielding affixed to the walls and ceilings of the hangars, work that had been conducted in secrecy by workers flown in from China. When the time came to leave the airport, an unexplained but severe fire would level both hangars, incinerating all evidence of the Russians and all trace of the EMP shielding. Then he and his prisoners would be away.

Oleniuk needed some "Yankee air", as he called it, and pulled a packet of American Marlboros from one pocket and a Zippo lighter from another. Lighting a cigarette, he pulled deeply. It was a beautiful day, and could only get better. He stared up at the white clouds drifting carelessly in the summer sky, the same sky that also stared down upon Russia yet seemed so much clearer, so much cleaner here in America, the land of the free and the home of the brave. His sat phone rang. '*Da?*'

'I have him. It will be done,' Akulov stated.

'You are positive?'

'One hundred per cent.'

'Very well. Go ahead, then return to base.' Oleniuk closed down and re-pocketed the sat phone. It was excellent news; soon they could evacuate. He flicked away the butt of his cigarette and tapped a new one out of his packet.

'Hey! Hey you!' A grey-haired man in blue overalls had appeared from the other side of the hangar. It was the caretaker, a man he had seen once before. The man held his arm up. 'Can't you read?' Oleniuk raised his eyebrows in incomprehension as the man spoke again. 'No smoking, son! Jeez, you want to set the place alight, is that it? Blow us all to smithereens?'

Oleniuk was tempted to say "yes" but instead regarded the large red sign above his head. 'I am sorry; I did not know.'

'Hm, well now you do. Enough vapours around here to set it all off, and then where would we all be?'

'Shuffling off our mortal coils?' Oleniuk paraphrased Shakespeare. The old man just scowled and placed his hands on his hips.

Chapter 15

British Embassy, Washington, DC

The taxi had started to attract too much attention. More and more of those out on the streets tried to stop it and now patrolmen flagged it down only to be waved off by Chang before it eventually arrived at the British Embassy. Chang attempted to drive through the security barrier but was told in no uncertain terms by the private security guard that he would have to leave it on the street, regardless of who he was. Chang squinted at the empty parking lot with bemusement before he reversed and parked in a space across the road. Chang led Tam around the barrier, through the empty lot, and into the embassy's main entrance, the taxi driver grimacing with each step on his bad ankle. The woman manning this reception desk attempted a smile. Chang returned it, recognising her from a few hours before. 'Any news on the ambassador?'

Karen King sighed. 'No, Detective. Would you like to speak with Attaché Filler?'

'Please.'

She stepped away from her station. 'If you'll wait there, I'll go and see if he is free.'

'Thank you.' Chang watched her walk away.

* * *

Eric Filler was at his paper-strewn desk. 'Yes, Karen?'

'Detective Chang is here again and he's brought someone with him.'

'Right, that's probably the second detective.'

'I don't think so. The second man is wearing a neck brace and handcuffs.'

'Ah, show them in, please.'

'Attaché Filler.' Chang dipped his head at the diplomat as he entered the office.

'Detective, do come in. And you are?'

'I'm an innocent man who is being held against my will by this police officer!' Tam protested, his voice indignant.

'Explain?' Filler eyed his guests guardedly.

'Attaché Filler—'

'Eric will do.'

Chang pushed Tam down into a chair. 'Eric, I believe this man – Li Tam – knows something about the disappearance of Ambassador Tudor, as well as what is responsible for the blackout.'

'The disappearance and the power cut?' Filler sat, putting the desk between himself and Tam. 'Go on.'

Chang gave a brief overview of what had happened so far and the evidence for his theory. He placed the sat phone on Filler's desk. 'Here.'

'This is all very cloak and dagger,' Filler announced with forced confidence as he examined the phone with both hands. 'It says no signal.'

'Must be a blind spot.'

Filler regarded Tam. 'You are a Russian agent?'

Tam, who had remained silent and impassive throughout Chang's monologue, now raised his eyes from his feet. 'I know my rights; I demand a lawyer.'

'Technically this is not US soil.'

Tam's left eye twitched and a half-smile parted his lips.

Filler addressed Chang as he attempted to comprehend the

situation. 'We've got one dead diplomat, a second missing, and what looks like the aftermath of a terrorist attack on the United States, utilising, you say, an electromagnetic pulse bomb?'

'That's about the size of it.'

Filler took a swig from a glass of water – he hadn't offered either guest one – then cleared his throat. 'Mr Tam, are you responsible for the murder of Major General Dudley Smith?'

'No.'

'I don't believe you.' Filler had noted a flicker of recognition in Tam's eyes on hearing Smith's name.

'Me neither,' Chang stated.

'I do not care.'

'Tam, you'd better tell us now, before things get uncomfortable.'

'I did not.'

'But you knew who he was?'

Tam shrugged. 'No.'

Filler leaned forward. Emboldened by outrage, his Yorkshire accent became thicker. 'As this is not US soil, I can have you transferred immediately to the UK.'

'Tam, we are going to find out eventually,' Chang said.

Filler scowled at Tam. Tam stared resolutely ahead, past the diplomat and out of the window. There was a knock at the door. A moment later it opened and Karen appeared. She was smiling. 'Attaché Filler, the ambassador has returned and is in his office.'

Filler let out a sigh, relieved. 'Well, thank the gods for that. Have you made him aware of the situation?'

'No, he wants to see you immediately.'

'I think it best if I stay here with Mr Tam, if that's OK with you?' Chang said.

'No, I have a better idea. Karen, can you escort Detective Chang and Mr Tam to the conference room?'

'Of course.'

'And can you make them some coffee?'

'We have no power.'

'Right.' Filler stood, Chang copied and pulled Tam to his feet. They left the room. Filler trooped to the end of the corridor, where the ambassadorial corner office was situated.

Anthony Tudor, the British Ambassador to the United States of America, needed a cup of tea, but without any power he was restricted to water or canned pop, and he disliked Coca-Cola with a passion. The office was stuffy; he had to let more air in. Still wearing his spandex cycling outfit and red-faced, he tried to push his window a notch wider but the safety catch tugged at the frame. He sighed. It was a beautiful August day in the US capital city, and he was in an overheated box. Below, he saw a handful of cars moving on the main road, including a dark SUV. This was in blunt contrast to the usual nose-to-tail traffic he would expect.

'Anthony?'

'Yes, it's me.'

'You're OK?' Filler asked.

'Just hot – this office is so stuffy. Look at this, it won't open more than three inches! It's "Health and Safety" gone mad! Does anyone actually believe that I could fall or would jump out? Rather than enjoying a "dangerous" natural breeze, I'm supposed to breathe in ice-cold, artificial air from a pump?'

'We've filed a missing person's report.'

'What? For whom?'

'You. I tried calling you and then even went to your house. Where have you been?'

'Away. I told you.'

Filler sighed. 'You said you might be staying at a place called Wide Waters.'

'I said Broadwaters, and we did.'

Filler nodded. Tudor had given him the wrong name but it made no difference now. 'I see.'

'It's a little place Janet found on the internet, with a wilderness bike trail.'

Filler was annoyed but showing it would make no difference, and now there were far larger issues. 'We couldn't contact you.'

'Ah, well I forgot my phone charger. Look I did try to call this morning. My sat phone was in the Range Rover and then that wouldn't switch on and the damn car wouldn't start. Janet, of course, blamed me and refused to come. She stayed at the guesthouse.'

'Anthony, I have something to tell you. You should sit down.'

'Whatever it is tell me now. Unless you are going to say that you've got one of our secretaries pregnant?' Tudor beamed.

Filler didn't. 'Dudley Smith is dead.'

Tudor stumbled, grabbed at the back of his chair and sat. Momentarily unable to find his voice, his mouth wobbled wordlessly. Finally he asked 'How?'

'The police believe he was assassinated.' Filler briefed Tudor on events thus far, including Chang's information regarding the Russians and Li Tam.

Tudor raised his arms expansively. 'So all of this is an attack by the Russians?'

'That's the current assessment.'

'Dudley was one of my closest friends. I'd known the family for years, and we were at school together. This is devastating, utterly devastating – on both a personal and a political level. World wars have started for less.'

'Let us hope it won't get that far. The police have no hard evidence that it was the Russians.'

'And of course now that all the electronics have failed, we may never have that concrete proof.' Tudor paused, rubbed his ruddy face with his hands. 'Do we have any means at all of communicating with home?'

'Not as far as I can tell.'

'So we can't implement our Critical Incident Plan?'

'I informed Whitehall late last night of Dudley's murder, but with time differences little was achieved in the five hours before the power went out. I imagined some frantic phone calls were going to be made and that someone was to be sent over here but . . .' He shrugged.

Tudor shook his head. 'If the phones don't work, how do we call everyone in? Do we mount bullhorns on bicycles?'

'I'm not an expert on bikes,' Filler mumbled humourlessly.

'Are any of our embassy vehicles operational?'

'None of those on-site will start. I can't vouch for any others. I would imagine that if they were operational, their users would be here already.'

'Where is our resident spook?' Tudor asked. 'He drives a Land Rover Defender – they're meant to be indestructible!'

'Simon hasn't made it in yet.'

'But he lives the nearest of us all to the embassy.'

'That's true.'

'I feel we need to discuss the Destruction Plan. How long would it take to complete?'

Filler mulled over the situation. The Destruction Plan was the last resort for any diplomatic outpost and, in short, was a schedule for destroying sensitive material. It was hour-based, meaning that the most sensitive documents and drives were destroyed in the first hour, and then the rest on an ever-decreasing level of importance. 'Without a shredder or the ability to power up the incinerator, we'd have to look at building a bonfire of sorts in the courtyard. I doubt that would destroy the data on our fireproofed military-spec thumb drives and hard drives.'

Tudor closed his eyes and sighed heavily. 'Have all staff that are present start filling burn-bags. I'll make a decision on this later. Did you say this Chang person and his charge are in the conference room?'

'Yes.'

'That then is where we shall go. It'll be a damn sight cooler than in here, with those big windows to open.'

'Of course.'

'You first. I'll be there in a moment.' Tudor watched his friend and colleague leave the room. As soon as he was on his own, he slumped back in his chair, engulfed in a wave of sorrow. He closed his eyes and took a deep cleansing breath – as his wife had taken to calling it. He had to rationalise his emotions. He was the diplomatic representative for his Queen and could not be seen to, in any way, appear weak but . . .

Filler shot a glance out of the window. On the road outside he saw an SUV moving. Did the suspected EMP only affect some vehicles and not others? It was something they would have to discuss further; perhaps the embassy could even purchase or commandeer the necessary vehicles to evacuate. The Evacuation Plan called for staff to be taken directly to Ronald Reagan Washington National Airport, which was less than a half-hour away, where they would be collected by a commandeered British Airways or a Virgin Atlantic Boeing.

Tudor left his office and descended the stairs. He saw Filler speaking with Karen at the front desk. He waited and Filler joined him at the threshold to the conference room.

'Shall we?' Tudor rapped his knuckles on the door in a perfunctory manner and entered. He saw two men. One sat with his head bowed while the other stood, leaning against the windowsill. Tudor addressed the man at the window without the handcuffs. 'Detective Chang, I'm sorry we had to meet under such circumstances.'

'Thank you, Ambassador.'

'And you, I presume, are Mr Tam?'

Li Tam stared deep into the ambassador's eyes. The Englishman blinked. Tam made no effort to reply.

'He is,' Chang clarified.

'Let us as least be civilised.' Tudor sat and gestured for Chang to join him.

'I'm happy to see that you have returned safely, Ambassador. We thought you'd perhaps been kidnapped or worse.'

'Enough about me; what happened to Dudley? Eric has explained your theory to me.' Tudor shifted his gaze from Chang to Tam. 'Did you have a hand in the murder of my friend?'

Tam remained silent.

'Answer me, damn it!'

'No, I did not. It was the Russians.'

Tudor and Filler exchanged glances. 'Moscow murdered the British Military Attaché?'

'Yes.'

Chang cleared his throat. 'What was your involvement?'

'I was their taxi driver.'

'You're starting that nonsense again?'

'I was their taxi driver. I was tasked with moving their men across the city.'

'Where to?' Tudor asked.

'The airport.'

'Which airport?' Chang snapped.

'I told you before, College Park.'

'Who gave you orders?'

'A man I never met. He was Russian.'

'If you never met him, how did you know he was Russian?' Filler now joined the questioning.

'I met his men – they were Russian.'

'Whoa.' Chang held up his hand. 'Men? How many are we talking about here?'

'I saw two,' Tam replied.

Tudor thought the man was lying, but carried on. 'Detective Chang, does your department still have a police sketch artist?'

'No, Ambassador, it's all done by computers nowadays.'

Tudor got to his feet; he needed some air. He stalked to the south-facing window and pushed it wide open. The thick, bullet-proof pane glided easily on its well-oiled hinge; being on the ground floor, there was no safety bar preventing it from doing so. The sky was a vivid blue and snow-white clouds floated high above. Tudor took a moment to gather his thoughts. What was happening around him in diplomatic terms was an "end of days" scenario. He was not going to be beaten by the Chinese, the Russians or whoever was behind this. Now resolute, he took a deep breath before turning back to face the others. 'Now listen to me, Mr Tam, you are damn well going to tell—'

There was a thud, a single round, suppressed. Anthony Tudor, the British Ambassador to the United States of America, sailed forward and landed face first on the floor, his head a bloody mess.

Chang dived to the floor, taking Filler with him. There was a blur in his peripheral vision, a sudden movement. Li Tam was on his feet and making for the open door. Chang scrabbled onto his side, reaching for his Washington-PD-issued Glock and raised it at the disappearing spy. Chang shouted a warning and pulled the trigger at the same time. 'Stop!'

The retort, flight, and impact of the round happened too quickly to be differentiated by the human eye. It was a single action, instantaneous. It caught Li Tam midstride, lifting him clean off his feet and pinning him against the wall. He slid down, leaving a bloody trail.

Crabbing across the floor, Chang pressed the Glock into Tam's temple. Hissing, his voice sounding distant after the Glock's roaring retort, he said, 'Move again and I'll put a slug in your skull.'

'They killed him . . .' Filler's voice trailed off as his eyes remained fixed on Tudor's lifeless body.

'Stay down!' Chang ordered as he darted to the window, giving Ambassador Tudor's corpse a cursory glance. There was no point checking for a pulse; half the skull was missing. Chang took a deep breath and inched his head above the windowsill. Outside, across the deserted parking lot, he saw a black SUV smoothly driving away on the all-but-silent street. A tinny trilling sound made him duck, made him flinch . . . The sat phone. Chang reached the table and lifted the handset. 'Yes?'

'Where are you?' The Russian-accented voice again.

Chang chanced a reply. 'I'm parked opposite the British Embassy.'

'You did not report the ambassador had arrived!'

Chang thought quickly; this was proof positive that the Russians were behind both assassinations. 'I did not see him arrive.'

'Were you asleep – is that it?' The voice sounded incredulous. 'In any case, he has been taken care of.' There was a long pause. Chang could hear a muffled conversation in what sounded to him like Russian and then the voice spoke to him again. 'You have new orders. Go to Location Three. We need a taxi.'

'Understood.' The line went dead.

'I . . . I can't believe this . . .' Filler was now on his feet but bracing himself against the wall with his left hand. He started to talk quickly, to himself. 'I bloody told him the windows were bulletproof for a reason, that he shouldn't open them, but oh no Anthony Tudor always knew best, told me to stop being an old woman. I should have insisted; I should have stopped him . . .'

'Filler!'

'What?' The diplomat looked up, his eyes wide.

'Do you have a secure area, like a panic room or a bunker?'

He frowned before he answered, as if momentarily not understanding the question. 'In the basement.'

'Get everyone there, now!'

'But . . . but, Anthony? We can't just leave him here!'

'He's dead; he can't get any deader.'

Without warning, Filler lunged at Tam. He grabbed the much smaller man by the lapels and heaved him up and off the floor. Arterial blood sprayed from Tam's leg, across both Filler and the meeting room. 'Tell me who did this, you bastard! Who shot my friend?' Tam's head lolled, his face ashen and his cream chinos turning scarlet. Filler shook him. 'Answer me, you little shit!'

'Back off!' Chang pushed the diplomat away and took hold of Tam, aware that he was losing him. 'Where is Location Three?'

'Washington . . .' His eyes were glassy, his face waxen.

'Where is it?'

'Fuc . . .' Tam's eyes rolled up and back.

'Tam! Tam! Stay with me!' Chang placed him back on the floor and grabbed his thigh, desperately trying to stem the blood loss.

A faint smile bent Tam's lips before his body went limp.

'He's dead?' Filler tried to control his breathing.

'Yes.' Chang raised his fist to punch the wall but thought better of it. His single round had clipped the femoral artery. He had killed his only lead. Chang started to shake. 'He bled out.'

'Good.'

Chang screwed his eyes shut. He was on duty. He'd lose his badge over this; he had killed an unarmed suspect. He was looking at jail time. Panic constricted his chest. 'I had no choice, he was running away. I had to stop him.'

Filler took a deep breath, regained his composure. 'We both believed he had a handgun, didn't we? We had no choice.'

Chang looked at the diplomat who was nodding. Chang took a deep breath. 'I agree with you – we had no choice.'

The room with the two men and two warm corpses became quiet.

'Who was on the phone?' Filler asked.

'His Russian handler.'

'The Russians did all of this.' It was a statement, not a question.

Chang tried to regain control. 'Eric, get your staff in the basement. There's nothing else you can do until we know it is safe outside.'

Chang could see Filler was at a loss. His friend was dead and they were cut off, under attack. Unlike their American counterparts, the British diplomatic mission did not have an armed corps of Marines guarding the embassy. The British had locally contracted private security guards, and as far as he was aware, only one of them had made it to the embassy. Was there any sense in local staff remaining on duty when the fate of their loved ones outside was unknown? Chang imagined they were not part of the evacuation plan; they would be left behind. No, he'd tell Filler to get everyone into the basement then decide what further action to take.

'How deep does an EMP reach?' Filler asked.

Chang shrugged. 'No idea. Why?'

'We have a secure cell in the basement, we call it "the bubble". I don't know if its air-conditioning system will be operating. It has a backup server . . . and I believe a set of secure sat phones.'

'Now you remember this? Really?' Chang shook his head slowly. 'Did no one check this earlier?'

'No.' A look of embarrassment washed over Filler's face. 'Gareth Moore is the IT wiz. I never really paid much attention to that side of things. He's on holiday and Simon Hunter has the spare key, but we could break the lock.'

'OK.' Chang studied Li Tam's sat phone. 'I should be able to get the number of this up somehow. There it is, I think. Write this down.'

Filler took a pen and a legal pad from the conference table as Chang relayed the number to him. There was a shriek behind them. Both men turned to see Karen standing with her hands held to her face and her eyes darting between the two corpses.

Filler stepped forward and put his arms around her. 'Karen, Anthony is dead and so is Mr Tam. We have been attacked. I need you to round up the rest of the staff and get into the bubble. Understood?'

Karen remained silent, her eyes fixed on the carnage.

'Karen!' Filler shook her by the shoulders. 'Do you understand?'

'Yes . . . but . . .'

'But what?'

'Simon has the key.'

'Take the fire axe and break it open.'

'Me?'

'Yes, you or anyone else who can lift the axe. We just need it opened. Understood?'

'Yes.'

Chang watched her leave. He rubbed his face. 'So what do I do?'

'What do you mean?' Filler asked.

Chang shrugged, an action that usually didn't inspire confidence in law enforcement officers. 'I can't call this in, and even if I could, the department and the coroner can't get here. For all I know, I may be the only mobile police officer in DC. Meanwhile, the Russians are running amok . . .' Chang needed a drink. Bourbon, neat. He'd been fooling himself to think he wasn't addicted. His ex-wife had known this even if he disagreed. But here he was, one week dry and making life-and-death decisions. And he'd just killed an unarmed man . . . a husband and father.

'Chang . . . Chang!' Filler snapped his fingers. 'You must go after the Russians!'

Chang agreed. He had to see this through to the end, even if it meant the end of him and his police career. 'The Russians are expecting Tam to drive to somewhere they call "Location Three".'

'Have you checked his sat nav?'

'His what?'

'His GPS. Don't all taxi drivers use those here now?'

'The lazy ones do. But . . .'

'But what, man – spit it out?'

'That doesn't sound like a very secure way of storing secret locations!'

'Does it need to be? It's hiding the information in plain sight – like a safe behind a mirror. Have you got any other suggestions?'

'No,' Chang agreed. 'And as his car and sat phone are in working order, we can expect that his GPS also has been unaffected . . . but I'm not Tam. They will be expecting him not me.'

'Tam's Russian handler didn't notice it wasn't Tam speaking when you answered. Perhaps they have several drivers, perhaps the people you are going to meet haven't met Tam?'

'That's a lot of perhaps.'

'Perhaps,' Filler said, with a thin smile. 'What else can we do?'

Run away, Chang thought. 'Nothing.'

Chang extended his right hand and shook Filler's. 'I'm sorry about the ambassador.'

Filler's eyes were moist but his voice was firm. 'Find them, make them pay.'

'I will,' Chang replied noting that Filler had not said "bring them to justice".

Chapter 16

Camden Hills Park, Maine

Tate pulled the Mini over at the side of the road, next to a pair of hikers.

'Good morning, folks.' Donoghue addressed them with a smile. 'You wouldn't have happened to see a black Chevy SUV on your travels this morning?'

'Yes, Officer,' the husband said, 'it was just inside the park back there.'

'Was anyone with the vehicle?'

'One guy, he sounded foreign.'

The wife glanced at her husband. 'I told you he was up to no good.'

'Thank you, folks, you've been very helpful.'

Donoghue nodded and Tate pulled away.

'It makes sense,' Tate said. 'It has to be an ERV. He'll wait for the rest of his team and then bug out.'

'And go where?'

Tate had been thinking about that. What was the Russians' exfil plan? 'I'll ask him.'

They passed a sign that read "Entrance to Camden Hills State Park 1,500 feet", and half a minute later Donoghue instructed Tate to stop the car. 'You stay here; I'm going in.'

'No,' Tate said. 'You are the law – I get that – but if the Russians are there, you can't just wander over, flash your badge, and ask them to come quietly.'

'That's exactly what I can do, Tate. You expect me to stay here? No way.'

'This is what I'm trained for – covert ops. I'll assess the situation. You need to stay with the car and keep the engine running. I don't know if this little beauty will start again.'

Donoghue sighed heavily; he could see the logic. 'OK, agreed.'

The two men got out of the car. Donoghue nodded at Tate as he headed off and then clambered into the driver's seat. With Edger's Glock held in a two-handed grip, Tate advanced towards the park's entrance road. The empty highway added to the eeriness of his approach. The only sound was that of the Mini's engine gently humming. He reached the entrance and stood stock-still behind a tree, the fat green leaves concealing him from anyone on the road. His black jeans and dark green shirt were not the same as tactical camouflage gear, but at least their colours were subdued.

He listened. The Mini's engine was now much quieter and probably would not carry past the tree line. There was no other sound. Although there was a slight breeze, it was not enough to swish the leaves.

Tate crouched and edged forward, further into the park, expecting at any moment to come across the Russians; he'd made himself a smaller target and would appear around the trees at a lower level than any sentry expected. He darted his head forward and saw an empty tree-lined path. He advanced, weapon up; he felt exposed. There was a bend ahead and he threw caution to the wind and jogged to it. Five paces out, he stopped and listened, and then he heard someone sigh. Tate went back to a crouch and eased himself forward around the trees. He saw the unmistakable shape of the black SUV.

* * *

Oleg focused on the screen of the American-registered Iridium satellite phone. The network had only gone down five minutes before. Had the effect of the EMP on low-orbiting civilian communications satellites been negligible or delayed? He didn't know, but surely the US military, as well as the Russians and Chinese, had others that would be immune. The probable cause of the network's abrupt disappearance must be governmental. Yes, that was it; he was certain that the US military had taken over the civilian network as part of their emergency contingency plan.

'Put your hands in the air!' the voice from behind his head ordered in a perfect St Petersburg Russian accent.

'What about the phone?'

'Keep it in your hand.'

The owner of the voice slowly came into view. Oleg was surprised to see the Englishman from the inn, aiming a Glock 17 at his head. 'I don't understand. Who are you?'

'I have the gun; I ask the questions. Who are you working for?'

'You don't know?'

'I am SVR and I know you are Oleg Sokol former GRU; what I am asking is which unit are you with now?'

Oleg's eyes went from wide to narrow. How did the man know his name? 'You are SVR? Prove it.'

'No. I have the gun. If I wasn't SVR how would I have known where to find you? This is your ERV for after the attack.'

'Yes,' Oleg admitted. 'Our rendezvous point was at the inn and we can't use that anymore.'

'You may lower your hands, but place the phone on the ground.'

'As you know, I am Oleg Sokol. What you may not know is that I am formerly of the Weapons Research Directorate.' Even now he felt a surge of pride as he stated this.

'Based at Arzamas-16?'

'Correct.' Anyone who was not from Russian intelligence would have used "Sarov", the name of the closed post-Soviet town in the Nizhny Novgorod region. Old habits were hard to break for

Russians; they didn't like using new names. Sokol frowned. 'If you do not know which group I am with, how do you know my plans?'

The man gave him an expressive "you know how it is" shrug and sighed. 'I was briefed by Moscow that your operation was taking place, but my superior did not read me in on which unit was carrying it out. He did not think I needed to know.'

'That sounds about right.'

'I was sent to monitor your group, assess how it carried out its duties, and, if necessary, act as over-watch in case you became compromised. That is why I was at the inn and why I had the same vehicle as yours.'

'Ah.' Oleg nodded; it seemed to make sense.

The man lowered his Glock. 'I'm sorry I had to point this at you.'

'It is OK. But you tried to stop me – you and the policemen.'

'I was trying to stop him. By the way, he'll live; he shot himself in the leg.'

'Not the foot?' Oleg joked.

'And so back to my question, which unit is undertaking this operation?'

Oleg nodded. 'I am not surprised that Moscow did not tell you – it is plausible deniability. I am a contractor working for the private military company Blackline.'

Tate nodded, as though he had heard of Blackline, but he had not. He knew the names of the top-ten Russian private military companies, these included Wagner, Cossacks, SlavCorps, Antiteror and MAR. All active in the conflicts of the past decade to a greater or lesser extent, but Blackline was not among these, and Sokol was not a soldier.

'So why exactly are you here now, and pointing a gun at me?'

'I was looking for answers,' Tate said. 'I can't get hold of my superior. The embassy has gone dark – hell everyone has gone dark.'

'Well, as you are here, we can both wait for Sergei and then head up to the regional operations centre.'

Tate frowned. He couldn't ask where this was, if he was meant to know about the operation. 'How much fuel do you have? I'm down to a quarter of a tank.'

'You will need more than that, and of course the gas pumps, being electronic will not pump. I have some spare fuel, but perhaps it is better just to take the one vehicle.'

'Agreed.' So the base was not in the local area?

'Where have you parked?'

'On the road; I'd better move it.'

'That is wise. I'm sorry, you have not given me your name.'

'Ivan Goncharov.' It was a name Tate had used before on an operation. He was familiar with the legend and if needed could be questioned about it. He extended his hand and Oleg shook it.

'Your watch – that is not standard issue.'

'I got it from a jewellery shop in Washington.' Not true, but near enough.

'It is a classic. I have often admired the watchmaker's skill. We were issued with these mission watches. The timers were synchronised, and there is a GPS tracker. I would have thought you would have been also issued with one in order to monitor our . . .' The Russian's words trailed off, and Tate saw that his deception was falling apart.

Tate cursed, pulled the Russian forward, and twisted behind him. He hooked his arms around the man's neck, put his left hand on the back of the head, and pushed the throat into his right forearm. Oleg started to struggle, but the simple *Adaka* chokehold had him lose consciousness in seconds. Tate laid Oleg on the ground as he searched for something to secure him with. In the trunk, next to a large black equipment bag, he found a plastic bucket of sundry items. He rummaged and discovered a roll of duct tape, which he quickly wrapped around Oleg's wrists and ankles. He then made an air hole in another piece and secured his prisoner's mouth. Once he was certain that Oleg was secure and breathing unimpeded, he hefted the Russian into the back of the SUV and laid him across the bench seats. As an afterthought, he secured him with the seatbelt before plugging it in.

Tate searched the vehicle. In the glove box he found a map with a location circled; it was the town of Houlton. The name didn't ring any bells to him. He took the map and went back to the trunk. He unzipped the black equipment bag. It held a full assault kit and extra ammo. He nodded approvingly and shouldered the Heckler & Koch 416. It was an A5-11 – the short barrel, Close Quarters Battle version. Although not the lightest weapon, it was a nice bit of kit. The Regiment didn't use it, but he'd trained with it. It was a specialised weapon and now there was no doubt whatsoever in Tate's mind that Oleg Sokol, former GRU, was involved in an active operation, even if he wasn't a shooter.

Tate continued to rummage through the bag; the hardware was new and US-made. Tate once more checked that the Russian was both breathing and secure before he took the key from the ignition, locked the Tahoe, and headed back towards Donoghue.

Donoghue heard the vehicle approaching before he saw it on the deserted highway. It only took a split second for him to make the decision to leave the car. He switched off the ignition and he was out of the Mini, Glock at the ready, and running for the trees. Reaching the tree line, he crouched and faced the road. As he did so, a black SUV crested the bend and bore down on his position. It came to a full stop next to the Mini. The window powered down and Donoghue saw the large Russian. He looked down at the car, saw that it was empty, then drove on into the park.

Donoghue followed on foot, as quickly as he could.

Tate dived into the trees as he saw the nose of the second Tahoe suddenly appear. He swore. Oleg was visible on the back seat of the other one for the entire world to see. There was no way he could talk himself out of this. He ran through his options as the

SUV stopped next to Oleg's, and Sergei stepped out and cricked his massive back.

From the trees Tate saw Sergei look around the clearing, searching for his partner. He then tried Oleg's driver's door before moving to the back of the vehicle. Oleg straightened up, and Tate heard him chuckle – a deep rumble that came from his belly. 'Wake up, old man!' Sergei knocked on the window, and then it was obvious he had seen that Oleg was gagged with duct tape.

Tate pushed out of the trees. The HK was up and zeroed on the big man. '*Ne dvigatsya!*' Don't move, he yelled in Russian.

Sergei examined Tate with dull eyes. 'Good morning.'

'Raise your arms above your head,' Tate commanded.

Sergei did as requested.

Donoghue now advanced from behind, panting, Glock trained on the Russian's temple. If he was surprised to see Tate wielding an assault rifle, he didn't show it. 'Down! Down on the ground now!'

'No.' The word carried no emotion.

'Down, now!' Tate repeated Donoghue's command.

'No. I will not lie down to die. If you are to shoot me, do it looking into my eyes, but know that I will come back for you.'

Donoghue stepped nearer and pressed the Glock into the back of the large Russian's neck. 'Get down. NOW!'

'OK . . . OK.' Sergei relaxed his shoulders and started to bend; as he did so, the Glock moved away ever so slightly, but it was enough. Sergei jerked his arm backwards and caught Donoghue in the chest with an elbow. Winded, Donoghue stumbled; Sergei grabbed the American's wrist and wrestled the Glock free. Tate dropped the HK. There was no way he could fire and not hit Donoghue; instead, he charged forwards and shoulder barged the Russian into the ground.

Sergei's head hit the gravel and he let out a grunt. Tate pushed his left hand into Sergei's throat and drew his right fist back to deliver a blow, but then the Russian's hand, still holding the Glock, connected with his temple. Sparks of blinding light erupted behind Tate's eyes and he fell sideways. Donoghue reached for the HK assault rifle but Sergei opened fire, a round missing the police chief's hand by a fraction of an inch.

'On the ground!' Sergei goaded as he stood. 'Let's see how you like it.'

Donoghue knew there was no point in attempting to reason with the Russian, so slowly and deliberately, he dropped to his knees and then stretched out with his nose in the gravel. He heard footsteps as the Russian drew nearer. And then there was a roar.

Tate, on legs of rubber, crashed his shoulder into the back of Sergei's right knee in a chop block movement, an old WWE move. The Russian yelled as the joint was dislocated and he fell on all fours, dropping the Glock. Tate staggered to his feet and glared at the Russian as blood streamed down the side of his face, like war paint. 'C'mon, big man!' he growled.

Sergei snorted; there was a white-cold wave surging up his leg, masking the pain in his knee, as a red-hot rage attempted to escape from behind his eyes. He forced himself to his feet, his left knee making a grinding noise like a car with a faulty transmission. 'You think you can beat me? One-on-one, man-to-man?'

'You'll never know,' Donoghue said as he pulled the trigger of the Glock and sent a 9mm round into Sergei's good knee. The Russian howled and collapsed, rolling twice before pulling himself into a foetal position.

Tate bent forward and put his hands on his thighs to steady himself. 'Thanks, but I had him.'

'Sure you did, Nature Boy.'

Tate tried to speak, but a wave of nausea caused him to vomit. He took several steps sideways before stumbling backwards into a sitting position.

'Tate, don't move. You're injured.'

Vision blurry, Tate batted away the words with his hand but said nothing.

* * *

Tate held the gauze against the side of his head. The cut was just in his hairline and, according to Donoghue, nothing more than a scratch. He'd stopped feeling dizzy but now a dull ache engulfed his head. It was a concussion, no doubt about it, but he'd had worse – much worse. Tate stood and took a deep breath. For a moment, the edge of his vision greyed out and then it was back. He'd be all right; he had to be. After treating Sergei's wound as best he could with a field surgical pack he'd found in the trunk, Donoghue had taken a Tahoe and doubled back to collect Officer Kent. Kent now watched over the two prisoners, whose duct tape had been replaced by police cuffs taken from Kent's Crown Victoria.

On the SUV's hood, Donoghue spread the map Tate had found. 'Yep, there's an airport at Houlton. It was bought by a Chinese investment company back in 2014. I can't recall the name, but I remember the uproar it caused at the time. Anyway they reopened it and brought in quite a bit of income for the local economy.'

'A commercial airport?' Tate hadn't heard of Houlton.

'No international carriers. Mostly private jets, and I think the occasional charter jet, but I've never been there.'

Tate looked at the circle someone had put around Houlton. 'So to get there, I go to Bangor and then take Interstate 95 north?'

'It's about one hundred and seventy miles; three hours or so driving time.' Donoghue frowned. 'Why do you want to go there?'

'The Russians wanted to.'

'You think this is where they planned to exfil?'

Tate nodded and wished he hadn't, as a dagger of pain stabbed his temple. 'They've got working vehicles so why not working airframes?'

'Something here does not add up. They're responsible for the attack, the lights out—'

'The EMP.'

'Right, and then they hang around afterwards to do what, exactly?'

'I have no idea. Oleg is from the GRU's scientific directorate. He's not a fighter; my guess is he was carrying out some type of experiments here.'

'On what?'

'You lot.'

'Bring Oleg over here,' Donoghue called out.

Kent did as requested and placed Oleg in front of them. The Russian looked at them with a quizzical expression on his face.

'Tell me exactly what you were doing here,' Donoghue ordered.

'In Camden?'

'Start with Camden.'

'And what if I don't? I know how policing works in the United States. I should have legal representation.'

Donoghue looked at Tate. 'Is he for real?'

Tate picked up his rifle. 'I think he needs to be persuaded.'

Fear now flashed across the Russian's face. Tate could see the man thinking furiously. 'Very well. You must understand, I am a scientist. Science is pure, not tainted with any bias or pernicious intent.'

Donoghue didn't look like he was following but said, 'OK, go on.'

'Science is science. My mission was to check our test equipment to see if it worked in the field after the EMP event and to assess the impact on unshielded local technology'

'You attacked the US to test your new equipment?' Tate asked.

'I did not attack, Blackline did . . .' Oleg's voice trailed off as he realised there was really no difference.

Donoghue pointed a large index finger at the Russian. 'Your employer attacked the US. You knew it was going to happen. That makes you complicit in a terrorist attack on the US!'

Oleg's eyes narrowed. 'I am a scientist; I am not concerned with war. I am interested in the phenomenon. That is what I study. I did not and will not kill anyone.'

'Your attack could cause the death of thousands,' Donoghue said, his anger increasing.

'I did nothing to cause any deaths!'

'And what about the killings?' Tate asked.

'What killings?'

'Darren Sant – a banker from Rockport, retired senator Clifford Piper, and General Colin Leavesley. They were assassinated by your team, were they not?'

'Assassinated?' The man's face was genuinely blank. 'I know nothing about any assassinations.'

'What was their mission?' Tate probed. 'Political assassination straight out of the old KGB playbook?'

'I know nothing about any murders, political or not. You must believe me, I am just a scientist. I observe, I record and I make a report.'

Donoghue shook his head and pursed his lips. 'We've got the two of you on conspiracy charges at the very least.'

'I think you should put them in your holding cells until you can contact the federal government.'

'I reckon that's all I can do.'

'But I have to leave!' Oleg said, astounded. 'You can't arrest me. I have diplomatic immunity!'

Donoghue and Tate exchanged looks; Donoghue spoke first. 'Is he being serious?'

'He really is.'

Donoghue addressed the Russian scientist. 'In order for you to have diplomatic status, you would have a diplomatic passport and the Russian government would also be required to log your details with the State Department. Now tell me, why would they have done that for someone working for a private military contractor?'

'But I was promised; it was all explained to me by the founder of Blackline—'

Tate cut the Russian off: 'And his name is?'

'Maksim Oleniuk,' Oleg said, as if Tate were simple.

Tate became quiet, as the events of five years before exploded into the present. Maksim Oleniuk! Tate remembered, in vivid detail the round that hit the GRU officer, the blood blossoming from his neck and the man falling. Oleniuk was dead. How could someone survive a 7.62mm round to the throat? Tate had to focus on the now and not the then. And did Oleniuk know about the operation with The Shadows in Ukraine? It couldn't be mere happenstance that he was leading a mission in Washington where Simon was stationed.

Oleg continued. 'There is a new, streamlined process. I could use my existing passport and his connections would talk to the relevant ministry.'

'Horseshit,' Donoghue stated. 'For someone who is obviously the most intelligent guy in the room, you are extremely dumb.'

'What?' Oleg did not follow.

'You do not have diplomatic immunity,' Tate stated.

Oleg's face fell. 'That cannot be correct. I am a valuable asset, not just to Blackline but to Mother Russia. No, you are not telling me the truth. My employer assured me that my diplomatic status would prevent me from being hindered in any way by US law enforcement.'

'And how is that working out for you now?' Tate said thinly.

'But my research, my evaluations!' Oleg looked down as realisation suddenly struck him. 'I've already sent my initial findings back to Russia.'

'How?'

'My Russian military satellite telephone was able to connect with one of our surveillance satellites. What a fool I have been!'

'Your sat phone works?'

'Yes, but it connects only with the Russian military.'

'What about the Iridium handset I found?' Tate had placed it in the trunk next to the weapons. 'Have you tried that?'

'It is operational, but there is no signal.'

'How were you to exfil?'

'You have the map,' Oleg pointed out. 'Our base is circled on it. A plane was to fly into Houlton.'

Donoghue looked at Tate. 'My priority is my town and my people. I'm going to take the Russians back to town, throw them in the cells, and commandeer their SUVs for Camden PD. Christ only knows how many other vehicles are working in Maine.'

'About ten per cent,' Oleg stated. 'That is the figure I was given. The older the vehicle, the more likely it works.'

Tate ignored Oleg's interruption. 'Chief, you take Sergei and one of the SUVs. I'm going to Houlton and I'm taking our new friend Oleg with me.'

'The hell you are.'

'Listen, Oleg knows the science behind all this. I have to get him somewhere where that can be used – and not by the Russians. I can pass for a Russian but the real Russians at the base know Oleg, not me. He's my ticket in there. If a plane lands, I'll hitch a lift and divert to London.'

'Tate, you're crazy.'

'I know what I'm doing.'

'You know, in theory I have jurisdiction over these two, right?' Donoghue said.

'This is not just about the law. It's not just national security, it's international security. Are we really getting into this?'

Donoghue chuckled. 'No, Tate, we're not. You can take our scientist here and one of the SUVs. And you didn't see me put a round in the other guy's knee.'

'No, did you?'

'No. I did not.' Donoghue extended his hand. 'I would say, see you around but that probably won't happen. Camden is kind of an out-of-the-way place.'

Tate took Chief Donoghue's hand. It was larger than his and rougher. 'Thanks. I hope Camden makes it. You've got a nice place there.' He let go of Donoghue hand's and started to push Oleg towards his Tahoe when he paused and turned. 'Oh and say goodbye to Sara for me.'

The police chief smirked. 'Do you want me to say goodbye to my stepson too?'

Tate opened the passenger door. 'Oleg, I think the SIS are going to want to talk to you and try to find out how on earth Blackline did this.'

'You are going to kidnap me?' Oleg said with a raised eyebrow. 'You are one man; how are you going to assault their base and steal an airplane?'

Tate smiled. 'Who dares, wins.'

Chapter 17

British Embassy, Washington, DC
Chang hurried along the corridor, across the reception area, and out of the front door. In case the main entrance was being watched, he walked away from the embassy quickly but smoothly. Each step, he expected a Russian-launched bullet to end his life. He gave the guard hut no second glance as he passed, wanting nothing more than to ask where the hell the man had been when the embassy had come under attack. The problem was that the round had been suppressed and the conference-room window had been on the south side of the building, visible from further around the bend but not the main entrance.

Chang reached the taxi and climbed in. He surveyed the street and the surrounding area. He saw no sign of any watchers. The GPS was in the glovebox lying on some loose papers, moved out of the way after Tam's crash. Something had become stuck to the bottom of the unit, a photograph that he had not seen before. Chang held it up; it captured what looked like a university graduation. Li Tam stood with one woman, presumably his wife, and a second younger woman, probably his daughter. Chang had just shot her father . . . He started to shake . . . He shook his head and snapped out of it – he had to keep it together.

A thought struck him: surely the mother must have known that Tam was a Russian spy, but had the daughter? Chang thought of his own, much younger daughter, a knot twisting in his stomach. She was out there somewhere with her mother, enjoying the Floridian sun courtesy of Robert – his ex-wife's new man.

He'd been a bad father, a bad husband, and a bad cop but now was not the time for self-pity. Now was the time for action, the time for redemption. Chang pressed the power button on the GPS and held his breath. It switched on. All he had to look for was an address on a taxi driver's GPS, one address among a thousand, the proverbial needle in a haystack. He had no illusions that it may prove a fool's errand.

He navigated the menu and scrolled through the saved addresses. There were only four of them, and they were numbered. The first was called "Home" and was an address outside the city, the second was for an upscale restaurant that was so popular even he knew of it, the third was a location in Georgetown, and the last was College Park Airport. Was it so easy, Chang wondered? Was there no code at all? Was Li Tam so confident of not getting caught that he hadn't bothered to hide the addresses? Was Location Three really the third address on the GPS? Was it Tam's decision or had he been given the GPS pre-programmed with his home address as a warning – "We know where you live?"

Chang would never know, but an old tactical mantra started to sound in his head. 'Keep it simple, stupid.' Simple and stupid would dictate that Location Three was the third address on the GPS.

Chang buckled up, started the engine and, out of habit, checked his mirrors. Seeing a deserted street, he pulled away from the kerb. The GPS informed him it was a ten-minute drive to Location Three, and he had already wasted more than fifteen minutes since he had been summoned. He turned onto the deserted main drag and followed the simple instructions from the GPS.

He passed a metro patrol car. It sat skewed at the side of the highway. Backup, that was what he needed. He was a detective and outranked the patrolmen. However, the Crown Victoria was empty. Further along, several more cars were parked at irregular angles as though they had rolled to a halt. Here and there he saw bewildered pedestrians. The only people who seemed unaffected by the EMP were bicycle couriers. Chang then saw a couple of cyclists wearing business suits.

Up ahead, a pair of figures stepped onto the road and held up their hands in the universal sign for stop. Chang didn't, but he did slow. Neither man was in uniform, at least not an official one, both wore dark suits. As he grew closer, the man nearer the meridian raised a sidearm and levelled it directly at him. Chang cussed; he couldn't stop, not now, not for anyone. He hunkered down and floored the gas pedal. The taxi's large engine growled and he was pushed back in his seat. The second man pulled his sidearm, also aiming it at him.

Chang tried to reason how far he would get, how far they would go to stop him. Did they want the taxi or did they want him? Were they part of the Russian team or someone else? If they wanted the car, not him, they wouldn't shoot out the tyres. If he kept on, they would have to move, have to give. Either way, his mind was made up.

The taxi closed the gap, and he closed his eyes. When he opened them again, the two men were on the ground in his rear-view mirror. He'd won this game of "chicken". Chang breathed out a sigh of relief and took a left and then two rights before the GPS told him he'd be arriving at his location on his left. Georgetown was an upscale area and this street was no different. What was different, however, was that there was a black Chevy Tahoe parked directly outside one of the town houses, the address on his GPS – Location Three. Chang brought the taxi to a gentle halt behind the large SUV. Time to become Li Tam.

His hand shot into his jacket pocket; he'd forgotten his badge and his Glock. He removed the leather wallet containing his ID and placed it in a door pocket then unclipped his pancake holster and pushed his sidearm under the seat. He took a deep breath to steady his nerves, wished he could have a drink, opened the door, and stepped out of the taxi. He could hear the Tahoe ticking; it hadn't been long parked.

Across the street, a door opened and a woman stepped out. 'I need to get to the airport!'

Chang grimaced and took in her appearance. She was large and carried an equally large suitcase. 'Sorry, already got a fare.'

'I'll share . . . I'll double, triple whatever they are paying!' She trundled down the path, the small wheels of her case rumbling on the concrete.

'No.'

She ignored his protestations and continued to advance. Chang turned his back on her and headed up the path to the target address. He was a couple of steps away from the front door when it was opened by a wide-shouldered man with short, black hair. He was dressed in black slacks and a dark blue windbreaker, similar to an FBI field agent's outfit but not quite.

'Get inside.' Chang noted the man's accent was Boston not Russian, and this confused him as he stepped into the dark hall. The door was immediately shut behind him. Strong hands clamped his shoulders, guiding him forward. 'Were you followed?'

'How? By bicycle?'

'That is funny,' the man grunted. 'I saw your taxi at the embassy. Why did you not inform us that the ambassador was inside?'

'I did not see him arrive. I don't think he came by car.' Chang's mind whirred; was this the assassin? Why wasn't he Russian?

'Never mind. It is done.' The man steered him into the living room. Two women sat on a toffee-coloured leather settee. Both were middle-aged, one had grey hair and the other's was an unnatural shade of chestnut brown. They were gagged, their wrists and their ankles bound. 'Ladies, your taxi is here.'

Chang was taken aback. He hadn't known what to expect, but

it certainly wasn't prisoners or hostages or whatever the women were. He thrust his hands into his pockets in an attempt to try to look casual as his heart pounded. His left hand closed around his disposable cigarette lighter. He'd never smoked but always carried a lighter. He'd once been told by a veteran detective that having the ability to light a suspect's smoke made you more likable. He hoped he seemed likable now, or at least not disagreeable enough to shoot.

Footfall sounded upstairs and then grew louder as its owner came down and entered the room. He was all but the twin of the man who'd met him at the door, Chang thought. They were even dressed the same except he was like a bonus box of corn-flakes – twenty per cent bigger at no extra charge. He didn't say a word to Chang. So far so good, Chang thought as neither man had questioned his identity. Perhaps they'd never met Li Tam or perhaps they'd worked with several drivers? Either way he had been accepted. Chang asked, hand still clasped on his lighter and as casually as his nerves would allow, 'Where am I taking them?'

'The airport,' the first man confirmed.

'College Park?'

'Where else? We can't very well put them on an Aeroflot flight to Moscow.' His tone was sarcastic. 'Deliver them to Oleniuk.'

Outwardly, Chang agreed but inside he wondered, who was Oleniuk? Was he the voice on the phone? 'Very well.'

The second man grabbed both women and yanked them up and off the settee. The first spoke again. 'Now Mrs Filler, Mrs Smith, Vlad will escort you to see Mr Oleniuk. Please behave yourselves.'

Chang's stomach pitched as though it were being poured into his shoes. Were the two women the wives of Eric Filler and of Dudley Smith, the slain British Military Attaché? He had to stop them being spirited away by the Russians to be disappeared or worse. But he knew his limitations; he'd had the basic hand-to-hand self-defence sessions with the Metro Police instructors, but both Russians were big, athletic men; more than likely Special Forces. Could he use their size to his advantage? He had no ideas at the moment and only about twenty-five minutes of travel time to come up with one that worked. Vlad started to remove the bonds on the grey-haired woman and then the brunette, leaving their gags in place.

'Please act normally and you will not be hurt, I guarantee it,' the first man reassured the women.

The grey-haired woman reached up slowly, but confidently, and took the gag from her mouth. 'Thank you, Ruslan.' Her polished English accent betrayed not a note of fear. The second woman made no effort to speak as she removed her own gag. Her eyes were wide and red-rimmed – she was in shock.

'Time to go.' Vlad gestured at Chang with his cleft chin, his voice seeming too high-pitched for a man of his size.

Chang was still trying to work out who the first man was. His name was Ruslan but he sounded American, perhaps his English was just that good? Chang opened the front door and did a double take at the large woman standing next to the taxi, suitcase on the ground, hands on her hips. He looked back at the two hostages and Vlad as the door shut.

'Move,' Vlad ordered.

'Ladies, I say ladies, you don't mind if I share your ride?' The woman's voice was loud and firm. Her eyes tightened as Chang neared. He willed her to go away but did nothing and got into the driver's seat. Making sure no one was watching him, he quickly reached under his seat, grabbed his holstered Glock and slipped it beneath his left thigh.

'I'm willing to pay!' The woman raised her voice.

'There is no room,' Vlad said. 'Be nice. Please go away.'

'I beg your pardon!' Her tone changed to disbelief.

Vlad stepped between the hostages and the woman. He opened the rear passenger door and shepherded them inside. 'No space. Go away.'

'You can fit three in the back and one up front. I don't mind sitting with the driver, and I'm willing to pay.'

'We have no room for you.' Vlad shut the door.

'What is it? Are you calling me fat?' The woman held up an accusative finger.

Vlad lost his temper and snarled. 'Go away, Elephant-woman!'

'How dare you!' The woman's face became purple with rage and she thrust her chubby arm toward Vlad. Vlad punched her in the face. She fell like a stone onto the sidewalk. He unzipped his windbreaker, drew a silenced sidearm from beneath and shot her. Even though the round was suppressed, Chang still heard a thud. Vlad opened the front passenger door, still holding the smoking pistol, and clambered into the taxi. There was barely enough room for his long, wide frame to fit. As was the Russian way, he made no effort to fasten his seatbelt. 'Drive.'

Chang bit his tongue. He shook with rage as he started the engine and pulled away from the kerb. The Russian had shot an innocent woman in broad daylight on a public street. A pernicious cocktail of fury and remorse threatened to overwhelm him. He should have, could have, said something to her, warned her to move away, but he had become mute. He should have pulled his Glock before Vlad got into the car, shot him there and then; it would have saved the woman's life. But he had done nothing. He really was not a good person. A whimpering from the back seat ended his thoughts of self-pity; he still had two lives he could save.

'You savage! You barbarian!' the grey-haired woman spat, her words tinged with malice.

'What can I say?' Vlad replied, matter-of-fact. 'I do not like fat Americans.'

'I hope your mother is proud of you!' Her sarcasm bounced off the back of Vlad's head.

'She is, and I am proud to kill for my motherland. I like close-up work, but Ruslan, he is good with the long shots and of course explosives.' He started to laugh humourlessly.

'And you are a party to this!'

Chang sensed her eyes burning into the back of his neck. He met her gaze in the rear-view mirror. 'Yes.'

'Disgusting!'

'That is enough chitchat.' The English phrase sounded strange from Vlad's lips. He waved the silenced Beretta at Chang. 'You just drive – that is your job. It is what we agreed with your bosses. Or am I to ask for a new man?'

Chang bobbed his head but didn't quite understand the Russian's wording: "your bosses"? Was he not controlled by the Russians? And if not, by whom? Was another foreign agent involved? He saw himself in the mirror as he checked behind . . . The answer was literally looking him in the face. The Chinese! Could he confirm this? He had to take another chance. He trawled his brain for the correct acronym. 'I apologise. The Ministry of State Security is very glad to be cooperating with you on this operation.'

'Ah, come on, my friend, we are all now members of the same club. Old MSS spies and former GRU soldiers. It is a dream team!' Vlad laughed. Like his voice, the pitch was too high, almost that of a teenage boy. 'Together we are Blackline!'

'You will never get away with this! You can't!' the grey-haired woman stated.

'Mrs Filler, shut your old face up!' Vlad raised his pistol as a warning of what would happen if she did not.

Chang's mind whirred as he continued to drive; he knew the SVR was the Russian equivalent of the CIA, the external security service, but what was the GRU? Was it military? This meant the Chinese and the Russians were working together, but Vlad had said "old" and "former". Was this non-governmental? Together we are "Blackline"? Was that some shadowy organisation? And why were these two specific nationalities working together? Both had large militaries, but he knew from documentaries on The History Channel that the Russian war machine was outdated.

And he knew equally that the Chinese were the globe's electronic powerhouse . . . So, had it been a Chinese bomb?

A heavy silence enveloped the taxi. Vlad watched Washington pass by, made a ghost town by the EMP, and Chang concentrated on devising a plan. The route to College Park Airport made him double back on the road he had taken half an hour before . . . and then he had an idea. He surreptitiously slid his left hand under his thigh, unclipping his Glock from its holster. He scanned the road and the sidewalks. No one around, no witnesses. He turned his head enough to see Vlad's face. The Russian was gazing sideways at the passing buildings, and not ahead. No seatbelt, no ballistic vest . . .

Chang's hands became slick with sweat and his heart started to pound; it was now or never. If this didn't work, he'd be dead, but Vlad could not be allowed to live. The anger, the outrage, the shame and the sense of helplessness urged Chang on, pushing him over the edge . . . He slammed on the brakes. Chang's seatbelt tightened against his chest, the tyres squealed, there was a scream from behind as the women fell forward, and a heavy clunk from his passenger in the front. Vlad's forehead smashed into the windshield, his suppressed Beretta falling from his hands. Ignoring the Russian's weapon, Chang let go of the wheel and withdrew his Glock, left-handed.

As Vlad started to turn toward him, blinking, Chang thrust the Glock into the Russian's side, and shot him at point-blank range in the chest. The retort was thunderous inside the taxi and the cloud of acrid propellant engulfed them. The Russian jerked sideways as the round escaped through his back and smashed the side window.

In the tinnitus silence caused by the exploding round, Chang pushed his door handle and scurried out of the taxi. He ran around the hood and opened the passenger door. Vlad half fell out; Chang dragged him the rest. The Russian was conscious but unable to resist. His body shook as it went into shock, and a sucking noise escaped from the wet mess of his chest as he battled to breathe. Chang heard distant voices, men were running toward him, but his blood was up and he couldn't stop. Vlad had murdered an innocent civilian, a woman, and he was not going to let the Russian get away with it! He fired again. Vlad's chest imploded. Chang had become judge, jury, and executioner. It felt good.

His breathing heavy and erratic, he turned to face the men. 'Metro Police!' Chang yelled, not fully hearing his own voice. He scooted back into the driver's seat and floored the gas pedal. The tyres chirped and the taxi shot forward.

Eventually, Helen Filler spoke; her voice was shaky but accusative. 'You shot him!'

'Yes, ma'am. He was a bad man, a murderer. He didn't deserve to live.'

'I'm not going to argue with you there.'

'You are both safe now. I'm taking you to the British Embassy.'

'I don't understand. Who are you?'

'I'm Detective Jon Chang, ma'am, of the Washington Metro Police Department.'

'Yet you shot him?'

'I did.'

'Can you explain to us what on earth is happening, Detective?'

Talking louder than normal, but not realising the fact, Chang related the events of the day and his understanding of them. He left out the assassination of the ambassador – that would be too much for his charges to handle. He wanted them to feel safe at their embassy. By the time he had finished his explanation and fielded questions, the taxi was pulling up again outside the British Embassy. He was glad to note that now a duo of patrolmen was manning the barrier.

'I'm going to need to see some ID, sir.' The fresh-faced officer peered into Chang's window.

Chang deliberately reached for his badge and held it up. 'What are you doing here, officer?'

'Brennon, sir, and it's our duty to protect and serve.'

Chang stopped himself from rolling his eyes at the eager officer's textbook reply. 'But why here?' Chang persisted. He was taking nothing and no one at face value today. 'Did you get orders from dispatch?'

'No, Detective, we were patrolling the area when our car just cut out. This embassy was unguarded so we used our initiative.'

'No security guards?'

'None.'

It was puzzling, but he had no time for jigsaws. Chang let his face soften a little. 'Good.'

'Attaché Filler has informed us of the situation.'

'Is Eric all right?' Helen Filler asked from the back seat.

The officer bent down, addressed her. 'Yes ma'am.'

'Well, thank the Lord for that.'

'Where is your patrol car?' Chang asked.

Brennon gestured up the street. 'Back there a way.'

'And it doesn't work?'

'Nope, as I told you, it cut out. Your taxi is one of the only working cars we've seen.'

Chang was interested. 'You see any black Tahoes?'

'Yes.'

'The shooter escaped in a black Tahoe.'

The officer stiffened. 'What are your orders, Detective?'

Of course, Chang remembered, he was the senior officer. 'Stay here, stay vigilant, and if you see a black Tahoe, tell me immediately. Do not engage. Got it?'

'Yes, sir.' Brennon's face became grave.

Chang gave a curt nod and drove into the embassy parking lot. This time he parked against the steps that led up to the main entrance. He helped the women out. They hurried into the foyer, leaving him locking the taxi. Chang let out a sigh. Now what? He'd been involved in more action in the last five hours than he had in the last five years. If this were a normal day, there would be procedures to follow, steps he had to take, an investigation by internal affairs, but now that nothing worked and no one could be contacted, he had no idea what to do. If he drove to the station, the chances were more than likely his commandeered taxi would in turn be commandeered by his captain, or the commissioner, or anyone else who outranked him. But here at the British Embassy, he was the ranking law enforcement officer, he was in charge. He heard a noise and reached into his jacket pocket. The sat phone was ringing. 'Yes?'

The voice was the same as before, but now the tone was angry. 'Where are you?'

'We are on our way.'

'What is taking you so long?'

'There was an accident – the road was blocked. I had to take an alternative route.'

'Your passengers are safe?'

'Yes, quite safe.' Chang felt his pulse quicken.

'Keep it that way.' The line went dead.

Chapter 18

College Park Airport, Washington, DC

The Russians had unceremoniously dropped him onto the concrete floor in a small room at the back of the hangar. Hunter's eyes were heavy. It took all his willpower to stop them from closing, and he knew this was an effect of the unknown drugs injected, against his will, into his system. The narcotics continued to make his temples throb; he prayed for it to pass. The most important aspect for Hunter was that Terri was safe, for the moment at least. She was by his side, her head leaning on his shoulder. Her eyes were closed and she was snoring gently, something she would never admit to.

Another diplomat, a Frenchman whom Hunter knew well socially, sat on his left. Each of them had their hands bound and legs hobbled, but they were not gagged and able to talk freely – as freely as their guard would let them. Hunter looked up at the surly, burly Russian who watched over them as his face, a mask of professional disgust, peered through the window in the door. His nostrils flared and he sniffed, as though checking the progress of wet paint drying, before he moved away.

'There was no warning, no nothing,' Remy Debois complained, his Gallic accent wafting off the walls. 'I heard a knock at the door. A big man stepped inside and hit me. I do not know why they want me; I mean what for? I am the French Cultural Attaché. What do they think, that I have the *Mona Lisa* rolled up in my pocket?'

Hunter smirked, in spite of the situation; he found it hard to take Debois seriously. Both men were members of the Washington Hash House Harriers, which was described as a drinking club with a running problem. They, and other expats, met up twice a month and ran a course around the leafy Washington countryside before stopping for beer and burgers. Burgers . . . Hunter heard his stomach rumble. 'I need to eat.'

'Ah, me too! I need my breakfast.'

'How many eggs does a Frenchman have for breakfast?'

Debois raised his eyebrow. 'I do not eat eggs.'

'Humour me, it's a joke.' It was best that they kept their spirits up. 'I ask you, "how many eggs does a Frenchman have for breakfast?" and you say "I don't know".'

'OK.'

'So, how many eggs does a Frenchman have for breakfast?'

'I do not know.'

'One. Because one egg is *un oeuf*.'

Debois shook his head.

'You Roast Beef have a funny sense of humour.'

'Do the French still call us that?'

'I just did, and I am the cultural representative for my country so the official answer from the French government is "*oui*", Roast Beef.'

They became silent as the guard passed again.

'This place is an airport, but it's too quiet,' Hunter noted.

'I agree. I cannot understand what is happening. It is a Monday morning and we should be hearing the sounds of planes, helicopters, but instead all I hear are your jokes about eggs.'

To Hunter's trained mind the silence was ominous, but he had no idea why. 'What do you know, Remy?'

'Know about what?'

'Confidential information, secrets about your embassy, your

government. What do you know that is so important that the Russians want to kidnap you for it?'

The Frenchman raised his bound hands to his face and rubbed wearily. 'I do not know. I am not a spy. Perhaps I was just an easy target? I live alone, no wife, no children.'

'For a normal kidnapping, yes, I'd agree but for an operation on this scale? I have my doubts.'

'They are Russian – who knows what their aims are. Perhaps they plan to claim Washington for "Mother Russia," to protect the Russian speakers in the District of Columbia?'

'Wait a moment . . .' Hunter remembered something they'd discussed over a beer. 'Didn't you back the boycott of that Russian soprano from performing in Paris?'

'You know I did. Valentia Smetaniuk – the crazy woman who sang in support of Russia's bombing of Syria. I did not merely back the boycott, I banned her from performing in all of France! Le Pen's National Front were not happy; neither was the Russian ambassador. But I do not see how that is connected to this. Valentia Smetaniuk was only an opera singer.'

'She was a Moscow mouthpiece, a favourite of the president; a ban on her was a slap in the face to the Kremlin.'

'So for this the Russian state kidnaps me?'

Hunter sighed. 'It sounds far-fetched, but what else can it be? I think we are both here because we've spoken out or angered the Russians in some way . . .' His voice trailed off as he understood completely. The drugs had slowed his mind, prevented his brain from seeing it all, but now as he reasoned it out with his French friend, the clouds were moving, the sky was clear. Hunter knew it was too much of a coincidence Dudley Smith's murder and his kidnap happening within hours of each other. The Russians had, he decided, murdered Dudley Smith – murdered him because in his official capacity as the British Military Attaché, Smith had been a vocal critic of the Russian regime. Hunter explained his theory.

'That is unbelievable.'

'I agree.'

'I have nothing against Russia or her people. Are you telling me that we are part of some "hit list"?'

'If they had wanted us dead, we would already be knocking at the pearly gates; they had plenty of opportunity. We are alive for a reason.'

'What reason? If it is information, I have none.'

'And nor do I.' It was a lie, a huge one. Hunter had information, too much information, about the SIS and especially about past E Squadron operations and the men who had undertaken them.

Debois asked, 'I wonder how many people they have kidnapped. You saw the other room, like this one?'

Hunter had noticed the second cell. 'Have you heard any noise from it?'

'I have heard nothing. Are we just to sit here and wait to be interrogated, tortured?' Debois rubbed his face again. 'I need a cigarette!'

'I need a drink.'

'What . . . what?' Terri sat up.

'You fell asleep.' Hunter stroked her head.

'We are still here – it's not a dream?'

'No,' Debois added, 'it is a nightmare.'

The guard appeared at the door. This time, however, he stepped inside the crude room and made to grab Terri. Hunter raised his arms to try to stop him. The large man brusquely brushed him aside.

'Simon!' Terri yelped as she was dragged to her feet.

'Where are you taking her?' Hunter demanded and tried to stand.

The Russian looked down; he was smiling. 'On vacation.'

'I demand you let us go! We have diplomatic immunity!' Debois's voice became indignant.

* * *

189

Oleniuk eyed the woman as she was brought before him. 'What have you learned?'

'Simon is trying to understand why you are holding him and Debois.'

'And why are we?' Oleniuk asked, noticing again that she used Hunter's first name.

'He thinks it is because he and Debois are enemies of the Russian state.'

'Hunter is extremely perceptive, rather a good job that he is an intelligence officer.' Oleniuk snorted at his own joke.

'Debois says he knows nothing.'

'That is true. Anything else?'

'They were talking about the other room.'

'Oh?'

'They were speculating if that too holds hostages.'

Oleniuk snorted at the word "hostages". The correct term was prisoners. 'And does it?'

'They do not know.'

'Good.' The cell held no one, but believing it did would increase their sense of unease. 'Are they aware of the EMP?'

'No.'

'Splendid. Go back. We have a little more time on our hands before I make my final decision.'

'Decision?'

'Whether or not I take both men to Moscow.' He noticed her mouth tremble. It opened and she was about to speak but then apparently thought better of it. Oleniuk gave a signal and the guard grabbed her.

Oleniuk sat back in his chair and laced his fingers across his stomach. He hated being a patient man. He hated having to wait with nothing to do. It was as though he were just as much a prisoner as Hunter and Debois.

It was almost midday and on a normal Monday morning he'd be about to start his three-hour lunch interlude. First would come a fine restaurant, where red wine and red meat would be consumed in large quantities, followed by a professional massage to loosen his war-weary body and relieve the twinges in his neck; and there were usually "extras". He wet his lips. The Chinese were good at that, or at least those he had encountered here in Washington on his many scouting and planning visits were. His mind wandered to his Chinese business partner, Chen Yan, and a smile crossed his face as he imagined himself with her.

He let out a sigh. The damned Chinese, he snorted. Yes, their progress and delivery of the EMP device was to be commended, but he hated their fake subservience, like a pretty, tamed tiger who, given the opportunity, would rip apart the hand that fed it. And rip apart Russia they would, if Russia dropped its guard. He was glad that Chen Yan had persuaded the Chinese authorities to allow Blackline use of their in-country deniable assets. These hangars, like others around the US, were leased or owned by Chinese shell companies. An excuse for Chinese pilots to come and go in private jets without a second glance. The fact that his own country no longer had the necessary assets in the US was by the by. He was a realist. He knew that despite the bluster and the Russian president's promenading, his country was poor and heading in the right direction to become Third World.

Oleniuk checked his watch again; the minutes ticked by sluggishly and the taxi driver had still not arrived. Something was definitely wrong. Something had happened to Li Tam. The more the day wore on, the more conspicuous a working taxi would be. The last thing he needed was for any of his vehicles to be seized by first responders, law enforcement, or armed citizens. In a country where the Second Amendment was sacrosanct, it wouldn't take long for armed mobs to replace the void left by the authorities. And nature did so hate a void. His men were professionals, hand-picked former Spetsnaz commandos who could easily shoot their way to safety, but he did not want any undue attention brought to the operation. If any of the planes were to be damaged or destroyed, it was a long walk home to Mother Russia.

The fate of the taxi driver did not concern him one iota. What concerned him was the fate of the man's passengers. The two women were integral to his plan. Without them or their dead bodies, it would not be complete. From a military point of view, the mission's objectives had been completed: the EMP had been deployed and deemed a success. Data on the EMP's effectiveness on unshielded technology had been collected and his side mission – those who had caused harm to the Russian state – had been liquidated. He could, and should, give the order now to pull out, pack up, board his executive jet, and return home after a fully successful mission; after all, he now had Simon Hunter.

But it would be a hollow victory if he could not make the Englishman accept, face to face, what he had been responsible for. First he would make Hunter suffer, demonstrate to him that his actions a decade earlier had-far reaching consequences. And those consequences were the death of all those he had ever admired or held dear. Oleniuk would finally get his revenge on the man who had stolen from him the only woman he had ever truly loved. Yes love was at the heart of Oleniuk's hate for Simon Hunter, and he very well understood the irony.

Oleniuk opened a drawer in his metal desk and slid out a thin steel case. Inserting a key, he unlocked it to reveal a second sat phone. This had been given to him by Chen Yan. It was for emergency usage only. He eyed up the strange-looking handset; it was not a brand he was familiar with.

Where was the taxi driver, Li Tam? Oleniuk had to know. He started to second-guess himself. He should never have agreed to work with the Chinese, but the decision had not been his. He had needed Chen Yan's money and Chinese scientific expertise. Without Chen Yan this chance would not have materialised. He closed the case and put it back in the desk. He refused to lose face to a woman. He marched out into the main hangar, ignoring the rise in temperature from that of his air-conditioned office, and over to the man operating his communications hub. Before the technician had a chance to speak, Oleniuk asked, 'Is it possible to track the whereabouts of the taxi driver's encrypted sat phone?'

'Only if he answers a call from us, sir.'

Oleniuk pointed at the machine. 'In that case, set it up so that my phone calls his.'

'Yes, sir.'

Maine

Tate motored the reverse route he had taken two days before, this time driving from Camden via Belfast to hit the I-95 at Bangor. Oleg sat next to Tate in the front passenger seat. His wrists were still cuffed together to the door handle. They passed the occasional car, and each time they did so, Oleg strained to see its make and model. Every now and then abandoned cars littered the verge, having come to a rolling stop.

They continued north on the rural 1A through green, rolling New England countryside and saw no other vehicles on the road with the exception of several pedal bikes. People came out of their homes in the hope that the Tahoe was either a rescue vehicle or law enforcement, but Tate did not stop until they hit Hampden and encountered a Crown Victoria parked across the entrance to a pharmacy at a strip mall. A pair of police officers stepped into the road and attempted to flag them down. Tate judged the angles and the width of the road; if the officers didn't dive under his wheels, he could get past them.

Oleg looked across at him, seeming to read his mind. 'Their standard-issue 9mm Glocks cannot penetrate our ballistic plates.'

'And you are sure?'

'Quite.'

Tate slowed the Tahoe to a walking pace and then just as the two officers stepped forwards, he yanked the wheel to the left and floored the accelerator. The tyres bit, the engine growled, and the big, heavy SUV jerked sideways before leaping forwards. Instinctively, Tate hunkered down in his seat, not trusting the armour plating as he aimed for the junction for the 202, which would take them to the I-95. Tate risked a glance in his rearview mirror and saw one of the officers shaking his head while the other lowered his Glock. Perhaps Tate could have helped or perhaps they just wanted to commandeer the Tahoe; he would never know.

'You are a very interesting man, Tate,' Oleg stated after several minutes of silence.

'The Camden PD were of the same opinion.' Tate concentrated on the road.

Oleg continued, 'You speak Russian like you come from St Petersburg. For a foreigner, that is unheard of. You learned this in the British Army?'

'I did.' Tate wasn't comfortable talking about himself but understood that if he was to get any intel out of Oleg, he needed to keep the conversation going, one operative to another. Give a little to get a little. 'The Regiment has language instructors who teach on intensive courses.'

'Regiment?'

'The SAS.'

'Ah yes, the British Spetsnaz. You were a Special Forces soldier?'

'I was.'

'So one can conclude that you operated in a Russian-speaking environment?'

'I did.'

'Ukraine?'

'Yes.' Tate's mind flicked briefly back to his mission with The Shadows and his shooting of Oleniuk before returning to his current predicament. Tate hoped he could use his language abilities when they reached Houlton, but he somehow doubted it.

'I did not agree with the annexation of Crimea,' Oleg stated. 'It was a folly to take the land from Ukraine.'

'I agree.'

'Our president was a lunatic; he still is. He is a survivor, but the end of his time is coming. He is still committed to the past and does not see that cooperation with China is the future. On the other hand, Maksim Oleniuk embraces this, and that is why he had to accept a deal with the Chinese.'

Tate glanced at Oleg. 'Had to?'

'Yes,' Oleg stated ruefully. 'Once, our scientists were undisputedly the best in the world. We, after all, won the space race. For scientists, at least our system – the communist system – worked, and its legacy continued to do so. Our science was science. It was for the greater good.'

Despite himself, Tate grunted with derision. 'Attacking another country is the greater good?'

'No, you misunderstand me, Tate. Let me explain. My research was into electromagnetic pulse weapons. While others worked on rockets or nuclear warheads with ever-increasing payloads, I was exploring how to beat an enemy without loss of life. Imagine, if you will, drawing a black line on a map around a target and knowing that all electrical equipment and motorised vehicles within that area are non-functional. That was the aim of our group, project Blackline from which the company takes its name.'

'Are you confirming that it was a Russian EMP weapon that was deployed against the United States?'

'Yes and no.' Oleg took a slow, deep breath. 'Alas I no longer have a wife, and when I die my line will end. Blackline have destroyed my loyalty with their lies. I have nothing to lose by telling you what I am about to. This is beyond classified. There was a virus in one specific, localised region of Russia. An outbreak of an unknown disease that hit hard. The young and the elderly were, of course, the most at risk. A small town with an overpopulation of elderly people was decimated. My research centre was in that town. Our scientists became infected. The belief was it was because they visited the shops and the markets, bought locally produced homemade produce et cetera.

'But this was not the case. In fact, it was the exact reverse. They transported the virus out of the base. We realised that we had created the virus, and that it had escaped from one of the classified chemical weapons research laboratories in Arzamas-16. So what did the authorities do? Calling it a "quarantine" exercise, they sealed our facility with us inside. I was fortunate not to be infected, and several other colleagues also recovered; however, many of the finest scientific minds of my generation perished, and their research died with them. The Kremlin officially lost interest in our research and shut us down.'

Tate could guess where the story was heading but wanted to keep the Russian talking, gaining his confidence. 'This is where the Chinese came in?'

'You are exactly right. A group of privately funded Chinese scientists, working under the employment of one of China's largest technology firms, had also been working on EMP technology. Somehow Oleniuk knew about the work of both sides and brokered an agreement that the two teams should work together to develop a fully functional EMP device. The Chinese had been focusing on a payload delivery system – which is what they detonated above the USA this morning, while in Russia, I had been exploring a man-portable device.'

Tate whistled. 'That would be a complete game changer.'

'And together, we had been developing EMP shielding.'

'But now everyone will include EMP shielding in their vehicles or garages as standard.'

'That is true, but how long that would take to implement? Also think of the benefits to law enforcement if a runaway or stolen vehicle can be brought to a halt with a simple, highly localised electromagnetic pulse.'

'Let me get this straight; what was the point of a terrorist attack on the US? A smaller scale test could have been carried out elsewhere and in secret?'

'I can see why you would call it a terrorist attack. As a scientist I demanded that I be included in a team on the ground here. And I am glad I was.'

Tate shook his head. 'So what's the end game? The US has been disabled and what, China steps in to clear up the mess?'

'Exactly. Russia can live with a strong China; it cannot live with a powerful USA. So Blackline brought both sides together, in a manner of speaking. It was better to be collectively strong than individually weak.'

'Isn't that the rationale behind communism?'

'It is.'

Tate again shook his head. 'But Blackline is a private military contractor, not a governmental agency.'

'Blackline is a power broker. Our two founders are well placed to coerce their governments.'

'Oleniuk is one founder, who is the other?'

'Chen Yan, a Chinese multi-billionaire.'

The name meant nothing to him. Tate read the road signs in silence. Whatever Blackline was, it was a menace. 'Now that it's just you and me, tell me about the assassinations.'

Oleg shook his head. 'That is something I have no idea whatsoever about.'

'You're being honest?'

'Of course.' He looked out of the window, as though he was trying to locate a memory. 'I did, however, hear Oleniuk once mention a "hit list", when he took a phone call during a meeting we had at the research facility.'

'Are you sure?'

'It was not verified, just a phrase he used. He could have been talking about the pop charts.'

'I see.'

Tate again became quiet as he concentrated on the highway. He still had no hard evidence that the assassinations were linked to Blackline. What he had was circumstantial; the timing fitted, and the vehicles matched and the victims themselves. 'Was there more than one team?'

'Two colleagues of mine, and by that I mean scientists, were also dispatched with men who were former soldiers. I do not know how many other groups there may have been, but what I do know is that the base at Houlton is large enough to accommodate many men.'

'Tell me what happens next. What's the next stage?'

'After the operation, we regroup at Houlton before flying out of the country.'

Both men fell silent. Tate agreed with the idea of non-lethal weapons, even though he couldn't condone the Russian's actions. Would Tate have accepted similar orders issued by his government? He would like to think not, but would he have accepted them if given by a private employer? His answer was a resolute no.

'Why are you in Maine?' Oleg asked.

'I'm here on holiday.'

'That is a silly cover story.'

'Silly or not,' replied Tate, 'it's the truth. I'd originally given myself a month to work my way down the coast to Washington.'

'That is a long drive. Why visit Washington?'

'My brother works there.'

'I see. The EMP was detonated above Washington. It is our ground zero.'

Tate felt himself go cold, but before he could ask anything more there was a sound from the glove compartment. He cast a glance at Oleg.

'That was the Iridium satellite telephone.'

'OK; can you take it out for me?'

'How? You have me chained up like a convicted felon.'

Tate took a deep breath. Oleg, he felt, was not dangerous. Even if he tried to escape, where would he go? He reached inside his jeans pocket and handed Oleg the keys. 'Undo the cuffs; I trust you.'

'Thank you, but what makes you think I will not hit you over the head?'

Tate focused on the road.

Oleg undid the cuffs, flexed his wrists, and retrieved the Iridium handset. 'There is a text message on this. It claims to be from the Department of Homeland Security.'

'Read it to me, please.'

Oleg read the message.

'*A national state of emergency has been declared and is effective immediately for the continental United States. Widespread power outages have been reported. For your safety, and the safety of others, all citizens are encouraged to remain at their residences and to avoid any form of travel until further notice.*'

'They are trying to be clever and not mention the EMP.'

'Perhaps they will not?' Oleg shrugged. 'The Soviet authorities did not acknowledge the Chernobyl reactor catastrophe immediatcly.'

'This isn't the USSR.' Tate had an idea. 'Your Russian sat phone can communicate with the other groups?'

'Of course, but we were instructed to keep complete radio silence.'

'Tell mc about the base at Houlton. Who is running it and what equipment and hardware do they have?'

'It is run by a former GRU major, who reports to Oleniuk; he has a team of six men. They have several SUVs like this, cars and trucks, as well as an arsenal of weapons.'

'What communications system do they have?'

'I don't know.'

'And your exfil is today by plane?'

'Yes, twelve hours after the attack.'

Tate checked his Rolex; they were an hour away. 'Piece of cake, we can make it.'

Oleg frowned. 'You want to make a cake?'

Chapter 19

British Embassy, Washington, DC

Chang sat in the sagging leather chair at the side of Filler's office. He was spent. Filler pushed a can of Coke across the desk at him. 'I think you need the caffeine.'

Chang agreed. 'I'd rather sleep.'

'Hm, no sleep for any of us for a while, I'm afraid.' Filler took a sip from his own tepid can, pulled a face. 'Tell me again what the Russian told you, the one at the house.'

'He ordered me to take your wife and Mrs Smith to College Park Airport, where I was to give them to someone called Oleniuk.'

'That's what I thought you said.'

'So why ask?' Chang asked testily before he raised his hand and smiled in the form of an apology.

'Oleniuk is not a very common Russian name; in fact, there are only two Oleniuks I have ever heard of. One was a general in the Great Patriotic War . . .'

'Great Patriotic War?'

'That's what the Soviet Union, and now the Russians, called World War Two.'

'I see.'

'And the other was a member of the GRU – Russian Military

Intelligence. They were related, father and son – Phillip and Maksim.'

'Were?'

'The son died in eastern Ukraine about five years back, or so we thought.'

'One of the Russians holding your wife said he was GRU.' Chang sighed; he hadn't been this tired since his daughter had been a baby. He took a deep breath. 'So the Oleniuk in the GRU is running the Russian operation here?'

'It appears so, if in fact it is the same man – back from the dead. And if it is, he is a heavy hitter. He was active in the Eighties and Nineties. His name used to pop up in briefings, et cetera. If now he has reappeared, something very big is about to happen.'

'Something bigger than today? Really?'

'That's my theory.'

'But why would he risk an operation here, in the US?'

'He likes to be hands-on?'

'He likes to be in control.' Chang nodded. 'Is this all usual for you?'

Filler frowned, his face darkening. 'What, the deaths?'

'No. Sorry.' Chang held up his hand. 'I meant the spy stuff.'

'Not at all. You're rushing around with a gun, tackling suspects with your unarmed combat techniques.'

Chang let himself smile, although he and Filler knew it wasn't funny. 'I did judo as a kid.'

'Wax on, wax off?'

'That's karate.'

'Were you any good?'

'No.' Chang shrugged. 'I was proficient at a couple of throws. But they were useful ones.'

Filler's face relaxed as he looked over Chang's shoulder. His wife entered the room. Chang turned in his seat and then started to stand.

'No' – she placed her hand on him – 'please sit. You must

be exhausted.' Chang didn't reply. He was too tired. Mrs Filler remained standing. 'Any word on Simon Hunter?'

Filler shook his head. 'We don't know.'

'Very peculiar.' She took a deep breath. 'Now if you'll excuse me, my friend needs me.'

Both men remained silent until they were alone once again. Filler spoke first. 'She's resilient, always has been.' Chang remained silent. Filler addressed the elephant in the room. 'So where is Hunter?'

'He's a diplomat; he's missing. Eric, do I need to join the dots?'

'Damn it, Hunter was a good man. They all were.' Mouth abruptly dry, Filler sipped from his can before he continued. 'None of this makes any sense to me.'

Chang had a moment of inspiration. 'Could it be that one operation has piggybacked on the other?'

Filler sat back in his chair then pointed at Chang. 'You mean like a Trojan Horse? The EMP blinds us to the acts of the assassin?'

'That would make sense. The Russians get to settle old scores without anyone being able to point the blame at them.'

'Until you got in their way.'

Chang felt the weight of Li Tam's sat phone in his pocket. He'd already missed two calls from Oleniuk. He raised his eyebrows. Things had been moving so fast that he hadn't wanted to think about that, about his own personal safety. But he wasn't the only link; he wasn't the only loose end. 'If they know I am here, they will assault the embassy. They will make sure that none of this ever comes back on them.'

Filler's face lost its colour. 'We have to get word out, somehow, and we have to do it now.'

'Without working communication equipment, we are sitting ducks.'

'Bollocks.' After finally getting hold of the emergency Iridium sat phones, Filler had checked and double-checked them. They had not powered on. 'Can we use Li Tam's sat phone?'

'Risky.' Chang retrieved it from his pocket. 'What if they are monitoring the calls?'

Filler's eyes went wide. 'Monitoring? What if they are tracking it? Turn it off!'

Chang shook his head. 'No. I can't do that; it may not power back on. We'll use it, but when we are somewhere the Russians can't easily get to us.'

Filler didn't look convinced.

'Tell me about your evacuation plan; how and where are embassy staff taken in the event of an emergency?'

'We go to Ronald Reagan Airport, where a requisitioned UK commercial airliner, either British Airways or Virgin Atlantic, takes us directly to London.'

'I can't see the UK government sending a commercial airliner into the unknown. We don't even know if Reagan's runway is clear.'

'Then it will be a C-130 military transport.'

'Again doubtful. They would have to scout the runway. And there is no guarantee that there will not be another EMP. No, if your government sends anything, it'll be something they can get in and out quickly.'

'And what would that be?' Filler slammed his fist on the desk.

'Eric, I'm going to make a suggestion and you are not going to like it.'

'Go ahead.'

'I evacuate your key personnel.'

'You?'

'Me in the taxi.'

Filler swigged his Coke, finished it, and threw the can at his waste-paper bin. It bounced off the rim – nothing was going his way. 'Who?'

'You, Mrs Filler, and Mrs Smith.'

'I can't leave my staff. I have a duty to the British government.'

'Eric, your life and that of your wife are in danger! You have a duty to yourself.'

'But—'

'Send your staff home. The Russians can't check up on every address, and why would they want to?'

'This is unprecedented.'

'Exactly.'

'What about our files? They haven't all been destroyed yet.'

'Is there anything life-threatening?'

'No.'

Chang's temper flared. 'Then screw your files, Eric!'

Filler's eyebrows shot skyward. 'And the dead? Li Tam and the ambassador?'

'Think about the living.'

The sat phone rang, causing both men to recoil. They exchanged glances. Chang let it ring out.

Georgetown, Washington, DC

The Tudors were away and had been all weekend, according to a very helpful, chatty neighbour. Ruslan Akulov smiled pleasantly and thanked the woman, who had told him to call her Nancy. She was often next door, sharing a glass of wine or three with Janet Tudor, she had said, now that she herself was a single, divorced woman. She found the couple to be extremely pleasant, but they were older than her, she emphasised. Nancy asked him if he knew anything about the blackout. Akulov said he had heard there was a problem at the local substation that would be fixed by the end of the day. Nancy accepted this and invited Akulov in for a drink, looking genuinely upset when he'd refused.

Akulov knew the effect he had on women when he used his smile. He beguiled them, won their trust. It was a tool, and a deadly one. He'd used it to enter the Filler house, which was how he had corralled the women and then bound them up. Many intelligence operatives were "grey men" – nondescript, unmemorable – but he was not. Unless he wanted to be. He thanked Nancy again and walked away from her house, which was next door to the British Ambassador's official residence.

It was odd, he thought, while the Russian residence was protected behind a large fence and had armed guards, the British diplomatic address resembled any other upscale detached Georgetown home. The security measures were electronic – digital rather than physical and now rendered utterly useless by the EMP. The street was quiet. On any other weekday, he would surmise that its residents were either at work or perhaps, as it was the height of summer, vacationing out of town. But today was not any other day. Were the locals staying inside, hiding? He didn't care; all that mattered was that he could return to his vehicle and drive away. He continued to walk along the tree-lined avenue, knowing that eyes hidden behind twitching curtains were watching his every step, but he had no choice. Akulov retrieved his sat phone and called Oleniuk.

'Da?'

'The target is not at the residence.'

Oleniuk swore. 'Do you have any idea where the ambassador's wife may be?'

'No. According to a neighbour she and her husband have been away all weekend.'

'Not good. Proceed to the British Embassy. If Li Tam is there, terminate him and reacquire the women.'

'They are not with you?'

'No. They are not.'

Akulov turned a corner and crested a rise. He could now see where he had parked his Tahoe. A small crowd stood on the sidewalk beside it. An elderly man with neat, grey hair placed his hand on the hood and gesticulated to another who had his hands on his hips. Several more locals stood a few paces away. Akulov weighed up the situation. He continued to approach the Tahoe as, one by one, the crowd turned.

'Hey, son, is this your vehicle?' the elderly man asked.

'Yes, sir, it is,' Akulov replied, his Russian accent completely hidden by a Boston drawl.

'It drives? I mean you drove it here, today?'

The gap between Akulov and the Tahoe lessened. 'I did.'

'Well, aren't you the lucky one!' The elderly man held out his hand. 'The name's Sam, Sam Wheat.'

'Nice to meet you.' Akulov shook his hand but did not offer his name. He waited to hear Wheat's proposal; he knew one was coming.

'I've been chatting to my neighbours here; none of our cars are drivable.' Wheat looked at Akulov, expecting a reply. When none was forthcoming, he continued, 'I have a medical emergency. I have an appointment today at the hospital that I can't miss and no one can get me there. Son, seeing as you have a working vehicle, and seem like a nice fellah, can you take me?'

Akulov studied the face of the elderly man and saw something he recognised, something he had himself lost twenty years ago. He sensed an emotion that he had been trained to suppress – remorse. In the last twenty-four hours, he had killed many men. They'd had no warning their lives were about to end. One moment alive, and the next eternal darkness. The old man, Sam Wheat, reminded Akulov of his great-uncle. A man he had loved like a father, the only relative he had ever known, lost also to the darkness. Akulov felt his resolve start to crack as the watery eyes continued to stare up at him pleadingly.

'I'd be forever grateful, son,' Wheat added hopefully.

Akulov dug in his pocket for the key fob, clicked the button and unlocked the doors. Wheat started to smile. Akulov pushed past the old man, climbed into the car and locked the door. Wheat's face, now perplexed, appeared at the window. Akulov started the engine and pulled away. He took a deep breath and focused on the road ahead. His great-uncle had been killed by an American, mown down by a drunk driver while on vacation.

It was less than a ten-minute drive to the British Embassy

on roads devoid of moving traffic. A few pedestrians tried to wave him down, but he encountered no real opposition. As he followed the leafy curvature of Massachusetts Avenue, the utilitarian-shaped British Embassy came into view. Akulov bumped up off the road and onto the sidewalk. Part hidden by the foliage of the mature trees lining the street, the dark Tahoe made a comfortable observation post. He swung a pair of field glasses to his eyes. He scanned the embassy building and saw a taxi in the parking lot. It had to be the one used by Li Tam. The man must be inside, with the two women.

He weighed up his options. It had been easy for him to take out the ambassador, luck rather than skill had come into play, but could he alone enter the building and abduct two British citizens? He now saw a pair of police officers by the barrier. Akulov knew his limitations, even if Oleniuk did not. If he was to assault the British Embassy, he would do so as part of a team and not like a one-man army. He called Oleniuk.

'Have you located Li Tam?'

'He is at the British Embassy.'

'Is it done?'

'No.'

'Why?' Oleniuk snapped.

Akulov took a deep breath. 'The task cannot be undertaken by one man. I need a team.'

'How many?'

'Three more.'

'Three?' Oleniuk paused. Akulov could hear him breathing heavily. 'They shall be there.'

Oleniuk shook his head and rubbed his neck. He had had enough of this. Everything was taking too long. His own embassy was less than a mile away from the building used by the British, but now as a private citizen he was not sanctioned to use its facilities, personnel, or hardware. He pushed open the door to the room where the prisoners were being kept and pointed at Terri and Hunter. 'Come with me.'

'Why?' Hunter was indignant. The guard accompanying Oleniuk hauled him to his feet.

'Time to talk.' Oleniuk turned on his heels and stalked back to his office. He sat heavily as his prisoners were hustled in. He spoke to the guard. 'Put him in that chair, hold her arms behind her back.'

'If you harm her, I'll—'

'Talk.' Oleniuk leered unpleasantly. 'If I harm her, you will talk.'

Hunter remained silent, his cheeks reddening as he took in the man opposite him. Oleniuk had gained a few pounds over the past five years and now sported two thin white scars on the left side of his neck thanks to his brother's work.

'Tell me please, Simon, what security personnel do you have at the British Embassy?' Hunter remained silent. Oleniuk sighed and addressed the guard. 'Punch her.'

'No!' Hunter yelled.

'Answer my question.'

'We have a team of four. Two are on duty at any given time.'

'Two men.'

'Two.'

'Are they armed?' Hunter didn't reply. Oleniuk waved his arm. The guard punched Terri in the lower back. She screamed and fell forward onto her knees. Hunter rose angrily from the chair. 'Sit.'

'You bastard.'

Oleniuk crossed his arms, leaned back in his chair. 'Are they armed?'

'Yes.'

'Sidearms or assault rifles?'

'Sidearms.'

'You are certain?'

'This is Washington, not Baghdad.'

'Are there any firearms in the embassy?'

'I don't know.'

'Now another question. Does the embassy have a secure area, such as a panic room?'

Hunter was too slow to reply. Oleniuk's eyes moved to the guard. 'No, don't!'

'Well?'

'It's in the basement. We call it "the bubble".'

'Very original.'

Oleniuk spoke quickly in Russian. 'Take them back and you, keep your ears open.'

Unseen, behind Hunter's back, Terri gave a slight nod.

Oleniuk again felt as though the mission was slipping from his fingers like the grains of sand he had played with on a Crimean beach as a child. He'd spend hours designing and building intricate sandcastles only to see them obliterated, wiped out, washed clean by the encroaching, unstoppable sea. Each time he would create a stronger fort, use driftwood, dig channels to divert the uncompromising waves, but the result was always the same; he suffered defeat. Today he would not be defeated.

Oleniuk picked up his sat phone. He would not admit it to himself, but he needed reassurance. He needed to hear it from someone he trusted. He dialled the number for his second-in-command, the man running the operation further up the coast, in Maine – Major Valentin Volkov.

'*Da?*' Volkov gave no name when he used satellite communications, encrypted or not.

'Progress report?' Oleniuk asked formally.

'All reports have been received. We have, however, lost contact with one team.'

Oleniuk glowered. 'A critical unit?'

'No. They completed their objective before they went dark.'

'Then that is acceptable.' Casualties were to be expected. 'Where did this happen?'

'Camden,' Volkov replied without emotion.

'Camden?' Oleniuk repeated the word, as memories of a successful operation in the other Camden flashed before his eyes. 'What was their last report?'

'Status green. Mission accomplished. Returning to base.'

'Could it merely be a communications failure?'

'It could be,' Volkov replied, his voice noncommittal.

'Inform me immediately should any new intel arrive.' Oleniuk ended the call. It really made no difference to him when or where the men had vanished. The US authorities were in no state to put two and two together. The training of the former Spetsnaz men was among the best in the world; it would take an extremely determined individual to stop them and a highly sadistic person indeed to get them to confess. However, the former GRU scientists were a different matter.

Chapter 20

College Park Airport, Washington, DC
'Wake up!' The Frenchman shook Hunter sharply.

It took a couple of seconds for the SIS man to remember where he was and then he jerked into a sitting position, embarrassed that the heat had made him sleep. 'What?'

'Pardon, not what.'

Hunter sighed; he wasn't in the mood for more of his friend's banter. 'What's happening?'

'I hear an engine.' Debois held up his index finger. 'Listen.'

'I can't hear anything.' Terri's face was turned away from the duo.

'Listen,' Debois repeated.

Hunter heard a faint, low rumble. 'Yes. I hear it.'

'See?' The noise changed in tone and then the clatter of a chain moving and a heavy hangar door opening. 'A plane.'

'We are at an airport, Remy.' Hunter yawned.

'*Oui*, but it is the first sound I have heard outside all day. It is odd, no?'

'No,' said Terri.

'Ah, you have been snoring, what do you know?'

'I do not snore!'

211

'You do, Terri,' Hunter added. 'That's two of us now who have told you.'

She ignored the insult. 'So what does it mean?'

'That you are either fat or your nasal passages are deformed,' Debois explained.

'Shut up, Remy!'

'It means that someone is getting ready to retreat, to pull out.' Hunter's tone was flat. 'What that means for us, I would not like to say.'

Terri experienced a wave of unease wash over her; she had a very clear idea what it meant for them. She moved nearer to Hunter and leaned against him. 'I'm scared.'

'It'll be OK. We are diplomats, remember? The Russians wouldn't dare hurt us.'

Terri could tell by Hunter's tone that he did not believe his own words. She was ten years younger than him, but he was the one who sounded naive. All was fair in love and war. The problem for her was that this was a war but she was in love, and with the enemy. It was something that she had been trying to suppress, something her instructors had drummed into her. She must not confuse her physical relationship with a target for an emotional one. If she engaged in sex, she must understand that it was work. It was a technique with which to mine more intelligence for her employer. Simon Hunter was the target of her operation, but Simon Hunter was also a good man who did not deserve to be tortured or worse by Oleniuk's department. She started to shiver.

She'd been stupid; she'd been used and now she felt like the lowest form of life. Lower than the drunks and addicts who had ogled her on the street as she passed on her way to university lectures. Lower still than the two boys at the military academy who had got her drunk, dragged her into an alley and held her down. Terri sensed a tear escape from her tired eyes; they had tried to rape her. She had been forced to kill them. The little

212

flick-knife she kept in her bag for slicing fruit had viciously sliced the groin of the first and then the neck of the second. Dark, arterial blood had discoloured the fresh Moscow snow as both boys writhed and died.

This canvas of killing had garnered the interest of the SVR, who spirited her away, trained her, and gave her a position as an undercover operative. She had been an intelligence agent for six years before meeting Oleniuk and leaving the SVR for his organisation. Her first assignment with Blackline had been Simon Hunter, and that had been a year ago. From day one she knew being with him was not like her previous assignment. She knew the time would come when she had to leave him, move on to her next mission, and break her heart in doing so. Oleniuk had made it clear: Blackline owned her heart. Her mission had been about monitoring and intelligence gathering. Terri had never once imagined that Simon would be in any danger, and that thought alone made her lose her mind. 'We have to escape.'

Hunter sat up straighter. 'Ssh – they'll hear you!'

'I mean it, Simon; I have a bad feeling about this.'

'And I do not have a particularly good one,' Debois added with a shrug. 'What do you suggest: that we wrestle the guard, or perhaps dig a tunnel?'

'We have to stay put and stay still.' Hunter squeezed Terri tighter. 'I'm sure we are too valuable a commodity to damage.' He made eye contact with Debois. 'Our governments will not let anything happen to us. They are looking for us; we are important.'

'I am very important, and I am still hungry.' Using the wall for support, Debois got to his feet. He banged on the door. Almost immediately the window darkened, the door opened, and the large Russian stood glaring at them. 'We need to eat.'

'Perhaps I should ring out for snails in garlic butter?' The Russian sneered.

'Why not?'

'Sit down.' The Russian shut the door.

'I like snails,' Hunter said, wistfully.

'I do not,' Debois said. 'It is like eating a sneeze.'

'Are you actually French?' Hunter chuckled mirthlessly in the gloom.

In the hangar next door, Oleniuk addressed the pilot. He was not happy that the Chinese element of his organisation had insisted on their own people flying the jets. The co-pilot was already at his seat in the cockpit. Oleniuk repeated his curt instructions: 'Pang, you are to collect Major Volkov and his men. Then you are to fly directly to Caracas. After that, your obligation to my operation shall be over.'

'Understood,' Chi Kong Pang replied.

'That is all.'

Oleniuk walked through the connecting door to the other hangar as Pang taxied away to the runway. Outside, not a single other electrically reliant item stirred. Neither planes, nor cars. The Russians stayed inside, away from the prying eyes of any watchers. Let potential eyewitnesses believe that the departure was a "one off" and that there was nothing else to see. Anyone who came knocking would be dealt with, like the caretaker who had been "disappeared".

Oleniuk checked his watch as he re-entered his office. He too would leave within the next three hours on his second jet. He would decide nearer the time exactly who went with him and who remained.

British Embassy, Washington, DC

Akulov continued to watch the embassy. Staff members started to leave in ones, twos, and small groups. One on a bicycle, the rest on foot. It was not a coordinated evacuation; the staff were not carrying boxes of belongings or files, and they appeared as though they were just leaving work early. He studied each face, mentally ticking them off from a memorised staff list. ID cards were updated periodically so the faces matched the digital images he had seen. What were they doing? Surely, as individuals, they were safer at the embassy than at home? Akulov sat up straighter as realisation dawned; the staff knew the embassy was about to be attacked.

Chang stood. 'We need to go.' He went to the window, gingerly raised a slat on the Venetian blind and peered out. 'It all looks clear to me.'

'Yes, time to go,' Filler declared with more enthusiasm than he actually felt.

They collected the two women and headed for the entrance foyer. The group crouched behind the large reception counter. Chang drew his Glock and handed Filler the silenced Beretta, taken from the dead Russian. Filler's hand shook. 'We don't have handguns in the UK.'

Chang rolled his eyes. 'That end goes bang when you pull the trigger. Only point it at something you want to kill.'

Filler's fear blocked out the sarcasm. 'Yes. Understood.'

'Eric, give that to me. You'll only end up shooting yourself.' Helen stretched out her hand.

Chang addressed the three Brits. 'Wait here, I'll make a run for the car. If anyone is out there, I'll draw their fire.'

'No you won't.' Helen Filler pursed her lips. 'They'll see you and know that we are coming. You'll give them time to prepare their shot.'

Chang agreed. 'OK, we go together, all at the same time. I'll lead, then Eric, and then you. Agreed?'

'Yes.'

Chang scuttled across the open foyer, hugging the wall, and peered out of the door. He could see the two police officers diligently standing by the barrier, talking to the last local embassy staff member to leave. 'Clear.'

They exited the embassy in a tight huddle. The taxi was a

matter of feet away – down three steps and immediately right. A breeze had picked up; the trees on the street outside gently swayed. Sunlight glinted on the windshields of stationary cars and the glass pillbox. The two police officers were still talking to the embassy employee. One of them pointed back at the embassy.

Chang tried to stay calm. He reached the first step, his foot struck the second step, but as he reached the third, something glinted in his eyes from behind the trees. Chang did a double take and tripped as he turned right. Falling forward, he landed heavily on his knees as a piece of brick was torn away from the wall where a moment ago his chest had been. Chang took a second to realise that he was being shot at with a silenced rifle.

'Move!' he bellowed at the others and scuttled the remaining distance to the taxi. Ducking down behind the wheel arch, he blipped the locks and opened the passenger door. Both women managed to get inside before a round thudded off the armour-plated hood. Eric Filler jerked backward, colliding with Chang. They fell against the outer wall of the embassy.

'I . . . I've . . . been shot . . .' Filler stammered.

Before Chang managed to pull himself out from under Filler, more brick disintegrated above them; another shot. Blood leaked from the right side of the diplomat's chest. 'You must get up, or you'll die!'

Filler grabbed the taxi door with his left hand, grunting with exertion as he pulled himself forward while Chang pushed him from behind. Filler fell across the rear passenger seat. Chang crawled into the driver's seat and started the ignition. A round hit the roof above Chang's head, making him duck, then another caused the windshield to craze like a spider's web. Chang put the taxi into drive and, tyres spinning, they leapt away from the parking bay. The taxi rocked as two more rounds hit it, but it kept on moving.

Up ahead, the police officers, sidearms drawn, had taken cover behind the pillbox. Unwilling to stop, the taxi ploughed past them and broke the barrier clean in two, adding another dent to the hood. Chang wrenched the wheel to the right and stamped on the gas. The modified taxi hit the street like a scalded cat.

Akulov was annoyed. He put his rifle on the passenger seat next to his empty first magazine and started the Tahoe. Never had he missed like this, not since he'd been a seventeen-year-old conscript! But something had made him pause, made him ensure that he did not hit the women and then the taxi driver had tripped; this he could not have foreseen. He doubted the taxi could outrun him, but there was no way he was going to lose it.

He swung the SUV back onto the road and accelerated smoothly in pursuit along the section of Massachusetts Avenue known as Embassy Row. He sped past the South African Embassy then the embassies of Bolivia, Brazil, and Italy before racing across the Massachusetts Avenue Bridge. Akulov smirked; 1600 Pennsylvania Avenue aside, this was probably one of the most secure streets in the capital city. Yet here he was, a former Russian intelligence operative, hunting British diplomats. The EMP really had crippled the most powerful country on the planet. Ahead, the taxi slowed to navigate around an abandoned station wagon. Akulov called Oleniuk.

'Where are you?' The voice was gruff, the tone impatient. 'Your backup is five minutes out.'

'South on Massachusetts Avenue, in pursuit of the targets.' The backup team was too late, he didn't add. 'They are in the taxi.'

'Who exactly is in the taxi?'

'Li Tam, the two wives, and Attaché Filler.'

'Stop them! Use deadly force.'

'On them all?'

'Wait! No! Terminate the driver, do not kill the others.' Oleniuk suddenly sounded panicked. 'That is all.' The line went dead.

The women did not deserve to die, which is why he had not aimed at them; however, Akulov had hit Filler. There was nothing he could do about that. He now hoped the injury was not critical, but doubted that the man could survive a .338-calibre round. He focused on the road ahead. The taxi had started to increase the gap. Akulov upped his speed, but the taxi continued to pull away. The Chinese had done a great job upgrading the vehicle. His .338-calibre rounds had not penetrated its ballistic skin, and from the way it was driving, he could see that the engine and suspension had also been much enhanced.

The vehicles hit Sheridan Circle Park then roared toward the Dupont Circle. The taxi drove the wrong way, darting through immobile cars, and flew onto Connecticut and North Street. Where the hell was the man heading, the Russian wondered – the White House? A large smile split his chiselled face; there would be no greater irony than to attack the targets outside the American seat of power.

Back inside the taxi, Filler lay sprawled across the entire length of the back seat, trapping the women beneath. Helen cradled his head with her right hand while she applied pressure to his wound with the other. Dawn Smith was silent as she held his hand. Filler had been both lucky and unlucky. The heavy .338-calibre round had hit him on the rebound, ricocheting off the taxi's hood and into his chest. It was a life-threatening wound, but a direct hit with such a large-calibre round would have ended his life.

Chang silently urged the taxi on as he kept the pedal flat to the floor. The nearest medical facility that could possibly save Eric was the George Washington University Medical Center. He'd have to double back, but could he get there with an assassin on his tail? The Mayflower Hotel flashed past on their left as the taxi sped on. Chang glanced back; they had increased the gap further back to the Tahoe. All he needed was a visual gap of a couple of seconds, a blind spot when the Russian would lose sight of him, and he could turn off and head for the hospital . . .

Trees! Ornamental trees lining the meridian now obscured his view of the Tahoe, and its view of him. Ahead, the crossroads with Farragut Square gave traffic the choice of three routes. Chang took a deep breath and jerked the taxi to the right, onto the wrong side of the road, straight into what on any normal day would have been oncoming traffic and a certain collision. More trees obscured his path and he powered on. It was now a direct sprint to the medical facility.

After a minute of watching his mirrors for the Tahoe, Chang was satisfied that he'd lost the Russian. He manoeuvred the taxi toward the wedge-shaped medical facility, ignoring the ambulance entrance, which was blocked by a white, blue, and red MetroAccess minivan, bumped up onto the sidewalk, and all but drove into the hospital lobby.

'Stay with Eric,' Chang ordered his passengers. After exiting the car, he made for the double doors of the foyer. Inside he saw structured chaos. Holding his badge aloft, Chang bellowed above the hubbub, 'Police emergency! Gunshot wound!'

Heads turned in his direction and an elderly woman shrieked. A white-coated doctor approached him.

'What have you got?'

'Male, late fifties. Gunshot wound to the upper right chest.'

'And he's still breathing?'

'Ricochet.' Chang didn't waste time with any further explanation. 'You need to see him. Now!'

'You know we have no power?' The doctor beckoned to an orderly. 'Grab Jones and grab a gurney!' Chang frogmarched the doctor outside. The physician's face took on a strange expression as he saw Filler through the open door. 'OK. We have to get him inside.'

The doctor moved sideways to grant the two orderlies access to Filler, then hung back to observe the street as his passengers and the medics went inside. He'd given the Russian the slip – but for how long? Chang noted the entrance to the underground car park; he'd hide the taxi there.

Chang closed his door; his hand hovered over the ignition. As a police officer what he was doing – risking his life for these people – was his duty, but Eric was the only witness to him killing Li Tam. If Eric died, he'd be in the clear.

But Eric was going to cover for him; Eric was one of the good guys. *Am I?* Chang asked himself. *I've killed two people today.* Whether it was fatigue, stress, or lack of booze, Chang didn't know but whatever it was had paralysed him. He sat, one hand resting on the wheel, the other holding the key in the ignition, unable to decide what he had to do. But then he heard a noise. He blinked, gazed around. On the street, pedestrians had started to move toward the taxi, like a scene from *The Walking Dead*, only they were talking and shouting at him. He needed to get the car away before he lost it by force or it was swamped.

Chang started the ignition, swung the car back onto the street, executed a tight turn, and cut into the underground parking lot.

College Park Airport, Washington, DC

Oleniuk was once again outside the hangar. The air inside was stifling. He no longer cared about being seen. He took a deep breath; the heat of midday had given way to what would become a glorious evening. It was almost a shame, he thought, that he was leaving for the heavy Moscow summer with its clawing, dirty air and morose residents. Almost a shame, but not quite, for this was the start of his ascent.

Failing health and one too many secret hair transplants had seen the incumbent president gradually remove himself from the eye of the people. The political strongman, who kept wild horses and boar at his dacha in Siberia, had not yet realised that it was time to abdicate power to the next generation. Oleniuk's operation would be enough to secure his place as the next leader of Mother Russia.

As Oleniuk stood alone in the deserted airport, the significance of its history became all the more ironic. It was here that

Wilbur Wright had taught Americans to fly, and it was here that Oleniuk had clipped their wings. With a deep breath and a smile, he checked his Patek Philippe wristwatch; his other tactical units, missions completed, would be airborne within the hour. And then he heard the all-too-familiar sound of footsteps behind him. 'Sir.'

Oleniuk turned and grabbed his sat phone, which was thrust toward him. '*Da?*'

'I have lost the targets.'

'Repeat that?'

'I have lost the targets.' Akulov's voice carried no emotion.

Oleniuk battled to control his rage. 'How?'

'Their vehicle was faster than I estimated. The taxi driver knew the streets; he lost me.'

'He lost you?'

'Yes.'

'What was their last known location?'

'Farragut Square.'

It made no sense to Oleniuk. First that Li Tam would take the women from the British Embassy, secondly that Vlad had been unable to prevent this from happening, and thirdly that the taxi would manage to outrun and evade Akulov, one of his most trusted men. 'Return to Filler's house. See if they are by chance there.'

'But—'

'But, what?'

'I hit Filler. If he is alive, he will need medical treatment.'

'No. The hospitals will be chaotic. Try his residence first. He only has one of those, compared to the plethora of medical facilities to search.'

'Yes, sir,' Akulov agreed, but did not sound convinced.

Oleniuk resisted the urge to hurl the sat phone across the tarmac. Instead, he made a beeline for his office. Opening the drawer, he regarded the case containing the emergency Chinese sat phone. He placed it on his desk, laid his palms flat across the top, and closed his eyes as though he were looking for answers from a Ouija board. He inhaled deeply, exhaled deeply several times. In . . . and . . . out, in . . . and . . . out . . .

He had two options. He could write off the hostages, leave them wherever they may be, and finish his mission – or he could attempt to find them. He knew which one made military sense, but that was not the option that satisfied him personally. He swiftly popped the catches on the case and retrieved the handset. It powered on instantly under his heavy index finger, and he called the only number saved on it.

'Yes?' The voice answered on the second ring. It was curt and without any discernible accent.

'I have lost track of your man – Li Tam.'

There was a pause. Oleniuk could hear a whirring noise. 'Lost track? What do you mean?'

'I do not know where he is.'

'So call him, not me!'

Oleniuk silently counted to five before he replied. 'He does not answer, and if he does not answer I cannot track him.'

'I will call you back.'

'When?' Oleniuk drew the phone away from his ear and glared at it to show his disdain. No one cut him off! He placed the device on his desk before reaching back into his drawer and removing a hip flask. He unscrewed the top and poured the clear liquid directly into his mouth. The Russian vodka burned as it slipped down. Instantly, he could feel his chest relax. He had promised himself that he would not drink until he was safely airborne, but damn it, he needed it now!

As he waited, he noted for the first time how quiet the hangar was around him. It creaked then groaned, sounding to his ears like the call of an elephant as a strong gust of wind rolled across the runway. Elephants indeed! Oleniuk shook his head; was imagining wild animals the first sign of madness? Well, if he was going mad, he perhaps could cure that with some medicine. He raised the hip flask, Doctor Vodka, and took another swig. He smacked his lips, "kill or cure" – that was the British phrase that sprang to mind.

The Chinese sat phone chirped. Oleniuk pressed it tightly to his ear. 'Yes?'

'We have located his vehicle.'

'How?'

'It is fitted with a tracking device of course.'

'Where is it?'

'The taxi appears to be stationary and in the vicinity of the George Washington University Medical Center.'

'Appears to be? What does that mean, exactly?'

'The signal is weaker than our technicians expected.'

'Hm.'

'Is that all?'

'Why is he there? What did he say? Have you given him new orders?'

'We do not know. He was given to you to use as you saw fit. We have had no contact with him.'

'He is jeopardising my mission!'

There was a pause before the caller spoke. 'The mission is completed and has been a success. My superior does not understand why you are not airborne.'

Oleniuk took a third swig of vodka. Battle lines were being drawn, which would have consequences for his Chinese partner. 'Loose ends.'

'Is that all?' the caller asked again.

'Yes.' Oleniuk pressed the "end call" button. No one cut him off.

Akulov was having to take increased care now with the roads, as more confused locals had taken to them. He had shot his way through a roadblock and used the nose of his Tahoe to nudge a pair of police cruisers out of his way. He was glad for the heavy ballistic plating on the vehicle, which in effect turned the SUV into a tank. A few fires started to burn in shop fronts. Looters who darted in and out.

He turned onto the main drag and headed toward the Georgetown address; there was a body on the road. Akulov slowed as he passed but then stamped on the brakes. There was something familiar about it. Turning off the ignition, he stepped down from the SUV and approached the corpse. His fears were confirmed as he crouched. It was Vlad. Two gunshot wounds to the chest, and he hadn't been wearing his ballistic vest. Stupid, stupid! Akulov's shoulders fell. The Werewolves had been a tight-knit unit of twelve men; Vlad had been a brother to him. They had lived and worked together almost since the day they were taken, as conscripts from the ranks, and put into Spetsnaz training. But Vlad had always been the most foolhardy and impulsive of the twelve.

Akulov's vision blurred. There was no shame in tears; real men wept when the situation deserved it. Vlad had not deserved this.

He returned to the Tahoe and retrieved a black body bag. Akulov manoeuvred his friend into the plastic cocoon before hefting the deadweight up and onto his shoulder. He placed him in the trunk and shut the tailgate as tears rolled down his cheeks, creating clean lines on his sweaty face.

How had this happened? Who was responsible? As Akulov dried his eyes, he knew that one man and one man alone must have done this. The taxi driver! Akulov resolved there and then that he would be the one to kill him. He climbed back into the SUV as a small crowd of pedestrians wandered toward him. *Is this the way it is going to be? Every working vehicle besieged by angry mobs?*

He pulled away at the same time as the first hands touched the rear of the Tahoe. He had to call this in. He had to explain to Oleniuk that Vlad had been murdered . . . but before he could, Oleniuk called him and gave him Li Tam's location.

Chapter 21

Tate had found a site for an observation post near the airport and was now assessing the target with a pair of field glasses. He had a direct line of sight to the airfield entrance, which consisted of a barrier and a guardhouse. By the look of it, they were not expecting anyone to try and break in. There was no sign of any sentries on the perimeter and the hangar looked deserted.

'You are really going to attack that?' Oleg asked, pointing at the aircraft hangar.

'I am, and you are going to help me.' Tate continued to watch the target.

'How?'

'You'll vouch that I'm SVR.'

'Pretending to be Russian may get you inside the building, but what are you going to do once you are inside?'

'Play it by ear.'

'Listen?'

'No, it means make it up as I go along.'

'Hmm, I see. Use the SUV as a weapon. It is armoured and you can run over any opposition.'

'That's an idea.'

225

'One question, Tate: what makes you believe that I will help you?'

'Oleg, you are a scientist and, as such, you told me yourself that the science is the most important part in all this. I can assure you that HM Government will be eager for you to share what you know and continue your research.'

'As a prisoner of the British?'

'In your sealed lab in Russia were you a free man? When you return to Russia after this secret mission will you be a free man? Will you be allowed to resign or walk away?'

'You are right. Very well, you have my word. I shall help you.'

Tate looked up at the sky; he could hear engines. 'I think that's your plane.'

From their vantage point, they saw a jet emerge out of the gloomy sky and approach the runway. As it neared the runway, lights flicked on as if the EMP had not happened almost twelve hours earlier. Tate looked back at the hangar. The large double doors opened and two SUVs tore out, heading for the runway.

'Right, we've got to get on that plane.' Tate started up the Tahoe, having already disabled the airbags and turned off the lights, and drove towards the airfield. He hit the barrier doing almost forty miles an hour and the pole splintered before bouncing up and over the roof of the SUV. Oleg let out a short yell as they carried on into the airport. Tate angled the SUV across the runway towards the oncoming jet and floored the accelerator. The plane was heading straight for them now, and unless he turned, he was going to hit it on the nose. He saw the massive tyres struggle to slow and the jet shuddered as it tried to steer away. Tate yanked the wheel to the left and passed by the jet. He was now behind one of the Tahoes and gaining.

'I thought we were going inside.'

'Change of plan. How good a shot are you?'

'I can fire a gun.'

'Then shoot out the rear tyre.'

Oleg glanced at Tate. 'You think I can hit that?'

'No. OK. Open the glove box and hand me a grenade.'

'You are going to blow them up?'

'Just the tyre, unless I am lucky.'

Oleg passed Tate the grenade.

'Here goes.' Tate opened the window and accelerated hard again. Up ahead, the lead Tahoe stopped dead and then turned before barrelling towards Tate. The closing speed between it and his own SUV doubled. 'Bugger.'

Tate pulled the pin, counted to two, and then threw it out of the window with his left hand before jerking the wheel to the right. There was a moment's pause and then an explosion. Tate didn't look back. He now turned the wheel again and aimed for the one remaining Tahoe, which had also stopped. 'Is there another grenade?'

'Yes.'

'Hand it over.' Tate lined up again and then once more floored the accelerator. Then he had a change of mind and headed for the plane. The jet was now stationary and the passenger door had started to open. He was nearer to it than the other SUV. A crew member wearing generic black trousers, tie and white pilot shirt started to walk down the steps. He looked Chinese. He had a submachine gun in a sling at his side. Tate slammed on the Tahoe's brakes and without pulling the pin, hurled the grenade. 'Catch!'

The man's eyes bulged as he saw the grenade. He dived off of the steps as it rolled inside the jet.

'Out, now! Follow me!' Tate leapt from the Tahoe and bounded up the stairs. He whipped the Camden-PD-issued Glock 17 from his pocket and checked the interior of the cabin. It was empty. He went back to the stairs as he saw Oleg reach the third step, and then the crewman opened fire from the tarmac. There was nothing Tate could do; a burst of rounds tore through the Russian and propelled him sideways. As Oleg fell, Tate saw the crewman and double-tapped him in the chest. More gunfire came from outside.

Tate darted back inside and sprinted for the cockpit door. He pulled the handle and ripped it open. The pilot thrust up his hands and said in American-accented English, 'Please don't kill me!'

Tate placed his Glock in the man's back. 'Raise the steps and get us airborne. Airborne now!'

The pilot nodded like a bobble head and started to turn the jet with the wingtips just missing the aircraft hangar. Once it faced the runway again, the pilot asked, 'What about the car?'

'Don't hit it.' The pilot did not reply as he concentrated on getting them into the air. Tate ran to check the fuselage door. He quickly searched for the grenade he had thrown, found it lodged against the underside of the nearest seat, and double-checked that the pin was still securely affixed. After making sure, he strapped himself into the empty co-pilot seat. The jet rocketed down the runway and then, engines shrieking, lifted into the sky.

Tate attempted to steady his breathing. 'How much fuel do you have?'

'Enough to get away from the USA,' the pilot said.

Tate nodded. 'Take me to Washington.'

'Washington?' the pilot replied, his voice concerned. 'Why?'

Tate didn't feel the need to explain. 'Do it; I have the gun.'

'Please, I am not your enemy. I didn't attack your country.'

'I'm not American.'

'Who are you?'

'I'm the right man in the wrong war.'

Chapter 22

41,000 feet above Maine

From the co-pilot's seat of the commandeered passenger jet, Jack Tate watched the August sky. It was a sea of blue. Sailing through it, he could have been forgiven for believing the events of the last twelve hours had not taken place, were just a false memory or a bad dream. The United States of America had been attacked by a Russo-Chinese private military contractor. The course of history and humanity had been forever changed by an electromagnetic pulse bomb, and he was bang in the middle of it all. Tate prodded the Chinese pilot with his Glock 17, 'Tell me what you know.'

'About what?' the pilot replied.

'Start with simple facts. What type of jet is this?'

'It's a Gulfstream G650ER.'

'What's its maximum range?'

'At Mach 0.85, 13,890 kilometres.'

Tate calculated the distance. 'So that's Beijing to Houlton, with give or take 3,500 k in reserve?'

'Yes.'

'You came from China directly to Maine?'

The pilot didn't reply.

Tate nudged him with the Glock. 'Did you fly directly from China to Maine?'

'Yes.'

Tate didn't believe him; there had been no tanker waiting to refuel the jet but he let it go for the moment. 'What were your orders?'

'Collect the Russians.'

'And take them where?'

'Moscow.'

Now Tate knew the man was lying. Without refuelling he'd fall out of the sky. 'This jet is configured to seat fourteen passengers. How many men were you expecting?'

'I don't know.'

'Who did?'

'The man you shot.'

'He shouldn't have pulled a submachine gun on me.' The man had sealed his own fate. 'Where are your parachutes?'

'W . . . why?'

'Because I can't fly.'

'There is a locker behind my seat.'

'Thank you.' Tate opened the cabinet. Inside he saw two parachutes, two life preservers, and a flare gun. He bundled a chute under his left arm. 'Now I'm going to ask you more questions and you are going to answer. And if you don't tell me what I need to know, I'm going to put a bullet in your left leg, then I'll move on to your right and if you still don't answer I'll shoot a hole in the instrument panel.' The pilot visibly stiffened, his face a mask of worry as Tate struggled into the snug harness. 'I can't fly a plane but I can fly a parachute, and I won't hesitate to open the emergency exit and jump if I have to. Do you understand me?'

'Y . . . yes.'

'Good.' Tate sat. 'Now, let's start with an easy question: what's your name?'

'Chi Kong Pang.'

'Which unit are you with, Pang?'

'Please, I'm just a pilot. My orders were to fly to Maine.'

'We both know that's not true.'

'I'm telling you the truth.'

Tate nodded. The man's hands were shaking on the controls, and sweat dripped down his face. 'Where are you from, Pang?'

'What do you mean?'

'Where were you born?'

'Shanghai.'

'How many pilots born in China speak English well enough to pass as Americans?'

'I don't know.'

'You fly a plane, you're part of a clandestine mission, and you speak English like a US native? That makes you MSS – Ministry of State Security?'

'No!' The pilot's eyes became wide. He took a moment to recover his senses. And then his mouth went into overdrive. 'Please I'm not with the MSS – you're wrong! I'm not a spy. I would never spy. I'm just a pilot. I used to work for Air China. The man you shot, he was ex-Chinese Air force – fast jets, not me. He had the gun – look at me? I'm just trying to fly this and to stay alive.'

'What's the airline code for Air China?'

'The IATA code is CA. And the ICAO code is CCA.'

'OK. Explain to me then why you are here.'

'The money of course.'

'And why is your English so good?'

'I studied at the Beijing Normal University, with the Princetown in Beijing programme.'

'OK, Pang.' He didn't want the man to lose control of the plane. 'I believe you. Now tell me about the EMP.'

'I swear, I didn't pilot that plane.'

'That's not what I asked.'

'The weapon was released at a specific point into the atmosphere in order to cover the continental United States.'

'What about Canada?'

'The splash radius will affect some parts of Canada and Mexico.'

'Are there any more, or was this a one-off attack?'

'I don't know.'

'Are there plans to attack the UK or Europe?'

'I do not know. I'm a pilot. I just fly the plane.'

Tate dug the Glock harder into Pang, who winced. 'I won't ask you again. Where did you fly in from?'

'Washington.'

'Thank you.' It made sense; a full tank of fuel would get the jet from Washington to Houlton and then to Beijing, or Moscow, and they'd just escaped the Russians in Houlton . . . 'Is there a second Russian base in Washington?'

'Yes.'

'Where?'

'I don't know.'

'Really? Don't lie. That's where you flew in from.'

Pang sighed, his defences defeated. 'College Park Airport.'

Tate frowned. 'Where?'

'It's outside the city, a small commercial place with a museum.'

'What were the targets in Washington?'

'The targets? I don't understand; the EMP targeted everyone.'

'OK. Take me to College Park, and remember, Pang, I have a chute on.'

'Please, you must understand! I am just like you. I am a working man, a professional just following orders.'

'That's what the Nazis said.' Orders, the word rolled around in Tate's head. 'How do you talk to the outside world?'

'The radio, of course.'

'No good,' Tate mused. The range was too short and it was hard to encrypt. 'Do you have a sat phone?'

'Of course.'

'Give it to me.'

Pang deliberately reached under his seat and pulled a large handset out from a Velcro pocket.

Tate grabbed the phone with his left hand, powered it up, and tapped in a number he knew by heart.

Pamela answered on the second ring: 'Newman.'

'It's Tate.'

'Jack, where are you?' Her voice sounded strained.

'I'm in a stolen Gulfstream somewhere above Maine.'

'Did you say stolen?'

Tate explained events since he had last spoken to her, mere minutes before the EMP hit the USA, and his suspicions of a Russian "wet" operation, the reappearance of Maksim Oleniuk and finally the loss of his witness, Oleg Sokol.

There was a pause as Tate imagined she processed what he had told her and then Newman's voice sounded hoarse as she replied. 'We have no contact with any of our staff at the embassy. GCHQ has detected a few transmissions from ham radios but apart from that, the airwaves are dead.' She paused; Tate could hear her sip what he knew would be chamomile tea. 'I imagine "the opposition" are listening in to this call, but I have no other choice. Jack, you are the only asset we are in contact with in theatre. We need you to re-establish contact with Opening Bat.'

'Got that.' Tate allowed himself a smile. SIS had given each member of the Washington Embassy staff code names derived from cricket, a sport that very few outside of the British Commonwealth understood and many within were baffled by. Opening Bat was the code name for Simon Hunter, stationed at the British Embassy.

'We have credible intel that Wicket Keeper is at risk.' The British Ambassador to Washington, Anthony Tudor, code name Wicket Keeper had been based in Moscow when Russia annexed Crimea. He had not held back on his disdain for the Kremlin's new foreign adventures and actively supported economic sanctions.

'Got that,' Tate said again.

'Jack, our closest asset to you is HMS Daring. She's attending festivities at Nelson's dockyard, Antigua. If I can re-task her, she's two days' sailing out of Norfolk Naval Base. Jack, this is down to you. Locate Opening Bat, extract Wicket Keeper and all other UK personnel.'

A thin, sardonic smile creased Tate's face. It was a huge task. His boss made it all sound so easy, but he did have a stolen executive jet. 'Will do.'

'Good luck,' Newman said, and the line went dead.

Houlton, Maine

Before the Chinese jet had approached, there had been no interest from the local population of Houlton, some five miles away, but the noise of its approach and departure had caused a steady stream of townspeople to descend upon the airport. They milled around outside the perimeter and a couple had attempted to clamber over the wrecked Chevy Tahoe positioned strategically in place of the shattered entrance gates. The Blackline team had withdrawn their serviceable vehicle into the voluminous hangar and kept watch from behind darkened observation windows. The door was secured, as was the team in their EMP-proofed operations centre.

Oleg Sokol lay on a military-style cot in the office at the rear of the hangar, which had been made into a temporary sickbay. He was conscious and due to the morphine flooding his system, felt no pain. He had overheard the team medic state he didn't know how much time he had left. Sokol's drug-numbed brain tried to understand what the man meant: time left for what? Was he going somewhere?

'How are you feeling?' a voice asked, without warmth.

'I am great, thank you for your concern.' His tone was jovial. The morphine made Sokol light-headed, ecstatic.

'My concern?' The voice belonged to Former GRU Major Valentin Volkov, a man Oleg knew reasonably well. Volkov sat on a chair next to the military cot. 'You are a traitor to Russia.

My concern only is the amount of damage you have caused. I am within my rights to have you shot, do you understand me?'

'*Da.*'

'If you cooperate, I may let you live. Who was he, the maniac who stole our airplane?'

Oleg smiled lazily. 'His name was Jack Tate.'

Volkov leaned forward in the chair. 'Who is Jack Tate?'

'The manic who stole your airplane.'

'Other than that,' Volkov snapped, 'who is Jack Tate?'

'He is an Englishman.'

'What?' Volkov's eyebrows shot skyward. 'He is not American?'

Oleg continued to smile; he couldn't help it. He was drifting on an opiate-created cloud. 'He is a British spy . . .'

Volkov's face flushed with anger. 'You have betrayed our mission to the British?'

'He discovered the mission. He captured me. I was his prisoner.'

'You were attempting to board the plane with him? You were trying to escape the USA!'

Oleg sighed. He couldn't lie – the morphine had loosened his tongue. 'I was going to fly to London and tell the British everything.'

'Is that where Tate is heading now, to London?'

'Perhaps; wouldn't you? I hear the beer is rather good.'

Volkov grabbed Oleg's head with his heavy hands. 'You are lying to me! The transponder is switched on; we are tracking the plane. It is not heading in that direction. Where is he going?'

Oleg did not react to the vice-like grip. He could not feel it. 'Perhaps then he is headed to Washington – his brother works in Washington.'

Volkov let go. Oleg's head fell back onto the thin pillow. Fresh bloodstains seeped through the field dressing on his chest. 'What have you told Jack Tate of our mission?'

'Everything . . .'

Volkov clamped down on Oleg's mouth with his thick palm.

Oleg found this to be a strange act. What was Volkov doing? And then the edge of his vision started to grey out. He tried to open his eyes wider but couldn't and then everything went black.

George Washington Medical Center, Washington, DC

Chang sat in the hospital corridor, head in hands. Both of the English women were sprawled out over several comfy chairs in the relatives' waiting room, trying to sleep. The doctor who had operated on Eric Filler confirmed that while not directly life-threatening – no organs had been hit – Eric did need to remain immobile. Battlefield surgery was the term Chang had heard used. Eric had been given painkillers, and of course no electronic equipment was available.

The fatigue was again getting to Chang. He glanced at his mechanical wristwatch; it was now past six in the evening. An entire workday had passed since the attack and still he and the nation were not safe, and that was why he was still on duty. He'd have to remember to put in for the overtime. He had left the sat phone in the car and gone down to check it. There had been no further calls and he hoped, as had been his intention, that the location of the parking lot – underground – had blocked the signal. Still the urge to use the phone to get help had been almost overwhelming, but Chang had resisted. Besides, he had no idea who he could call. He presumed that most news organisations would have sat phones, yet none of the channels were broadcasting. The same for government agencies, but every contingency plan he had ever seen relied on the use of electronic devices, vehicles at the very least.

He felt trapped. The three Brits were alive because of him but what more could he do to protect them? Chang decided he'd outlived his helpfulness here. His duty was to the police department, to protect and serve the citizens of Washington, and that's what he'd do. He'd report for duty, help in any way he could, use the functioning taxi as an official vehicle . . . but . . . but he had killed two men.

Chang stood, drifted to the window and gazed out at the city below. The shootings had been justified; he would write them up as such.

Chang took the stairs down in the direction of the underground parking lot. With the elevators out of order, his progress was slow, as the stairwell was busy with medical staff and concerned relatives. In his light sports jacket and slacks, he looked more like a doctor than some of the white-coated staff and had to fend off an elderly gentleman enquiring about his sister.

The jostling intensified as he reached the lower, busier floors and then he froze. He recognised the face of a man climbing up toward him. Their eyes locked and Chang knew that he had less than a second to react. Chang grabbed the shoulders of the woman next to him and shamefully shunted her forward. She shrieked and fell, arms flailing towards Ruslan, one of the two Russians who had kidnapped the women.

At the same time, the Russian was reaching for his silenced Beretta. He thrust his left arm up, but it was too late to fend off the impact. The woman collided with him, causing the Russian to spin backward, hit the safety railing, and tumble down several steps.

Chang turned on his heels and pumped his legs; he was four steps away from the nearest floor and a door. He burst through and sprinted along the corridor. It was dim without its strip lights as all the doors were closed and the only light came from a window at the far end. There was a second stairwell to the left of the window; if he could reach that, he had a chance of getting away, but if the Russian caught up with him before he got there, he'd be an easy target.

Chang had an idea. He'd open the doors, use them to confuse his pursuer or perhaps draw people out into the hall. He ran, slipping and sliding on the institutional linoleum, his loafers struggling for grip. He passed the first door – it was too near to the stairwell so he ignored it – and flung open the second. The room inside was dark and seemed devoid of life. He opened the next and as he was about to open his third, the fourth door along, there was a crashing noise behind him.

Chang turned to see the stairwell door rebounding against the wall and Ruslan entering the hall, pistol in hand. In panic, Chang tried to increase his pace but careered into a medical cart he'd not spotted in the gloom and lost his footing. He went down hard. Winded, he scuttled behind the cart, now trapped in the darkness with only stacks of paper towels, bottles of surgical spirit and other supplies for cover.

Chang knew he was going to die; time seemed to slow. Chang allowed himself a resigned smile, perhaps things were preordained? Perhaps he was meant to die here as a coward running away from his duties? No. He still had time to change that; he could go out as a hero! A police officer doing his sworn duty, or he could break the rules and try to survive . . . An idea entered his head. It was crazy, it was dangerous and it was illegal but it was the only way he could see of getting out of this.

A silence hung in the air. The hall was still and dark. The last light of the day from the window at the opposite end made it hard for Akulov to pick out any detail, but he knew someone was there. The taxi driver wasn't an athlete, he couldn't have gotten far, and the door to this hall was the nearest and most obvious choice for an escape route. He was going to have to hunt the man.

Akulov cocked his head to one side and listened. Voices carried from the stairwell behind, but nothing from within the hall. He noticed the outlines of several open doors and cursed, silently as he realised his quarry could have hidden in any of the adjoining rooms. He scanned the space. There were at least ten doors on each side. If he ventured into one room it gave the other man a chance to get to the opposite stairwell and away. But what if the man wasn't running? What if he was waiting to strike?

On instinct he ignored the first door and then was about to

enter the second when he froze. A noise, ahead. He edged along the wall, raised his Beretta and fired two supressed rounds at a dark outline. The first round made no noise as it impacted into something soft, and the second sparked as it hit metal and ricocheted. Akulov paused. And waited. There was still no movement. He took a chance and went through the open door into the dark room. He carved arcs with his Beretta, left to right. No target. A conference table and six chairs sat in the middle. He went prone and looked under the table. His eyes – now more and more adjusted to the half-light – confirmed that the room was empty.

Quickly, up on his feet, he swung back into the hallway and advanced, weapon up. One step, two, three, he was level with a third door . . . and then his eyes tracked an object arcing towards him . . . an object he was familiar with. It was bottle-shaped and had a flaming end.

He tried the door next to him, but it was locked. As the object neared, he took three fast steps and ran at a door on the opposite side of the hall. It gave way and he crashed into the room just as the object landed on the linoleum, shattered and sent a sheet of flame racing in all directions.

Chang, shaking now with anger rather than fear, held a second glass bottle of surgical spirit in one hand and his lighter in the other. He moved the flame towards the wad of paper towels he'd stuffed in the open end. He silently chuckled to himself. He hoped the Russian liked to drink, because he was about to be served another Molotov Cocktail!

Akulov ran from a room on the left side of the hall. Chang hurled the improvised explosive directly at the assassin and ducked back into cover. He waited for the explosion.

Immediately after hearing the *"whompf"* of the spirit igniting, and using every last ounce of his courage, Chang rose back to his feet and, expecting to immediately be hit in the chest with a bullet, adopted the police department's preferred two-handed

Weaver stance. His Glock pointed back down the hall, towards the wall of flames. His finger was tense on the trigger. But then barely audible above the roaring of his own blood in his ears and the crackle of the flames, two rounds flew at him.

Chang felt superheated air pass over his left cheek and something tug at the lapel of his jacket. Heart now beating in his chest, like a deranged death-metal drummer, Chang's feet scrambled backwards across the slick, institutional linoleum and towards the door to the stairwell as he tried to escape the line of fire. He was level with it when the exit door opened and a pair of orderlies stepped out. Chang yelled, 'Get back! Metro Police!'

Eyes wide at the scene before them, they darted back inside the stairwell. Chang's finger overcame the second resistance on the Glock's trigger. He fired. His unsuppressed round left the barrel with a seemingly thunderous retort that echoed off the bare walls and floor. The Russian appeared, charging at him through the flames. The round hit Ruslan in the chest. He jerked backwards and sideways, stumbling into the wall, but did not fall.

Chang's eyes widened as the Russian carried on striding forward, his Beretta now held in one hand. Chang tried to relax and remember his training. He fired a second, a third and a fourth round. The first two went wide, as the Russian jerked sideways, contemptuously, out of their path. But the last one struck him again in the chest. The Russian fell to his knees, but as he did so, he sent a volley of rounds back at Chang. His left shoulder was jerked backwards and he collapsed onto his back. He heard the window behind him shatter as the remaining Russian rounds flew through it.

Chang felt no pain, just anger. He frantically moved his feet, pushing at the linoleum with his hands, and managed to get back to his feet. The Russian was on his feet too but bent forward. The big man charged at him like a linebacker, like a wrestler. Chang felt himself relax; he had this. He knew what to do. He took a step backwards, taking himself nearer to the broken window. The

Russian was almost upon him, rage in his eyes. Chang met the much larger man, grabbed him and using his opponent's own momentum threw him up and over his shoulders. The Russian crashed into the remaining wooden frame of the window but continued on, through the gap, and out into the night.

Chang rolled over onto all fours, panting like a crazed dog. 'Wax on, wax off.' He mumbled to himself. He moved his hands to get to his feet and his left one touched something. Chang shook his head. It was the thick plastic casing of a Chevrolet car key. He pocketed it and stood.

Chang looked out of the broken window, but couldn't see the Russian's body below. He sighed. What had he done? What was he doing? What he had to do was contain the fire. The flames in the hallway had not yet taken hold of the entire space. He had to tackle them. He grabbed a fire extinguisher from its mounting next to the exit and started to spray foam over the encroaching fire. Although the linoleum had melted, starting to release a foul-smelling smoke, and the paint on the walls had blackened, nothing else had caught fire. Chang dropped the depleted extinguisher and felt extinguished himself.

It was then that he noticed a dull ache in his shoulder and remembered he'd been shot, but he had full motion of his arm and shoulder. What had happened? Using his right hand, he probed his left shoulder. There was a tear in his jacket and through this he gingerly pushed his finger and felt his skin. He pushed gently. The pain flared but was bearable – a flesh wound.

Chang let out a sigh and looked at the broken window. He'd now murdered three people; it was getting easier and he was getting better at it. No, Chang reasoned, they had not been murders, they were justifiable homicides. All three suspects had resisted arrest and pulled weapons on him. If anything, he should get a commendation for finding and shooting the Russian killer.

Chang nodded, and said aloud, 'Justifiable homicide.'

Chapter 23

College Park Airport, Washington, DC

Oleniuk sat massaging his neck. He too had made a decision. It was all or nothing now. He would take the diplomats' wives and Simon Hunter. They would prove to be his insurance should anyone attempt to disappear his jet. The Frenchman was of no further consequence to him; the man had insulted the President of Russia so deserved to be shot. Yes, Oleniuk decided he would do it himself, in front of the other hostages as a warning to them. The Chinese sat phone rang. Oleniuk snatched it up from his desk. 'Yes?'

'Do you understand what you are asking me to do?' The caller, this time, had some emotion in his voice. 'You are asking me to murder one of my own pilots, and shoot down a multimillion-dollar aircraft to kill a single man?'

'I am fully aware of the consequences of my request. Blackline will compensate you for your loss.'

There was a silence, punctuated by the warbling on the encrypted line.

'My operations centre will directly guide your helicopter in on the jet.'

'Thank you, comrade.' The Chinese were still communists after all.

'Now that is all. Our cooperation is at an end. This line will no longer connect.'

Oleniuk glared at the Chinese sat phone as the call finished. Their cooperation was at an end? Hm, he'd love to see the expression on the fool's face when Chen Yan reminded him of his duties. Oleniuk had been made to seem a fool by relaying to the Chinese the news Volkov had given him: a British spy named Jack Tate had hijacked his jet! There was no way that Oleniuk would allow this man, whoever he was, to blow his operation. No way at all.

Once he had confirmation that Tate had been eliminated and the women were returned, he would depart. Oleniuk pursed his lips. How had a member of British Intelligence or someone masquerading as one discovered the existence of his operation? At a later date he would look into it.

31,000 feet above Pennsylvania

The note of the engines changed as the executive jet started to gently descend. Both of its occupants were silent. Pang focused on flying while Tate thought about the mission ahead. The flying time from Houlton to Washington was two and a half hours. His Rolex told him he had just over half an hour to go. Looking through the canopy, he took in the Appalachian Mountains stretching out below.

He'd seen his first mountains when he'd joined the British Army. As kids all he and Simon had near London were hills and on his family trips to North Wales his parents adamantly refused to take him anywhere near the Snowdonia National Park. He envied those who grew up with the great outdoors as their backyard. The Appalachians were ancient, untouched and unaltered by the march of humanity. Anyone out trekking or living amongst them was likely still unaware of the chaos in the rest of the country – a country over-reliant on electricity and digital connectivity. Perhaps when this was all over he'd quit, get a log cabin, and live by a lake.

Tate's mind snapped back to the present and his mission. He noticed that Pang had started to look nervous; minutes out from their destination, the pilot was scanning the sky more than before. 'Problem?'

'What do you mean?'

'I mean what are you looking for, Pang?'

'We are nearing Washington. I am checking for other aircraft.'

Tate said nothing, and as they continued to lose altitude, he searched the skies for himself. International aircraft that had been en route at the time of the EMP, but out of the blast zone, would have already diverted. Was Pang looking for backup, for another Chinese aircraft? Before Tate could demand an answer from Pang, he saw a reflection off his port side, sunlight glinting on a piece of metal. He squinted, another flicker . . . and then he recognised the distinct shape of rotor blades. The helo climbed, the custom paintwork on its fuselage making it all but undetectable against the sky. The model he did not recognise, but what was slung underneath he did. Air-to-air missiles . . .

There was a flash and a sleek shape rocketed toward them.

'INCOMING!' Tate yelled.

Pang, eyes wide, pushed the nose of the Gulfstream down to gain instant speed. Their stomachs tried to escape through their chests. Pang stabbed at a button on the dashboard. A flare and then a cloud of metal foil burst from the rear of the jet – countermeasures retrofitted by the plane's owners. There was an explosion behind them, violently rocking the Gulfstream. The jet dropped through the clouds, and both men saw the ground, a dark mass of greens and browns, growing increasingly larger.

The engines whined; Tate swore. He imagined he could hear the rivets popping off the fuselage as the Gulfstream continued to dive. He had no idea where the helo was. If it fired again, everything ended; they could outrun the helo but not its payload.

Pang yanked the Gulfstream to starboard and then tried to

pull the nose up. The engine note changed to an angry roar – the executive jet had not been designed for this.

Tate caught a glimpse of a distant smoke trail . . . A second missile was inbound. They couldn't escape. The jet was doomed. It was a modified commercial airframe, not a fast-jet – it had an emergency exit but no ejector seats. Tate had one option, and it would kill Pang. He had no time to warn, no time to explain, no time to apologise. Tate undid his seatbelt, aimed his Glock at the glass – the only barrier between him and the outside world – and squeezed the trigger. The Glock boomed, a hole appeared in his part of the screen, cracks instantly spread across its entire length like bolts of lightning, and the howling slipstream ripped away the panel. Tate was viciously tugged forward by invisible claws and hurled into the void . . .

Head hunkered into his shoulders, eyes screwed shut, Tate spun. Two seconds, three, four . . . He thrust his arms and legs out in a starfish shape to create drag and control his fall. Opening his eyes, they immediately streamed as the frigid air attacked. Above the thundering of the wind in his ears, there was an explosion; the jet and Pang were no more. Tate's rapidly stiffening fingers found the toggle on his harness and yanked it. He felt as though he'd been punched in the gut as the canopy deployed and he instantly slowed.

Tate was helpless, defenceless as he floated ground-ward. He searched, with streaming eyes, for the helo. Had his attackers seen him escape before the missile struck? There was nothing he could do either way. A crosswind picked up. He had to concentrate on his landing. Tate saw empty fields and buildings devoid of light. He was short of Washington, but how short he had no idea. As he started to feel ground rush, he heard rotor blades above, but to look up now would be fatal. A road appeared, dissecting the fields. He managed to ride the wind, crabbing away from a fast-approaching homestead and over the now defunct telephone lines toward a green field. As he prepared himself to land, the retort of a heavy machine gun filled his ears and rounds ripped through his silk canopy . . .

Tate dropped, his feet lost in the heads of a tall crop. He stumbled, tumbled, fell. Landing heavily, the air was forced out of his lungs as he was dragged forward by his billowing parachute. Head dizzy, Tate struggled with the release mechanism, finally managing to undo the harness. He squirmed free and lay still, crop heads fluttering above him, peering down, seemingly indignant to his unannounced and uninvited arrival.

The helo passed overhead. He had to move. 'Who dares, wins,' Tate muttered to himself, and with a monumental effort pushed up onto his haunches. Through the crops, he could see the helo sitting in the adjacent grassy field. As the rotors slowed, three figures dressed in black fatigues and helmets got out, the commando manning an exterior-mounted 0.50-calibre machine gun from one side and two passengers from the other. They tactically advanced toward his parachute, which had come to rest further ahead in the crops.

Tate turned his head. Behind him stood the road, and beyond that another grassy field with a driveway gently sloping uphill to trees and a large house. He was in the only bit of cover. He was a sitting duck and they'd find him sooner rather than later. Tate slowed his breathing; if he made a dash for it now, perhaps he could get across the road and partway up the drive before they opened fire?

Tate pushed off. One . . . two . . . three strides, increasing his speed through the thigh-high crops. There was a shout from behind. Four . . . five . . . six . . . He broke free onto the road. A metallic bark and something pinged the blacktop in front and to the left – he powered on. Another shout and more rounds raked the road. Tate reached the other side. Oblivious to the incline, he pounded up the driveway. He stumbled on a piece of loose asphalt and fell forward, catching a glimpse of the scene behind; one of the gunmen had returned to the helo while the other two tore after him.

Tate ran on. His body recognised no pain, no fatigue as the adrenalin fuelled his charge. He made it to the tree line and burst through the other side and into a turning circle outside the house.

The homestead loomed large in front of him, a handsome, hefty wood-panelled house, at odds with the semi-rural DC countryside. He had to get inside. It was his only hope, and his attackers would be forced to follow him in. He just hoped that his SAS training would mean his close-quarter combat skills were better than theirs.

As he pelted towards the house, Tate saw no signs of life from within; none of the curtains twitched and there were no cars or vehicles parked outside. He swerved to head for the stoop that led up to the front door and as he did so rounds raked the steps in front of him. Cursing, he increased his pace even more and jinked to the left of the building, taking the access road to the back between the outer wall and tall, mature trees. At the back of the house, the trees gave way to a large yard with a barn on the left, open countryside ahead and the nearest neighbour half a mile away to the right and parallel to the road. Tate took a sharp right.

The back door looked less sturdy than the front but further on past this an extension, an orangery with oversized, sliding glass patio doors had been added. The wood around the windows was thin and the paint flaky. It didn't seem that solid, looked like a DIY job. It was Tate's best chance of entry. Ducking his head down and pumping his arms, Tate powered towards the extension. He launched himself into the air and hit the central glass pane with his right shoulder and elbow. For a moment it was almost imperceptible; the glass flexed, held firm, then shattered. Tate crashed into the kitchen. Flooded with adrenalin, he felt no pain as he skidded across the tiled floor before coming to a halt with a jarring thud against an island. If the place wasn't empty, he'd soon know.

Panting like a dog on a hot day, but knowing that he couldn't pause for a single breath, Tate grabbed at the top of the kitchen island for support. His hands were slick with blood from the crash but he managed to pull himself to his feet. He was unarmed. The Glock had been whipped away in the slipstream as he'd escaped the doomed Gulfstream. Eyes darting around the duck-egg-coloured country kitchen, he searched for a weapon, anything. A set of kitchen knives sat on the worktop to his right, safely sheathed in a wooden block. He grabbed the entire thing then made for the kitchen door, which led – he presumed – into the house itself. The door was wood, locked. He booted it just below the lock and on the second attempt it swung open. Stale air and dust immediately attacked his nose.

Tate now heard noise outside, the slapping of feet on the hardstanding. He spun and dived back into concealment, behind the island. Tate pulled two knives out of the block. The first was small, with both the top and bottom of its blade sharp and curved like a spear. The second was a stubby oyster knife. He discounted the oyster knife. Outside, feet scuffed on the concrete as his pursuers came to a stuttering halt. He imagined the lead gunman aiming his firearm into the room, assessing the scene and seeing the open door at the far end. He'd either enter the building with caution or speed, and Tate guessed the guy would use speed – knowing that he had the advantage of tactical equipment, backup and most of all an assault rifle.

'*Davai! Davai!*'

There was a crunching of glass and then scratching as the lead commando's rubber-soled boots dragged the glass across the kitchen floor. Tate got to his haunches ready to spring up. The first commando sped past him, through the door and into the hallway beyond. To Tate, time slowed. In his head he counted twenty seconds, but it felt like twenty minutes.

The first commando called back to the second: '*Chisto!*' Clear.

More glass crunched as the second man entered the kitchen. Tate pictured him, weapon up, advancing tactically, moving past the island towards the door, relying on his comrade's call of "clear", falling into the trap of tunnel vision as he focused on the space ahead and ignored the room that was already "safe".

This was Tate's only chance. If he ran he'd be cut down either by the unknown remaining number of gunmen in the helo or by the two in the house. He had to attack, and attack now. He sprang up behind the second commando and with furious speed his left arm looped around the man's neck, his left hand grabbing his face, clamping his mouth whilst at the same time his right drove the spear-pointed paring knife into the commando's head directly behind his right ear. The knife sank up to its hilt; Tate twisted it for good measure and the commando immediately started to drop but not before his finger tightened and sent a burst of rounds from his stubby rifle down the hall. Tate tugged the rifle from the dead man's grip, noting the body armour he was wearing under his black coveralls, and went prone on the kitchen floor next to him.

He waited. There was a shout from inside the house and then the first commando appeared, leaning over the bannister on the stairs at the end of the hallway. Tate depressed the trigger and a line of rounds slammed into the man's centre mass. Before the lead commando had finished falling, Tate was on his feet, weapon up and sprinting towards him, knowing that if he too was wearing body armour, he'd be injured perhaps but definitely not dead.

The first commando lay sprawled on his back, half on and half off the stairs. His rifle had landed out of reach near the front door. He was starting to regain his senses, and trying to fight gravity and reach back up the stairs to his thigh for his secondary weapon – a handgun on a leg holster.

He made eye contact with Tate and said in a pleading voice, '*Niet!*'

'*Da,*' Tate said, and shot him at point-blank range in the face.

There was eerie silence. The thunderous retort of rounds fired in a confined space and the heady stench of gunpowder mixed with the stale air made Tate's head throb. He put his arm out against the wall, to ward off the dizziness that threatened to engulf him. His body screamed at him to stop, lie down and rest. But Tate knew there was no rest for the wicked, and the very wicked were outside, and they had a helicopter.

He wobbled back to the kitchen and quickly rooted around for something to numb the pain. Inside a cabinet, above a kettle, he found a Tupperware container. He opened it. Ignoring the prescription codeine tablets, which he'd love to take but couldn't because of the drowsiness they'd induce, he took a packet of generic ibuprofen and a blister sheet of paracetamol. He popped three tablets of each into his mouth then moved to the kitchen sink and let the water run. He bent down and filled his mouth. The water tasted wonderful but the tablets scratched his throat as he swallowed them in one go. Gulping another mouthful, he then splashed his face before he knelt down next to the corpse of the first commando.

As quickly as he could he removed the body armour from the corpse and strapped it over his own clothes. He then searched the webbing and found a spare magazine. Tate exited the kitchen, shut the door as best he could and went back into the hall. He collected the second man's rifle. Like the one he was holding, it was the short-barrelled HK416 A5-11. Exactly the same weapon he'd taken from Oleg Sokol's Tahoe. Tate collected a further two spare magazines that protruded from this man's webbing and then jogged up the stairs.

The team in the helo knew he was in the house, and as both dead commandos were wearing comms they had to know their two men were dead, or incapacitated at the very least. This gave Tate time whilst they regrouped. Tate had no idea how many more commandos were in the Bell. It could hold up to seven passengers plus the pilot, but how many had been dispatched to shoot down the Gulfstream? They'd only really needed the pilot and the gunner – who could have also acted as a spotter. Why bring an assault team, unless they were on their way somewhere else or perhaps wanted to come along for the ride? So how many more men were there?

From experience he knew that soldiers, especially Special Forces operators – which these guys he presumed had once been – were a strange, superstitious lot. Odd numbers were messy, and mess was the enemy of discipline. They liked routine and even numbers. If he counted the pilot, the gunner and the two whose bodies were littering the house that made four. So it was either no more commandos, two more or four more. Would the assault team just count themselves and ignore the pilot?

Tate realised that fatigue and pain was creating in him a strange type of delirium. All he could be sure of was that whoever entered the house next was not coming to sell him a time share in Marbella.

A door met Tate at the top of the stairs. He kicked it open – a bathroom. Tate turned right on the landing and saw four more doors, two on his left and two straight ahead. He quickly opened each and peered in – three bedrooms and a study. The first bedroom was painted pink and the second blue. He entered the third room, the largest upstairs room. It was pastel peach and had an outsized bed in the middle with a gold headboard and black bedding. A wide window with a wooden window seat covered with cushions gave him a view back across the road to the field he'd landed in. His abandoned parachute rolled and bellowed in the gentle breeze.

And past that, rotor blades turned and the Bell rose into the air, slowly like a boxer beating a ten count. It approached the house. Tate now identified it as a modified variant of the Bell 429 GlobalRanger, modified because of the two empty missile carriers but more importantly and urgently now because of a figure manning a 0.50-calibre machine gun out of the starboard side.

Tate moved to the window, broke the lowermost pane with the butt of his HK and then dropped to his knees. In the room there was three foot of wall before it met the window, Tate rested his HK

251

on the cushions and trained it on the Bell as it grew larger. The gunner swung toward the house. The Bell cut its speed, rearing back and up, like a startled horse, and the gunner opened fire. Heavy rounds slammed into the front of the house below the window. Any one of those would rip him in half. Tate tried to screen out the danger, the fear and concentrate on the gunner. The HK416 A5 wasn't a precision rifle, especially with the shortened eleven-inch barrel, but he was a skilled shooter, a trained sniper and the range was shortening with each millisecond.

Tate acquired the gunner's face, a flesh-coloured smudge between black coveralls and helmet, and squeezed the trigger. Rounds raced towards the Bell . . . and then the magazine emptied. Tate cursed and rolled away at the same time as the helo turned. Fatigue had made him sloppy. Tate sat with his back against the exterior wall and changed magazines. He had three full magazines and whatever was in the second weapon – that would be his last resort, his Hail Mary. Tate took a deep breath and felt a stabbing pain in his chest. He hoped it was just bruising. He darted out of cover to see the Bell retreating. He'd driven them back, for now.

Tate stood, knowing that if he stayed down he'd never get up. He saw his reflection in the mirrors of the built-in wardrobes opposite the bed. He had the hair and clothes of a tramp and his eyes were manic. Then he heard the helo again. The sound of rotors got louder and then it swooped past the window, this time without the gunner hanging out and so close that the downwash made Tate all but stumble. There was a moment of calm and then an explosion on the ground floor.

'Diversion!' Tate shouted, at himself.

He flattened himself on the floor next to the bed and readied the HK. The Bell came again, fast, buzzing the house, dust swirling across the room but Tate ignored it. This was the time for the attack. Footsteps sounded on the stairs, almost undetectable amid the noise from outside. Tate caught movement. It wasn't a target . . . it was a concussion grenade . . .

The flashbang sailed into the room. Tate forced his palms over his ears, and shut his eyes intuitively. In the SAS he'd had been on the other side of the equation, the one throwing the stun-grenade, the one clearing the room with an HK416. He knew what to expect, but even so, the effect of the flashbang was debilitating. Searing white light and an ear-splitting explosion filled the room.

A second without senses and then the gunmen rushed into the room, professional, trained, their short-stock machine pistols tracing arcs. They were fast but a split second too slow. Tate fired from the floor, his rounds striking the lead commando's shoulders and then his neck, throwing him backward. The second commando, a step behind and to the left, swivelled and opened fire. Tate scrabbled into cover under the bed as the floorboards splintered around him. Tate flicked the fire selector to full automatic and fired blind up through the mattress, emptying the magazine. His target grunted and fell.

Tate dragged himself back out and threw the empty HK at the commando who was clutching his arm and using his feet to push himself out of the room. The weapon hit him in the face as Tate rushed forward. Using both hands, Tate grabbed the commando's throat and squeezed. His eyes widened, he bucked, and his arms flailed as he tried to dislodge Tate. A fist connected with the side of Tate's head, the exact same place the Russian in Camden had hit him. Twice in one day. Not good. Potentially lethal. His vision dimmed, he felt himself drop to the side . . . and then he saw a glint, a blade.

Acting on instinct alone, Tate rolled as a serrated-edged knife passed his cheek. Groggy, he grabbed at the furniture for support. Tate got to his feet with his back to the door. The room was silent save for the laboured breathing of both men. Six feet apart. His opponent had dark eyes, and the flat forehead and wide cheekbones of Russia's Far East. He now knew the men were undoubtedly Russian, probably former Spetsnaz.

'I'm not who you think I am!' Tate said, in his St Petersburg accented Russian.

Furrows appeared on the commando's forehead as his arm swayed and the knife glinted.

Tate held up his palms. 'Oleniuk sent me!'

'Oleniuk?' The commando's frown deepened and for a split second his eyes flicked away as he repeated the name of his boss. But a split second was all Tate needed. He snapped his right arm forward, connecting with the commando's wrist, knocking the arm wide, and then followed up with a straight kick to the groin. The man folded. Tate grabbed the fist holding the knife, jerked the man's arm backward, twisted it, and heard a satisfying pop.

The commando screamed. Tate dragged the injured arm forward, clamping his own fist over the commando's and drew the knife across his neck. The scream gave way to gurgles and the commando fell limp. Tate swayed, his legs trying to give out. He staggered backward, his eyes now resting on the body of the other commando whose glassy eyes stared at him accusingly.

Tate fell to his knees, exhausted – more than exhausted. His body swayed. How many more people would die today because of him? He didn't know and part of him didn't care. He felt no remorse; every man he'd put down had been trying to kill him. He heard a voice. It wasn't his conscience, it had a tinny tone and came from the comms set. Tate studied the nearest man he had killed; his throat mic was drenched in blood – the sound came from his earpiece. Tate stumbled back towards the window, located the first commando's mic, and carefully pulled it and the helmet containing the earpiece away.

'*Dolozhyt.*' Report – one word, barked in Russian.

Tate used one Russian word in reply: '*Chisto.*' Clear.

'*Prinial.*' Got it.

Tate heard the Bell return. How many more men were outside? The pilot only or the pilot and up to three more commandos? That wouldn't make sense. Tate decided it had to be either the pilot only or the pilot and one more man, the gunner. Unless the gunner had been one of the two he'd just shot? Tate took a deep breath. He didn't have time to debate with himself. He had a minute, maybe less, and only one option of getting out. He quickly undid the dark coveralls of the dead commando next to him and took them from the still-warm body. They were plastered with blood and gore, but he didn't care. He pulled them snugly on over his own clothes and placed the sweaty helmet squarely on his head. His boots were a giveaway, but the disguise needed only to work once and for a few seconds.

Tate left the room, cradling the rifle from one of the dead Russians. He took the stairs down. He was finding it difficult to breathe. He didn't know how much longer he could keep going but the need to get to Washington, the will to reach his brother drove him on.

He walked out, visor down, through the shattered back door and into the large yard. The Bell 429 sat in the middle, the pilot alone seated inside and staring at him. It had been five. An odd number, if they included the pilot, but they were soldiers and hadn't. Tate breathed deeply, to steady his racing pulse. It was he who had the machine-pistol, not the pilot. Tate closed the gap, opened the front passenger door. A question formed on the pilot's mouth.

Tate jabbed the stubby HK into the man's gut and said, in his perfect Russian, 'Take me to the British Embassy.'

Chapter 24

George Washington Medical Center, Washington, DC
The post-surgery recovery area was down the hall. Chang knocked and entered. Janet was sitting in a chair, holding her husband's hand. Eric was ashen-faced but he managed a smile.

'Jon. Thank you.'

'For getting you shot?' Chang replied flatly.

'No, for getting me here.'

'You've not seen the cheque yet – the meter's still ticking.'

Janet was terse. 'Eric has left something important at the embassy.'

Chang had a sinking sensation. 'Oh.'

Eric wet his lips with his tongue. 'You told me to leave my papers . . . the stress you see, when I came round I suddenly remembered.'

'The morphine,' Janet stated, 'it jogged your memory.'

It was a peculiar observation, but Chang let it go.

'There's a file. It isn't mine, you see? So I didn't think about it before we left. It must still be in Simon Hunter's office. It's one of his files. He has a secure, locked metal drawer in his desk, but as he wasn't there he couldn't clear out his files.'

Chang said, 'The file is important?'

'Yes.'

'How do you know it's there?'

'It's not allowed to be removed.'

'I see. What's in it?'

'That's classified.'

Chang sighed heavily. 'And if this file falls into the wrong hands?'

'People will die. It's a Secret Intelligence Service file.'

Chang didn't bother to reply.

'Do I have to spell it out to you, Detective Chang?' Janet asked, sounding exasperated.

'You want me to return to the British Embassy and collect this file?'

'Yes,' Filler said, weakly.

'OK.' Chang took a deep breath. 'Tell me exactly what this case looks like.'

'It's in a red folder.'

Washington, DC

The painkillers had started to numb Tate's battered body, but he had no time to slow down. He needed to keep going; he needed to get to the embassy. He greedily emptied a water bottle commandeered from the Russian pilot as the Bell continued toward Washington. Pressing the HK rifle into the man's side, Tate learned that the main Russian command centre was at College Park Airport, a little outside Washington. An incoming call on the pilot's radio curtailed the questioning.

'Sasha, report. Has Jack Tate been liquidated?'

'Confirm I am dead,' Tate snarled before he let the pilot broadcast a reply.

Sasha paused. Tate pushed the HK harder into his side, and Sasha pressed the send button. 'Tate has been liquidated.'

'Excellent.' Oleniuk's voice became jolly. 'You have loaded his body?'

'Yes.'

'Return to base.'

Sasha made no further reply as the transmission ended.

'How does he know my name?'

Sasha didn't reply.

Tate prodded him harder with the HK.

'The commander of the Houlton base,' Sasha grunted. 'He claimed you attacked his airfield and hijacked his plane.'

Tate scowled. 'How did this commander know my name?'

'A traitor named Sokol told him.'

'Sokol is alive,' Tate muttered to himself.

'I do not think so. Traitors are not permitted to live.'

Tate cursed. He'd left Sokol for dead, bleeding out on the runway. He'd had no choice but to escape. It wasn't that he had any remorse for abandoning Oleg Sokol, rather, he felt anger for losing what would have been an invaluable intelligence asset for the British government. And now the man had identified him to the Russians.

'Tell me about Blackline.'

'If I tell you that I too become a traitor.'

'I won't tell anyone.'

'You are a funny man, Jack Tate.'

'So, Blackline?'

'It is an employer, like any other.'

'Very insightful. It is run by Maksim Oleniuk?'

'That should not surprise you.'

'It does as I shot him dead five years ago.'

'Then you must be a very bad shot.' The pilot snorted. 'Oleniuk is a pompous fool. Me? I am a simple man, I just do this for the money – for my family you understand, but Oleniuk? He has great big plans, aspirations.'

'Give me an example.'

'Huh, it is no longer a secret, he plans to become the next President of Russia.'

'He's planning a coup?'

'No he may be a fool but he is not crazy. He will become the next president when this one eventually loses an election, or steps down. He is looking at the long game.'

'I see.'

'So, Jack Tate, do you have children, a wife, a family?' Sasha paused, expecting Tate to reply. He didn't, so the Russian continued. 'I have a wife but I do not get the chance to see her.'

Tate didn't continue the conversation. He sensed that Sasha wanted to lull him into making a mistake, to lower his guard – lower the HK. Tate was tired but not stupid. He said nothing and the interior of the Bell fell silent, save for the rhythmic thud of the rotor blades. Their flightpath had taken them across dark countryside but now Tate saw the occasional glow, the EMP having taken out all electrical lighting. Eventually the outskirts of a city loomed into view below, darker objects against the grey.

'So you have a family, Jack?' Sasha asked again.

'I have no one,' he lied. His eyes noted a grey freeway, its turnpikes and interconnecting streets leading off like veins. The helo started to lose altitude; Tate smelled a rat. He saw the unmistakable shape of an airfield in the distance and nudged Sasha harder with the HK. 'What's that?'

'An airport.'

'Which one?'

'A small private place.'

'College Park?' Sasha did not reply. Tate jabbed again. 'Answer me! Is that College Park?'

'Da.'

'Pull up and take us past.'

'Or you will do what, exactly?'

'I'll make sure you're dead before this thing hits the ground.'

'You joke. That would be your own death sentence.'

'Ah, but I have no one. You have a wife.'

'I lied,' Sasha grunted.

'Right or left?'

'What?' The pilot was confused.

'Which leg is your favourite?' Tate shifted the HK, now digging it into Sasha's thigh. 'You may get lucky; I may miss your femoral artery but then again I may not. Either way, you'll lose a leg.'

'OK,' the Russian said sourly as the helo turned away from the airport. 'Your embassy is eight more minutes south-west.'

Tate remained silent as he continued to scan for threats in the dark skies above grey streets below. He was unnerved, floating above a seemingly sleeping city; not sleeping, he corrected himself, awake but blind. Dim lights flickered in the fast-approaching twilight from more buildings now, and he saw a couple of sets of headlights.

'Down there,' Sasha indicated. 'To your right is the embassy.'

From above, the British Embassy seemed like an empty, topless cube made up of four wings built around an inner courtyard. On three sides, the building was bordered by a parking lot, and on the other by the sweeping tarmac of Observatory Circle. Tate knew that as soon as the helo set down, it would draw attention from anyone within a half-mile radius. This included personnel at the Naval Observatory and guards at the neighbouring embassies.

Tate saw no letter "H" denoting a landing pad. Sasha read his mind. 'Where shall we land?'

'There, out the front.'

Faster than Tate would have imagined possible, the Bell dropped and came to a rest in the parking lot, which was empty save for an abandoned taxi.

'Remove the keys and hand them to me.'

Sasha switched off the helo and moved his hand toward Tate. 'There.'

'Drop the keys on my lap. Now give me your sidearm.'

'I am unarmed.'

'Don't lie.' Tate had no time for pretence. 'Give me your sidearm.'

Sasha reached down to his side and extricated a sub-compact Glock from a holster. 'Here.'

'Toss it in the footwell.'

The Glock made a loud clunk as it collided with the bare metal.

'Get out and walk around to my side. Just remember you can't outrun a bullet.' Tate let Sasha exit the Bell, grabbed the Glock 29, thrust it into a pocket, and then quickly climbed out. The Russian appeared in front of him a moment later; his arms were raised. Tate gestured with the HK. 'Lead me to the embassy.'

They crossed the lot and started to climb the stairs, the twilight hiding the fresh strike marks in the walls from an earlier shooting. Sasha stopped at the double doors. 'They are open.'

Something was wrong. Tate did a three-sixty scan of the scene. He saw no visible threats, but without power it was dark enough inside the embassy to hide an army. 'Then go inside.' Once through the doors, Tate took three steps away from Sasha. He scanned the empty foyer, opening his mouth slightly to eliminate interior sounds. Silence. 'Where is everyone?'

'They are gone.'

'What do you mean?' Tate knew the Foreign Office emergency protocols; he also knew that the means for an evacuation did not exist.

'They left earlier.'

Tate struggled to control his anger. 'Why didn't you tell me?'

'You did not ask.'

Tate crossed the floor to the high reception desk, covering both Sasha and the entrance with the HK. 'Where is Simon Hunter?'

'Who?' Sasha replied too quickly.

Tate couldn't read the man's face in the dark but picked up on his tone; he was lying. 'Simon Hunter.'

'I don't know who that is.'

'Drop your weapon! Now! I will shoot,' a voice with a Washington accent ordered from the shadows.

'If I drop this, it will go off,' Tate lied as he switched from Russian back to his native tongue.

'Place it slowly at your feet.'

'OK.' Tate lowered the HK, his eyes now wider, the rods in his peripheral vision picking up a figure with its arms extended, pointing a handgun.

The piercing beam of a flashlight appeared on the counter, pointing upward, like a lantern. As Tate squinted, his eyes battling to readjust, the man's face became visible. He was Asian.

'Who are you?' Sasha asked.

'I'm one of Oleniuk's taxi drivers.'

'Oleniuk told us you had disappeared.' Sasha was confused.

'No. I was delayed by the British. Who is this man?'

'He's a British spy. Oleniuk wanted Hunter to see his body. Perhaps as a warning, perhaps he knows him?'

Tate felt his jaw slacken; the Russians had Simon?

'But he's not dead,' the man holding the gun stated.

'You can correct that, now,' Sasha sneered.

The man's face remained impassive then his arms twitched and without warning, his Glock spat two rounds into Sasha. Tate lunged sideways, away from the commando, but a third round just missing his right foot made him stop. 'My next bullet won't miss. Hug the ground, now!'

Tate complied. He was all out of plays and by the look of it, he was also out of time. He lay on the corporate-grade flooring, still warm from the hot August day. 'Where is my brother?'

'How would I know? Who is your brother?'

There was a groan from the gloom. 'You shot me . . .' Sasha's words were slurred and in Russian. 'You little shit—'

Tate heard another round and then silence. The commando's feet came into view. 'Who are you?'

'Like he said, I'm a British spy.' Who was this man?

'A British spy, huh?'

'Secret Intelligence Service.'

'MI6?'

'Well, that's one name for it.'

'This is a trick. You were both speaking Russian. You are one of them.'

'If I was Russian, why was I holding him at gunpoint?'

'You tell me.'

Tate raised his head enough to see the man's face; he was all but convinced the man wasn't working with the Russians. 'I'm British. My name is Jack Tate. I'm looking for my brother Simon Hunter. He works at the embassy; he will confirm who I am.'

'Jack Tate?' The man repeated the name, like a crossword clue. 'That means nothing to me.'

'I am MI6. He was telling you the truth.'

'Get up.'

Tate dragged his weary body up from the floor and stood facing the shorter man. 'I'm just here to find my brother.'

'What were you doing with the Russians?'

'Taxi service.'

The man's eyes flashed and a smile almost formed on his lips. 'You have any ID?'

Tate let a sarcastic snort escape. 'What are you, a cop?'

'Yes. ID?'

'Let me check.' Tate had no idea if he still had his passport 'I'm going to reach into my shirt pocket.'

The man said, 'Slowly.'

'Slowly.' Tate ran his hand under the combat coveralls and the ballistic vest into his left breast pocket of his shirt. He undid the button and levered out the sturdy board document.

'Open it.'

'You can read in the dark?' The man remained silent as Tate opened his UK passport and held it spread between both hands.

'Don't move.' He stepped forward, Glock still fixed on Tate's centre mass but eyes now on the passport.

Tate lowered his arms a fraction. The man took another step

and then Tate shot out his left leg and twisted to his right. The shorter man's legs were swept away and he instinctively threw his arms out to brace his fall. Tate reversed direction, followed the right hand – the one that held the pistol – pinned the forearm with his knees, and ripped the weapon up and away.

'Now you tell me, who are you?' Tate asked, breathing deeply.

'My name is Jon Chang; I am a detective with Washington Metro PD.'

'ID?'

'My badge is in my jacket.'

Tate dug the Glock into Chang's neck and with his left hand retrieved the badge. 'Why did you shoot the pilot?'

'I've had enough of Russians trying to kill me. I didn't want to give him the chance.'

'I can understand that.'

'Can I get up now?'

'Go ahead.' Tate edged back, but kept the Glock pointed at Chang. The sound of gunfire would have kept any onlookers' heads down for a while, but Tate knew they were exposed. 'Why are you here?'

'I was sent by Attaché Filler.'

'Filler? You know Jim Filler?'

'I know Eric Filler.'

'Correct.' It wasn't much of a test but all he could think of.

'And his wife is called Janet.'

'Why did he send you?'

'To retrieve a file. It's over there on the counter.'

'He'd forgotten it?'

'Yes.'

'That sounds like Filler. Where are the embassy staff?'

'They went home. Eric was shot – he's in the hospital.'

'Who shot him?'

'The Russians.'

'So Simon Hunter's at home?'

'No. I mean I don't know.' Chang met Tate's eyes. 'He hasn't been seen since before the EMP happened. I think the Russians may have him. They like taking diplomatic hostages.'

Tate shuddered, suddenly cold. Oleniuk knew. He had to know about Ukraine and he had to know about Simon's involvement, but he didn't know Simon was his brother. Tate let out a sigh. Sod it! He had to stay focused. 'Where did you get the torch from?'

'Torch?'

'The flashlight?' Tate pointed.

'I took it from one of their vehicles.'

Tate held up his palm. 'Explain to me how you know Eric.'

Chang took a breath and briefly recounted his dealings with Filler and Hunter at the embassy over the last day. The news of the assassinations of Military Attaché Dudley Smith and the British Ambassador Anthony Tudor, hit Tate like hammer blows. He leaned against the counter and lowered the Glock. His mission was already a failure. Tate pushed the Glock along the bar toward Chang; he had no reason to doubt his identity. 'I need your help.'

Chang studied him. 'You need a doctor.'

'That can wait, but what can't is rescuing my brother.' Tate needed a way into the airport, a way to get as near to Simon as possible before the Russians spotted him. He looked out of the window. 'Can you fly a helo?'

'No, but I can drive a Tahoe.'

'You have one of their Tahoes?'

'Yes.'

'That'll work.'

Chapter 25

College Park Airport, Washington, DC

Oleniuk's world became an unnatural shade of green as he switched on his night vision goggles. Although not yet dark, the summer sun was finally slipping away. He stood outside the hangar and stared across the expanse of grass-lined runway to the innumerable American homes beyond. It was silent. He cocked his head a little; had he heard distant rotor blades? He held his breath and opened his mouth to lessen any internal interference or bone conduction. Had he heard it again, lessening, moving away?

Oleniuk was puzzled; were there other helicopters in the area, and if so, whose? Could a carrier have repositioned itself near enough to launch search parties, rescue parties? He presumed that the American president was in his bunker, unable to leave for Camp David with the EMP having grounded Marine One. The more he thought about it, the more it made sense. The rotors must have been a Navy airframe. He did not fear the American military; they had no idea his team existed.

Oleniuk searched the skies. No lights; in fact, the only manmade illumination came from the houses out past the perimeter of the airfield. Dim flickering in windows, a mixture of paraffin and candles he imagined, but none of them had the intensity to cause his optics to flare. His stomach churned; it wanted more alcohol. His hip flask was long since empty, but there was a celebratory bottle of Wild Turkey on his jet. He wouldn't drink that until he was in the air, and then it would taste somewhat sour.

Objectively, the mission had been a success. The casualties sustained, while higher than he had imagined, were acceptable. Men were just men and irreplaceable, even Major Volkov was merely a soldier . . . no. He was wrong. One of the men was not just a man, he was the best of the Werewolves and he was irreplaceable. Ruslan Akulov had not checked in since he'd ordered him to the hospital to execute Filler. He didn't know how the bloody taxi driver had done it, but he knew that somehow he was responsible for squirrelling away his missing diplomats. Oleniuk was no fool, although if he had taken an objective look at the orders he had dished out, he would have to agree that he had acted like one. It was time to let go what was unsalvageable.

Oleniuk did not believe in myths and legends; such things to him were mumbo-jumbo but he did know that if he lost a Werewolf, he would be haunted. They were a small unit and fiercely loyal to each other. He would do well not to incur their wrath. He turned back into the expanse of the hangar. 'Grisha!'

Moments later the bearded commando, who had acted as his personal bodyguard, appeared. 'Sir.'

'Listen to me. You are to take the last remaining Tahoe, my personal escape vehicle, and go to the George Washington Medical Center. That is the last known location of Ruslan Akulov. You are to return with Akulov, if he is alive, or his body if he is not. Have I made myself clear?'

'Yes, sir, but what about your personal safety?'

Oleniuk snorted. 'I am quite safe here, unless Simon Hunter sends me a strongly worded diplomatic letter! Now go!'

He watched Grisha hustle out of the hangar then heard the V8 of the Tahoe growl and the tyres chirp as he pulled away. The confirmation that Tate had been liquidated had raised his sagging spirits. As soon as the men on the helicopter and then of course Grisha returned, he'd issue the command to exfiltrate. Inside the second hangar, the second Gulfstream was ready with a matter of minutes' notice to roll out across the taxiway, sprint along the runway, and leap into the dark summer sky. No. There was no way he would be stopped now.

A wide grin spread across Oleniuk's face. The next time he returned to Washington, it would be as a benign benefactor leading the reconstruction of his country's arch enemy. What imbeciles these Americans were with their open arms and "reset buttons". This would be a reset, all right.

Soon Oleniuk would finish enacting his own personal revenge. He would relish explaining to Simon Hunter who had been responsible for the Camden, UK, bombing. And then he would present him with the reason why. And then Hunter would crumble. Oleniuk felt dizzy with the inner power that only true vengeance could unlock. And then what should he do with Hunter? Killing him was too merciful. He would bleed him first, physically and psychologically. In Moscow Hunter would talk, and spill his intimate knowledge of the twenty-first-century British Secret Intelligence Service, their operations, their agents and of course their secretive E Squadron. Oleniuk realised he was breathing fast. He took a deep breath, and after Hunter had divulged all he could then, and only then would Oleniuk finally execute him.

Oleniuk tentatively stepped back inside the hangar, his balance off due to the NVG's lack of depth perception and, he had to admit, his own fatigue. Two men stood by the prisoners, who now kneeled on the floor in the centre of the empty hangar. The Frenchman was slumped forward, chin resting on his chest while the other two leaned against each other for support.

'I must apologise for being such a poor host.' In the total darkness, the Frenchman raised his head, and the others, eyes white in green-tinged bodies, squinted blindly in his direction. This would not do at all. For his judgement to be effective it had to be witnessed, and for this to happen there had to be light. 'Turn on the lights.'

'Sir.' The nearest commando flicked the switch.

Oleniuk removed his goggles. The generator powered, commercial overhead lighting making him blink, but not as much as the unfortunates before him. 'Now that's better. We can see each other, eye to eye.' Oleniuk chuckled; no one else did.

'What do you want from us?' the Frenchman asked, surprising Oleniuk.

'I think you know why you have been brought here.'

'I most certainly do not.'

'No? A little bird overheard you talking to Hunter about what you had done wrong.'

Debois frowned. 'I do not understand.'

'You insulted a close, personal friend of the President of Russia. A very close and personal friend, and that is something neither she, nor he, can ever forgive.'

Debois's forehead furrowed, frowned. 'This is about Valentia Smetaniuk? The opera singer?'

'And there we have it,' Oleniuk stated flatly.

Hunter found his voice. 'This is outrageous.'

'I agree with you,' Oleniuk stated.

'I do not understand.' Debois's face showed incomprehension. 'You have drugged me, abducted me and held me against my will all because your president and this singer are upset I banned her from performing in France?'

'Yes,' Oleniuk said.

'It was my right to so do!' Debois said defiantly.

'That is of course your opinion, but not ours.'

'And what is it you want? Do you expect me to change my mind? Rescind her ban? Apologise to the lady and your president? To repent?'

'I do not expect you to do anything.' Oleniuk held his hand out toward his nearest commando. 'Give me your sidearm.'

'Sir.' The guard unclipped it from its holster and placed it in Oleniuk's palm.

Oleniuk turned the pistol one way and then the other in his hand as he took his time to study it. 'We Russians make excellent assault rifles, but in terms of pistols, there is nothing finer in my opinion than a well-balanced Italian Beretta. Oh and the retort it makes is just exquisite – it is such a shame to dull it with a suppressor but I am mindful of our neighbours.' Oleniuk thumbed off the safety toggle. 'Simon, say goodbye to your friend.'

Hunter's eyes went wide. 'What?'

Oleniuk fired a double tap into the Frenchman's chest. '*Au revoir.*'

Debois fell sideways and a wave of exhilaration crashed over Oleniuk. It washed away his weariness but replaced it with rage.

'You're crazy!' Terri screamed.

Oleniuk's eyes narrowed. He was impressed by her acting ability.

Simon all but spat his words at the Russian. 'You'll pay for this, Oleniuk!'

Oleniuk handed the pistol back to the commando. He was no longer able to trust himself with it. 'Not in your lifetime. Take them back to their cell.'

The two commandos lifted Hunter and Terri to their feet, but Hunter twisted, broke free and threw himself at the older, heavier Russian. Oleniuk sidestepped Hunter and, as he passed, jabbed the Englishman's nose with his right fist. Stunned, Hunter fell as blood streamed down his face. 'I boxed at school, Simon, but even then you English toffs wouldn't accept me. I was undefeated. I beat the living daylights out of the older boys, yet they deemed it unsporting behaviour! You see, I would not accept their white towels. I demanded a knockout. In the real world one does not simply suspend hostilities because the other side are weak! One continues until the enemy is crushed.'

Hunter was on his knees. He coughed, the metallic taste of blood in his mouth. 'You are pathetic. Is that what this is all about?'

Oleniuk slowed his breathing, and took longer breaths as he

attempted to calm his ire. When he spoke it felt as though his voice was not coming from his own mouth but emanating from somewhere far away. 'I have a question for you, Simon Hunter.' He paused. He could feel his body starting to shake and hear a rushing of blood in his ears. 'Did you love Sofia Antonova?'

Hunter looked up from the floor. Through the blood Oleniuk could see the shock register on his face.

Oleniuk ground his teeth, flexed his fingers. His voice no more than a whisper he said, 'Answer me!'

Hunter coughed. 'Yes.'

'Why did you kill her?' Oleniuk hissed. 'You killed Sofia Antonova!'

'I didn't. I loved her,' Hunter replied. He had started to shake and tears now streamed and mixed with the blood on his face and dripped on the hard, concrete floor.

'Pick him up, take them to their cell,' Oleniuk ordered.

As one commando dragged Terri away, the other lifted Hunter. This time he did not resist. Once inside their small room the door was locked again. Terri put her hands to Hunter's face. He pushed her away, leaned against the wall and slumped down into the corner.

'Simon. Please. Simon, talk to me?'

Hunter didn't reply. He couldn't. He felt his body start to shake as the sins of his past reappeared.

Simon Hunter had met Sofia Antonova after he graduated. He was a young SIS officer and she had worked for a law firm. They'd met over a lunchtime sandwich in the park. He had never told her he worked for the SIS. She thought he was a regular FCO junior civil servant. They had been together for fourteen months when the car crash happened. It had been after a summer party. Both of them had been drinking. Hunter had told her they'd take a taxi. But Sofia was too strong-willed. She asserted that her Russian genes gave her the ability to hold her booze far better than he could. Vodka did not get her pissed.

And like a fool in love, Hunter had drunkenly accepted her assertions because he had seen her in action on numerous occasions; plus she became very angry when he argued with her. Sofia drove fast, she always did, just above the speed limit, always slowing just in time to beat the speed cameras and all the while singing along to Alicia Keys at the top of her voice. This time, as she was singing and driving above the speed limit her Fiat 500 ploughed into the back of an unforgiving, slow-moving truck.

Hunter had awakened two days later to see his parents sitting at his hospital bedside. It had been what the police called a FATACC – a fatal accident. Sofia had died instantly at the scene. He had blamed himself – he should have stopped her from driving, he could have, but he didn't. Legally he was in the clear but morally he knew he was not. Nothing anyone could say would stop him from blaming himself.

He knew that part of the guilt he'd felt had been because Sofia had loved him perhaps more than he had loved her. She had wanted to get married, dropped subtle and not so subtle hints and he had not been man enough to say no. She'd introduced him to her mother, who explained that Antonova was her maiden name. Sofia's father was an abusive man they'd left in Russia. Hunter liked both mother and daughter but felt trapped, and then the accident had freed him.

Hunter realised Terri was talking to him, questioning him. How could he possibly reply to her, how could he possibly tell her? He knew he had to. She deserved to know the truth. His confession spilled out in one concise sentence, like an intelligence report. 'Sofia Antonova was my first love and she died in a car crash because I let her drink and drive.'

British Embassy, Washington, DC
Tate stood in the dark, empty embassy foyer and dialled Vauxhall Cross on the Russian sat phone taken from the Tahoe. Pamela answered on the third ring. 'Yes?'

'It's Tate.'

'Jack, where are you?' She sounded on edge.

'Washington.'

'Sit rep. Have you re-established contact with Wicket Keeper and Opening Bat?'

'Negative. Wicket Keeper is dead.'

The line warbled, bleeped. 'Repeat?'

Tate was tired. He was finding it hard to stick to protocol. 'Blackline have assassinated Wicket Keeper and abducted Opening Bat. Maksim Oleniuk is in Washington.' Tate explained the situation as succinctly as he could.

'Jack, stay where you are and wait for assistance.'

Tate snapped, 'Wait for what, the bloody cavalry? They have my brother!'

'Jack! You must keep your head!' The line bleeped again. 'Things have developed since last we spoke; we are discussing an evac mission with the Canadians.'

Tate fumed. He had wasted too much time coming to the hospital, but at least he had located Filler's party. 'Filler is safe. Filler will continue to be safe. You know where he is; send the Canadians here. I have to go after Simon. Oleniuk may leave at any moment.'

'Jack, that's a negative. Listen to me, you must stay . . .' Another bleep and Newman's voice faded.

Tate scrutinised the display; a battery icon flashed and then the screen went blank.

Chang handed him the keys to the Tahoe. 'You'll need these. It's around the side.'

'Thank you.' This was it. This was the end. He was going to save his brother. Tate hurried down the steps in search of the Tahoe.

Arriving at the SUV, Tate saw that Chang had followed him. He held out his hand to Chang. 'Thanks, thanks again. What you did today was above and beyond the call of duty.'

Chang's eyes darted to Tahoe and back as he shook the much taller man's hand. 'Killing people?'

'Saving people.'

Chang shifted from foot to foot for a moment. And then he nodded. 'I'll come with you, as backup.'

'I can't ask you to risk your life for my brother.'

'I have a duty, like you said, and it's to "Protect and Serve" any way you need me. I've got an idea how we can get into the airport,' Chang explained.

Tate smiled.

The pain told Akulov he was still alive. It seemed to come from all over his body at once. He opened his eyes and found himself looking at a star-speckled sky. He was outside on the flat roof of a building, but which building was it? His arms were by his sides, his fingers splayed and pressed into the pitch-covered felt. He looked past his feet and now saw another part of the building rising at least eight storeys higher.

And then he remembered being shot, twice in the chest. The taxi driver somehow countering his attack and throwing him over his shoulders with a simple judo move. The pain became less vague, more focused. Akulov coughed and felt as though he'd been stabbed in the solar plexus. Broken ribs, a cracked sternum? He would need to see a doctor. But he was in a medical centre. He moved his arms and felt his chest. What he immediately felt were the two holes in his windbreaker and underneath his ballistic vest, which had saved his life, caught the two 9mm rounds and held them.

Tentatively Akulov tried to move his head. From side to side was fine but lifting it caused a violent pain. He could move his legs. He rolled slowly onto his side then pushed himself up. There was a pain in his chest but he felt nothing move. That was broken ribs ruled out then. He took a deep breath and as he inhaled felt the pain grow in his chest; a cracked sternum, possibly. Cracks healed on their own. He managed to get up to his knees, his head hammered and the world around him spun. Akulov got to one foot and stumbled forward, managing to now push against the exterior wall of the main hospital building to leverage himself to his feet like a drunk.

He felt a roaring in his ears. The deformed rounds dropped out of the bottom of his windbreaker, causing dull thuds on the roof. He peered up and acknowledged the broken window two floors above, which he'd fallen from. He felt the back of his head; there was a painful lump. He realised that he must have taken the brunt of the fall on his back and shoulders; if he'd landed on his head, he would without a doubt be dead.

Akulov moved along the roof until he was on the outside of another window. Inside it was dark and he saw no movement. There was no way to open it, so he kicked it with his booted foot until the glass gave way and he pulled himself inside. He dropped feet first into the carpeted room and fought the urge to lie on the large, padded couch that took up one side of what he imagined was a consultation room. Akulov walked across the room to the door. He swayed but didn't fall.

So he'd been shot in the chest twice, thrown out of a window and survived. Was this his second chance? He fancifully thought about the money in the bag, in the locker at the airport. It was enough to live on for a while, perhaps even to start again? But he was in Washington and the money was at College Park. A twenty five-minute drive. No problem on any other day. Uninjured he could run it, or walk it but now? No this wasn't a second chance given him by some divine being – it was the new ballistic vest. He had worn his, but Vlad had not; he was alive and Vlad was dead in a body bag in his Tahoe in the underground car park. He felt in his coat and then his trouser pockets for the keys. They weren't there.

Akulov opened the door and started to walk. He breathed deeper, felt the pain, used it to sharpen his mind and found stairs leading down. The stairwell was dark but he could just about see the steps. He used the handrail for support, but felt stronger, steadier after each floor. He reached the bottom and took the door into the underground car park. And there he saw not his Tahoe, but an empty space and next to this a taxi. He hauled himself towards the taxi and realised that it was the same one he had been chasing. He tried the door. It opened. He clambered inside, dull needles of pain probing his chest. The key was in the ignition. He turned it. The engine tried to start but could only cough. The fuel warning light was on. The policeman had taken his Tahoe and left his useless, fuel-less taxi.

He slammed his fists against the wheel in anger and climbed out. He leaned against the roof of the car to support himself, and through the pain, inhaled deeply. He had failed.

A car horn sounded. Akulov opened his eyes, and realising he'd passed out, found himself on the concrete floor of the car park as the bright lights of an SUV washed over him.

'Ruslan?' a voice he recognised called out to him and then the bearded face of Oleniuk's bodyguard appeared in front of him. 'Are you hurt? Can you walk?'

'Help me up,' Akulov said.

Grisha grabbed the Werewolf's arms and pulled him to his feet. 'What happened?'

'The taxi driver is not a taxi driver. He is a policeman and he shot me twice in the chest.'

'You are wearing your vest?'

'Yes, I am wearing my vest.'

'Oleniuk sent me to bring you back to the airport.'

'The policeman has taken my Tahoe. I presume he's also taken the women and Filler.'

'We must update Oleniuk.'

Chapter 26

College Park Airport, Washington, DC
In the summer night, the line of light spilling from under the hangar door acted like a beacon. It was visible to Chang and Tate from across the other side of the airfield, unlike their Tahoe, which was hidden behind them in a dip.

'NVGs,' Tate said as he lay on his stomach in the grass. 'I'm praying they don't have NVGs.'

Next to him Chang agreed. 'If they do, we are screwed.'

They had stuck to a road named The Paint Branch Trail, which wound through the woods immediately opposite the airport and was separated from the runway by a thin forest and a wire fence.

'You ready?' Tate asked, the sound of nothing but the wind carrying across the open ground ahead.

'Yep.'

'You can still change your mind.'

'Why would I do that? I told you, Jack, I have a duty as a police officer. Besides, I also have an armour-plated Tahoe between me and the bad guys.'

'True.' Tate took a deep breath and let it out slowly. 'Give me three minutes and then make your move.'

'Got it.'

Tate got up to his haunches and within seconds was lost to the night.

Oleniuk stroked the nose of his jet. It was a moving monument to US commercial success. He chuckled nervously; it was probably the last remaining working jet on US soil. He had grown impatient and a nagging sense of doom crept into his consciousness like an uninvited guest to a family party. The helicopter had not returned. This could, of course, mean many things, but to Oleniuk it meant one thing and one thing alone: Jack Tate was alive. What was it about this man that made him indestructible? Oleniuk refused to let one unimportant, inconsequential individual prevent him from completing his mission, from achieving his destiny. He knew now that Akulov had survived and as soon as he and Grisha returned he would tell the Gulfstream pilot to prepare for take-off.

He returned to his office to make a cursory check of its contents. He collected the case containing the Chinese sat phone, held this in his left and clasped the Russian one in his right. As he re-entered the hangar containing the jet, he shouted an order for the main hangar doors to be opened, on both hangars. He refused to hide anymore. Within twenty-four hours, he would have swapped this dump for his dacha; he would enjoy a well-deserved rest before meeting with the president and handing him the list of his foes he had eliminated on his behalf.

The EMP attack and subsequent assassination by Blackline was a private operation. He had no mind to link the two for the president; he would simply state that he had contracted an assassin to undertake the kills for the good of Russia. The former KGB strongman would appreciate Oleniuk's gesture; after all it was something the president would have done. And the man would then be indebted to him. While this would not make him step down, it would force him to back Oleniuk in the first future presidential election he could not contest. Then of course the fool would jump on the bandwagon when North Korea was denounced as the aggressor.

A shrill note echoed in the hangar, catching Oleniuk unawares. It took a moment for him to realise that his sat phone was receiving a call. He inspected the display, and his nose wrinkled. The missing taxi driver! 'Where have you been?'

'I was detained by the Washington PD; I am now on my way to you.'

'You were at the British Embassy; you helped the hostages escape!' Oleniuk yelled.

'That is not what happened. This is urgent. I have urgent intel. I am here now – let me explain.'

'You are where?' Oleniuk asked, but the caller had cut the connection. Oleniuk stared at the screen as though it may come back to life and explain to him what was happening. The man driving the taxi he now knew had not been Li Tam, but rather a police detective. So what was it that the fraudulent taxi driver had to say, and how was he going to get to the airport? Before Oleniuk had time to ponder this further he heard a car horn.

Tate lay on the dew-covered grass and counted again the number of men around the target. The overspill of light from the interior of the hangar silhouetted them as they worked. One was standing by the open doors of each hangar, while four others kept guard, sweeping the area with assault rifles. It wasn't until he saw one of the sentries in profile that he realised the man was wearing NVGs, the optics flipped up to save his night vision in the high-contrast environment. Tate was pretty sure that he was invisible, resting as he did in the slightest of depressions in the grass a metre in front of the perimeter fence, but he wouldn't bet his life on it.

Tate swore silently. One gun against six was not good odds, but he would dare and he would win or be cut to ribbons. Tate fixed his eyes on the empty space past the hangars, where Chang would appear in the Tahoe. It may have been his imagination, or the sound may have carried on the warm, night air but Tate thought he heard a telephone ring. Moments later, things went noisy. A yell from inside the hangar and then the sound of a car horn heralded the SUV as it burst into the pool of light, its own headlights now on full beam. This was his chance, and he was going to take it. Tate sprang up and sprinted in a straight line toward the hangar.

Striding outside, Oleniuk found his men, weapons ready, tactically facing an oncoming Tahoe. He knew what he was seeing but found it hard to understand. He asked his men, 'What is it?'

'One of our Tahoes, sir,' the Russian nearest to him stated. 'It could be Grisha.'

The Tahoe drew nearer but instead of slowing it accelerated and Oleniuk realised it was not his personal SUV. 'Shoot the damn thing!' Oleniuk roared.

A hailstorm of bullets hit the fast-approaching sedan, but the standard jacketed rounds were deflected by its ballistic plating. Oleniuk sensed movement, and then there was a flash. The barrel of a firearm flared in the darkness, and a commando twisted to the tarmac. Before he could issue an order, a second fell. The remaining four men realised what was happening. One went to ground behind the door, the second ducked back inside while the third and fourth rushed toward him.

'We are being attacked!' the first commando to reach him yelled. 'Get inside!'

No words came from Oleniuk's mouth as the larger, younger, and much fitter men hustled him back into the safety of the first hangar.

'Shut the doors!' Oleniuk ordered. 'They must not hit the plane!'

'Sir.' The commando reached up for the door closure button, but a round pinging off the metal inches away from his hand forced him back.

'Do it, you fool!' Oleniuk bellowed.

The commando reached out again; this time he was hit in the throat. He fell to the floor, directly on the door runners.

Oleniuk took a deep breath. He would not be beaten like this! He had not been in combat for five long years, not since he had been shot by a man working for Simon Hunter's E Squadron. Oleniuk felt his anger rise again, but this time he would let it explode out of him with devastating results. His two remaining ex-Spetsnaz commandos ran into the hangar and joined their colleague to make an arrow formation around their principal. Oleniuk nodded; the odds were still in his favour. Three highly trained men, plus him against whoever was shooting and whoever was in the vehicle. It was a fight all right but one that he would not lose. What puzzled him most though was who was attacking him and why? They couldn't have come for Simon Hunter, surely? And of course no one knew about his operation . . . except Jack Tate . . .

The lights in the hangar went out. Oleniuk pushed his NVGs down over his eyes and the darkness around him became shades of green once more. Walking like a man on a rolling ship, he scampered towards the weapons locker, all the while being protected by his last three men. Oleniuk opened the locker and reached for a Beretta at the same time as one of his men opened fire. He turned just in time to see a projectile sail into the hangar. Behind his NVGs Oleniuk's eyes widened and he shouted, 'Grenade!'

A monstrous-sounding explosion rocked the interior of the hangar. The thunderclap reverberated off the metal walls, ceiling, and concrete floor and was immediately followed by a flash of blinding white light. Painfully dropping to his knees, nauseous, Oleniuk had the presence of mind to keep moving forward, with his rifle, away from the percussion grenade.

Jack Tate flicked the lights back on and scanned the space. There had been four targets before he had thrown the flashbang he'd found in the glove compartment of the Tahoe. He acquired one of the commandos lying on his back; he had been hit in the knee. With his NVGs on his face and arms and legs thrashing he resembled some sort of large beetle. Tate unleased a short burst from his HK416 directly into the man's face and the beetle stopped moving.

He now saw another body, lying motionless in a pool of blood. Tate moved quickly to the body and dropped to his haunches, his eyes searching the rest of the space for threats. It wasn't one of the commandos; it looked like a civilian. Who was it? Tate scanned the hangar – it was empty. That meant the three remaining targets, Oleniuk and his last two men must be outside.

Tate pushed back up to his leaden feet and made for the door when a pair of shots rang out. The first one hit his thigh, making him twist, and the second was like a hammer blow to his back, propelling him forward. Tate dropped and, arms not moving quick enough, was winded as he hit the unforgiving concrete floor with his chest and then temple . . . He groaned more with annoyance than pain; he'd come so close, it couldn't end like this.

'Welcome,' Oleniuk's voice boomed, 'you are very good. You almost had us beaten with your little assault, but we are Blackline and you are, well, who are you exactly?'

Tate used the palms of his hands to push himself forward, to drag himself away from the voice that mocked him, but boots appeared by his face, and then two sets of muscular arms hauled him up to his feet. Tate was manhandled to face the Russian spymaster. Tate muttered, 'Hello.'

'Hello? Is that all I get from you, an informal greeting?' Oleniuk tutted as he ripped off his NVGs and tossed them to the ground. He blinked, still feeling the effects of the flashbang. 'You have killed too many of my men. Who are you?'

Tate looked the Russian in the eye. 'I'm Jack Tate. I've come for my brother.'

'Brother?' Oleniuk's eyes bulged and then he seemed to understand, but asked Tate the question regardless: 'Who is your brother?'

'Simon Hunter.'

'Hunter has a brother? How was it that I did not know about you?'

'Perhaps Blackline is not as great as you think it is?'

'I am truly happy that you are here. It is highly fortuitous.' Tate waited.

'You have impressed me, unlike your snivelling brother, Simon.'

'If you harm him, I'll kill you,' Tate hissed through the pain.

'You both like to make threats!' Oleniuk raised his Beretta.

'I'm not going to tell you again. Let my brother go, Oleniuk, and I'll let you live.'

'Ha, ha! What fun, as we used to say at school!' He switched to Russian. 'Let him go.'

The commandos loosened their grip, and Tate stumbled to his knees. Blood ran freely from his thigh onto the floor. Tate switched to Russian; it seemed only polite to do so. 'Why do you want my brother?'

'Bravo, you speak excellent Russian, of course you do; I should have expected no less,' Oleniuk's eyebrows arched. 'From a member of E Squadron who operated in Ukraine! Am I correct? Or are you just a skilled amateur? Come on, a man with your skills and determination? Do not now play dumb with me, Jack. I should liquidate both you and Simon for pitching E Squadron against my Ukrainian operation, for directing The Shadows, for meddling in the sovereign affairs of Russia! But I want intel, a bargaining chip, leverage.'

Tate's mind struggled to comprehend the words. Oleniuk knew about the special operations group, whose existence was above classified – but more worryingly, he knew that Simon and he had been a part of it. The realisation made Tate shudder; there was a Russian mole somewhere within SIS or her close allies. Tate said, with more conviction than he felt, 'You are delusional, Oleniuk!'

'It has to be.' Oleniuk's eyes narrowed as his left hand stroked the scars on his neck. 'I saw you – I remember you now. I know it was you. You gave me this.'

'For a dead man you look well.' Tate wanted the Russian to know what he had been responsible for.

'I am just glad you are an awful shot.'

'You moved.'

Oleniuk's nostrils flared. 'It is easier to hit a stationary target, as you will soon see.' His left hand started to crawl toward his neck, but he caught himself and formed a fist. 'I asked your brother questions; he wasn't very helpful, but he will be.'

'I'll never talk.'

A sneer formed on the Russian's lips and he slowly shook his head. 'This is why your journey finishes here, today, and your brother will travel with me to Moscow.'

Tate battled to control his anger. His life was one thing, and he knew it would end in violence; Simon deserved more. 'This isn't Ukraine, Oleniuk. You can't cross the border, kidnap foreign nationals, and place them on trial in one of your kangaroo courts.'

'You are correct, that would have proved too problematic even for me, which is why six targets were executed.' Oleniuk paused. 'I want to make certain that you understand the full magnitude of your failure before you die. Six men are now dead and the world will never know who was responsible.' Oleniuk looked, in Tate's opinion, manic.

'I will hunt you down.'

'Really? From beyond the grave?' A frown passed over Oleniuk's face. He looked at one of the commandos behind Tate. 'Go outside, check where that damn Tahoe is!'

'Yes, sir.' The commando exited the hangar.

'You will not be around to tell anyone about my operation, Tate. No witness, no crime.' Oleniuk's right arm moved; his Beretta acquired Tate as its target. 'But what is the point of killing you now, when I can do it in a few minutes' time in front of your brother?'

* * *

The shooting had stopped. Did this mean Tate was in the clear? Chang had passed the two hangars, turned the wheel sharply, causing the heavy Tahoe to pitch and stutter before the traction control switched on. It came to a halt at the end of the access road but facing the giant tin boxes. He waited a minute, saw no movement, and waited a minute more before driving onto the grass and happily breaking through the perimeter fence. Now the Tahoe was hidden again in its original position. Chang hoped the diversion had worked.

Chang lay in the grass, not far from where Tate had before, and did his best to blend into the darkness. There was still no movement outside the hangars. Where was Jack? Chang decided that even though Tate had told him to stay put and stay safe, he was doing no good hiding in the long grass. What kind of law enforcement officer was he? Chang had to find Tate; he had to help him. He rose to his feet. In his left jacket pocket, he had Akulov's silenced Beretta and his hands held out his personal Glock 19. He started to move forward towards the hole in the fence when he saw a figure, one of the commandos, dart out of the nearest hangar.

Chang threw himself down onto the damp grass. He lay flat, just raising his head enough to look ahead. He saw the commando tactically moving and sweeping the terrain with an assault rifle. He abruptly halted and aimed his rifle in Chang's direction, at the hole in the fence. The commando started to walk across the grass, then bent down and inspected it before turning back towards the two hangars. Chang followed him with his eyes as he walked in the opposite direction of the open hangar door and disappeared into the dark shadows.

Chang got to his feet, and jogged across the grass. On hitting the tarmac he quickly scuttled into the shadow at the side of the hangar. He stealthily edged nearer to the open door, and when he had taken a large breath to calm his nerves, peeped in. Inside but still far away, due to the hangar's voluminous construction, he saw

Tate. One commando stood behind him, and another was talking to an older man. That had to be Oleniuk. As he watched, one of the commandos walked away to the other side of the hangar and momentarily disappeared behind a two-metre-high wall. He could hear the faint murmur of words being exchanged between Tate and the older man but nothing more. The commando returned pushing a blonde woman and a dark-haired man, Simon Hunter.

Chang considered his actions. He had shot and killed three men thus far today, so he wasn't afraid of using his sidearm; however, that had been at close range, in daylight and the men had not been armed with assault rifles as the two commandos were. Chang didn't know much about weapons, it had never really been his bag, but what he did know was that the rate of fire from an assault rifle was much higher than his Glock or Beretta. If he was going to attempt a rescue he would have to get nearer and surprise them.

He took a deep calming breath and started to move nearer. Then he heard an engine. He cocked his head. It was a rumbling, roaring V8. High-powered lights exploded from around the other side of the hangar as a large, dark shape appeared. It was another black Chevrolet Tahoe and Chang had no idea who was inside it. He ducked back into the shadows.

Oleniuk exchanged looks with his two remaining Spetsnaz commandos. He gestured to the one on Tate's right. 'Check that out, it could be Tate's accomplice returned or perhaps it's Grisha and Akulov.'

'Yes, sir.' The commando jogged out of the hangar, weapon up for the second time.

Oleniuk once more raised his Beretta. 'Do not get any ideas, gentlemen. I may not be a crack shot but at this range I cannot fail to at least hit one of you, perhaps even the lady.'

'You harm her and I'll kill you!' Hunter said, with venom in his voice.

'Ha. That is right, you would not want to be responsible for the death of *another* woman!' Oleniuk switched his focus to Tate on seeing his expression darken. 'Correct, Jack. I know all about Sofia Antonova.'

'You have no right to say her name!' Hunter said, his voice now wavering.

'I have the most right in the world to say her name!' Oleniuk, pointed the handgun at Hunter and hoped that Tate was thinking about making a move.

'Sir.' A voice called as three men entered the hangar.

'Ah, you have returned.' Oleniuk felt relief and a surge of energy from within at the sight of the commando returning with Grisha and Akulov. He took in the assassin's appearance. The Werewolf's face was pale but he was standing unsupported, yet what Oleniuk noticed most of all was that his gaze was focused on the woman. 'Hunter, Tate. This is the end – you can see that you have lost.' Tate frowned and this made Oleniuk smile. 'What, chaps, no jolly quips? Tatiana, what about you?'

'I've got nothing to say.' The woman Oleniuk knew as Tatiana, and Hunter knew as Terri replied.

'Nothing to say?' Oleniuk demanded, then switched to Russian to emphasise her true identity. '*Nichevo?*' Nothing.

'*Nichevo*,' Tatiana replied, with a Muscovite accent.

Hunter's mouth fell open. His shoulders slumped. 'Terri?'

'Grisha, go to the jet and tell the pilots to prepare for take-off.'

'Understood.'

Grisha exited through the connecting door to the second hangar. Oleniuk smiled ruefully at Hunter. 'I do not blame you at all for falling for her, Simon. She is exceedingly beautiful and from past reports, a real tiger in the bedroom!' Hunter's face was pale. 'It is funny, don't you think, that once she opened her legs for you, and now you will open your mouth for us? She is a swallow and you'll become a parrot! You will be highly helpful to Blackline.'

Hunter was shaking. 'Terri . . . I don't understand . . . why . . .'

'Did you love her, Simon? More than you loved Sofia Antonova?'

Tate took a half-step forward. Intuitively Oleniuk opened fire. Two rounds kicking up the concrete millimetres in front of his feet. 'Do not move.'

Grisha rushed in, weapon raised.

'Stand down. All is OK.'

'Understood.' Grisha stood again next to Akulov.

Oleniuk looked at his assembled audience. He was writing and directing this Greek tragedy, and it was time to end the last act. His eyes flicked between them, Grisha his bodyguard, Akulov his Werewolf, the seemingly indestructible Jack Tate, Simon Hunter the snivelling excuse of an intelligence officer, Tatiana his "swallow" and finally, slightly away from the others, his two remaining Spetsnaz commandos.

'Simon, I'm in love with you.' It was Tatiana who spoke. 'I really love you, you must believe me! I never knew any of this would happen, what he would do, what he had planned. I was just meant to give him information.' Tears started to form in her eyes and she struggled to speak. 'But then I fell in love with you!'

'How touching.' Without warning, Oleniuk jerked the Beretta, pulled the trigger twice and sent two rounds into Tatiana. Both shots hit her in the chest, shredding her heart and catapulting her backwards. She was dead before she hit the floor.

Tate started to move but so did the Beretta. He stopped. Hunter collapsed to his knees. Akulov's eyes narrowed, and his jaw clenched.

'Simon, did you love her? Did you really love her more than you loved,' Oleniuk screamed the last two words, 'MY DAUGHTER!'

Hunter looked up and blinked.

'Sofia Antonova was your daughter?' Tate asked, his voice low.

Oleniuk, eyes wide, moist, nodded. 'Yes.'

There was a yell from outside followed by a single shot. It

hit Grisha in the centre of his forehead, instantly flooring him. Akulov dropped into cover. Tate dived on top of his brother, to shield him. Oleniuk darted to his left, and further away from the open doors; the two Spetsnaz men followed, one facing him and the second facing back the way they had come.

Tate was light-headed, struggling to concentrate. He saw the man Oleniuk had called Akulov was already by a locker in the corner. Akulov was retrieving a weapon, an HK416. He met Tate's eyes. 'Stay down, and I will not shoot you.'

'Why?' Tate was confused, by both the man's words and his accent. He sounded American.

'You saw what Oleniuk did? He killed one of his own, one of us. He murdered Tatiana like she was nothing! And if she is nothing then I am nothing,' Akulov spat, his disgust evident. 'He has broken the code. Our code.'

Tate's head was spinning and he could think of nothing more eloquent to say than: 'Yeah.'

Akulov disappeared through the door to the next hangar.

'Jack, you're losing blood!' Hunter struggled away from his brother.

'I'm OK.'

'No you are not. Give me your belt.'

Tate understood what Hunter wanted to do but did not have the energy to reply verbally. He undid his belt and Hunter helped him pull it off, and then tightened it around his thigh, above his bloody leg wound.

'Simon, Jack!' Chang slowly advanced into the hangar, his arms extended and weapon up in a textbook two-handed Weaver stance.

'That was you who fired?' Hunter asked.

'I saw Oleniuk shoot her, he was too fast . . . I tried to hit him but I missed and got the other one.' He shook his head. 'I'm sorry, I should have been faster.'

The booming whine of jet engines started from the neigh-bouring hangar, followed by an exchange of gunfire.

'Help me up,' Tate said.

Chang eased him to his feet.

Tate slapped his own face and roared, 'C'mon!'

Hunter knelt by Terri's body. He touched her face. His shoulders shook as he closed his dead girlfriend's eyes. 'The man is evil, evil! A deranged . . . We have to stop him!'

'We will.' Tate looked around for his HK, couldn't see it. He hobbled over to the same locker Akulov had been in. There was an array of 9mm handguns, and one more HK416. He picked up a Beretta, stepped back to Hunter and held out the weapon. 'Simon, take this.'

'I'm not a shooter.'

'That's why you're not coming with me. Jon, where's the Tahoe?'

'By the trees with the taxi.'

'Take my brother, lock yourselves inside then drive it back here.'

'No. I'm coming with you!' Hunter said.

'No. You're the brains, remember? Go!'

There was more gunfire and Tate made for the door. He advanced, stiff-legged, into the second hangar and immediately tracked to his left and ducked down behind a stack of wooden crates as a round pinged off the doorframe behind him. Adrenalin once more flooded his system, pushing the pain and fatigue away. To his right and behind another stack was Akulov. The man met Tate's gaze, and nodded slowly. Each man now seeing the other for the cold-blooded killer they had become. Could Tate trust the Russian? All he knew was that they now both sought the same enemy and he was in front of them trying to escape.

Tate cautiously peered around the top crate. One of the commandos was on the floor, behind his rifle, inside the open door of the Gulfstream. The second commando had crawled behind the airstairs, but had left a bloody trail across the concrete. Tate saw a shadow move past one of the jet's large oval portholes, halfway along the length of the jet. Akulov sent a burst of rounds at the shadow; several hit the porthole and pinged off. He fired again and hit the next porthole, but neither shattered. Akulov whistled to Tate. Tate looked over. Akulov made hand signals and pointed at the open door. Tate nodded, slowly – it hurt and his head was still heavy – but he understood. Oleniuk must not get away.

He rose to his haunches, but before he could advance there was a flash to his right as Akulov sprinted towards the Gulfstream. The commando behind the airstairs swung into view. He and Akulov exchanged fire; the commando went down, twisting, his finger still on the trigger spraying rounds in an erratic arc as he did. Akulov reached the bottom of the airstairs and powered his way upwards. Tate trained his HK on the open door. Both he and the last commando fired at the same time. Both weapons found their targets. The commando's head dropped, and his rifle fell out of the jet, but he had not been aiming at Tate, his target was Akulov.

Akulov carried on forward as his legs gave way. He had been travelling too fast to stop and pitched over the edge of the handrail. He fell, landing heavily on his back.

On his feet now, Tate shifted as fast as his fatigued and injured body would allow. He grabbed the handrail with his left hand and hauled himself up. Ahead he saw a darkening in the doorway as a figure tried to close it, but the dead man was in the way. One-handed, arm straining with the weight and torque of the HK, Tate send a wild shot into the empty space and the figure ducked away. And then the dead commando was shoved out of the jet and onto the airstairs. The body tumbled forward, a deadweight knocking Tate in the process. Tate's HK was ripped out of his hand and crashed to the hangar floor. Tate was pushed against the same rail that Akulov had fallen over. Looking down, Tate's eyes met the Russian assassin's, who lay on his back – a trail of blood seeping from his mouth.

'*Davai! Davai!*' Go, go – Akulov mouthed above the roaring engines.

Tate, ignoring the wet, white pain in his leg, the pressure in his chest and the hammering of his head, half dragged, half climbed up the three last steps. The door had started to close, Tate sprung off the railing and barged it with his right shoulder. He fell inside the executive jet. The door slammed shut behind him and he saw one pilot secure it as the other scrabbled away from him into the cockpit.

'Oleniuk!' Tate roared, and hauled himself to his feet by a leather chair back. The cabin had been configured to carry fourteen passengers with wide spaces between the seats and a pair of tables midway down the cabin. It was a sea of cream leather and walnut wood.

At the far end of the cabin Oleniuk stood, in front of a bar, pointing his Beretta. 'Here.'

Tate knew it was stupid, he knew it was senseless but he had no other choice. He started to run towards the remorseless Russian. Stars flashed before his eyes and his vision dimmed. Oleniuk kept the Beretta aimed in his right hand and beckoned Tate forward with his left. The Gulfstream was not the smallest of planes, still nowhere near commercial size, but what should have been a five-second sprint turned to ten as Tate found it harder to make his legs move.

His vision started to turn grey at the edges and then he blacked out. His head hit a padded, executive seat sending a hot white spear of pain down his spine. His eyes snapped open and he found himself lying sideways in the aisle, with the tables directly ahead of him. He blinked trying to make sense of what was happening as the noises around him had changed. One was the roar of the Gulfstream's jets as it started to taxi and the other was Oleniuk as he laughed a huge guttural laugh.

He spoke in Russian now. 'Look at you, Jack Tate, you are dying. Lying there on that bespoke carpet bleeding out. You haven't got long to live. So I am going to drink this very fine bottle of Russian vodka and smoke this exquisite Cuban cigar and watch you drift away into the kingdom of Hades.'

Tate could hear the runway rushing beneath him, and then a slight lightness as the Gulfstream attempted to become airborne. Tate grabbed at the chair, clawed at the table in an attempt to get back to his feet, but his arms seemed to belong to someone else.

'And now I will take my seat. Don't die before we level out – that would be extremely impolite.' Oleniuk sat, in a deeply padded seat, facing Tate from the far end of the cabin.

Akulov knew he needed medical attention but he could wait. He had to get away. He stumbled back into the first hangar as icy daggers seemingly stabbed him in the chest and neck, a sure sign of internal injuries. The space was empty. Dizzy but determined, Akulov padded towards a pair of lockers. The first one hung open. It was the one containing the weapons. This time he opened the second and retrieved his bag, the bag that insured his financial future. He winced as he lifted it, the weight was reassuring, but it was also almost too much for him to carry in his weakened state. Akulov swapped his HK for a fresh Beretta from the other locker.

He looked over at the broken body of Tatiana as an emptiness filled his injured chest. There was nothing more he could do here.

Outside the Gulfstream was still moving away from them down the runway.

'We have to stop it!' Hunter said.

'It has to turn,' replied Chang. 'We'll stop it then.'

'How?'

'You ever play chicken?'

'No?' Hunter shrugged. 'Is that wise?'

'This is an armour-plated full-size SUV,' Chang replied. 'South of a tank I think it's the best bet.'

Hunter screwed up his eyes, then opened them. 'Do it, ram the bastard!'

* * *

Oleniuk settled himself in the plump leather seat, and swigged vodka directly from the bottle. He had no time for delicate crystal – he was a warrior not a woman. The Gulfstream abruptly jerked to a stop, making him slip forward in his seat. He cursed in Russian, 'Suka! What is going on?'

Seconds later, the door to the cockpit opened; the co-pilot appeared. 'There is an SUV on the runway, coming toward us.'

Oleniuk sighed and waved his Beretta. 'Take off, you idiot!'

'But, sir—'

'TAKE OFF NOW!' Oleniuk roared.

'It's moving again,' Chang noted. 'This is going to be fun.'

'What if it explodes?' Hunter asked.

'You've seen too many bad movies. How many times do planes or cars explode in real life?' Chang said.

'I see your point,' Hunter conceded.

The Tahoe's V8 growled and it leapt toward the Gulfstream. This was the second time today Chang had played chicken; this, however, was the biggest game of his life. The jet grew larger, both vehicles accelerating, their closing speeds dangerously increasing.

'This is going to hurt!' Chang stated.

'We only need to clip the end of the wing. They'll move – they'll have to.' Hunter did not sound convinced.

The Gulfstream's tyres started to rise, as it left the ground then crashed down again. It was still coming straight for them and then the Tahoe started to shake.

'Shit,' Chang said.

'What?' Hunter asked, but had a feeling he knew.

'We're out of gas!' Chang uselessly jabbed his right foot at the pedal as the Tahoe slowed.

'No.' Hunter slammed the dashboard with his fist. The fuel light was on.

'Simon, it's still coming!'

Hunter's eyes went wide and he suddenly realised what was happening. 'Get out! GET OUT NOW!'

'What?'

'JUMP!'

The two men dived as best they could from the still-moving, but rapidly slowing SUV. Chang landed heavily and was barely able to drag himself onto the grass. Hunter, more athletic but injured, collapsed beside him. The pair looked on, powerless, as the Tahoe finally came to a halt in the middle of the runway. The Gulfstream was seconds away from colliding with it when its undercarriage left contact with the ground and it soared into the air.

Chang pulled the Beretta from his pocket and emptied the magazine at the retreating target. But the Gulfstream continued to climb, immune it seemed until it was out of small-arms range. Chang's chest was tight. He fell onto his back. He'd failed. 'I'm sorry,' Chang said.

'You didn't let him go. You didn't give up.'

Chang didn't know what to say.

The jet went into a steep climb. Tate was pushed back against a chair and managed to clamber into it. Over the roar of the blood in his ears and the jet turbines he could hear another sound, a hiss. He saw the Perspex on the porthole nearest to him vibrate. He smiled at Oleniuk, whose expression had turned to anger.

Oleniuk bounded from his seat even before the jet had attempted to level out. He still had a cigar in one hand and a bottle of vodka in the other. Tate saw that the Beretta was hastily pushed into the waistband of his suit trousers. It poked into his stomach in the gap his ballistic vest left exposed. He closed the distance to Tate. 'And now, Jack Tate, I shall enjoy my booze and smokes whilst watching you die!'

Tate opened his mouth to reply; however, then a sudden, searing rush of air slammed into his face and whistled in his ears. The oval, panoramic porthole just in front of his head had given way. Oleniuk's head snapped to his right and his jaw opened, the cigar falling to the floor. Tate now saw what he was looking at. Several small holes had appeared in the next porthole, which was in the door of the over wing emergency exit. Akulov's rounds! The firefight in the hangar. The integrity of at least two of the aircraft's sixteen, twenty-eight-inch-wide portholes had been compromised.

Tate sprang up at Oleniuk and barged him back into and over the table. The Russian rolled until he fell onto the floor trapped between the table and a seat. Tate followed him over the table, landed on top of him in the confined spaced and pummelled his face with heavy fists. He felt Oleniuk's nose give way, and his jaw click, but the Russian was not finished yet. Oleniuk twisted to his left and pinned Tate against the huge, leather seat.

Oleniuk still had the vodka bottle in his hand. He raised it to strike Tate, the dregs of the alcohol splashing over both men. There was a cracking sound and then a second, larger rush of air. The bottle was torn from Oleniuk's hand and sailed out of the failed porthole of the emergency exit. Tate could hear a warning claxon sound from the cockpit and the Gulfstream suddenly dropped and turned to starboard.

Tate bucked away from Oleniuk and pulled himself to his feet. But Oleniuk was also standing. Both men were of equal height but the Russian was the heavier, and not all of that was flab. They stood facing each other, their heads inches away from the interior ceiling. As the jet tilted and the air continued to rush in, Oleniuk came at Tate with his fists raised. His eyes were wild and his face a bloody mess, but he was grinning.

'I boxed at school, Tate, I was undefeated.' He threw a quick jab in Tate's direction and then tried to land a left hook.

Tate defended, mirrored the boxing stance but not quickly enough as Oleniuk shot out another jab, hitting him on the jaw. Tate absorbed the extra pain and now brought his fists back up to his face. Oleniuk saw the schoolboy error and stepped in ready to deliver a blow to Tate's unprotected body, but Tate had changed the game, and the sport. He threw a hard, straight, karate kick at Oleniuk with his right leg. Tate's foot connected with his target's groin. The Russian crumpled.

Tate held on to the nearest chair to steady himself, his left leg slick with fresh blood and threatening to give way, then he saw Oleniuk's hand move shakily towards an object lying under the table. The Beretta. Tate fell on the hand with his knees, crushing it into the carpet and grabbed the gun first. He pulled the trigger, the raucous retort momentarily competing with the whistling air. The round buried itself in Oleniuk's stomach, in the exposed gap below his ballistic vest.

Oleniuk then did something that took Tate completely by surprise. He started to talk. His voice was barely audible above the rush of the air. 'Listen to me, there is something I need to say.'

Tate looked the Russian square in the eyes. Was this where the madman begged for his life? Tried to justify his actions? Momentarily it appeared as though Oleniuk had shrugged off his injuries as his eyes seemed to shine. 'I am responsible for the Camden bombing that killed your parents . . .'

Tate felt as though he'd been hit in the chest with a sledge-hammer. Using a surge of strength created by pure, primeval rage and hatred, he grabbed the Russian by the neck, hauled him to his feet, all but slamming his head into the ceiling. 'What did you say?'

'I killed your parents.' A large smile split Oleniuk's battered and bloodied face. 'It was my plan, and it was my men. You had to pay for the death of my daughter . . .' Oleniuk started to cough.

'Who planted the bomb?'

Oleniuk's eyes were wide. 'You do not know?'

'Tell me.' Tate now grabbed a hold of the Russian's hair with his left hand and thrust the Beretta tight into the underside of his jaw.

'I want you to live the rest of your unimportant life knowing that my man did this, and you let him escape . . .'

'Who!' Tate demanded, breaking Oleniuk's skin with the Beretta's barrel.

'He designed the bomb and he drove the van that day . . .'

'Give me a name!'

'Ruslan Akulov!'

Tate dropped Oleniuk and stumbled back against a seat. 'Akulov.'

'My assassin, my Werewolf . . .' Oleniuk started to cough; blood foamed around his lips. 'What is it like, to know you have been played for a fool? You have the blood of your parents and all of those innocents from the market on your hands all because your brother killed my daughter . . .'

'Simon did not kill her!' Tate was shaking. He knew his body was about to shut down, as was the plane, which was juddering erratically.

Oleniuk continued, 'And then you did my bidding in Chechnya by liquidating such a troublesome terror group! That was pure ecstasy to me . . . I've beaten you, Jack, and I've beaten your pathetic brother, and now I shall soon see my daughter again.'

Tate raised the Beretta, his hand shaking.

'Do it, kill me like a man.'

'No.' Tate pocketed the Beretta and grabbed Oleniuk. He hauled him to feet his feet once more and with his vision dimming manhandled him towards the broken porthole.

'What are you doing? T . . . Tate, are you mad?' Oleniuk bucked and struggled, but he was a spent force.

Tate elbowed the Russian in the gut to double him over, then slammed him against the emergency exit, jamming his head and shoulders into the gaping hole. Oleniuk's body shook, his feet drummed on the carpet, his arms pushed weakly against the door and then his body went still. Like roadkill, like the result of a bird strike, he hung suspended from the porthole.

The roaring of the slipstream was halved. Tate again could hear the alarm from the cabin. Grabbing every single piece of furniture for purchase, Tate edged towards the cockpit door and slammed it with his fists. 'Take us back! Get us down!'

The door didn't open but he felt the Gulfstream bank. He lurched to the left and fell into the nearest seat. Tate pulled the seatbelt tight around himself, snapped the clip shut, and then his vision went black . . .

Epilogue

Three months later

Georgetown, Washington, DC

Simon Hunter gazed out of the window of his rented Georgetown townhouse as his neighbour walked his poodle in one direction and a fat man in a tracksuit wobbled in another. He sighed. Nothing had seemingly changed in this sleepy, salubrious part of the capital city since the EMP attack, but he had. He'd lost a woman he had loved, a woman it turned out he didn't know at all.

Debriefed and then signed off to recover, Hunter mentally and Tate physically were both recuperating. Tate had recovered quicker than expected from his surgery, but unexpectedly he'd chosen to spend the rest of his downtime with Hunter. Hunter didn't know how to thank him.

Hunter sipped his milky tea and couldn't help a sudden smile from forming on his face. He moved to the settee and sat. His stomach rumbled as the greasy, delicious waft of a full English breakfast drifted in from the kitchen. He picked up the TV remote for his new set. It was the same brand as his old one that had been rendered useless by the EMP, but a different model. He fumbled with the unfamiliar buttons and managed to find BBC World. Milky tea and the BBC, it was like being back in Camden as a kid, but not quite.

It was a quarter after the hour on a Friday morning. On screen a journalist reported on the continuing efforts of the international community to aid the rebuilding and re-plugging of the US after the "EMP terrorist attack of August". The banner under the reporter's name gave his location as Arlington Assembly, Arlington, Texas. It was where the US car giant GM manufactured, amongst other vehicles, the Tahoe.

'*Of course, Martin,*' the BBC correspondent replied to the studio anchor, '*the true cost to the US economy can only at this point in time be estimated. But undaunted, the president as we know has promised to rebuild it stronger and greater than ever before.*'

The studio cut away to the well-used footage from several weeks before, which showed the President of the United States and the Prime Minister of Canada at a joint press conference. They smiled broadly and shook hands and posed for photographs all the while standing in front of a huge banner which read, "Making North America Great Again".

'MNAGA,' Hunter said, and took another sip of tea.

'Here.' Tate appeared from the kitchen. He was holding two large plates.

'Thanks.' Hunter took one and placed it down on the coffee table in front of him. His brother sat at his side and did the same. Hunter studied his breakfast: eggs, bacon, sausages, baked beans, mushrooms, tomatoes, fried bread, and black pudding. Gourmet.

The brothers ate in silence, listening yet not listening, as the news report continued. An info graphic showed the number of new businesses that had been set up, with federal government grants, to handle the huge demand for the replacement and fitting of wiring looms to salvageable vehicles. It then displayed the import volume of vehicles from manufacturing plants in Canada and Mexico. A new table depicted, with mini-flags, the percentage by country of electronic components shipped to the

US. Percentage wise, the biggest winners were the Germans, the Japanese, the Koreans and the Taiwanese.

'*The Chinese too, have played their part,*' the correspondent stated. '*However, with the unusual omission of one of China's largest and most respected electronics manufactures, CY Holdings, from the US tender process, speculation has increased regarding the disappearance, of its multi-billionaire owner, Chen Yan. The Electronic Princess, as she has been dubbed by the international business press, has not been seen since late August. And now the business world is asking why.*'

'What a pity,' Tate said.

'She needs to be found,' Hunter replied.

The visual feed returned to the correspondent in Arlington. '*Of course, it will continue to be the United States armed forces which will have the most spent on it. All branches have suffered huge technological losses, with everything from field radios to cruise missiles inoperable and aircraft carriers reduced to floating barges. But NATO and her allies have rallied round, adopting a status of high alert whilst the US remains vulnerable.*'

'*What's the latest from Moscow?*' the studio anchor asked, as though the question had not been rehearsed.

The feed switched to footage, taken in September, of the President of Russia returning tanned, fit and fresh from his summer holiday at his dacha in Siberia.

'*Well, Martin,*' the correspondent continued, '*the Russian president has issued an official statement that Russia is a true friend of the West and will do all it can to help its great strategic ally rebuild.*'

'On condition that we hugely relax sanctions against them,' Hunter scoffed, through a mouthful of egg.

'I grew out of politics,' Tate said, as he bit into a piece of toast.

'I know you haven't grown out of this.' Hunter changed the channel and the familiar logo of the WWE filled the screen.

'Ooh yeah!' Tate said, with an exaggerated drawl.

'Wooooo!' Hunter replied.

After losing themselves in the world of sports entertainment for the best part of an hour, Tate sat in the passenger seat of Hunter's rewired Land Rover Defender as they weaved their way out of the city. It wouldn't have been Tate's choice of vehicle, but his brother always had had odd tastes.

Their destination was the Appalachian Trail in Virginia. As they moved farther and farther away from the city, the Friday morning traffic began to ease. In the three months since the EMP attack only a small percentage of the population had managed to regain their independent mobility. Ironically these tended to be those at the bottom of society, with older vehicles not affected by the EMP, and those at the very top who had instantly ordered new, replacement cars. This was the new normal, for a while at least.

They passed a roadside billboard with the slogan "Make driving great again, buy your rewired, cherished car today!"

'MDGA,' Tate said.

'Sorry,' Hunter said, with a shake of the head, 'I was miles away.'

'Just keep your eyes on the sat nav.'

The brothers remained silent for the majority of the trip. The drive from Washington into Virginia to reach this part of the Appalachian Trail took just over an hour before they pulled into an empty car park at the bottom of the trail.

The pair climbed out, zipped up their coats, shouldered their day sacks and set off. The trail meandered and sloped upwards, at first an easy hike but becoming increasingly difficult and Tate, used to leading from the front, pulled away.

'Jack, slow down!'

'Come on!' Tate called back to his brother.

'Look, I can't keep up – you may well be bloody superhuman but I'm not!'

'I thought you were a runner?'

'I am, but not uphill!'

Tate stopped and looked back down the blustery mountain trail. It was part of the same range he had flown over three months earlier in the commandeered Gulfstream jet. He wondered where the wreckage had landed, and he hoped it hadn't injured any civilians. His leg still ached from the gunshot wound inflicted on that very same day, but it was bearable – it had to be if he was going to regain and even surpass his previous fitness levels.

Hunter caught up, panting. 'A normal person would now be recuperating on a desert island with a vodka martini.'

'You want to look like a normal person, act like a normal person.'

Hunter rolled his eyes. 'Jack, stop it with the clever quotes.'

'Ah, you don't know who said that, do you?' Tate tutted. 'I'll give you two guesses.'

'OK,' Hunter said, still battling to regain his breath, 'it was either Gandhi or the Dalai Lama.'

Tate shook his head with exaggerated slowness. 'Mike Tyson.'

The brothers started to laugh. Tate retrieved his water bottle, had a swig and passed it to Hunter. Hunter took a mouthful and then pulled a face. 'This is water.'

'What did you expect?'

Hunter frowned. 'Something medicinal perhaps? We're in the mountains so I'd have chosen bourbon; that's what "Mountain Men" drink, isn't it?'

'We're here to get healthy, not hammered.'

Tate put away his water bottle and looked wistfully north: the entire Appalachian Trail was over two thousand miles long and if they trekked the entire length, they'd end up in Maine. Perhaps he'd revisit Camden one day.

'What are you thinking, Jack?'

Tate lied. He didn't want to mention the EMP. 'I'm just taking in the scenery. Look around, this place hasn't changed in millennia.'

'True.'

The brothers stood in the stillness as the November winds rolled around them and threatened to bring the first snows of the year.

'I miss her, Jack.'

Tate nodded, but remained silent, not wanting to stop his brother from opening up but also not wanting to say the wrong thing.

'I loved her. I really loved her.'

Hunter's eyes became moist. Tate hoped it was the increasing wind but knew it was not. He wasn't good with emotions, well apart from anger. He said all he could think of saying: 'I'm sorry.'

'Jack, there's nothing for you to be sorry about. Oleniuk killed her, murdered her like he murdered our parents . . . If I had just . . . if I could have . . .'

Tate drew his big brother close and embraced him. 'You'll never lose me, Simon. Not again.'

'Thanks, brother.'

Jack Tate felt his own eyes water, and this time he knew it wasn't the wind. Regardless of who their parents had been, Jack Tate and Simon Hunter always were and always would be brothers. 'Sod it. That's enough for today – let's go back down, find a bar and drink some bourbon!'

Acknowledgements

Like long-distance running, writing can be a solitary process, but I have drawn both strength and inspiration from those around me who have by turns inspired and supported me along my journey. Firstly, I need to thank my wife Galia, for without her support I would not have been able to carry on. My sons, Alexander and Jonathan who tell everyone I'm a famous author.

I'd like to thank my editor at HQ, Finn Cotton, and my agents, Justin Nash and Kate Nash, for believing in my work and wanting to champion me and publish it.

I'd like to thank my friends both inside and outside of the book world for putting up with me rabbiting on about my next book, my next idea, and for being vocal supporters. This is a long list but includes: Neill J Furr, Liam Saville, Steph Edger, Paul Grzegorek, Alan McDermott, Charlie Flowers, Stephen Leather, Jake Needham, Tom Wood, Rob Sinclair, Lee Child, James Swallow, Simon Toyne, Duncan Falconer, Michael Ridpath, Ali Karim, Noelle Holton, Jacky Gramosi Collins, Louise Mangos, Rachel Amphlett, Alistair Church and superfans – James Brocklehurst, David Dobiasek, and Karen Campbell.

If you loved *Total Blackout*, don't miss book two in the explosive Jack Tate thriller series!

TOTAL FALLOUT

Jack Tate thought his war was over . . .

Former SAS trooper Jack Tate is running a black op for MI6 when he learns that the man who killed his parents has been found.

On a quest for revenge from Monaco to Qatar and into the US, Tate must stop at nothing if he is to catch the world's deadliest assassin.

But his target is hunting too. Members of his old unit, The Werewolves, might hold the key to the London bombing which has bound him and Tate together for the last four years.

As Tate tracks the Russian, the lines between friend and foe, and good and evil starts to blur. Now Tate must pick a side in order to avenge his family, no matter the consequences . . .

Perfect for fans of James Deegan, Tom Clancy and Mark Greaney, this is an explosive action thriller you won't be able to put down.

Dear Reader,

We hope you enjoyed reading this book. If you did, we'd be so appreciative if you left a review. It really helps us and the author to bring more books like this to you.

Here at HQ Digital we are dedicated to publishing fiction that will keep you turning the pages into the early hours. Don't want to miss a thing? To find out more about our books, promotions, discover exclusive content and enter competitions you can keep in touch in the following ways:

JOIN OUR COMMUNITY:

Sign up to our new email newsletter: hyperurl.co/hqnewsletter

Read our new blog www.hqstories.co.uk

🐦 https://twitter.com/HQDigitalUK

f www.facebook.com/HQStories

BUDDING WRITER?

We're also looking for authors to join the HQ Digital family! Find out more here:

https://www.hqstories.co.uk/want-to-write-for-us/

Thanks for reading, from the HQ Digital team

If you enjoyed *Total Blackout*, then why not try another gripping crime thriller from HQ Digital?